The
LIGHT
THAT
BLINDS
US

The LIGHT THAT BLINDS US

ANDY DARCY THEO

GALLERY YA

First published in Great Britain in 2024 by Gallery YA,
an imprint of Simon & Schuster UK Ltd

1 3 5 7 9 10 8 6 4 2

Simon & Schuster UK Ltd
1st Floor, 222 Gray's Inn Road
London WC1X 8HB

Simon & Schuster: Celebrating 100 Years of Publishing in 2024

www.simonandschuster.co.uk
www.simonandschuster.com.au
www.simonandschuster.co.in

Simon & Schuster Australia, Sydney
Simon & Schuster India, New Delhi

A CIP catalogue record for this book is available from the British Library.

PB ISBN 978-1-3985-3177-2
eBook ISBN 978-1-3985-3184-0
eAudio ISBN 978-1-3985-3183-3

Typeset by Sorrel Packham

Printed and bound in the UK using
100% Renewable Electricity at CPI Group (UK) Ltd

For 13-year-old me.
We did it.

AUTHOR'S NOTE

This book is full of paradoxes, but so is the human condition.

Prepare for laughter and revenge, love and loss, light and dark. In times of humour there is sadness, and in the greatest moments of despair there is hope.

Alexis's psychosis is based on my own family history, years of extensive research, and my experience as a senior clinical psychology assistant and healthcare assistant in a psychiatric hospital. Alexis's symptoms, cognitive profile and mannerisms are inspired by real-life encounters to reflect an authentic experience in a fantasy setting. His journey to understanding himself and living with his mental illness is raw and tumultuous and incomplete, as it is for so many of us.

I hope you love reading *The Light That Blinds Us* as much as I loved writing it.

Welcome to the Elemental world.

Take care on your descent into darkness.

ALEXIS

*I'll drown you
in your own blood*

MICHAELS

DEMI

*Don't make me
tell you twice*

NIKOLAS

BLAISE
*I'm sorry that
I'm beautiful*
ADEMOLA

CAELI
*I'd rather die
than apologise*
DORAN

PROLOGUE

Eleven years ago

Alexis Michaels's parents were certain their son didn't know what he was doing when he tried to drown his therapist.

They were wrong.

Alexis knew exactly what he was doing.

Not that he wanted to kill anyone – he was only six. But even by that age, Alexis had long grown accustomed to doing things he didn't want to do.

And he would do anything to silence the *Shadow Man*.

Dr Carl Dash didn't know this when he arrived for a psychiatric consultation with a boy tormented by nightmares. The appointment, like all of his assessments, began with him thinking of a single word to describe the patient. An outdated method perhaps – but Dr Dash liked to think of himself as a good judge of character. And after thirty-seven years of experience, he wasn't going to change now. People weren't as complicated as they liked to think.

He didn't know it at the time, but the boy standing before him was an exception.

Dark curly hair fell in unruly waves over the boy's tanned forehead, covering much of his eyes and face. He stood in the open doorway and looked up at the doctor.

Dr Dash smiled. 'Hello, young man. And who might you be?'

Before the boy could respond, winter's icy whisper howled, sweeping through the quaint suburban cul-de-sac of Valerian Lane. Dr Dash shivered as he buried his chin into his scarf and pulled his long woollen coat across his chest. The boy, however, didn't flinch. He only waited for the wind to withdraw before he spoke.

'Alexis.'

Alexis brushed his hair from his eyes, revealing their colour – an inner ring of icy blue, surrounded by a thicker band of obsidian black. *Central heterochromia*, the Doctor thought – rare. He had never seen anyone with eyes like this before. They were as beautiful as they were unsettling, in the way all unnatural things are.

'Alexis!' A man rushed into the hallway behind the boy, followed by a woman carrying a baby. They smiled at Dr Dash in greeting before the man crouched down to Alexis's level and placed his hands on his son's shoulders. 'What did we say about opening the door to strangers?' he asked gently.

Alexis nodded and retreated inside the house. *Interesting child*, Dr Dash thought. What word would best suit him? *Peculiar, unnerving, melancholy* all came to mind, but none were quite right.

'Sorry about that.' The boy's father stuck out a hand. 'You must be Doctor Dash?'

'Yes. And you must be Mr and Mrs Michaels?'

'Mr and *Doctor*,' said the woman, failing to stifle a grin. 'Didn't do all those years of medical training to not have the title. But call us Stephanie and Jackson. It's nice to meet you, doctor. Please come in and have some tea.'

'*Bold*' was the word for Stephanie Michaels. Dr Dash liked her already.

Untouched by the pollution of Central London, and free from its crowded confinements, the houses of Valerian Lane stood proudly against the great expanse of Protegere Forest. Set back and guarded by gates, the Michaels' home was as picturesque on the inside as one would expect from the outside, with morning sunlight spilling into the tall windows and conservatory where they settled.

Jackson poured them cups of Earl Grey tea. Then he took the baby while Stephanie grasped the teacup with both hands to absorb the comforting heat. They were a young couple – an attractive couple – and very much in love. Dr Dash could tell just from the way their bodies found a way to always be touching, even if it was just at the elbows. Yet there was a worry between them, and it was more visible now.

The doctor was the one to break the burdensome silence.

'Alexis looks a lot like you, Jackson. And yet – he's adopted, isn't he?'

Stephanie's response flew out, drenched in maternal defence. 'Yes. Why do you ask?'

'I understand the circumstances were rather unusual,' he replied calmly. Stephanie's leg was bouncing nervously, but Jackson placed a reassuring hand on her knee and it stilled. 'Would you mind telling me a bit about it?'

It was Jackson who answered, looking at his wife between sentences, every so often glancing at Dr Dash's notepad. 'It was around a year ago. Alexis was five at the time, although we're not certain of his exact date of birth. It was after that mega-tsunami in the South Pacific Ocean. We were in Australia for our honeymoon, but luckily weren't near the shore when it hit. Stephanie and I went to volunteer; she helped the medics and I helped the survivors. That was when we met Alexis. His parents had both died – that's what the officials presumed. We bonded with him instantly, as if we were meant to be there to find him. As someone raised in the system myself, I couldn't leave him.'

Jackson shifted the weight of the baby in his arms. 'I'm sorry, but what does this have to do with Alexis's current issues?'

'It is helpful to get a sense of history to understand the present.' Dr Dash loosened his shirt collar. 'But let's move on. Could you tell me about Alexis's presentation and the reason you called me? You mentioned he suffers from nightmares?'

'Every night,' Stephanie began, setting down the empty drink. Without anything to fiddle with, she interlocked her hands and tucked them beneath her chin to hold up her head. 'Wakes up screaming and crying. Sometimes he even hurts himself in his sleep, scratching his chest and arms, making them bleed. We've tried everything to help him. We even have him in our bed now, but nothing seems to stop them.'

'Does he tell you what these night terrors are about? A particular worry?' Stephanie shook her head. 'I understand he has been diagnosed with retrograde amnesia and doesn't remember anything before the tsunami.'

4

'Not even his name,' said Stephanie with a sad smile. 'But the nightmare is always the same. It's always him falling off a cliff.'

Dr Dash added to his notes and then stood up. He didn't want to speak too much longer in case he had any preconceived ideas when he spoke to Alexis, but there was one more thing they hadn't discussed – the thing that had led him to take their case in the first place. 'And what about his hallucinations?'

The word alone brought over a cloud of disquiet for both Stephanie and Jackson. Even the baby sensed the change, squirming in his father's arms. Jackson tried settling him as he began crying, but soon handed him to Stephanie.

'Excuse me,' she said, standing also. 'I'll let you explain, darling.'

She left the room, soothing the baby. The distant wailing soon subsided.

Dr Dash turned back to face Jackson. His eyes had followed after his wife as she left, brimming with adoration and concern. It was that look alone that helped Dr Dash find Jackson's descriptive word: '*Guardian*.'

'The hallucinations?' he prompted gently.

'Sometimes he looks like he's talking to someone who isn't there,' said Jackson. Through the glass table, the doctor could see his fists clenched so tightly they shuddered. 'He's better in the mornings and when he's around Jason; Jace, he calls him. But at night, he's . . . he says he talks to a man. A man made of shadow. He said the man tells him to do things, bad things.' Jackson met the doctor's eyes, finally sucking in a long breath. 'We're so worried about him, that he's going to hurt himself or his brother. The last two psychiatrists that came refused to medicate him, saying he was too young, but we can't risk anything happening to him. Please, doctor, you have to help us. I–I'm powerless here. I can't bear to see him in pain any longer.'

Dr Dash could see the desperation, the pain, the exhaustion. 'I think it's time I talk to Alexis.'

Jackson led him towards the bright living room where Stephanie sat on the cream carpet, Jason resting in the crook of her arms. Alexis was crouched over his brother, letting the baby hold his finger, swaying it back and forth in the air. The corners of his eyes were crinkled from smiling so widely.

Alexis's face was a portrait of unconditional love. It was enough to make Dr Dash wonder if he and his wife had made a mistake in deciding not to have children of their own. The thought was only fleeting, however, for his attention shifted towards something odd – a bucket of water beside the mother and sons. A blue stone pendant cut into an inverted triangular shape floated on its surface, bobbing up and down.

Alexis glanced up, catching him staring. Alexis snatched the pendant out of the water, hastily pulling the chain over his head to conceal the pendant beneath his collar.

'What are you doing to your toys there?' Dr Dash asked, tucking the notepad away in his pocket. Jackson and Stephanie had reluctantly agreed to give him a few minutes alone with the boy. Now Alexis was entertaining himself by dunking three small plastic figurines into the pail of water beside him. Each time he submerged them beneath the surface, he too held his breath, pinching his nostrils closed with his free hand.

Two red blotches dotted Alexis's tanned cheeks until he finally gasped for air. He pulled the toy free from its underwater capture and placed it dripping on the carpet. Dr Dash was about to repeat his question before Alexis replied, his blue eyes still focussed on the water's surface.

'They're my friends. I'm seeing how long they can breathe underwater.'

'Why would you want to drown your friends?'

Alexis looked up at him, his eyebrow arched. 'Obviously they're not real.' He went back to playing with a slight smirk to himself.

'Obviously,' Dr Dash muttered, feeling humbled. 'So, do you have any other friends? Maybe from school?'

A long exhale slipped out as Alexis shook his head, his smile waning. 'I don't go to school.' He suddenly shut his eyes. His face contorted and his shoulders shot up as if to cover his ears from an inaudible, sharp sound. It was only brief, for he soon opened his eyes and added, 'I don't go anywhere. Mummy and Daddy don't let me out. I have no friends.'

'That's a shame,' Dr Dash said, making a quick note. 'It's good to have friends your age. Friends can be some of the best people in our lives. I'm sure that when he gets older, you'll find a friend in your brother.'

Alexis didn't seem to have heard him. He was looking past Dr Dash, somewhere over his shoulder. He looked like he was listening to something, or rather trying to ignore something. Dr Dash tried his best not to, but he couldn't help but turn around. There was nothing there, of course, but a coldness had descended on the room, and he felt prickles on the back of his neck. There must be a draft coming from somewhere.

Dr Dash turned back. 'Alexis? Did you hear me?'

The boy didn't blink. He seemed transfixed. Scared. And as the clouds outside came together, unleashing a tide of rain that thrashed down on Valerian Lane, the natural light in the Michaels' home fell dark, and Dr Dash shared in Alexis's unease.

'Alexis,' he said quietly. 'Is there someone behind me?'

Alexis nodded.

'I can't see or hear him, but can you?'

The boy nodded again.

'Can you feel him? Can he touch you?'

Alexis's throat bobbed, his eyes threatening to spill with tears.

'Is he your friend?'

Alexis shook his head. He clutched the pendant through his T-shirt. When he spoke, his voice was barely a whisper, almost as if he was frightened of being overheard. 'It's the *Shadow Man*. It is real and it is not my friend.'

'Can I see your necklace?' Dr Dash asked, hoping to distract the boy.

Alexis shook his head. 'It's an amulet.'

'Did your parents get it for you?'

'No. It's mine. It floats sometimes.'

'I saw. I'm sure it's a very special necklace, then,' said Dr Dash, before correcting himself. 'A very special *amulet*.'

He received a smile from Alexis in return, a smile that revealed his dimples. This was a boy who didn't smile often, Dr Dash observed with sympathy. There was a vulnerability to the joy, a hesitancy to be happy. Dr Dash wanted to do whatever he could to help make this rarity a reality.

'Here,' said Alexis, broken from his trance. He handed the doctor a toy. 'Who are you?'

'Thanks,' said Dr Dash, looking down at the battered figure. He began to walk the toy playfully across his knees. 'I'm a doctor.'

Alexis grinned widely. 'My mummy is a doctor. She fixes hearts.'

'I'm a different kind of doctor.' Dr Dash tapped his temple. 'Your mother treats people's bodies. I treat people's thoughts and feelings, to make them feel better. I have helped many children just like you, in fact.'

Alexis looked at him thoughtfully. 'You're here to help me? To help *us*?'

Before Dr Dash could reply, Alexis gasped and recoiled. He squeezed his eyes shut, clamped his hands over his ears and shook his head from side to side. All the while, he repeated the same two words over and over again, his plea nothing more than a whisper.

'Please stop, please stop, please stop.'

'Alexis?' Dr Dash spoke loudly and firmly. 'Alexis, do you know what I do when an upsetting emotion takes over? When I want to focus on the here and now?'

Dr Dash didn't know if his voice was louder than the one Alexis was hearing, but it was enough to make Alexis crack open his eyes. The doctor rolled back the sleeves of his own sweater. Slowly, he tapped each finger against his thumb, repeating the action over and over, rhythmically, purposefully. 'Can you copy me?' he asked.

Alexis watched for a while before imitating him, concentrating intently until he became familiar with it. It seemed to help, pulling his focus back and grounding him to a calmness.

Dr Dash handed him back his toy. 'Does the *Shadow Man* talk to you?'

The rain outside had fallen still, silenced by the clouds above. In the absence of all sound, the darkness of the sky held a noise of its own. Low. Persistent. Hostile.

Alexis's eyes were locked onto the water within the bucket. The surface was disturbed, rippling. Dr Dash didn't recall Alexis knocking the bucket at any point. 'It used to be a *voice* in my head. Now it's real. It scares me.'

'And what was he saying just then, Alexis?'

Alexis dropped his toy and looked straight at Dr Dash. There was a sorrow to his voice when he spoke, a guilt. Regret, not for what he had done, but for what he was about to do.

'It told me to drown you in your own blood.'

And Alexis lunged.

A strangled, gargling scream echoed throughout the house. Jackson had been waiting outside and flung the door open the second he heard the commotion. His heart thundered in his chest at the prospect of his son in danger, but what he found was the very opposite.

Alexis was holding down Dr Dash's head in the pail of water, pushing with all his weight. The old man's arms thrashed, scratching out at Alexis and drawing blood, but Alexis didn't move. His eyes were wide and unblinking, lips trembling.

Somehow charged with unnatural strength, the boy fought against the old man's resistance.

As Jackson rushed towards them, he noticed where the pail's rim had cut into Dr Dash's throat, deep enough to spill his own blood into the bucket where he was drowning.

Jackson hauled Alexis away with both arms, restraining his son as he screamed in defiance.

'I have to! I have to!' Alexis cried, fighting with a strength Jackson didn't know was possible for a six-year-old.

Stephanie ran into the room just as Dr Dash swept the bucket away, gasping for air, his thin, white hair plastered to his forehead. A mixture of blood and water dripped down his face, staining his shirt and sweater.

'I'm sorry!' Alexis bawled, rubbing his eyes with his knuckles before pressing his palms against his ears. Jason's cries in the distance rang out as Stephanie inspected Dr Dash for signs of major injury. He was cut and shaken, but he was going to be okay; just.

Alexis twisted in Jackson's grip, staring up at his father. '*It* made me! If I don't, *it* hurts Jace.'

Stephanie and Jackson locked eyes with one another from either side of the room. It had been bad before, but never as bad as this. As the seconds rolled out – seconds of disbelief and wordless deliberation – Alexis's resistance grew futile, his strength depleting. Soon, the exhausted child crumbled.

'I don't want to,' Alexis whispered, tears streaming down his face as he buried it into Jackson's chest. 'I just want to make it stop. Please . . . make it stop.'

Dr Dash batted off Stephanie's hand as he struggled to

his feet, breathing raggedly. He ignored her as she began to apologise. Everyone was silent, watching the small boy clutching his blue amulet between his hands as if that would save him. As if that would somehow grant him sanity and safety.

Another delusion. Another fantasy.

Dr Dash realised in that moment that Alexis Michaels was beyond his help, possibly beyond anyone's.

He shook his head and backed away. He had to get out of this place.

He said only one thing before he had left, the one word to describe Alexis.

'*Doomed.*'

PART I

DEMI
Fated to fall
'I am more than my emotions'

1

NOCTIPHANY

Noctiphany (n.) *Latin and Greek origin*
An appearance of something that occurs only at night

Eleven Years Later

Each night, at dawn's first light, Alexis Michaels had the same nightmare.

The nightmare that tormented him like a plague, ever since he was a child. The nightmare that didn't feel like it was a dream at all, but rather a distant memory, something that had been buried deep in his unconscious and resurfaced only in his sleep. Feeling like an imposter in his own body, he braced for the pain that would inevitably come to wake him, unable to do anything to stop it.

He stood at the cliff edge overlooking the ocean, its waves crashing against the shoreline far below. Even from a distance, he could feel the cool salty spray dampening his curly hair and plastering it against his golden-toned skin. There was something tranquil about being surrounded by water, peaceful. The rhythmic pulling and pushing of the waves had an order that made sense to him. The ocean made him feel small – made his worries and pain insignificant. Things that could be swept away by the current. Inhaling as the waves drew back

15

and exhaling with every broken crest, the boy closed his eyes to savour the perfect synchronicity.

But, as usual, the moment of peacefulness, of tranquillity, did not last.

The colour of the scene around him drained away, tinting all that he saw grey. His body plummeted – cold as ice as a violent, explosive pain struck him like a tidal wave from within. He gasped at the intensity of it and clawed at his face and neck, trying to exorcise the pressure.

But the pain only grew, snatching the air from his lungs as it did.

His vision blurred as pools of red bled across his body, pulsing out through the tiny pores of his skin. It was unbearable. It flooded his consciousness and his sight, forcing him to buckle over.

Alexis tried to call out for help, but even his voice had abandoned him in his suffering. He stumbled back. He had to get away. But in his struggle he had forgotten where he stood, remembering all too late once the ground disappeared beneath him. Fighting to regain his balance with only one foot left on the earth's edge, he cast a final look towards the vacant cliffside.

A second boy with striking white hair appeared in the distance. He was running towards Alexis, his face aghast in horror.

The boy desperately called a name, '*Nero!*' and reached out, but at that point there was nothing to catch but air. Alexis disappeared over the edge of the cliffside.

The bitter sea air stung his blood-soaked body as he fell, twisting and turning in his attempt to somehow slow his descent, his eyes upon the element that would seal his fate.

The black surface of the ocean rushed towards him. Waves crashing. No longer peaceful. No longer tranquil. No longer safe.

Nero closed his eyes as he met the darkness.

Alexis bolted awake, sitting up straight in his bed as if to stop himself from hitting the water. The afterimage of the dark ocean remained at the forefront of his mind for a while, determined to linger as his heart pulsed in his throat. Yet with the light from the sunrise shining into his room, illuminating the walls with a warm orange glow, the darkness of the nightmare was forced to recoil, releasing Alexis from its clutches.

He used the back of his hand to wipe away the feverish sweat that glazed his skin and spent a couple of minutes tapping his fingers to his thumbs, timing each brief pressure with the regulation of his breathing, just like a doctor had shown him years ago. To settle his mind, he reached out for the book on his bedside table and removed the bookstore receipt that served as a bookmark.

Despite every effort to stay awake, his eyelids began to droop. The nightmare only came once at sunrise, so it wouldn't disturb him again. He must've drifted because he was once again startled awake, only this time it was by the frustrated shout of his mother.

'Boys! If I have to call you one more time, you're getting a bucket of cold water over you. I come home and no one's even loaded the dishwasher.' The sound of her tutting somehow managed to carry up the entire flight of stairs. 'Alexis, get a move on or you'll be late!'

A bucket of cold water didn't sound too bad, Alexis considered, but a hot shower would probably be a more relaxing option.

Alexis stared unblinking into the mirror as he brushed his teeth. Although the *Shadow Man* was long gone, he was still haunted by its remnant voice. It was one of his more unusual superstitions, the distrust of his own reflection, wary that if he blinked, the *Shadow Man* would be able to reach him again. He was probably just being paranoid – points for consistency. A short blow of air from his nose indicated that he at least found himself funny.

The moment the shower water touched his body, he instantly relaxed as the previous night's disturbed sleep washed away. Under its near-scalding temperature, Alexis's amulet remained cold. The small, blue gem sat in the centre of his chest, droplets falling freely from the bottom point of its shape.

After quickly dressing and throwing on a hat to cover his messy dark hair, he picked up his pre-packed suitcase and shut the door to his room. He pounded his fist against the door of his younger brother's room and pushed it open before he continued downstairs.

There was a grumble in response. Probably a swear, but Alexis didn't catch it.

The kitchen doors swung open and Stephanie Michaels burst through them, a wooden spoon held out like a weapon in her hand. She stopped when she saw him. 'Lexi, there you are.'

He gestured to the kitchen utensil. 'That for me?'

'Not now that you've come down,' she said, flashing him a grin. 'Come on – if you insist on going on this trip, you need to make sure you eat something before you go. You know Dad will nag you otherwise.'

'Morning, son,' Jackson said as Alexis joined him at the table. 'How did you sleep?'

The lie came to Alexis as easy as breathing. 'Fine.'

When the hallucinations had stopped a few years back, his parents had assumed his nightmares had gone too. Alexis had let them, because the endless trials of medicine and countless child psychologists had become unbearable for them all.

He was protecting them. They deserved peace of mind after everything he had put them through. Besides, he hadn't hurt himself – or anyone else – for years now; it was easier to pretend the nightmare of Nero had disappeared along with the *Shadow Man*.

Alexis watched as his dad stood and pulled his mum in for a kiss. 'Sit down and rest, darling. The boys and I will clean up,' he said, trading places with her behind the counter. 'Right, have you packed a coat in case it gets cold or rains?'

'Dad, it's basically summer,' Alexis replied in between mouthfuls of scrambled eggs. 'We'll only be gone for a couple of days for this stupid geography coursework.'

'Doesn't matter. It's windy on the Jurassic Coast. Do you need any money?'

Alexis shook his head as Jason thundered down the stairs. His younger brother trudged into the kitchen, dragging his feet across the tiles, still in his superhero pyjamas. He had inherited his father's blue eyes and mother's dirty blonde hair and short height. Otherwise, he looked no more biologically related to them than Alexis did.

'Why do I need to get up so early?' Jason moaned. 'I don't have to be at school for another hour.'

Stephanie kissed the side of his head as Jackson handed him a plate of breakfast. 'Didn't you want to say goodbye to Lexi before he goes?'

'I don't care,' Jason mumbled.

'*I don't care,*' mimicked Alexis, exaggerating the crack in Jason's voice, making him scowl.

Alexis moved over to the sink to wash his empty plate. His mother joined him. As she took the plate to towel it dry, she quietly asked him for the twentieth time that week, 'Are you really sure about going?'

'Mum, I'm seventeen and it's not like it's a holiday – it's for school. It's compulsory if I want to get top grades. If it makes you feel any better, Demi will be there.'

'I know,' his mother replied, nodding to herself. 'That's the only reason we're allowing you to go.'

Alexis's parents had always been strict, especially with him. They had eased off a little over the years, especially when he had joined Bishop's Secondary School, but they were still over the top. Alexis understood, however. He hadn't been the easiest child growing up.

'I've barely left Protegere all my life. I promise I won't wander off or get into any trouble.'

Stephanie took his hands, squeezing them tightly in her steady surgeon ones. 'Maybe you should take some medication with you, just in case.'

'I've been off them for years now, Mum. With no episodes or symptoms, bar the odd delusional thought, but I hear

20

that's common for teenagers.' Alexis grinned, hoping that in convincing her it was no big deal, he too would be reassured. 'I'm not going to suddenly lose my mind.'

'I know, I know.' She looked sheepish for having brought it up. 'It's just . . . to me, you will always be my little boy who hated letting go of my hand and would never let me say "love you more" without saying it back.'

'He's a young man now, Steph,' interjected Jackson from the other side of the kitchen. 'He knows how to look after himself. Besides, Alexis, what do we say if we ever see the *Shadow Man* again?'

Alexis got into the fighting stance his dad had taught him years ago after he told him he was getting bullied at school for being adopted. Swinging punches at the air in front of his mother's face, he said, 'I didn't come this far just to come this far.'

Stephanie was so used to them shadow-boxing that she didn't even flinch.

Jason scoffed. 'I don't know what's weirder: how overprotective you are or the fact that Lexi used to *see things*. Oh, and that no one knows about it except us.'

Alexis didn't need a second's thought to react. 'What's weird is that at eleven-years-old, you still cry if there's no night-light in your room.'

'Mum said you can't joke about that anymore!'

'Lexi!' Stephanie tutted.

'What? He shouldn't start a fight he can't win.'

Thankfully, the doorbell rang. Demi Nikolas had come to Alexis's rescue. As Stephanie left to answer the door, the two brothers scowled at each other.

'We battle at sunset,' Alexis said, pointing an imaginary sword at his younger sibling.

Jason failed to suppress a smile, raising an invisible weapon of his own. 'Farewell, brother, enjoy this day for it shall be your last.'

That was all the goodbye the Michaels brothers needed.

Alexis wheeled his suitcase into the family room. Demi was laughing at something his mother had said, and with that laugh, she brought in the warmth of summer.

'At last.' She threw her arms up when she saw him. Her voice was raspy and laced with a faint Greek accent. 'I'm sure I spend half my life waiting for you.'

'Some of us take longer to make ourselves look pretty,' Alexis replied, flashing a grin so wide that his dimples showed.

Demi's bronzed skin brought out the bold green of her eyes, which looked brighter still framed by her unruly brunette curls, worn loose as always. Two pendants hung from her neck, a horizontal golden crucifix that sat on a shorter chain and another that was concealed beneath her T-shirt. And she was smiling. Ever since her family moved from Greece into Valerian Lane a few years ago, they seemed to have brought a warmth and lightness with them that was more beautiful than the wisteria and lavender that decorated their front garden.

At the boundary between spring and summer, Demi looked particularly radiant, although Alexis would never tell her that directly. Instead, he fist-bumped her and rested his arm over her shoulder until she shoved him off.

'Give us a hug before you go,' Stephanie said, pulling Alexis in for a fierce embrace.

22

Jackson followed, hugging Alexis and whispering, 'Be safe. Look after my boy, Demi.'

'I always do.'

Alexis's parents stood in the doorway as he and Demi walked down the drive. He knew they would watch long after he had vanished from sight.

'I love them,' Demi said, her face tilted up as she admired the lush canopy of Protegere Forest.

'They're full on,' he said affectionately. They had good reason to be, he supposed, but Demi didn't know why, nor would she ever. 'But I love them too.'

They started jogging when they saw the coach waiting at the stop opposite their cul-de-sac, its engine rumbling gently and their teacher, Ms Mason, pacing in front of it. She shook her head when she saw them arrive.

'What time do we call this?' she chastised them in a voice so high-pitched Alexis was surprised the local dogs didn't start howling. 'Now we're going to be stuck in rush-hour traffic.'

Alexis went to open his mouth to take the blame, but Demi beat him to it. 'I'm sorry, Ms Mason. It was my fault completely. Kallisto took a fall this morning and I had to make sure she was okay. I'm sorry for holding us up.'

Ms Mason's hawk-like face softened. 'That's okay, dear.' Alexis had to bite his inner cheek to not crack a smirk, his eyes fixed on the ground so he wouldn't look at Demi and laugh.

Ms Mason stepped aside as Demi boarded the coach. Her stern look swiftly returned as Alexis went to pass her. 'Give me your earphones. That way I can make sure you are paying attention to for once.'

If only you had something interesting to say, Alexis nearly blurted out, before he decided it was better to just nod and hand them over without complaint.

There was no cheering of Alexis's name like there had been for Demi's when she'd gotten on the coach, but he hadn't expected any. He had already pulled out his actual headphones. Ms Mason had the faulty pair that had been in his bag for weeks.

When he was younger, earphones had drowned out the *Shadow Man*, but now he wore them more out of habit. He had just started to play an audiobook when he heard his name.

'Lexi!' called Demi, waving him over to a pair of vacant seats near the back of the coach.

Demi had that rare but endearing quality that made her liked by everyone who knew her. It made her offer even more sincere that she chose to sit next to him over anyone else.

'I can't believe you used your sister's blindness as an excuse,' Alexis said, taking the window seat so that she could chat with her friends in the aisle.

Demi pressed her lips together. 'I know; I feel really bad for it. I *did* have to help her get ready this morning though. And at least it got us out of trouble.'

'Demi Nikolas lying?' Alexis gasped, feigning shock as he tucked his earphones into his pocket, knowing that no matter how long the journey, they would not run out of conversation. 'What's next? Swearing? Violence?'

Demi threw her head back to laugh. The coach suddenly jolted as it took off, and she grabbed Alexis's hand to steady herself. He held it tightly in his, feeling its warmth until he let go. 'Sorry,' she mumbled, as did he.

Alexis leant back and looked out the dirty window as Valerian Lane disappeared. For the first time since he could remember, he was leaving Protegere. He was going to be further from his parents than he had ever been.

With a pang, he realised he never told his mother he 'loved her more,' this time.

Demi straightened her golden cross at the base of her neck, and then pulled out the second necklace that sat beneath it. Despite seeing it a hundred times, Alexis couldn't help but stare at the small green pendant that hung from its chain, the triangular emerald stone identical to his own, save for the colour. Demi caught him looking and smiled.

Even now, years after, Alexis remembered their meeting on his first day at secondary school. They had been paired together, the boy who had been home-schooled and the girl whose family had recently moved to the country. She had approached him just as he found an empty table to sit at alone to eat his lunch. When she neared, both their amulets had suddenly flickered alight, shining as though powered by a supernatural force that had stirred to life. Like an evanescent flash of light from a distant star, moving through the darkness and igniting the stones for only a moment. Just long enough to leave an imprint.

'It's meant to be,' Demi had told him, her accent thicker then than it was now. 'We have to be friends now.'

It had been six years since they first met and the amulets hadn't glowed again since. Over the years they had convinced themselves it was just a trick of the light. It had also become easier to explain it as some sort of friendship jewellery to those who noted their likeness, even though Demi's was a family heirloom and Alexis had had his since before he was adopted.

And yet Alexis cradled that memory, never allowing it to be forgotten. The amulets glowing, the sudden lightness in his chest. How it felt as if it was the universe's way of telling him he had made it out of the darkness and had found someone with whom he belonged, a guide to a better life. How it was the very day the *Shadow Man* finally disappeared, cast into the darkness of Alexis's mind from where it came. Never to stand in the light again.

2
DUYÊN

Duyên (n.) *Vietnamese origin*
A predestined affinity; the force that binds people
together as friends or lovers in the future

They had been driving for a few hours before a student decided to projectile vomit. She swore it was travel sickness, but Alexis didn't need a detective as a father to know from the smell that it was more likely due to the concealed bottle of vodka and orange juice she had been guzzling.

While the girl retched and students shrieked, Alexis and Demi climbed on top of their seats to open the window which barely moved more than a couple of inches, sucking in precious gasps of fresh air.

Demi pressed both hands against the window to steady herself.

'Don't you throw up as well,' Alexis warned, unsure of whether to rub her back in circles or dive over the chair in front to escape the line of fire.

Demi didn't seem to hear him, however. Instead, she was staring at something in the distance, a blur of grey that stood out against miles of field. 'Is that Stonehenge?'

Despite the chaos around them, an uncommon silence

passed between Alexis and Demi. As they pulled closer, the famous stone circle became clearer, sharpening into focus and standing tall against the throngs of tourists surrounding it. There was something about it that demanded Alexis's attention too, so much so that he didn't notice the coach screeching to a stop.

'Everybody out!' demanded the coach driver, a burly man who stunk of cigarette smoke. 'Go get yourselves sorted. Out now!'

The students scrambled out, herded by Ms Mason whose shrill voice instructing them to stay by the coach was drowned out by the commotion. After pausing to pass a bottle of water to the girl who had thrown up, Alexis evacuated last.

Once outside and in the fresh air, an unfamiliar sensation washed over Alexis, one that he couldn't attribute or explain. The only thing that was certain was that he had to get closer to Stonehenge.

He rounded the back of the coach and began to head for the site. Someone caught him by the arm.

'We're supposed to stay by the coach,' said Demi, eyebrows furrowed.

Alexis looked back and saw Ms Mason with her hand over her nose and mouth, ushering the sick-covered girl out. She wouldn't notice.

'Don't you want to see it properly?' he asked, noting the glint in Demi's eye every time she glanced at it. 'Come on, we'll be back before they even know we've gone.'

He turned back to the road. This time, Demi joined him. 'This better not get me in trouble.' Then, almost as an afterthought, she added, 'Mum said we should take a look if we went past.'

The walk was farther than Alexis had anticipated. The warm summer sunshine washed over the pair as they hurried towards the distant structure, soft grass replacing the unyielding concrete. Something was making Alexis feel unsettled, although he wasn't sure what it could be. Was he homesick already?

'Did you hear me, Lexi?' Demi touched his shoulder, and he realised she'd been talking but he hadn't heard a word. 'I said, do you know why it was built?' she repeated.

'I'm not sure. I read somewhere that it's to do with the summer and winter solstice – you know, the longest and shortest days of the year. The sun lines up with it apparently. That's all I know.'

When they finally reached the stones, they found dozens of tour guides explaining its origins, what kind of stone it was, and how it had decayed with time, but Alexis knew they didn't have the time to stay to listen. Taking Demi's hand, he weaved seamlessly through the crowds of chattering tourists and ducked beneath the barrier that blocked pedestrians from getting close until they reached the simple rope fence that guarded the ruins' circumference.

He'd seen pictures, but Alexis wasn't expecting the monoliths to be so impressive. The giant standing stones were embedded into the ground in a broken circular arrangement, balancing the remains of the lintel rocks between them. It looked . . . powerful.

And Alexis could *hear* something.

At a frequency that he wasn't quite sure was audible, Alexis heard it somehow – a humming. The sensation was as ineffable as it was daunting. His thoughts raced dangerously beneath the surface of his expressionless façade. One thing was clear – this shouldn't be happening. He shouldn't be hearing noises that couldn't be real. He knew what it signalled.

Demi cupped her hands over her ears. 'I don't know if my ears have popped, but I swear I can hear humming.'

Alexis felt his chest deflate. It wasn't just in his head. There must be a speaker or a radio somewhere. Although that didn't explain why he felt so drawn to Stonehenge. He looked longingly at the stones and felt a strong urge to touch them.

'Should we ask someone to take a picture of us?' Demi suggested. As she turned, she bumped into a tall girl about their age with long platinum blonde hair who was in the middle of a debate with a handsome dark-skinned boy.

'It wasn't made by aliens,' the boy chuckled. 'Oh, watch out.'

Demi stumbled backwards. Alexis caught her before she fell, taking a step back as he did to balance himself, his body passing the decking rope guarding Stonehenge.

'Watch where you're going,' snapped the girl, scowling at Demi through hooded stormy grey eyes.

'Sorry, my bad,' said Demi as the broad-shouldered boy raised his hand in apology. Demi turned to thank Alexis.

It was as if all her breath was stolen from her lungs. She didn't say anything. Instead, her eyes widened, fixed upon his chest.

Following her gaze, Alexis looked down to see his amulet

glowing beneath his black T-shirt. The stone shone with a fierce blue light, growing brighter still as he pulled it out to examine. He went to say something to Demi but was interrupted when her own pendant sparked in response. The stone glimmered with a deep, brilliant green.

'Caeli, what the hell is this? Wait . . . what?' Alexis turned to see the muscular boy staring at him, maroon eyes wide with shock. Golden clips decorated his box braids, glinting like burning embers as they reflected the red-glowing amulet hanging from his neck. 'You've got them too?'

'What's going on?' said the silver-haired girl, Caeli. She held up a pendant of her own that pulsed with a steady grey light and looked between her boyfriend and Alexis and Demi. 'Where did you get yours?'

'I've had mine since I was born,' Demi replied, her voice thick with confusion. She took a step closer to them, pulling Alexis with her. As she did, Alexis felt a surge of energy flowing between his amulet and theirs. The pendants simultaneously lifted from their chests in search of one another, like magnets drawn to the opposite pole.

'Is this a prank?' laughed the boy.

'Has yours glowed before?' asked Alexis, inching his hand closer to his own amulet.

The boy shook his head.

'Once,' corrected Caeli. 'The day I met Blaise.'

'Same here,' said Demi. 'Although this feels . . . *stronger*.'

Four stones, all glowing. Two inverted triangles, and two unturned.

As if in an unspoken agreement, without question or

hesitation, the four teenagers allowed the glowing gemstones to meet, the edges of each lining up to make a large diamond that flashed white when they all connected. The joined amulets then pointed towards Stonehenge, and the humming sound that Alexis and Demi thought they heard earlier grew deafeningly loud.

'Seriously,' said Blaise, looking between them. 'How is this happening? And Cae, don't even say aliens.'

Before she could answer, the amulets yanked the four teens to the ground. Alexis could hear blood thundering in his ears as his metal chain cut into his neck and pulled him over the grass as though he weighed nothing. Demi gasped for air beside him, tears dotting her eyes. Somehow, she had not let go of his hand.

The massive rocks of Stonehenge loomed ahead, reverberating as they were dragged towards it by an invisible force. Caeli managed to escape first, ducking out of the way. She rolled past the others, her amulet continuing to fly ahead freely.

With bloodied fingers, Alexis managed to untangle Demi's necklace. The amulet's chain rolled from underneath her chin and she bundled to a stop. At the same moment, Blaise came free just ahead, swinging out to knock Alexis's amulet off-course but failing to connect.

The outer ring whizzed by Alexis as he neared the centre of Stonehenge, the harsh sides of the fallen rocks scraping the bare skin of his arms, his vision darkening where the chain cut off his circulation. The others' amulets had secured onto the base of the stone in the very centre, fitting perfectly into white-glowing hollows that had been carved out in the arrangement of a compass.

Blaise's red stone fastened itself to the south-facing position, Caeli's grey to the east, and Demi's green to the north. Kicking off the ground in one last desperate attempt, the chain came loose from Alexis's neck, and he rolled free only seconds before his amulet slammed into the rock, completing the diamond formation, facing west.

The others joined Alexis in the centre of Stonehenge, staring at each other incredulously. Caeli waved her arms at the crowds of tourists surrounding them, trying to get their attention. 'Are we invisible or something?' She raised her voice. '*Hello?*'

'This can't be real,' Alexis murmured, his hand going to the place on his chest where his amulet had always been. 'This can't be—'

He broke off as an explosive white light burst from Stonehenge, so bright it blinded the four of them and shook the very earth beneath them. As the light hit him, a spasming sensation rippled down Alexis's body. The feeling of untapped energy coursed through him as if it was contained within his blood, his brain, transfixing his body to the spot beside the others. The power flooded his senses until it was too much to comprehend.

The monoliths of the outer ring of Stonehenge rose steadily into the air, summoned by the skies. As the pillars hung above the ground, glowing with a light brighter than the sun, a thunderous chime rang out in waves, undulating across the fields into the horizon.

With each chime, a ripple surged across the earth within the halo of Stonehenge, crumbling the ground beneath the four teens. The earth fell in on itself, breaking away before dissipating into a hollow pit of darkness.

And yet all this time, not a person from outside the structure batted an eyelid. It was as if the spectacular phenomenon occurring to them was nothing but a projection of their minds, a tangible yet imaginary hallucination, one that Alexis could recognise all too well. One that Alexis thought no longer plagued him.

Damn, he knew he should've listened to his mother.

Holding tightly onto each other, the strangers formed an unbreakable connection as the ground disappeared beneath them. When Stonehenge chimed a final time, they plummeted into the dark abyss together.

3
MOIRAI

Moirai (n.) *Greek origin*
The Fates; goddess of fate and destiny

Once the lights faded away and the quaking of the earth drew still, the first noise that followed was that of Caeli moaning.

'I think I'm dead. This is not what I thought heaven looked like.'

'I think we've gone in the wrong direction for heaven,' said Alexis, slowly sitting up.

'And for God's sake, these boots were brand new!'

Blaise threw a handful of damp soil at Caeli. 'Never mind your boots! What the *hell* just happened?'

Following his gaze, Alexis looked skyward to see the huge open hole from which they had fallen. Untethered from power, the bright glow of Stonehenge receded as the structure rebuilt itself, burrowing back into the soil metres above them. The earth's surface was too far for them to reach without climbing, even if they helped each other. They were trapped like prey in the pit, with no sign that anyone would come to their aid.

Alexis took a quick scan of their bleak confinement and saw Demi and Blaise slowly getting up, Caeli remaining sprawled dramatically on the ground until Blaise hauled her to her feet. Aside from the dull ache from landing and the dirt that marked their bodies, they appeared free from injury.

Alexis's relief was short-lived. Sweeping across the pit crawled a blanket of shadow. Visibility in the cave disappeared once the earth sealed above them like a lid closing, plunging them into pitch-black darkness.

'And now we're buried alive!' Caeli cried, trailed by a low thud as she whacked her hand against the wall of mud. 'What is going on? I'm not dying down here.'

'I love your optimism,' Alexis mumbled as his eyes adjusted to the darkness.

All his life, Alexis had worn his amulet. It was the only thing he had left from a time before he was adopted, the only link with his biological parents, whoever they were and wherever they may be. He felt its absence as if it was a lost limb. 'We need to stay calm and find a way out.'

'We should at least start digging,' Demi added, turning on her phone torch. Alexis soon heard her muttering something under her breath as she ran her hand against the edges of the earth. He didn't need to listen for long to know she was praying.

'Do you think this is some sort of trap?' Blaise asked, kicking at the soil with his foot.

'Seems like it.' Alexis dropped to his knees, running his hands across the ground. If this was still a hallucination, it was the most vivid one he'd ever had. On the off chance, the tiniest chance that it could be real, he had to take it seriously.

He couldn't explain it, but even in the darkness, he was

starting to feel an affinity with the strangers, just as he had the first time he saw Demi. He wouldn't let that fool him into letting his guard down though. Probably just danger-bonding. Who knows, maybe they had something to do with it? He doubted it, judging by the shock on their faces and the fact that they were buried in the cavity with him.

Demi was still whispering. Alexis reached for her blindly in the darkness, finding her shaking hand. He placed his own on the small of her back and felt her breathing slow.

Alexis spun round when he heard Caeli thrash out at the wall she had been picking at. Her fear and frustration was turning into wild panic as she began shrieking.

Demi rushed towards her, stepping between her and the wall. 'Hey. *Hey*. Calm down. Caeli, right? Cae?'

'Yeah,' she said, struggling against her.

Demi didn't budge. 'I'm Demi, and this is Alexis. We've probably got our whole class from school looking for us right now. We're going to get out of here. But there's only so much oxygen in here; you'll use it all up screaming like that.' Her soothing voice seemed to resonate, and Caeli soon stopped resisting. Demi turned to the others, speaking with conviction. 'We *are* getting out of here.'

There was a faint skittering noise, the sound of falling earth. Whether by coincidence or luck, a portion of the pit started to loosen, crumbling away in chunks that landed at their feet. Once the dirt settled, what remained was a tunnel entrance, one that led to a brightly lit man-made pathway which slanted deep underground with no end in sight.

Blaise backed away. 'Isn't this the part in the movie where

you scream at the characters to *not* go down the hallway that likely leads to hell?'

'And then they go anyway, don't they?' Alexis replied with a shrug. 'There's no other option.'

'Do you think it leads to a panic room or something?' Demi asked, treading dirt onto the pristine white-glowing floor.

Caeli snorted as she finished wiping her knee-high boots with her sleeve. 'Don't need a room to do that.'

For minutes they walked, barely saying a word, silently searching the pathway for any sign of escape. Blaise bumped into Alexis several times, saying he was worried in case he took a step out of line and risked getting blown up or decapitated. Alexis would have found it annoying had it not served as a distraction from his thoughts.

In the back of his mind, he was trying to silence the fear that had settled there. Was all this his mind playing tricks on him, punishing him for the last few years of thinking he was safe and sane? It wouldn't be the first time that the line between reality and his imagination had blurred for him.

Yet his hallucinations were always of darkness, of shadows. The white-glowing walls of the tunnel had no place in it. This was different somehow. The presence of the others and absence of the *Shadow Man* was enough to prove that, wasn't it? Before Alexis could dwell on the thought, the end of the tunnel came into view.

Approaching with extreme caution, the four teenagers entered a massive white space that looked more like a laboratory than anything else. White and pale blue light shone through the glass panels, not a scratch or an edge along them as they curved to meet the ceiling, illuminating every corner of the room. Metallic high-top tables held dozens of monitors that were faced away from them. Cool air was blowing in from somewhere, sweeping away the oppressive, musky smell of the dank pit they came from.

The room was completely empty, but an open journal with an uncapped pen sat on the main desk, a shot of espresso still steaming beside it.

Someone had been here recently.

In the bright lights, Alexis took a moment to survey the two strangers he was now stuck with. Both were beautiful in the way Demi was, with striking eyes and symmetrical features. Caeli's porcelain pale cheeks were flushed red beneath her high cheekbones. Her manicured eyebrows narrowed as she inspected the room. She caught him looking at her and glared until he averted his eyes.

'Hey, I'm Blaise,' said the boy, leaning over to address Demi with a charming half-smile. He extended his hand, and she shook it. Alexis counted the seconds he held it; it was longer than necessary. Alexis noted his strong jaw and broad shoulders, accented by a tight designer t-shirt, and felt a rush of heat prickle the back of his neck at the way he looked at Demi.

Demi smiled politely and then returned to Alexis's side.

'This looks like some sort of lab or government headquarters,' said Caeli, shouldering past Blaise as she made to move towards the computers. 'Where are w—?'

A low growl rumbled through the laboratory, freezing Caeli mid-step. The only other entrance – or exit – was through the double doors at the far end of the room, and looming beyond was a creature. A snow-white wolf, larger than Alexis thought was possible. It was as beautiful as it was dangerous as it bared its ferocious teeth and approached them with long, heavy strides.

Blaise gasped and pulled Caeli back by the waist. 'Is that a *wolf*?'

'It's definitely not a Chihuahua,' Alexis retorted, wishing he had a more useful response to threat than sarcasm.

The animal neared, lowering its body to the ground and locking its stormy eyes with Alexis. It snarled again, saliva dripping with every step. It was preparing to attack.

Before Alexis could stop her, Demi stepped out between them and the wolf. She reached her hand slowly to its nose and spoke in gentle tones. 'Hey, boy. We're not going to hurt you, we promise.'

The wolf's ears softened slightly, the growl dwindling in its throat. But before Alexis could relax, the doors to the laboratory burst open again.

This time, it was a man, a man so beautiful he looked like an angel, with neatly cropped white hair and piercing blue eyes that sparkled in the artificial light. His face was full of colour as if he had been running. He skidded to a halt and beamed at the sight of them.

'About bloody time you guys showed up! You have no idea how many decades I've been waiting for you.'

Even though Alexis knew he had never met the man before, there was something familiar about him. Maybe it was the smile on his tanned face, the complexion similar to his own, or how the light seemed to reflect off his ivory robe to make him look like he was glowing.

'*Gibbous*,' the white-haired man said sternly, crossing muscular arms. 'Be nice.'

The wolf, Gibbous, retreated, and stood by the man's side.

Despite everything that had happened, the first question that Blaise asked was, 'Your wolf is called Gibbous?' Then, after a beat, 'What've you been feeding it?'

The man chuckled. 'Named after one of the moon's phases. And he eats anyone who wanders into the lab . . .' Met with a collective gasp, the man raised both hands. 'That was a joke; poorly timed, I must admit.'

'What did you mean you've been *waiting* for us?' Alexis asked.

'Are you the one who trapped us here?' Demi added.

'That? It wasn't a trap,' the man replied, amused. 'It was to bring you here safely.'

'Drop us into a pit and bury us alive?' Caeli said, her face upturned with doubt. 'Who's in charge of health and safety around here?'

Alexis interjected. 'Who are you? And how do you know us?'

The man considered the four teenagers. He took in their appearances one by one. He examined Alexis last, staring at him for a few seconds longer than the others, his face concealing whatever he was thinking with an easy smile. Alexis didn't take it personally; he had learnt that the black and blue heterochromia of his eyes usually made people stare.

'Alexis Michaels. Blaise Ademola. Caeli Doran. Demetria Nikolas.' The man recited their names like he had known them for years. 'I wouldn't expect you to remember me. You

41

were mere minutes old when we last met. My name is Incantus Arcangelo.'

Incantus held out his hand and the loose sleeve fell away from his wrist. A white glow spread over his open palm, emanating from his fingertips to his wrist. From behind him, suspended in the air as if held by invisible strings, the four amulets floated towards him.

The pendants continued to glow dimly, supercharged under Incantus's invisible touch; blue, green, grey, and red. Incantus gestured them forward to claim their stones.

'I gave you your amulets on the days you were born. But it was Stonehenge that brought them here. And fate that brought you all to Stonehenge today. Gibbous, go say hello, you big softy,' he added, seeing the wolf's tail wagging at Demi who smiled hesitantly at him. Demi stroked his head before he rolled onto his back to expose his belly. She brushed his silky white fur with her nails.

'This still doesn't make sense,' said Alexis, fingers tapping his thumbs behind his back.

Incantus nodded. 'Why don't you all have a seat? There is a lot to cover.'

None of them sat. They just stood there, waiting for Incantus to begin. Finally, after a deep breath, he began.

'There is no easy way to say this, so I'll just . . . say it. Stonehenge brought the four of you here because you are the Children of the Elements. Your arrival here has been expected for some time, because it was foretold in the Prophecy of Light and Darkness. The prophecy says that you – the four of you, with your Elemental powers – are destined to destroy Mortem and the Darkness.'

Demi let out an involuntary laugh, Caeli scrunched her face up in disbelief, and Blaise swore. Alexis said nothing.

A long silence ensued as Caeli picked neon pink polish from her fingernails.

Incantus sat patiently, waiting for one of them to respond.

Alexis turned the amulet over in his hand. In the centre of the blue stone was a delicate engraving of a drop of water. *The Children of the Elements.* Alexis knew what element he would be linked to even if he didn't have the amulet. His obsession with rain and the ocean. Powerful, chaotic, dangerous.

He couldn't deny it. Ever since the white light struck him at Stonehenge, he had felt something coursing through him. As if his blood was amplified. As if there was a power contained within, something that had been locked away all his life but now urged to be unleashed.

But it made no sense. Caeli and Blaise were strangers. How could they have been drawn together? What could this man possibly mean by saying that they were *destined to destroy the Darkness*? And who in the hell was Mortem?

Eventually, it was Incantus who spoke again, his deep voice rich with enthusiasm. 'Even though what I am saying sounds completely implausible, deep down you all must know it is true.' The teens exchanged silent glances. 'Everything that has happened today is because it was meant to happen that way. Not coincidence, but fate. And now that you have come to Stonehenge, your power is finally accessible.'

Caeli peered around as if looking for hidden cameras and whispered, 'Do you think this is some sort of reality TV show?'

Blaise laughed, eyes shining with excitement. 'You're telling me you don't feel different since Stonehenge? I feel like my heart is beating so fast it's on fire.'

'That's just heartburn,' Caeli countered. 'Doesn't mean that he's telling us the truth. We weren't even supposed to be here. We stopped here by chance for a break.'

'I feel it as well,' Demi spoke up.

Caeli frowned. 'You can't be that naive?'

'I thought it was fear or adrenaline at first, but it's more than that. It's in my bones,' Demi continued, unshaken. 'It's as if they're . . . vibrating with a kind of energy. Don't get me wrong, I don't know if I believe in whatever this prophecy is – no offence, sir – but I can't ignore what I feel.'

Caeli stared ahead, her grey eyes unblinking. Then, with a long sigh, her chest deflated, and she turned to meet Demi. 'My lungs,' she said quietly, glancing between them. 'My lungs feel . . . bigger. I feel as if I've never taken a proper breath until right now.' Although she didn't exactly break a smile, the crease between her eyebrows faded.

Alexis felt their attention shift to him.

He knew the warning signs of his psychosis: avolition, decline of his personal hygiene, paranoia. Yet he had never felt more alert. The daily experience of life had never felt so vivid, so tangible. Was there a chance this could be real?

'You are not alone,' Incantus reassured them, encouraged by their gradual acquiescence. 'There are others who possess powers. We are called Elementals. But since the First Borns, no one has ever been born with the powers of the *first four elements* until you.' Incantus paused, looking between each of

44

them with a knowing smile. 'I assume you do not need me to tell you which power you each possess.'

The four stared at their amulets. Caeli's the colour of a windstorm, Blaise's bright as a flame, Demi's a bold forest green, and Alexis's sparkling ocean blue.

'Mr Michaels, I didn't meet you at birth to give you your amulet like the others; I met you a couple of years after. It was then that I, with the help of another Elemental, placed the block that would shield you from your powers and this world. It is nice to finally meet you again, Alexis.'

Alexis sighed. Of course he had to be the one different from the rest, even in a fantasy world. He then realised something – the sequence of time laying out before him, or rather behind him.

'Was it before I was adopted?'

He noted the eagerness in his voice, and instantly felt guilty. It wasn't that he wasn't proud of being adopted. He couldn't dream for better parents. It was just that his whole life he had wondered who his birth parents were. Incantus could know that. It was the only time in years that he could grow closer to finding out a little bit about them, and in turn, about himself.

Incantus shifted his weight, tucked his hands into his pockets. 'I believe it was after,' he said.

Alexis shook his head. He had too many questions and no idea where to begin.

As if reading his mind, Incantus smiled, and the hallway he had come from lit up behind him. 'I will explain everything. But first, you need to be proxied.'

4

QUERENCIA

Querencia (n.) *Spanish origin*
A place from which one's strength is drawn, where one feels
at home; the place where you are your most authentic self

Incantus led them through a labyrinth of brightly lit corridors
towards what appeared to be the heart of the huge underground
compound. Gibbous strode by his right side, turning round
every so often to remind Demi to keep petting him.

The wolf kept its distance from Alexis, as if he had sniffed
something on him he didn't like. What about Alexis could hope
to unnerve a beast so big? Instead, Alexis focussed on trying to
memorise the route they were taking, just in case they needed
to go back for any reason. All the while, he quietly watched
Incantus, waiting to see if his benevolence was just an act.

'What exactly is being *proxied*?' asked Blaise excitedly.

'Well, a proxy is a sort of clone for an Elemental,' said
Incantus.

'How do we get them?' probed Caeli. She was still yet to
smile at the man, seemingly as cynical as Alexis. 'There's no
research on human cloning trials yet as far as I know. And why
do we need one?'

'If you consent, you will need to live and train here for the next few weeks,' Incantus answered. 'Your absence, I'm sure, would not go unnoticed by your loved ones. Your old lives should not end just because you are making new ones. So, I can create a single proxy for each of you. A perfect replica to take your place.'

'I'll believe it when I see it,' said Caeli.

Incantus seemed impervious to her pessimism, his cheerful smile unwavering. 'You soon shall, Miss Doran.'

'How do you do it?' Demi asked brightly. 'Is it one of your powers?'

Incantus didn't turn around as he replied. His voice, however, dropped an octave. 'No, it was my father's. He had the power to replicate himself countless number of times. He carried out many experiments, trying to see if he could also create proxies of others. He never succeeded in his lifetime, leaving in his wake only death.' Incantus paused. 'He couldn't figure out how to stop the body from ripping apart to create the proxy or how to have control over it. It meant any successful clone would also share their power and could choose not to return to the Elemental. I've since figured it out, ensuring a safe procedure that is widely used in our community. Ah, here we are.'

Alexis once again found himself lost for words. They stood at the top of an enormous beehive structure carved entirely from white marble stone. Dozens of suspended golden bridges crossed over the open, hollow core of the complex, interconnecting the different sides and levels of the hexagon-shaped compound.

Incantus flung his arms wide. 'Welcome to the Haven.'

As they leaned against the balustrade, a holographic projection of the Haven appeared before them, displaying the five levels of the seemingly infinitely sized facility.

'There's a sixth floor,' Incantus said. 'This floor, but that's reserved for me alone.'

Alexis peered at the labels. The ringed levels that encircled the central hive consisted of anything a person could conceivably need, from a Healing Sanctuary to a Training Academy to the Hub, which sat at the bottom of the core. It was like an entire village.

But it wasn't just the size of the Haven that amazed Alexis. It was the *feel* of it. Static energy coursed through his body the moment he arrived, making his skin tingle in equal parts trepidation and exhilaration. Did it have something to do with meeting the others – or possibly Stonehenge or the Haven itself? Was it his power?

'It's like we're in an underground Mount Olympus,' Demi marvelled, with a wide-toothed grin of wonder. 'It's incredible. Who are all those people?'

'Other Elementals,' Incantus said, gesturing to the tiny figures roaming on the ground floor. 'Most Elementals develop their powers during puberty and their parents often send them here to train, learn and live away from the human world. The Elemental bloodline is inherited, you see, but only a small number of our kind possess powers.'

'So you built this place for them?' Caeli asked.

He laughed. 'I built the Haven primarily for *you*, the four of you, for the time when the stars deemed it right for you to find me. Decades passed. I– *we*, thought it could be used for more.

48

That it *should* be used for more. For a long time now, the Haven operates as a teaching and training facility for Elementals who will use their powers to protect others from the creatures or criminals of our world that may seek to harm them.'

Light seemed to spill out of Incantus when he spoke to them. Each time he felt his eyes on him, Alexis couldn't and didn't want to look away, as though he was the sun, with the power to cast away the shadows of doubt and distrust in Alexis's mind.

'When you say creatures, what do you mean?' Blaise asked.

There was a twinkle in Incantus's eyes. 'Mythological creatures, you'd call them.'

Blaise swore in disbelief as Alexis smiled and instantly thought of his brother, of how much he would love it here. As annoying as he could be, he felt a surprising pang of longing for Jason.

'Come along,' Incantus said, marching onto one of the suspended marble pathways that bridged the Haven's core, unhesitant as if two steps to the side wouldn't have him tumbling over the edge. Gibbous trotted after him, equally as unfazed.

Caeli was the first to lead the others, striding down the path as though it was a catwalk, seemingly fearless of heights. About halfway across, she stopped to turn back.

Demi hadn't yet taken a step, her hand still gripping the railing, eyes blinking rapidly at the floor hundreds of metres below.

Caeli extended her hand to Demi, offering an encouraging smile. 'Thank you,' Demi whispered as she let Caeli guide her across, Alexis and Blaise following.

'How could we have gone our lives not seeing anything like this if we're Elementals?' Demi asked, her voice shaking as she kept her gaze straight ahead. 'You said our powers are hereditary. Did our families keep it a secret from us?'

'My parents never mentioned I got my amulet from a stranger,' Blaise added. 'Although they always told me I was meant for greatness. Can't say the same about the rest of you yet.'

Alexis felt his jaw tick, but he didn't retaliate.

Incantus helped them off the pathway at the other side of the Haven. He directed them down another long, high-ceiling, white-walled corridor.

'I'm not here to disclose whether or not your parents are a part of this world, that is not my truth to tell. However, at your births, and some time after you were adopted,' he added, nodding at Alexis, 'I gave you the amulets owed to you as your birthright. Then, one of my associates placed an inhibition block on you all to prevent you from developing your powers and seeing into this world.'

'Why?'

'For your safety,' Incantus answered simply. 'Like humans, not all Elementals are good. Every Elemental knows of the Children of the Elements and the Prophecy to destroy Mortem. Some would like to prevent that. Your powers would act as a beacon. The block stopped you from accessing them – and stopped Mortem from being able to find you. The Prophecy stated you had to be raised apart from this world. When the time was right, you would find your way back to us.'

The corridor led to a set of sealed golden doors which opened automatically at their arrival, revealing a large circular office.

Alexis was hit with the welcoming smell of old paper and wood. The two-tiered room had a vintage library-like feel to it; worn brown leather sofas lined the edges of the walls beside the ash-marble fireplace, and over a dozen stacked bookcases zig-zagged across the opposite side. Along the spines of some of the older books were titles in languages he couldn't read, possibly ancient Greek or Latin, Sanskrit or Arabic or Hebrew.

To Alexis, *this* was heaven.

Gibbous curled himself in front of the white-burning hearth, his huge back expanding with every breath as he started to snore. A wide wooden desk covered with scattered maps and books sat towards the back of the room, and Incantus perched against it. Underneath a map that had vaguely pinpointed the four compass directions across the globe were sketches of mythical creatures. From a glance, Alexis saw what looked like a grey-scaled Chinese dragon.

'Mr Arcangelo–Incantus,' said Alexis as they took a seat on the welcoming sofa opposite Incantus. 'What *is* the Prophecy?'

Incantus was quiet for a moment, and when he spoke his tone was gentle, like Alexis's mother's when she was on the phone, delivering disappointing news to a patient.

'The Prophecy of Light and Darkness speaks of six individuals with powers no one has ever had since the First Born Elementals aeons ago. The four Children of the Elements, each possessing one of the four primal elements; an Elemental with the power of light, me; and another with darkness. Mortem possesses the ancient shadow power, and with it, he wishes to dominate our people and replace our governing body, the High Order, to command over us. He hopes to achieve this by covering the world in eternal shadow. The Prophecy states that only you have the power to stop him.' His gaze dropped. 'That's all I can tell you, I'm afraid.'

'Why can't you tell us more?' asked Caeli. 'It's about us so why shouldn't we know our fates?'

Incantus suddenly looked weary. Older. 'No one should know their future,' he said. 'It has driven wiser people mad as they try to actualise or avoid it. I'm sorry, but know this is from a place of care, not control.'

Alexis swallowed hard. He knew himself well enough to know his insatiable curiosity likely wouldn't accept the ignorance of not knowing. If one could be intolerant to feeling naive, Alexis would be deathly allergic to it.

'I can tell you one more thing,' Incantus decided, making them lean in towards him. 'I believe that it is only through our *combined* powers that we can stop Mortem. And this must be before the next solar eclipse, here at Stonehenge.'

The pressure in the room seemed to slowly intensify. *The next solar eclipse*, thought Alexis. He wasn't sure who had asked when that would be, but he wished they hadn't.

'On the summer solstice,' said Incantus. 'In one month.'

5

SELCOUTH

Selcouth (adj.) *Old English origin*
Unfamiliar, rare, strange, and yet marvellous

If Incantus had anticipated questions, complaints and outright protests, then he could add fortune-telling to his list of powers.

'Your power will come to you naturally!' he assured them, rising from his seat. Encumbered by his robe, he shrugged it off, revealing the silvery-white bodysuit that clung to every muscle on his body. It seemed to cause them to forget whatever they were saying, although Alexis wasn't convinced it had any stun-like properties. 'Your powers are innate. It's more a case of learning how to use them. It isn't ideal, but you will have the very best trainers in the Haven – including me.'

'Modest of you,' mumbled Caeli.

'Who is Mortem?' Alexis asked. 'Before we get proxied or go any further, tell us why we have to do this. Who is he and why does he want this?'

'He was once one of us,' said Incantus, wringing his hands at the apparent memory. 'I trained him and, in turn, he worked with me and my allies in some of our greatest battles for the High Order. For the longest time, he was believed to be

53

the first of the Children of the Elements, the one with the power of the water.'

Everyone turned to Alexis. He felt himself growing red. 'I–I thought you said no one has had our powers before.'

'That is true for the others, but not for you. I am still yet to understand how or why. All I know is that Mortem became seduced by the powers of darkness and sacrificed his control of the water to enable these to grow, allowing another of only Elemental blood to be born with this ability in line with the Prophecy.' Incantus scratched his jaw. 'Mortem was obsessed with becoming the most powerful Elemental in the world, stronger than I. He wanted to impart onto the world the pain and suffering he had endured in his youth – not to seek change or to bring about justice, but for no other reason than revenge. He murdered any that stood in his way to acquire control and power – mortals, Elementals, friends.' He let out a deep breath. 'Even family. It's why he *must* be stopped.'

'What happens if we say no?' Demi asked softly. 'If we don't want to put ourselves in the way of this person?'

Incantus's look was grave. 'That is, of course, your choice. But I have studied the Prophecy all my life. Only through the power of your amulets can I hope to thwart him. Without you, we will lose everything.'

Blaise stood abruptly and stalked over to the burning fireplace, his hands extended to the flames.

'What are you doing?' Caeli asked through gritted teeth as though he was embarrassing her.

Blaise's jaw was taut, his eyes narrowed in concentration. 'I'm calling his bluff.'

There was a beat, and then the air in the room stilled. The fire that had been burning brightly in the hearth faltered, suddenly losing its colour. The white coal sizzled as the fire waned until extinguished. Gibbous huffed disappointedly at the sudden lack of warmth.

There was a flash of red out of the corner of Alexis's eye. It had come from Blaise's amulet which glistened on his chest like a luminescent ruby.

Blaise gasped, holding his hands out before him. They glowed scarlet, as though he had just plunged them into the fire itself. When he clicked his fingers, sparks of orange flew from them.

Caeli jumped to her feet. 'No way!'

Incantus chuckled with joy as he went over to the fireplace to reignite it for Gibbous. 'Do you believe me now, Mr Ademola? Your elements *want* to be used. Power pours from your fingertips.'

In spite of everything, this was the first true sign that what Incantus had told them was real – that they really did have powers.

Blaise spun to the others. 'Feel them,' he said.

Caeli tentatively reached out to touch his hands. 'They're still warm!'

Alexis couldn't help but notice Blaise's amber eyes were brighter in colour, his skin seeming to glow, although he wasn't sure whether it was with pride or with power. He was happy for Blaise, he really was, but a small a part of him felt disappointed that he hadn't been the one to use his powers first. He knew it wasn't a competition. But if it was . . . Blaise was now in the lead.

'How about we save any other questions for later,' Incantus suggested, heading towards the back of the office. He pulled away one of the bookshelves with ease as though it didn't contain dozens of heavy-bound books to reveal a short hidden passageway. 'Ready to make your proxies?'

'A secret passageway?' gasped Demi. She dragged Alexis up with both arms. 'This I have *got* to see. '

The teens fought to go through first, cramming themselves through the doorway into the adjoining hidden room. This time, the chamber was practically bare and far smaller than the office. Inside were only two things: a wardrobe-size silver machine that somewhat resembled a vertical sarcophagus, and a small shallow pool built into the ground. As they neared, Alexis saw that it didn't contain water at all, but rather a denser, pale substance. The pool's still surface was a liquid mirror that reflected the ceiling, which was engraved with a series of interlocking triangles.

'This is the Proxying Chamber,' Incantus announced. He gestured to the machine which opened on command, folding away on itself to reveal a space large enough for a single person to enter. 'Your proxies will take on your current memories and thoughts to act in the way you would. It will allow you to essentially live two lives, in both the human and Elemental world. They do not experience emotions in the same way that you do; they are merely simulacra, illusory representations of you. When you wish to become one, you can make the proxy return to you, taking on board the memories and experiences it made as if it were your own.'

Blaise held up an imaginary drink. 'Here's to never revising for an exam again!'

Caeli scoffed. 'I'm sure you'll make great use of those extra ten minutes a month.'

Incantus continued. 'When you enter, you will be scanned and given a proxying serum. Its effects are immediate, so you must then submerge yourself in the Kathreftis straight away.' He nodded at the pool.

'Kathreftis,' Demi repeated, her head tilting as she stared at the reflective pool's surface. 'Greek for "mirror." My sister and I were raised in Greece before our parents moved here. It's my first language, then Arabic, then English.'

'Well done, Miss Nikolas. It is extremely important to submerge yourself completely in the Kathreftis,' Incantus instructed. 'That liquid will ensure your body doesn't, ah, destroy itself in the creation of the proxy.'

'Yeah, we wouldn't want that,' said Blaise. 'Al, tell us how it feels, will you?'

Alexis pulled a face. 'Wait, what? Why should I go first?'

Blaise shrugged. 'I've proven I'm an Elemental. This is your chance.'

Alexis glared at the grinning Blaise, trying to figure out if he was going to like or loathe him. Although he did have a point. He didn't want Demi to trial it and risk getting hurt. Rather he than her.

'If you're scared, you should've just said so,' said Alexis. Blaise snorted, but Alexis saw the fire in his eyes. *Two could play that game*, he thought.

Incantus led Alexis over to the machine where he stepped inside. For a moment, Alexis was sure he saw a flash of worry on his face – belying his usual calm confidence. Maybe it was because it was the first time proxying one of the Children of the Elements, or maybe the procedure as a whole wasn't as straightforward as he had made it sound. Either way, it was too late for Alexis to turn back. It was time to test the reality of Incantus and the Elemental world for himself.

'It shouldn't take a minute,' Incantus said, offering him an encouraging smile.

The space was small and dark, but it wasn't until the door was secured after him, locking him away from the outside, that Alexis began to feel suddenly claustrophobic. *Stupid to have gone first*, he thought, tapping his fingers to his thumbs to calm himself.

Alexis held his breath as multiple red laser lights scanned the length and width of his body. Then a small syringe appeared from a hole above him. It pierced the skin of his neck, injecting him with some sort of thick potion that he could feel seeping into his bloodstream.

Within seconds, Alexis felt it flooding his brain, jostling the delicate stability of his mind as a wave of nausea rippled down the length of his body. The syringe retracted and the door snapped opened. After the darkness, the bright light of the room was blinding.

'Don't worry, Mr Michaels, the pain and dizziness will subside,' said Incantus, sounding like he was a couple of metres away.

Alexis barely heard him. He had doubled over, clutching the sides of his head. He could feel a strong arm wrap round his waist – Demi. 'Is it supposed to hurt this much?'

Incantus's unsure silence was an answer. 'Get into the pool,' he said, his voice calm but with a note of strain.

He doesn't know if this will work, Alexis thought.

The others looked away while he clumsily undressed. Then, with both hands gripping the rail, he stumbled down the steps leading into the thick white liquid.

The Kathreftis was warm to the touch, like candle wax. He walked further down the steps, the surface passing his knees, waist, shoulders. Taking a deep breath, he dived his head under, running his hands across his body so that not an inch was left dry.

'Whatever you do, don't panic,' he heard Incantus say, his voice distorted through the viscous liquid.

Alexis broke the surface, breathing heavily and blinking wildly, his bottom half still submerged. He was glaringly aware of Demi's eyes on his chest, arms, lower stomach. He didn't have time to ponder why she was blushing so deeply.

A violent ripple shot through Alexis, forcing him to buckle as he felt suddenly aware of the number of cells, nerves and muscle fibres within him, a number that was doubling to the point where his skin could no longer contain it all. Before his very eyes, Alexis watched in equal parts horror and awe as his skin became malleable, translucent almost, like liquid glass in the sunlight.

And then, without a drop of blood, a human hand emerged from his chest.

It didn't hurt, simply slipped through, taking his migraine with it. Another hand followed, its weight becoming tangible once free, making Alexis stumble to keep his balance. And then, in one great final release, the rest of the body followed.

Alexis opened his eyes to see his body untouched, not a scratch or break on his lean frame. In front of him stood another person sharing his height, his build, even the moles on his arms and faint freckles on his cheeks. The only thing it didn't share was his amulet.

Standing before him, looking as shocked as he was, was *another Alexis*.

6

IKIGAI

Ikigai (n.) *Japanese origin*
A reason for being; the thing that gets you up in the
morning; purpose in life

'This can't be real,' said both Alexis and his proxy in unison.

Blaise was jumping on the spot in excitement, jostling Demi and Caeli's shoulders. 'No way. No way! All right, now I believe you, Mr Angel.'

Caeli was shaking her head in disbelief. 'There's . . . there's *two of him*. Do you know how much stuff I could get done if there was two of me?'

Alexis had always wondered what he looked like from someone else's perspective. Now he could see, more clearly than in a mirror. For a few seconds, all he did was stare at his proxy, taking in the curve of its shoulders, the narrowing of its waist, the swell of muscle bulging from its chest. Tanned skin, full lips, dark hair.

Neither spoke. Alexis remembered Incantus saying that proxies didn't feel emotions in the same way as their counterparts, but did this being share his memories, his fears? Its blue and black ringed eyes were locked onto his. For reasons he couldn't explain, just as he would when looking at his reflection in the mirror, Alexis looked away before blinking.

Suddenly, Alexis realised how exposed he was. 'Er. Could I have my clothes?'

Incantus stepped forward, his mouth stretched into an easy smile. 'If you decide to stay, I was hoping you could wear this.'

He held out a seamless full-body suit, similar to the one he was wearing, only it was threaded with the colour of midnight. A rich sapphire blue seam ran across the hems, cuffs and a single diagonal stripe across the torso. Another three lay in a pile on the floor, with corresponding vermillion, forest green, and dusty rose coloured detail, pairs of sturdy boots beside them.

Alexis hadn't seen such material before, but it looked comfortable, both weightless yet tough, tight but breathable. He pulled the black suit over his body with ease. It adapted to his shape as if it were enchanted, moulding to his form. As the neckline reached his throat, Alexis pulled his amulet free before resting it against his chest.

'I want to speak to whoever designed these,' said Caeli as she snatched hers up. 'They are so lush. And pockets! They have pockets!'

'Raeve and Taranis designed these suits to be adaptable to your powers,' said Incantus as Alexis passed his old clothes to his proxy. 'Resistant to attacks, particularly human weaponry, it will also modify to different environments to maintain your core vitals. It's all you'll need to be wearing during your training and . . . after.'

He cleared his throat when he noticed Alexis and his proxy playing rock-paper-scissors, Blaise beside them mesmerised when they kept drawing. Demi came to inspect them with her eyes closed, trying to sense which one she knew to be her Alexis. By his aura, or possibly that when he laughed it sounded more sincere, she managed to correctly identify him, her success making Alexis smile to himself.

There was a glimmer in Incantus's eyes, making Alexis wonder how long he had been waiting for them, whether they were what he had been expecting. Whether they were *enough* for whatever was needed of them. 'Once I make proxies of Miss Nikolas, Miss Doran, and Mr Ademola, I would like you to suit up to meet with the Leaders. Once there, I promise all your questions will be answered.'

It was approaching an hour later before all four teenagers were proxied and suited up.

Demi stretched and squatted as she tested her suit's range of motion. 'It's like a second skin. Good thing, too, because I bloat *all* the time.'

'More importantly, we look *good*,' Blaise added. He did a ninja pose, and then threw in a karate chop at Alexis for good measure. Alexis couldn't deny that he was beginning to find him entertaining. He blocked it and returned a strike, play-fighting with him the way he would with Jason.

'If you two are finished with whatever you are doing,' Incantus said, looking slightly concerned. 'It's about time the proxies were sent up.'

Incantus removed a flat silvered disk from his pocket. At his touch, a holographic screen was projected. He swiped at the display and a large round platform lowered from the ceiling, untethered by any strings or machinery. As the replicas began walking towards the podium, Alexis pulled his proxy aside.

'Take care of them,' Alexis whispered. 'Mum and Dad and Jace. Call me if anything unusual happens . . . to them or to you.'

The proxy nodded reassuringly. 'I will look after them as if they were my own.'

His proxy squeezed his hand before joining the others, finding its place beside Demi's replica who was chatting with Caeli and Blaise's proxies.

Light escaped from Incantus's palm and the disks hummed, glowing with energy. The proxies' bodies flickered, and a moment later, they vanished into thin air.

'They have reappeared on ground level not far from Stonehenge and will be doing exactly what you would do in this situation,' Incantus informed them, heading out of the room.

'I hope they're okay,' said Demi, biting her lip. 'I don't want to make her do something she doesn't want to do, even if she – *it* isn't really real.'

'They are not people in the way you think,' Incantus said. 'They have no life without you, no aura or soul. Think of them as reflections, that's all.' His eyes softened. 'But your concern for them says a lot about the person you are.'

Demi broke into a slight, shy smile. Incantus's light seemed to be infectious, and Alexis found himself desperate for his approval. Maybe in this world, there was a chance at being accepted.

'Come,' said Incantus. 'Let us go meet the Leaders.' Gibbous stirred at their presence and got up to join them. They exited the long, wide corridor before beginning their descent down the Haven, walking around the huge gold-banister spiral staircase that encircled the hollow hive centre.

Elementals of all ages, suited in similar all-black training suits, walked past, greeting Incantus with familiarity and respect as one would a boss or headteacher. Alexis realised that some were looking at the foursome, their eyes fixed on the amulets. A chorus of whispers and gasps followed them in recognition of who they must be.

Caeli ran her hands down her new uniform to ensure there were no creases. 'Not going to lie, kind of loving this attention.'

'They've probably noticed the mud still in your hair,' Blaise mumbled, laughing as she violently combed through her silver-blonde hair.

They exited the level that read 'Student Dormitories' along a narrow walkway. Splashes of coloured sketches decorated the sides of the walls, some finely detailed, others more childish, drawn in crayon. A theme soon evolved, with each depicting four beings with a coloured stone in their hands that illuminated the surrounding black shadow.

'I guess we're kind of a legend,' Blaise said, realisation dawning on him. 'The Children of the Elements.'

'We have been waiting for you for a long time. Ever since Mortem revealed his darkness powers.' Incantus's reply was short, but carried the weight of significance. Gibbous's ears pricked up at the mention of Mortem, and only lowered once Incantus stroked his head.

Demi paused in front of one of the drawings, stroking the cracked paint. 'Why us four, Incantus? What makes us so special? How did all of this come to be?' Alexis noticed her free hand was holding her crucifix, tugging on the chain slightly, testing its strength, and with it, her faith.

'It is because you are the direct descendants of the First Borns. The first Elementals, created by the Elemental Gems.'

'The Elemental Gems?' Alexis asked.

'Ancient primordial gemstones born from the Darkness, hosting the first four elements, *your* elements, and their states of matter.' Incantus gestured to the glowing stones held by four female figures. 'It's said that the Women of the Elements, each representing a Gem, used their limitless powers to create all that we know. They chipped away a portion of their Gems to carve your amulets, sharing with the First Borns one power each to defend their creation. At the site of Stonehenge, the First Borns joined their powers to make light, and sacrificed their lives to destroy the Darkness. Stonehenge remains their resting ground.'

Without having realised he had been slowly walking, Alexis found himself staring at the last piece of art on the wall. It showed the faint outline of four individuals, each in a different colour, standing within the broken ring of Stonehenge. There were no more drawings after that.

Caeli shook her head in confusion. 'If they died, how do Elementals exist today? And how did the darkness or shadows or whatever come back?'

'We're not sure,' Incantus admitted. 'We will likely never know how it survived. As for Elemental-kind, the First Borns had children before they died. Your amulets remained buried here, and once I found them, I held onto them until the world saw the birth of the Children of the Elements, their direct heirs.'

Alexis found himself lost in thought as they walked on. For as long as he could remember, he never considered himself someone who was special for the right reasons. Growing up, the things that made him different were the things that made him feel alone. And yet within the space of a few hours, he was expected to believe there existed an entire hidden world where people had been waiting for his arrival for centuries before he had even been born.

After a lifetime unsure whether the shadows he saw were real or not, it was second nature for Alexis to be distrustful, especially of the things that appeared most wondrous. He hated that he wasn't as innately trusting as Demi was, but he hadn't had the luxury of always believing the things he saw and heard.

They arrived at the end of the hallway where there were four short flights of stairs leading in opposite directions. Each door was engraved with one of the classical symbols for air, water, earth or fire.

'The Leaders are waiting for us in here,' said Incantus, stopping by a door with an upturned triangle, the sign for water. He patted a nervous-looking Gibbous. 'Off you go, friend, you do not need to come in.'

Suddenly apprehensive, Alexis followed Incantus inside, and found himself star-struck once again. It was an enormous room, far bigger than it looked from the outside. The faint bluish hue and the coolness of the air was the first thing he noticed. The second thing was the swimming pool. It divided the upper and lower halves of the room, arching across in a half-circle, a single lane. A short flight of stairs crossed over the centre, leading toward the elevated bedroom area, complete with a king-sized bed, wardrobes, and an adjoining bathroom. Beneath the suspended staircase trickled a single, metre-high waterfall that flowed into the pool, the gentle sound reminiscent of the rain. Alexis longed to touch the water. It seemed that unleashing his powers had made him even more drawn to his element.

There was something, however, that held Alexis's attention more so than anything else. Sitting before the pool, in the mostly cleared lower section of the room, was a huge mahogany table, and standing around it were three individuals. They stopped mid-conversation at the silent entrance of the Children of the Elements. Alexis could feel the power radiating from them, making the hairs on his arms stand up.

Intimidating. Important. Powerful.

'Children,' said Incantus proudly. 'Meet the Leaders of the Haven.'

7

NODUS TOLLENS

Nodus Tollens (n.) *Latin origin*
The realisation that the plot of your life
does not make sense to you anymore

The Leaders didn't look like anything Alexis had expected. Then again, he didn't know what he *had* expected. They were similarly dressed in the Haven uniform, only theirs were deep grey in colour, as if they had been woven with threads of malleable titanium.

He leaned into Caeli who he thought would appreciate the joke. 'I wonder if they get an offer on the suits when they buy in bulk.'

She snorted. 'I'm growing to like you.'

The first Leader came forth, speaking with a faint Caribbean accent. 'We got your message and came immediately, Ian.'

Ian? Alexis snuck a look at Incantus. He wondered whether it was a nickname or possibly Incantus's real name. *Didn't sound as cool*, Alexis thought.

This Leader looked older than Incantus, somewhere in his fifties or sixties, and was probably the largest person Alexis had ever seen. His bald head was creased with deep wrinkles, his silver beard neatly cropped, a stark contrast to the warm brownness of his skin. Despite looking like he was a semi-retired, steroid-fuelled bodybuilder, loose caramel and beige robes were draped over his suit, the juxtaposition between the two looks oddly complementary.

The second Leader fidgeting beside him couldn't be more different. His frame was lean, his blond hair gelled meticulously upward as if he had been shocked by lightning. His blue eyes were flecked with yellow, darting excitedly. 'Is this them? I can't believe they're here!' Alexis wasn't sure if his eyes were deceiving him, but it looked as if the outline of his body was *flickering*.

The woman had raven-coloured hair pulled into a tight ponytail that fell to just below her shoulders. Swirling lines of black and gold ink curled round the base of her neck. But it was her eyes that entranced Alexis into a stillness. Her gaze was hypnotic.

'They look strong,' the woman said. 'Untrained, but strong.'

Incantus was beaming as he explained, 'The Leaders help me run the Haven and train Elementals to use their powers. They each represent one of the three sectors our Elementals can specialise as when they graduate: Scholar, Fighter or Healer.' He brought forward the muscular bald man, resting his hand against his boulder-sized shoulder. 'This is one of my oldest and dearest friends, Akili Pierce, who guides the Healers.'

Towering over the young Elementals, he shook each of their hands, his grip surprisingly delicate. 'It's nice to finally meet you. I know that with a bit of training, you can become the best of us. You are everything we have hoped for and more.'

'Akili has the power of telepathy, empathic manipulation,

and astral projection – I'm telling you now to save yourself any trouble if you try to lie to him,' said Incantus lightly.

Alexis shivered as he felt Akili's eyes rest on him and narrow slightly. Could Akili hear his thoughts? If that was the case, was there a way for Alexis to hide anything from him?

Barely after Akili stepped aside, the tattooed woman stepped forward, her eyes raking up and down their bodies in assessment. 'Your potential is *undeniable*.'

'Raeve,' Incantus announced as she bowed. 'Master weaponist and a powerful witch – she is particularly adept in stunning her opponents into a hypnotic stillness with one glance using her Concilium charm.'

'That's just natural beauty, sir,' said Raeve, the corner of her mouth tugging into a smile.

The blond man greeted them last, no longer able to contain his elation. He attempted to shake all their hands at once with both hands, and spoke with an Australian accent. 'Hey. Hi. How you doing? I'm Taranis, meaning thunder.' Crackling in his palms, blue and yellow electricity sparked. 'Lightning. Thunder and lightning.'

'Descended from a powerful bloodline of weather Elementals, Taranis oversees the Scholars and is our youngest and most enthusiastic Leader, a mere fifty years in age.'

'Fifty?' Demi blurted out. Taranis looked about half that age.

'What face cream do they use?' Caeli whispered to Demi.

'Elementals age slower, as you might have guessed,' Incantus explained. He glanced at Akili. 'These youngsters have many questions.'

Akili nodded. 'I can *hear*. But the most important question is what they are here to train *for*. The Quest.'

A purple illumination grew around the table, and within seconds, wooden chairs manifested into thin air. Flicking her hand, Raeve made them skid across the floor to Alexis and the others who slowly took their seats.

'What quest?' Alexis asked.

Incantus perched against the large mahogany table, his square jaw set as the tone of the conversation intensified. 'You recall the Elemental Gems I told you of, the stones that bestowed the power of the elements to the First Borns?'

'Yeah,' Blaise answered. 'Where our amulets came from.'

Incantus's lips pressed together into a line. 'Well, the first stage of the Prophecy involves finding these Gems.'

'You don't know where they are?'

'Not entirely. They have been lost ever since the First Borns' sacrifice, scattered by the Women across the world to keep them safe, and guarded by the creatures of our world that would die and kill to protect them. This is where you come in. We need you to go on a quest to retrieve them. To find the lost Elemental Gems. Only when you have possession of them, will you unleash an unlimited supply of your pure powers which we can use to defeat Mortem.'

Alexis didn't have time to process what had been said before Caeli spoke, her voice dripping with unimpressed disbelief. 'So in one month, you expect us to learn how to use the powers you hid from us to go on a mission to get some magical rocks so you can kill some evil monster who wants to cover the world in shadow due to some unresolved childhood trauma?'

The Leaders hesitated, sharing incredulous looks between one another and Incantus.

Demi winced and quickly added, 'What we mean is are you sure we can handle all this? How are we expected to find these Gems if no one else has all these years?'

Taranis was the one who answered, speaking rapidly. 'Only you can retrieve them. Each Gem will only reveal itself to the person who inherited its power and bears its amulet. We have managed to pinpoint the general location, but we can do no more. Your amulets will lead you to the lost Gems in the same way you were led to Stonehenge.'

Blaise rubbed his neck. 'I hope not in *exactly* the same way.'

'And these are scattered around the world? So we'll be travelling?' Demi said excitedly. She'd always longed to travel, Alexis knew, as did he.

'My idea of travelling is backpacking around Europe or Asia for a few months – not travelling the whole bloody world in a weekend on a blind treasure hunt,' Caeli countered. 'Is this going to be dangerous?'

Raeve cleared her throat, her expression set as she spoke with little sympathy. 'Most definitely. You'll have to defeat the Creatures of the Elements that defend them, if the legend is true, and ensure you bring them here before Mortem can steal them from you. He'll know you're after them – or suspect at least.'

'Great,' muttered Caeli.

'But to succeed is to survive,' Raeve added, 'and to fail is to allow the world to fall into darkness and chaos.'

'No pressure, then,' said Blaise.

Akili rested his huge hand on Raeve's shoulder, which somehow didn't budge beneath the weight. 'What our passionate Raeve is trying to say is – do not underestimate your abilities, your powers. I can appreciate how this must be making you feel, hearing for the first time that there is a story written about the events in your life you are yet to experience. But you may also find comfort in such a belief.'

There was something about the way Akili spoke that lessened the tightness in Alexis's chest. Maybe it was his deep voice or the way that he spoke as though he had considered each word before saying it. Or maybe he was using his powers to make them more passive and agreeable. Whatever it was, it was what Alexis needed to calm the whirlpool that was his mind.

Blaise leant back in his chair, twirling the golden clips of his braids. 'So what you're saying is, it's dangerous and we don't have much choice.'

Incantus nodded slowly. 'I'm so sorry. I wish there was another way where I could go in your place, but it has to be you. Without you and the Gems, we have no hope. And that won't just mean the demise of our world, but of the mortal world too.'

As the seconds drew out, the four teenagers looked between one another, uncharacteristically quiet for the first time since they met, a time that seemed so long ago.

Alexis found his voice. 'We need time to decide. Alone.' He was surprised at how confident he sounded.

Incantus offered Alexis a gentle smile. He really did look like he was carved by angels, Alexis thought, someone from a pristine painting of undeniable beauty. And yet he still couldn't shake why he looked so familiar.

'Of course,' Incantus said, rising alongside the Leaders and heading to the door. 'I'll have someone bring you some food as you process all of this. If you are still here by morning, I will assume you have made your decision, and your training shall begin.'

Akili Pierce's steady voice filled the room before he closed the door behind them. 'Good idea, Miss Nikolas, to start practising your powers.' Demi blushed deeply as Akili appeared to have read her mind.

In the wake of their departure, an oppressive silence descended upon the four strangers.

Alexis looked around at the others. He felt torn between fear and a sense of tremendous responsibility, between realisation and disbelief. He had already made his decision. He would do whatever it took to save the world his family lived in.

An icy chill crawled up Alexis's spine at an old memory – holding a man's head down into a pail of blood and water.

Small acts of kindness would not pardon him from his sins, but maybe this would. Maybe this would be his way of proving he wasn't a bad person, his chance to forgive himself for the things he had done wrong. He willed himself to believe it would.

'I say we do it,' said Blaise, folding his arms across him in the way Akili had. 'We do this and we'll be remembered as the people who saved the world. We've already been proxied and suited up.'

'Process of gradual commitment,' said Alexis, staring at the pool, longing to dive in. 'When you agree to a series of small

75

requests, it becomes harder to refuse more extreme orders.'

'So you're saying we shouldn't do it?'

Alexis shook his head. He had spent his whole childhood observing the world as an outsider, not trusted to go out and experience it himself. He no longer wished to be a spectator of life. 'I think we should. I think we have to. And I want to. But I don't want to pressure anyone into it if they don't. If any one of you wants to leave, I've memorised the route back to the tunnel.'

Caeli scraped the hair from her face, tying it into a high ponytail that accentuated the sharp angles of her cheekbones. 'Look, I'm not one to trust others,' she began, resting her elbows against her knees. 'And I don't even know either of you. I want to make sure I actually have these so-called powers before I sign a death sentence. I don't care whatever you choose to do, I'll decide for myself only after that.'

'Something tells me you're an only child,' Alexis commented.

Caeli raised an eyebrow but didn't deny it.

Blaise shrugged. 'I've already proved I'm a Child of the Element or whatever. If we've all got amulets, odds are that you are too.'

Demi was the only one who hadn't yet spoken. Her hand was at her chest – not to her amulet, but to her crucifix, her fingers running the length of the small golden cross. 'I'm scared,' she said quietly, pinching her full bottom lip. 'But I've been scared a lot of times before and I've never let that stop me. I know it's the right thing to do. We have a responsibility to do it,' she said with finality.

'Exactly!' said Blaise. 'I didn't have any plans for this summer anyway.'

Caeli and Blaise left after agreeing to meet for dinner. 'Do you think they're together?' Demi asked once she and Alexis were finally alone.

'Hard to tell with the way he was staring at you.' He was surprised at the bitterness in his voice.

Demi waved her hand dismissively. 'Notice how he looked at you whenever he made a joke? I think he wants to be your friend.'

'I've already got you,' said Alexis, as though she was everything he would ever need.

She was. Whether she had initially befriended him at her parents' request to be nice to their neighbours' quiet son, they were good friends now, possibly best friends. That was all she wanted from him, he was sure of it.

And yet, Alexis replayed the way Demi had looked at him when he had been topless in the Proxying Chamber. How she couldn't meet his eyes for a long while after.

'You're allowed more than one friend,' Demi said gently. She regarded the rest of the room. 'Caeli seems like a tough one to crack, but that just means I'll have to try harder to be her friend. *Kill them with kindness*, Mum says.' She glanced at Alexis. 'The two of you seemed to hit it off. You also looked smitten with the woman with purple hair and tattoos. Raeve.'

Was Demi jealous? Alexis wondered. A tiny part of him guiltily wished that she was, that there was a reason jealousy was called the green-eyed monster. He nudged her and said, 'You know I have a thing for powerful women.'

Demi laughed and pushed herself up from her seat. They walked alongside the swimming pool as he escorted her to the door. Just as Alexis was imagining swimming in the pool, he felt her hands press against his back. Before he could move out of the way, he was shoved off his feet, falling into the water. It was refreshingly cool, so clear that it was as though he was looking through air – although he wasn't sure if that was the water or his awakening powers.

'I thought you looked like you wanted a dip!' called Demi, eyes shining with mischief.

'That's how you want to play?' he laughed as he broke the surface. With all his might he sent a wave, soaking her up to her waist, making her scream.

'Oh please, you were staring at it the entire time. Besides, I was only helping you *use your powers*.' She extended her hand to the wooden door and closed her eyes in wilful concentration. The door shuddered briefly, before flinging open wide, nearly ripping off its hinges.

Demi squealed and turned to see his reaction. Her amulet was bright jade with the use of power for the first time, her cheeks flushed.

'I'm so proud of you!' Alexis celebrated, applauding her as she curtsied.

'I'm going to check out my room! Enjoy the swim, Lexi.'

With the sound of her laugh echoing in his head, Alexis undressed down to his underwear, leaving his suit on the side before going underneath again. The fresh water relaxed him, healing his troubled and frantic mind, settling it into order. If there was a way he could spend his whole life in its soft embrace, he would do anything to make it become a reality.

Of all his thoughts, there was one that couldn't be shaken now that Alexis was underwater. A memory that had long been lost to him. Of being very young and far away, scared and in the water, cold to his core – as though the blood in his body was freezing to ice.

For his whole life, Alexis had known he was adopted, found by Stephanie and Jackson Michaels in a shelter after a great tsunami. He had always wondered about his birth parents. Whether they had perished in the tsunami or if they had discarded him in the commotion of the disaster. The latter became easier to believe over time. His mind often clung to the most negative thought.

Now, in the clear water, a sudden realisation hit him with a fierce chill. The thing that tethered it all together. His element. The powers of the seas.

The tsunami.

Could that have been his doing?

Incantus mentioned he had sealed off his powers *after* his adoption. Before that, would they have been wild and uncontrolled?

The sinking feeling of dread plummeted in his stomach as he asked himself the question: *had he killed his birth parents?*

The surface of the water heaved above him, rippling outward in small waves as though it had been disturbed despite Alexis having not moved. Pulled away from his thoughts, he glanced down to see his amulet glowing faintly, shades of blue swirling within the ancient stone. He knew that he had been changed since Stonehenge, his senses acute as if tapped into an awareness beyond the external world into something deeper.

He recalled how Incantus had used his power by waving his hand, and he tried doing the same.

Something happened – but it wasn't what he had expected.

A violent shudder shot through Alexis as a tide of shadow exploded across his vision. The cold sea of black washed over his body, wrapping around his limbs, stealing his breath. Somehow, beyond it, he knew lay his true powers, waiting to be reached. His lungs burned as he fought to not inhale the blackness, as he fought to make it past the wall, as he fought to survive.

With his final breath, Alexis screamed and commanded the use of the water.

A current gushed away from the body of water, rippling out wildly. It shot up into the air, climbing higher and higher until it almost reached the ceiling before it lost its momentum and splashed back against the wooden floorboards.

Alexis gasped for air as the darkness dissipated, recoiling out of sight. He swam to the side of the pool and lifted himself onto the ledge, his legs dangling in the water as he panted, his chest rising and falling.

He hadn't anticipated just how much it would take out of him to use his powers. It looked easier when Blaise and Demi had done it, as if it were second nature. His seemed a harder fight, like he had to cross some sort of mental barrier to access it. The cold shadow that was all too familiar.

Should he ask the others if they had also seen the darkness that blocked them from their powers? He quickly suppressed the idea. It may have been a hallucination, something he hadn't experienced in years, something no one except from his family, not even Demi, knew about.

Alexis just prayed it wouldn't happen again, that it only happened because it was the first time he had practiced his abilities. He couldn't imagine ever wanting to use his powers again if it did, not if the *Shadow Man* returned with it.

8

ÉNOUEMENT

Énouement (n.) *French origin*
The bittersweetness of having arrived in the future, seeing
how things turn out, but not being able to tell your past self

A knock at the door disturbed Alexis from the hour of
continuous swimming, pulling him out of his daydreams.

'One minute,' he called as he got out of the pool and rifled
through the wardrobe for a towel.

A woman's high-pitched voice came from behind. '*Holy
First Borns*. I'm so sorry! The door was ajar and I-I thought you
said to come in.'

In the doorway stood a short Indian girl around his age
with dark hair tied up in a tight bun, wearing a loose-fitting
sweatshirt with "HAVEN" printed vertically down the
middle. The tray of food in her hands wavered as she turned
away from his dripping wet body.

Alexis hastily wrapped the towel round his waist. 'It's okay,
I'm covered. Hi.'

She stumbled over her words. 'I was just bringing you some
food – the others said you were in here.' Her large, rather
owlish, eyes settled on his amulet and widened further. 'Wow,'
she breathed. Alexis made his way over to the table, clearing

space for the tray of plates covered entirely in piles of steaming hot food that she nearly dropped as though in a hurry. 'I didn't know what you would eat so I grabbed a bit of everything. Veggie, vegan, halal, kosher.'

'I usually take a girl to dinner *before* I let her see me with my clothes off.' Alexis smiled, even though he hadn't done either of those things. She snorted loudly then covered her rounded face with her hands. 'Alexis, the sarcastic one,' he said, extending his hand. 'Nice to meet you.'

She shook it, still avoiding eye contact. 'I'm Ziya. Ziya Parashakti.'

Alexis passed a chair to Ziya before sitting himself. It wasn't until he started shovelling food into his mouth that he realised how hungry he had become after not eating anything since breakfast.

'So . . . first day,' Ziya began, her huge eyes not leaving his amulet. 'Technically. How do you feel? Did you know of your powers before coming here? What did you think of Incantus? He's great, isn't he? And the Leaders. Have you had a tour of the Haven yet? Did you know the others before today?'

'Um,' said Alexis through a mouth full of chicken and rice, swallowing painfully before she fired another question. 'What was the first question again?'

'Sorry!' she said, getting up abruptly. 'I'll let you eat in peace.'

Was this the effect he should expect to have on everyone, being one of the Children of the Elements? Or maybe that was just Ziya? He quickly decided it was probably both.

'Please stay, I'd love the company. So . . . what powers do you have?' he asked.

Ziya shifted in her seat, tidying frizzy strands of hair that had escaped her tightly knotted bun. 'I . . . well, I actually don't have any powers.' She gave an embarrassed laugh. 'I'm not sure why, just unlucky I guess. My younger sister has – she's just developed the ability to manipulate matter which is so cool and super rare. I missed out.' She shrugged, seemingly used to the idea that not having any powers was what made her different from everyone else. 'But it's fine, what can I do about it?'

'I'm assuming your sister inherited it from your parents?'

'Only our mother was Elemental. She was supposed to have been one of the best of her time, but she disappeared when I was young.'

Alexis stopped eating. 'I'm sorry.'

'One day we just woke up and she was gone. It wasn't long after that Incantus and Akili came, offering to take me and Parvati to the Haven. Dad didn't seem to care so we went and have been better off ever since.'

'Did you ever find out what happened to your mum?' Alexis asked gently.

Ziya swallowed, and for the first time, albeit only fleetingly, she met Alexis's eyes. 'In the end. Incantus didn't tell me till I was older, but Mortem either *imprinted* her or killed her.'

'Imprinted?'

Ziya chuckled like he had just asked a silly question. It wasn't meant mockingly, but Alexis still felt embarrassed for knowing so little. When she realised the question was genuine, she explained, 'Mortem can insert darkness into those he wishes to control, using them as his slaves by hijacking their brains and bodies. My mother was an Elemental with powers no one had ever seen before. So unless Mortem wanted to imprint her to use her, she's likely dead. Honestly, I like to think it was the second option.' Ziya shook her head. 'Enough about me! What about you? You've cut it close to the solar eclipse to find your way here!'

Alexis smiled to himself. 'Sorry,' he said. 'We had homework.'

Ziya was in the middle of telling Alexis about something called the Elemental Tribes – who worshipped the Gems in isolation from the rest of the world – when the door to Alexis's room swung open without a knock or a call. Blaise, Caeli and Demi strolled through.

'Hi, Ziya,' said Demi with a wave.

'Door's bent,' Blaise observed, largely ignoring Ziya as he sat beside Alexis and picked at whatever remained on his plate.

Ziya had already got to her feet. 'I'll leave you guys to it.'

'Stay if you like, Ziya,' Demi automatically offered. She had always taken in the strays, making anyone feel welcome and wanted. It was one of the traits Alexis loved most about her.

But Ziya was already halfway across the room. 'It's okay! I'll see you tomorrow – if you decide to stay that is.' Just before she shut the door, she added quietly, 'I really hope you do.'

'Sorry we interrupted your date,' said Blaise. 'The girls kept going on about Incantus and the lightning guy and I got bored.'

Alexis had managed to find a T-shirt and shorts from the wardrobe, and after dusting them off, they had been a comfortable fit. He found himself oddly protective of Ziya. 'She's genuinely so nice. She told me all about the Haven and how anyone can specialise as Scholar, Fighter or Healer regardless of their powers. She's only nineteen, but Incantus still made her his protégé over everyone else; must mean he sees something in her.'

Caeli didn't mince her words when she said, 'She doesn't have any powers, apparently. Not sure we want to hang out with someone like that.'

'Don't be rude,' said Demi, launching a slice of bread at her.

Caeli instinctively raised her hands. A gust of wind swept from behind her, blowing the bread across the room where it splashed and sunk in the pool.

She let out a surprised laugh as Blaise's clapped her back. 'Anyway, let's go to my room,' she said. 'The four of us have a lot to figure out before the night is over. And the view is to die for!'

Caeli's room didn't feel like a room at all.

For starters, it had no ceiling. The grey walls climbed high until they disappeared beyond glowing lines of white markings. Where the roof should've been was a view of the night's sky, midnight blue and dotted with stars that were much larger than Alexis had ever seen them, almost as though they were high up a mountain.

He was certain it was an illusion at first until he felt the light gales ruffle his drying wavy hair. Mesmerised by the impossibility of it and wondering if it had anything to do with the glowing white lines, he took the blanket Caeli offered him and wrapped it round himself without a word. They sat in pairs on the plush suede sofa that curved round a circular glass table in the centre of the room. Demi shuffled close to him and spread out their blankets over them both.

'Warm enough?' she asked. Her face was free of makeup and her hair was down in damp curls, smelling lightly of lavender.

Alexis preferred the cold, but knew Demi was the opposite. He put his blanket round her shoulders.

'So what's the verdict?' asked Blaise. Caeli sat cross-legged beside him as she brushed her long hair with methodical purpose. 'Do you guys have powers?'

They all nodded. Alexis wanted to ask if any of them had sensed a dark force blocking their powers, but again decided against it.

'Does that mean we're all in agreement?' said Demi. 'We stay and train – and go on this quest for the Elemental Gems?'

Caeli let out a long exhale through her nose. She tipped her head back to look at the night's sky and said, 'I'm supposed to be at a festival right now making bad decisions like getting on topless boys' shoulders and drunk confessing I have daddy issues. My proxy better not make a fool of me.'

Blaise patted her knee. 'You do that all by yourself.'

'Can I ask,' said Demi curiously. 'Are you guys . . . you know.'

Caeli and Blaise looked at each other, laughed, and then a pulled a face of revulsion.

'A couple? Don't flatter him,' said Caeli with a shake of her head.

'You wish,' Blaise retorted. 'I'm too outspoken to be controlled by you.'

Caeli made a noise at the back of her throat. 'And I'm too intelligent to be charmed by you.'

Alexis was surprised – the palpable chemistry and familiar bickering between their two new companions made them seem like they were a long-surviving married couple. Then again, maybe they thought the same with he and Demi.

'I used to date one of his friends and he's dated half of my dance squad,' Caeli explained. 'We go way back though so I've never been able to escape him. Our parents took us to the same nursery.'

Blaise grinned. 'And she was self-righteous even as a two-year-old.' He frowned, fiddling with the clips that decorated his box-braids. 'Do you think our parents brought us together on purpose?'

Caeli shrugged. 'Who knows? Maybe. What do you guys think of Incantus?'

The wind whistled across the open sky above. Demi drew closer to Alexis, burying her chin into the blanket. 'I trust him.' She yawned. 'Everything he's told us so far has been true.'

'I think there's more than meets the eye with him,' Alexis weighed in thoughtfully. In his memory, every image of Incantus was light with the faint glow of his aura, an aura that was encouraging and inspiring and uplifting. But there was a dullness in his voice when he spoke about Mortem, and in his eyes a pain that Alexis recognised. Of someone who had forever been changed by suffering.

'You're being paranoid,' said Blaise, and Alexis flushed. 'What about this quest? I say we do it. It would make for a good story.'

'We're putting our lives in danger and your justification is that "it will make for a good story?"' Caeli asked incredulously, tossing her hairbrush onto the table. 'Raeve said something about the Creatures of the Elements that guard the Gems. Can't imagine it'll be easy if we need the top bosses to train us.'

'And with Mortem after us as well,' Demi added, shivering despite the layers of blankets over her.

They fell into an uneasy silence. Alexis looked at the others. Demi he trusted with his life – but Caeli and Blaise were still unknown. At that moment, Blaise looked up and their eyes met.

Fire and water, Alexis thought. He wondered which was stronger.

Fire may burn boldly, but lest he not forget that it was water that extinguished it.

'Anyone interested in showing each other what we've managed to do with our powers so far?' Caeli said, breaking the silence. 'I'm hoping by the end of the night I'll be able to blow-dry my hair.'

The four teens spent the next couple of hours getting to know each other while testing the extent of their untrained abilities. Their powers were not limitless, however, and they soon grew exhausted.

Each seemed to respond according to their element. Air-element Caeli grew breathless and complained of vertigo, Demi claimed her bones and muscles ached as if they were laden with a great weight, Blaise swore at fiery pins and needles that stabbed along his arms, and Alexis felt desperately dehydrated as if he'd gone a week without water.

Alexis couldn't help but notice the rivalry growing with

Blaise as they tested the limits of their powers. They strained to outdo each other, silently competing for greater feats. When Alexis manipulated the water from Caeli's glass to tip over, Blaise made sparks fly that caught fire to the edge of his blanket. When Blaise made the candlelight flare into a column of yellow flame, Alexis nearly blacked out after gathering a billow of rainclouds to drizzle from the sky above. That was when Caeli kicked them all out.

Alexis crept into his enormous bed feeling utterly drained. The moment he lay down, his body relaxed until he felt like he was floating in a sea of clouds. There was something about the bed that seemed healing, as though it had some sort of restorative powers. He laughed sleepily to himself. Even the beds were designed to heal them and optimise their training potential over the next few weeks.

He rolled over and slipped his hand beneath one of the pillows to get comfortable. Something cold and thin scratched his fingertips.

He pulled it out and examined what appeared to be a black-and-white photograph, its edges having crumpled over time. The image showed two young boys, their arms round each other in loving affection. He was about to put it away when he noticed something that snapped him wide awake again.

The younger boy looked just like him. Or, at least, how he had looked as a child. His parents didn't have many photos of him until later in his childhood, but the resemblance was remarkable. So much so that Alexis immediately wondered if it could be him, taken from a time before he had been adopted.

He turned the photograph over and on the back of it, scribbled in small cursive handwriting, was written, 'Ian and Nero. 1923.'

Nero. It was as if someone had squeezed the air out from Alexis's lungs. Nero was the name Alexis had been called in his nightmare, the name that echoed around his head every time he awoke just as he hit the water.

It didn't make any sense. The photograph of the boys from his dream was dated over a century ago. There was no way it could be Alexis, no matter how similar they looked or how much the dream felt like a memory that was his own. This boy had lived a hundred years ago. It must be of someone else. But of who? And how could he dream of someone he had never met before?

Alexis then remembered the person who once possessed the power of water before relinquishing it for the darkness.

The photograph fell from Alexis's hand. It hadn't even touched the ground when he came to the sinking realisation that after years of searching, he might have finally just discovered who his birth father was.

And how he desperately wished he hadn't.

9

NIGHTHAWK

Nighthawk (n.) *English origin*
A recurring thought that only seems to strike you late at
night; a person who stays up late in the night

Alexis didn't get much sleep that night. Not even the enchanted bed could calm his restless mind. He flipped the pillow for what must have been the hundredth time to try to find the cold side, and when there wasn't one, he hurled it across the bedroom. Hearing a splash in the distance, he groaned.

Sleep came only after he accepted that the one person who could possibly answer his questions was Incantus.

Ian – that was what Akili had called him. That had been the name of the other boy in the photo with the white-blond hair. The other boy in the dream, calling out for Nero, trying to save him from falling.

Maybe Incantus had concealed just how close he had been to his enemy. Maybe the reason Incantus seemed so betrayed was not because his student had turned against him – but because his brother had.

Although Alexis couldn't see or feel the warm glow of sunrise, he was nonetheless ripped from his slumber by the nightmare at the break of dawn. He knew there was little chance of him going back to sleep. Instead, ensuring his door was locked, Alexis stripped off his clothes and dove into the pool.

The water instantly rejuvenated his body. He closed his eyes as it washed away the previous night's questions. He got lost in the motion of the water, swaying with the movement of it, swimming as effortlessly as he could walk. Yet he knew he couldn't stay for too long.

Showered and suited in his black Haven uniform, he was reading a huge dusty book called *Origins of the Elemental* by the time there was a knock at the door. With no bookmark on hand, he used the blade of a dagger he found in the nightstand to save the page.

He opened it to find Raeve before him. She stood poised in her grey suit, zipped all the way up so only the corners of her black and gold tattoos at her throat were visible. Two curved swords flanked her waist, somehow attached without clip or strap, gleaming under the white ceiling lights.

'Morning, sweetheart,' she said with a nod. Her purple hair was tied in a taut ponytail, formal and practical. 'I see you have decided to stay. I knew we could count on you.'

'Do I need to bring anything with me?'

'You're all I need.' She smirked, catching his eyes. Alexis realised what she was doing a moment too late, that her powers could hypnotise him into a stillness through eye contact alone.

Despite being bound in content suspension, he was able to move his lips. 'Now's a really inconvenient time for my nose to starting itching.'

Raeve gave him a genuine smile and freed him. 'After

you.' She followed him down the short flight of steps to join the others already there waiting outside their rooms. There weren't many things Demi would compromise her sleep for, but even she seemed bright-eyed and excited, grinning widely at his arrival.

Raeve led them down the outer ring of the marble staircase that encircled the Haven's hollow core. As they descended, Alexis saw that the majority of the base level was taken up by an enormous flat stage the size of a stadium floor. Elementals were already practising, some as young as seven or eight, others looking fresh out of a retirement home. He watched them open-mouthed, astounded by their powers. The way they flipped around the room effortlessly, blades clashing so fast it was blurry to the eye. One managed to turn her whole body invisible, striking her partner from behind, whilst another threw away a full-grown man with just the wave of their hand.

Jason really would love it here, Alexis thought, wishing one day he could show it to him.

They walked down the corridor the level above the ground floor where a series of doors labelled 'Training Academies' appeared lining the walkway. Raeve stood in front of one of the rooms, spinning around to address them, her movements as agile as a cat's. 'Your first few hours are with Mr Arcangelo. He's waiting for you inside. I'll see you this afternoon. Ensure you are prepared, sweethearts, for I promise I won't be going lightly on you.'

She bowed before turning on her heel, striding back the way she came.

After yesterday's revelations, Alexis thought there wasn't

much else that could take his breath away. That couldn't be further from the truth.

It wasn't a room they walked into, but rather a white-metal arena, its ceiling almost too high to be seen. The floor was divided into quarters, with four raised platforms at the corners of the room surrounding a single, larger training ground in the centre. Lining the sides of the central training space were a series of gym equipment; weights, cardio machines and something else: a tall, simple-looking machine that appeared to have a camera lens. Alexis assumed it was a projector of sorts, although he had no idea why it was there.

Instead of a solid wall at the back of the room, the great training hall fed directly onto an empty green field, the sky above beginning to turn blue in the early sunlight. From where Alexis stood, he could feel the warm morning breeze and the scent of fresh grass. A white glowing chalk line ran across where the metal ended and the field began, such like the lines around Caeli's ceiling.

Approaching from the field in the distance came a figure, instantly recognisable in build and stride as Incantus Arcangelo. When he crossed over the border, the chalk line glowed fiercely and the white walls of the Haven brightened at their creator's return.

'Teleportation lines,' Incantus clarified when he reached them, gesturing to the glowing white lines. 'Engineered by some of the Elementals that have been taught here. On this side is the Haven facility, and on the other is one of the limited destinations we can choose from.'

He swiped his finger across the silver command device in his hand and the landscape beyond the teleportation lines shifted before their very eyes, like the changing of TV channels, from a snowy mountain range to a bleak desert, and then, before returning to the green field, an active volcano site.

'This is the coolest thing I've seen,' Blaise confessed, tugging Caeli's sleeve.

She batted him away. 'I have eyes; I can see it too.'

Incantus bowed. 'Welcome to one of our private Training Academies. This is where you will spend at least twelve hours of your day.'

'Twelve hours?' Caeli asked, dipping her head. 'Is it even possible to train for half the day?'

'We have to make up for lost time. You'll have all the time you want to make friends, explore and do anything else you so wish *after* your quest.'

She sighed. 'Yes, boss.'

Incantus began strolling around the room, indicating for them to follow. 'Your time training as a group will be divided between myself and the Leaders. What I want you to remember, more than anything, is that the four of you are stronger when together. You add to each other's aura, as you add to mine, and I add to yours. Training together will therefore not only accelerate your learning but, most importantly, your confidence. As such, I am happy to inform you that I hope to join you on the quest to retrieve the lost Elemental Gems.'

A flood of relief passed over Alexis. Knowing that the most powerful Elemental in the world would be there to guide and protect them on their journey made it seem slightly less terrifying.

Besides, there was something about Incantus's aura that made him want to stay close to him. Maybe it was the warmth. Maybe it was the light.

Maybe it was the fact that he could be his paternal uncle.

He pushed the thought away.

'Thank goodness,' Demi exhaled. 'And thank you!'

Incantus's eyes crinkled as he smiled. 'Each training session will take about three hours. First thing in the morning will be with me, teaching you how to control your elements and master your environments. What separates you from the four isolated Elemental Tribes that you were descended from is your ability to not only manipulate and control your element, but also create it from nothingness. But for that, you will need the Gem's powers. Whilst the Leaders oversee their own specialisms, they will focus on preparing you for your quest. Akili will teach you the ways of battle, particularly strategic fighting against other Elementals, and also how to control your energies and aura against much greater opponents.'

'The Creatures of the Elements,' said Alexis. He thought of the sketch of the grey-scaled Chinese dragon in Incantus's office. 'What exactly are they?'

'I know little more than you regarding them, I'm afraid,' Incantus said. 'They are largely believed to be nothing more than myths and legends passed down over generations – but, then again, so are we. For this reason, we cannot ignore the possibility of encountering them. And then there is another threat.'

'Oh, good,' said Caeli. 'I was hoping there would be more.'

'Mortem may already know you are here and seeking the

Gems. He likely would've sensed what happened at Stonehenge, that the Prophecy is unravelling. He may send his followers, the Shadowless, to prevent this from happening.'

'How can you be shadow-less?' Blaise muttered under his breath, getting a shrug from Demi in response.

Alexis added it to the list of things to ask Ziya.

'Come.' Incantus led them onto the larger training podium in the centre, his hands clasped behind his back. 'Weapons can help channel your strength, especially when your element is not present to manipulate. This is what Raeve will teach. And Taranis will take you through the tools that will help you in our quest and improve your overall fitness to ensure you have the stamina for all that is to come.'

The platform underfoot suddenly shuddered awake, causing the young Elementals to crouch to keep their balance. Pulled by nothing, the platform slowly rose, lifting them above ground level.

Eyes twinkling with delighted anticipation, Incantus said, 'Your first lesson is about to begin.'

The raised platform swept to the side. All but Incantus fell off their feet and fought to cling to the flat surface. The dais soared towards the teleportation line at the back of the room. As they passed the glowing white line that adorned the wall, they were hit with a cold salty sea breeze. Dark blue waves now chopped below as Alexis looked over the edge to see that they were flying over endless miles of nothing but ocean. They glided away from the teleportation line, the image of the Haven's Training Academy shrinking in the distance.

'Ordinarily we would take your training slowly,' said

Incantus, shouting as the waves crested and crashed around them. 'But we don't have time for that. The first lesson I learned from my mentor and that I will teach you is to always be aware of your environment and of how you can utilise it to manipulate your power.' He stifled a chuckle. 'The only way to do this . . . is to throw you in the deep end.'

The platform tilted to the side. The four teens let out a chorus of screams as they skidded off, falling through the air before crashing into the ocean.

Beneath the surface of the seawater, Alexis saw nothing but a dark emptiness below with no end in sight. Kicking his legs with ease, he resurfaced and saw the others' heads bobbing above the water. Caeli was swimming fine, but Demi and Blaise were kicking laboriously, gasping for air.

Alexis shouted, half-spitting and half-swallowing as he fought the surging tide. 'Where the hell are we?'

'Somewhere off the coast of Ireland, the Atlantic Ocean,' Incantus called. 'You need to build up your endurance, and practise in environments both favourable and unfavourable to you; to learn how to survive in each other's elements.' He bent down to his knees. 'You are no longer four strangers, but rather four parts of a whole.'

'Blaise isn't good at swimming!' Caeli shouted. She wiped at her face and her hand came away blackened from where her mascara ran. She let out an audible groan. 'I spent ages doing my eyeliner this morning!'

'Your counter elements will weaken you,' Incantus continued. The worry that Alexis had seen yesterday was there again. *He didn't like seeing them struggle*, Alexis thought. 'Find strength in each other! You are far stronger together than apart.'

Alexis found himself growing sturdier in the water, and although the thrashing waves tried to beat him down, he somehow felt taller, his strength greater. He swam over to Demi and supported her, wrapping his arm round her waist to steady her.

'That's enough!' Blaise stuttered, his lips purple from the cold. Every so often his head would go under and he'd resurface, spitting out salty ocean water. 'Come on, boss, this is unfair!'

'I'll be okay,' Demi gasped to Alexis. 'Help him.'

Alexis frowned. 'Demi . . .'

'You heard what Incantus said,' she said, glaring at him with stubborn green eyes. 'We are stronger together. Drop the ego battle and help him.'

Alexis looked over. Blaise was barely treading water. His arms flailed erratically which was more successful at splashing a nearby Caeli than keeping himself afloat.

'Here to brag?' panted Blaise as Alexis swam over to him.

Alexis took Blaise's weight in his hands. 'Here to help.'

Blaise had no other choice but to trust him.

'Lean back,' Alexis said, and, slowly, Blaise relaxed enough to let Alexis support him. He was heavier than Alexis was expecting and keeping them both afloat was a struggle, but he didn't let him go.

There was a splash behind them.

'Please don't be a shark!' Caeli screamed, covering her head with both arms.

Incantus broke free from the ocean's surface, sweeping his

white hair out of his eyes. 'I do not want to be your boss,' he said, swimming effortlessly, taking Blaise's weight in one hand from Alexis. 'I want to be your Leader, your mentor. I promised myself that I would never train you in the merciless, unforgiving approach I experienced, no matter how little time we had together.'

Through haggard breaths as she barely kept afloat, Demi still managed to thank him.

'Now you are going to swim back to the Haven.' Incantus silenced their protests with a flash of his hand. 'You have to rely on and trust each other as you would your own limbs. The weight of the world lies on your shoulders and if one of you falls to your knees, the rest has to push harder. Sink or swim – no will dive in to rescue you. You need to save yourselves.'

With another bright flash, he sent a wall of white energy into the back of them, shoving them into action.

'Feel the water, Alexis,' Incantus called over the crashing noise of the tide. 'How your body falls into synchrony with it. How you move through it. Before you use your powers, you have to know the mechanics and properties of your element – the most fundamental level. Focus on wielding it, using it to support your desires. Think of how you will get it to do as you command.' He nodded at Alexis. 'Give it a try.'

Trying to block out the chaos of the sea and his concern for Blaise and Demi, Alexis focussed on the qualities of his element; its fluidity, its coherence. He moved his hands in the water, urging it to carry him.

A surge of water propelled into Alexis, sweeping him up in a current of his own making. He laughed with disbelief and turned back to see Incantus gleaming with joy behind him and the others cheering.

'I did it,' Alexis whispered to himself, recognising that the feeling in his chest was one he wasn't used to: pride.

'Take me with you, Al!' Blaise yelled, losing his rhythm and clutching his mentor.

'Not for now,' Incantus told him. 'You need to learn how to survive the hostile environment by yourself.'

'What about that whole *share the weight of the world* stuff?'

'Support each other, trust each other, you are nearly unstoppable when together. But you should never become dependent on another person to save you.'

They swam on, all of them struggling except Alexis.

'Miss Doran,' called Incantus to Caeli. 'How you could make this easier for yourself?'

In short gasps, Caeli answered, 'Don't tell me. Use the wind?' She looked around desperately. 'How exactly will the wind help?'

'What was the first lesson?' Incantus asked calmly.

'Surroundings!' Demi shouted from behind.

Caeli looked up for the first time to see the dais that had carried them from the Academy was following overhead, just a few metres above. 'It's too far away! I can't reach it.'

'Then make it within reach.'

Caeli extended her hands toward the platform, straining in focus as she curled her fingers.

'That's it,' Incantus encouraged, modelling with his hands. 'Breathe out as you force it to submit to your wishes.'

Slowly but surely, the stage began to lower to the ocean's

surface, close enough for Caeli to clasp onto its edge. She struggled to lift her own body weight, her thin arms shaking from the strain. Blaise splashed towards her and shoved her up onto the platform from behind, a movement which sent him under the water again.

Alexis summoned his remaining strength and sent a wave that flung Demi and Blaise up into the sky. They landed heavily on the drifting platform. Caeli went over to check on Blaise as he coughed up water whilst Demi leant over the platform, reaching a hand out for Alexis to take. With surprising might, she hauled him up in one swift motion.

Alexis collapsed half on top of her. His muscles were too sore to use, and hers must be too because Demi made no attempt to push him off. They panted, breathing the same air as water droplets fell from his lips onto her face. They had never shared a closeness like this before.

Alexis could see the yellow and brown specks that dotted her green eyes; it was like looking into a kaleidoscope of the beauty of the forest, of the very essence of nature.

Incantus clapped from below, and they finally rolled apart. 'Utilise your strengths, aid each other's weaknesses. Well done, my children! Rest until we are back inside the Haven.'

'You okay?' Alexis asked over his shoulder to Demi.

She nodded. 'I am now.'

Blaise called down to Incantus, 'You're not allowed up! You can keep swimming!'

Incantus laughed, grinning a bright, wide smile before taking off at an unnatural speed toward the teleportation line, somehow beating them to it.

10

EQUANIMITY

Equanimity (n.) *Latin origin*
Mental calmness, composure, and evenness of temper,
especially in a difficult situation

By the end of their training with Incantus, sweat was
pouring from Alexis's body in a seemingly limitless supply,
exhaustion tugging at his muscles. The environments beyond
the teleportation line had been transformed three more times,
changing from a dense rainforest to the frozen hills of a snowy
desert, and finally to a suspended mountain far beyond the
cloud line.

Akili Pierce arrived the minute the third hour ended,
again sporting loose brown robes over his sleeveless all-in-one
titanium suit. He walked in to see the four young Elementals
laying scattered across the central training podium, as if they
were toys who had just had their batteries removed.

Through the environmental shifts, with breaks no longer
than five minutes in between, Incantus had talked. He spoke
of ancient warriors, the truth within myths and legend, and
even creatures of old times, those that would come to their aid,
remain neutral or seek chaos, joining Mortem. It had been a
lot to take in, especially when the air was so thin it was hard

to breathe or so hot it burned their faces, but Alexis held onto every word Incantus said, wanting to consume it all, to learn everything there was to know and not stop until he did.

'Incredible progress,' Incantus told Akili, looking delighted. 'Each with their individual strengths: Alexis's instincts, Blaise's passion, Caeli's reactions and Demi's resilience. A formidable team when working together.'

'I've trained for marathons but that doesn't come close to how tired I am now,' Caeli groaned.

'My muscles feel like they're on fire,' Blaise added. 'And not in a good way.'

'I'm hungry,' said Demi.

Alexis was too tired to laugh. 'I need to wee again.'

'They've had ten minutes rest,' Incantus said, ignoring their complaints. 'It's time for them to get up. My friend, perhaps you might *convince* them?'

Akili had come to stand over them, his size casting a huge shadow, the light reflecting off his bald head. Bulging muscles flexed beneath his suit, veins protruding across his biceps in a spiderweb of strength and power. His arms extended towards them and an undulating wave of clear energy washed over them. As if listening to a deep narration in his head, Alexis heard Akili's commands as clearly as if they were his own thoughts.

'Recover. Restore your commitment. Remember why you are training so hard and what you are training for. Motivation is fleeting, discipline is consistent. Your body may tire, but your spirit won't ever. Tell your body what it needs to do. And now – get up.*'*

It wasn't that Akili had forced him to do it, but his voice

had been so overpowering, so persuasive, that Alexis *wanted* to obey. Alexis heard the voice as if it were a stream of whispers, replacing his own thoughts which told him his body was too tired to move. It convinced him that he had rested enough, making him get to his feet, the others doing the same. The minute he stood up, Akili's voice disappeared, fading away into an echo, but his message remained.

'Did you just *mind-control* us?' Caeli gasped, shaking her head as if to get him out. 'What's to say you won't do that to get us to do whatever you want?'

Incantus went to speak, but Akili raised his hand. 'I didn't mind-control you. I spoke to your subconscious mind and convinced you of what you already know but were too lazy to do.'

Alexis shivered. Akili had definitely been in his head. What if he discovered Alexis's revelation about the photograph? Mortem and Incantus possibly being brothers? As well as Alexis's theory that Mortem might just be his father?

'We've been training for, like, three hours straight,' said Blaise, folding his arms to mimic the larger man.

'Some battles have gone on for weeks and months,' Incantus countered. 'Akili is not only telepathic, but he can also influence your behaviour through cognitive and emotional persuasion. In this case, he just increased your motivation to continue your training.'

'Doesn't mean he made us any less tired,' Caeli grumbled.

Akili inclined his head. 'Our healing crystals and those in the Healing Sanctuary can repair your bodies.' He smiled. 'Although Incantus's presence is already helping with your recovery.'

'Ziya told me you have healing abilities and magic in addition to light,' said Alexis, steering the conversation away from hearing voices in one's head.

Incantus paused. 'My healing abilities are tethered to my lifeforce,' he said simply, as if there was anything simple about it. 'Using it on anyone other than myself drains my immortality. It's therefore not something I do often, particularly if there is another way.'

'Sorry,' Alexis said awkwardly, knowing it was only a matter of time before his curiosity crossed the boundary to being nosy.

Incantus shook off his apology. 'Enough time-wasting.' He went to the central training podium, standing on one of the platforms situated in the corners of the room.

He picked up a sword that he wielded with the elegance and speed of a trained expert. 'I want to see how they face up against the *bots* by the end of your lesson. Mr Pierce, run the projections.'

Three hours later and Alexis and his friends lay in the same positions as they had done after their first training period, panting, sweating and, in Blaise's case, sulking.

'He didn't have to hit me that hard,' Blaise grumbled, still clutching his chest. In spite of their suits' protective qualities, he was acting as if he had been hit by a truck.

Although, looking at the size of Akili, and how far Blaise had been thrown, Alexis wasn't sure in this case if Blaise was downplaying it.

Their session with Akili had been as gruelling as their

training with Incantus, only this time, the focus was on their bodies and breathing, rather than on their powers.

'What do you mean we need to know the importance of breathing?' Blaise had asked at the start of the session, his face upturned. 'It's what we do every second of the day.'

'To breathe is the first thing you ever do in your life and the last,' Akili said simply. 'Breathing corresponds to how you feel: you inhale when excited, exhale when relieved, and hold your breath when anxious. Being able to control it is key – to breathe is to energise your body, heal your soul and channel your powers.'

Alexis hadn't expected meditation to be a part of his Elemental training, but he was more than happy to take up the offer. Anything for some peace and quiet – minus Demi's intermittent snoring every time she dozed off.

Akili then took them through some basic self-defence, how to block and attack with the body. Alexis found himself familiar with much of it, having been trained by his father for years. With an hour to go, Akili switched on the projector Alexis had noticed when he had first entered the room.

The camera lens flickered to life, projecting a metallic white laser light display on the ground before it. Bleeding from it came an enormous holographic display, growing taller with each passing second. At first it was a mass of shimmering light, but as it grew in size, the projection began to solidify, the image holding a stable shape. Soon it started to resemble an arrangement of large monolithic boulders. In less than a minute, the projection was instantly recognisable as the circular ruins of Stonehenge.

'Did you just teleport it down?' Alexis asked with wild

fascination. He placed his hand against one of the stones to feel its rough, solid texture.

'It is, in fact, a projection,' Incantus answered, looking up from the Haven command device.

It was identical. The only thing different about it was the way that it made him feel. Rather, how it didn't make him feel anything. When he had been beside the real Stonehenge, he had felt its power even before his amulet had flown towards it. This structure had no such effect.

Demi pressed her palm against the sandstone surface. 'How can a hologram be *solid*?'

Incantus lay his tablet down. 'These machines can three-dimensionally print an entire object, or even environment, with astounding detail, making it appear as if it were real. It can project whatever display the person who casts it wishes.'

Smaller projection lines shot out from the camera lens and swiftly morphed into four humanoid figures, their bodies a pale off-white colour. The area where there should have been a face was blank – no eyes, nose or mouth, just an unnervingly smooth surface.

'The projections can also produce humanoid bots,' Akili informed them, flattening his robes over his muscles. 'Extremely useful when training. A darker colour indicates their increased difficulty setting out of seven. Unlike sandbags, these have the ability to dodge *and* strike back.'

The hologram of Stonehenge flickered away, leaving just the training bots.

If the training earlier had been tough, fighting the bots was exhausting. Alexis found himself bent over, chest tight, a painful stitch at his side. He looked at Demi, who was hugging the bot, trying to keep on her feet, and then at Blaise, who lazily shoved his bot away every time it advanced. Alexis needed to figure out a way to stall Akili before he caught them.

'Excuse me, Mr Pierce,' gasped Alexis. 'You know how you can control people's minds and stuff?'

'Not control,' Akili corrected him, guiding Caeli's wrist to help her throw a proper punch. 'I can encourage certain lines of thoughts and increase particular emotions to influence behaviours.'

Still breathless, Alexis said, 'Yeah, that. Well, why don't you just fight using our bodies as vessels? You could read our opponents' minds and win the fight before it even starts.'

The four teens collapsed into a seating position on the floor, glad to have a break. Demi flashed a thumbs up in thanks, her chin already resting against her chest in the hopes of taking a nap unnoticed.

'I bet you're a Taurus,' Caeli muttered under her breath, making Demi grin sleepily.

'Because you will not learn that way,' Akili replied, as if it was obvious. '*Making* you do something is very different from teaching you *how* to do it yourself. And I cannot impose my approach onto you. I only encourage your own unique style. For example, in the last half an hour I can quite clearly see you each have different approaches to combat.'

'Like what?' asked Alexis, curious.

'Well, Blaise relies on his strength, throwing himself in without thought of what could happen if overpowered. Caeli here takes an offensive approach, but she never gets too close, ensuring she has her own space. Demi is the opposite, preferring to fight up close albeit more defensively. Alexis, your approach seems more fluid – you adapt your style to match your opponent's. I take it you have trained before?'

'My dad showed us a few things,' Alexis explained. He could sense Incantus's eyes on him from the corner of the arena, his attention focussed like a spotlight. 'He's a homicide detective, but he's trained all his life, mixed martial arts and stuff like that. He explained fighting once to my mum by saying that to approach each case using the same technique would be like treating each disease with the same antibiotic. A personalised approach is an effective one.'

'A very insightful man,' Akili said with an impressed smile. 'It is the same principle here. Whilst I could tell you how you should fight, it may be more detrimental than useful. I may not always be there to do so, in which case you need to learn for yourself. You must find your own way.'

'And what if we fail?' Caeli asked, picking dirt from beneath her fingernails.

Akili paused before speaking, his deep, Caribbean accent resonating with Alexis. 'It is only through trying and failing and trying again that any of us succeed at becoming someone worth remembering.'

'I haven't seen *you* fight yet,' said Blaise. He wiped away the sweat from his forehead. 'You look like you've done about a million steroid cycles, but you act like a yoga teacher or a priest.'

'Want to see if you can land a hit?' Akili asked, trying to conceal a smirk.

Caeli sniggered. 'Don't encourage him.'

111

Incantus strolled over, 'Mr Ademola, if you last more than one second, I will make it my personal goal to get you swimming lengths in a lava pool by the end of the month.'

'You're on,' said Blaise. Before Blaise could even raise his fists, Akili had swiftly jabbed at his chest, sending him flying back. Everyone burst out laughing as Blaise lay groaning on the ground, clutching his chest.

'I wasn't ready,' he gasped. 'Not fair.'

Akili shrugged in response. 'Your opponents will not wait for you to be ready,' he said, pulling the hood up of his brown robes before striding away.

'Go to the Hub and get some food in you,' Incantus laughed, using his powers to lift them to their shaky feet. He cast away the projection of their training bots with his hand. 'Have an hour's lunch before returning, but from now on, make sure you eat breakfast too; you will need it for energy and muscle growth. Oh, and if you are late, I'll tell Raeve not to bring the healing crystals. And trust me, you'll need it before her lesson.'

11

APANTHROPINISATION

Apanthropinisation (n.) *Greek origin*
The resignation of human concerns; withdrawal
from the world and its problems

On cue, the door to the Training Academy creaked open
and Ziya hesitantly appeared. As she stepped into the huge
stadium, her large eyes darted over the scene excitedly. She
brushed away her fringe so she could see it all.

'Sorry I'm late,' Ziya apologised. 'Got waylaid with Taranis. He
was showing me how he does the surveillance. Honestly, his brain
goes faster than lightning when it comes to anything technical.'

'And yet I'm sure you managed to keep up with him,'
Incantus replied. 'If you're not busy, would you like to show
the Alpha team to the Garden? Try to prevent them from
getting swarmed. It seems as though the news of their arrival
has spread even before sunrise.'

Blaise perked up at their new nickname. 'Alpha team?'

Incantus rolled his eyes. 'It's only because your names
happen to begin with the first four letters of the alphabet.'

Blaise winked as he got up. 'Okay, boss, if you say so.'

'Thanks for showing us the way; you didn't have to,' Alexis
said as they headed out.

'I did, otherwise you would've got lost,' said Ziya matter-of-factly, speaking in her typical rapid fashion. 'And I'm happy to. Besides, Incantus is right. Everyone wants to meet you. I don't like change, but I like—'

The door to the Academy room opposite creaked open and a tall, young man came out. His lanky frame was dressed in an Elemental suit, his pale skin contrasted against the mop of dark hair that half obscured his face.

He pulled the door shut, locking it, and his gaze landed on Ziya.

'You're not obsessing over the newcomers already, are you? They deserve better company than you.'

'Crawling out of your cave, Ezra?' Ziya retorted, her cheeks flushing as she glanced at Alexis and the others beside her. 'Still jealous that Incantus chose me over you as his protégé?'

Ezra folded his arms and leant against the wall of the corridor. He didn't blink for an uncomfortably long time. 'His biggest mistake was picking a powerless girl like you. I actually contribute around here instead of following Incantus around like an abandoned puppy, desperate for validation. He's already got one beast for that.'

Ziya went to reply, but her words caught in her throat. Meanwhile, Ezra eyed the rest of them up and down with a smirk on his face.

Alexis knew a bully when he saw one. Through gritted teeth, he said steadily, 'Who the hell are you to speak to her like that? Apologise to her. Now.'

Ezra huffed, brushing the hair out of his eyes. 'So you're it? The Children of the Elements?' He sounded dissatisfied, scratching the edge of his impossibly sharp jawline. Glaring at Blaise, he added, 'You don't exactly look like you can take on Mortem.'

Blaise's jaw ticked. 'I look like I can take on you, whoever you are.'

'Ezra Alastor,' said the tall teenager as if his name meant something. 'Teleporter and portaller, one of the few. My family helped to create the teleportation lines everyone uses so regularly. I was just checking up on them.'

'Not interested, babes,' Caeli said. Much to Alexis's surprise, she hooked arms with Ziya. Demi made her way next to her on the other side, forming a trio.

'You can go now, Eczema,' Alexis added, not taking his eyes off him.

He glared back, squinting with distaste. 'It's *Ezra*.'

Alexis shrugged. 'That's what I said.'

Ezra took a step closer to the girls. 'Got your boyfriends here?' He licked his lips and extended his hand towards Demi's side, his crooked fingers brushing the curve of her waist. 'I could have you and go before they even blin—'

Demi reacted before Alexis could. In one motion, she slapped his hand away with her left and punched him with her right, rocking Ezra back against the wall. 'Don't ever try to touch me again.' She shivered, recoiling as she shook the blood from her hand.

Wide-eyed, with blood dyeing his yellow-stained teeth, Ezra took a step forward, fist pulled back. 'You stupid bi—'

A gust of wind catapulted Ezra to the side, launching him down the hallway. He had barely landed before Caeli spoke.

'Finish what you were going to say, I dare you,' she thundered, her hair blowing in the stirring wind, amulet shining grey.

One moment Ezra was laying on the ground, the next there was a whooshing sound as the outline of his figure glinted bronze. In the blink of an eye, he had reappeared just in front of them, his bloodied face pressed into a scowl.

The door the Alpha team exited from swung open. Incantus caught Ezra's fist just before it connected with Caeli.

'I *know*,' said Incantus, his grip tightening round Ezra's wrist, forcing him to submit, 'that you aren't about to attack one of the Elementals of *my* Haven.'

Ezra reeled back, clutching the hand Incantus had held as though it had burned him. 'Sir, they attacked me first. Look!' He wiped the blood from his chin and flicked it on the walls.

'Do you want me to call Mr Pierce to find out just what happened?'

The thought of Akili poking around in Ezra's head seemed to petrify him more than anything.

'If I ever see you go to strike one of these Elementals, or anyone for that matter, you will suffer the consequences with me. Now go to the Healing Sanctuary. You're bleeding on my floors.'

With an incensed glare at Alexis and the others, Ezra disappeared, his body gone in a flash of bronze before another drop of blood reached the ground.

Incantus turned to them, the remnants of his anger fading. For the first time, Alexis feared the harm he could cause to someone should he choose to. Having heard so much of the legend of Mortem, Alexis wondered if the legend of Incantus

Arcangelo was even greater. 'I see you have settled in well. Not five steps from the Academy.'

'It was my fault,' Ziya blurted, stepping forward. 'I think I embarrassed him in front of the others for not being picked as your apprentice.'

'It was me who punched him though,' Demi admitted. 'I'm sorry, I know I shouldn't have hit him. It's really not like me to do that.'

Incantus nodded, his lips pressed into a line. 'I will have a word with him. But, Ziya, you have to start standing up for yourself too. You will always face others who will try to put you down to make themselves stand taller, who will fight to extinguish your light because they think it will make theirs shine brighter. Never compromise who you are or be any less proud of the achievements you have earned.' He rested a hand on Ziya's shoulder, making her look up and eventually nod. 'Now go and eat, and please try not to beat up anyone else on your way.'

The five young Elementals headed down the corridor, their heads lowered. Just before they turned the corner, Incantus added quietly, 'Well done, Miss Doran.'

He didn't see it, but Caeli had smiled.

'Thank you for defending me,' Ziya said the moment they were out of earshot, awkwardly pulling down the long sleeves of her jumper. She was seemingly one of the few Elementals of the Haven that didn't wear the training suits. 'I'm sorry I got you in trouble.'

Demi took her arm. 'That's what friends do.'

'He deserved it,' Caeli added, tying her silvery-blonde hair into a messy bun. '"Eczema."' She chuckled and extended her hand for Alexis to shake. 'At first I thought you were odd, but now I think we'll get along just fine.'

'Your hand okay, Demi?' Alexis asked. Her smile helped his anger dissipate, although not entirely. 'Is there a way we could euthanise him?'

'That would be murder, Lexi,' she chastised.

Alexis made a face. 'So you're saying it would be frowned upon? What's his problem, anyway?'

They crossed the interwoven pathways that connected the huge expanse of the hive. One-by-one, the Elementals below somehow noticed their arrival. Maybe they had been waiting for them. Maybe they sensed them. They gathered around, tiptoeing to get a better view of the Children of the Elements and their amulets.

'Ezra grew up in the Haven,' Ziya explained. 'His parents left him here when they went out on missions, you know, as peacekeepers sent by the Haven on behalf of the High Order. One night, years ago, they died fighting against a horde of Nekro.'

'Nekro?'

She nodded pensively. 'The undead that Mortem has partial control over. Incantus took Ezra in then and helped him develop his rare teleportation and portalling powers. It was around the same time that I first arrived. We all thought he would be Incantus's apprentice, but for some reason he chose me. He's only allowed to remain here because of a promise Incantus made to his parents. That was about a year ago and he's kind of secluded himself since then. He should be gone by his twentieth birthday.'

Alexis felt suddenly guilty for mocking the boy who had lost his parents. A history of pain had convincing and cruel ways of shielding itself.

Blaise, though, seemed to have only paid attention to one part of the story. 'Mortem can create *zombies*?'

Ziya did her best to lead the Alpha team through the masses, but they were swarmed immediately. Alexis looked for Demi, knowing how she thrived when meeting new people, but her attention was focussed on one person only; Caeli.

The taller girl had become quiet in the crowd, her eyes darting between the surrounding people as they invaded her personal space, restricting her movements. Demi had taken Caeli's hand in hers, sticking out her other arm to keep people from getting too close, grinning all the while. It wasn't much, but it gave Caeli the air she needed. Soon enough, Caeli was smiling just the same.

Eventually, they reached a gigantic stone archway which stood just behind the main training arena of the Hub. It seemed older than the polished marble walls of the rest of the facility, made of a different stone that had crumbled with time. Its rockface was engraved with carvings of animals, mundane and magical alike, with round fruit sprouting from trees in between.

As he neared, Alexis noticed the familiar white chalk line that ran along its edge, illuminating the archway and the pale-white threshold beneath it.

An explosion of colour and nature lay beyond the doorway as the Elementals passed through. A park-sized clearing sat just beyond the portal face, hugged by a forest of flourishing trees that stood tall in the sky, bursting with fruit and decorated by giggling tree nymphs made of leaves or bark.

Swathes of Elementals roamed leisurely and ate in the summer heat. In the distance, only a couple of hundred metres away, Alexis sensed a large body of water settled within the canyon, and he yearned for its touch.

This place was breathtaking in its beauty, magical in vibrancy.

'Some call it Paradise or Nirvana, some say it was once the Garden of Eden,' said Ziya. Demi reached for her necklace in wonder, eyes shining bright. 'Most of us just call it the Garden.'

There were long countertops overflowing with food by the portal and a looming, large-bellied man bounded over.

'Welcome! I am Libero, head chef.' He rubbed his hands. 'I would love to serve you! I want you to try a bit of everything.'

Before Caeli could convince him that they could manage, Libero had assembled huge lunches and brought them to a long carved wooden table. Gibbous had been strolling around and made himself comfortable beside Ziya.

'Well?' said Libero, watching them eagerly as they dug into a mountain of seafood risotto with a Greek side salad, topped with feta and cucumber and tomatoes.

'Delicious,' Demi assured him and he beamed with pride.

'Zee, why didn't you tell me you were with them!' A young girl who appeared around Jason's age appeared in front of the group, with dark hair and familiar large eyes.

'Parvati, leave them alone,' Ziya said. 'Sorry about my sister. She's been excited to meet you.'

'Just show me one of your powers,' the girl begged excitedly.

The new Elementals could not refuse.

'Alpha team,' announced Incantus, arriving sometime later. The crowd moved to allow him through. 'Looks like you're enjoying yourselves.'

Walking behind him was another, hunched, figure.

'There's someone very important I want you to meet,' Incantus said, stepping aside. 'One of my oldest companions. Meet Teller Sagen.'

12

MÄRCHEN

Märchen (n.) *German origin*

A story or tale

'Well aren't you a striking bunch,' said the man in a thick Nordic accent, his mouth turning up into a crooked grin.

Even though he looked much older than Incantus, old enough to be his father, he had the charm and confidence of a once handsome man. Grey had replaced the blond, but the sharpness of his green eyes hadn't faded. He extended his hand, his grip surprisingly strong despite it wavering in the space between them.

'Teller was one of the most prominent members of the Haven and High Order,' said Ziya, taking his hand with the familiarity one would share with a grandparent as Alexis offered him a seat.

'I still am, don't forget that,' he corrected her with a playful smirk. 'I grew up with your mentor here. We were companions in the Quinate!'

'What's the Quinate?' asked Demi.

'The most famous warrior group of modern times,' Ziya answered on his behalf. Teller sat back and nodded for her to continue. 'Made up of five of the most powerful Elementals of their generation: Incantus Arcangelo, Akili Pierce, Serena Aevum, Darcy Raphe, and Teller Sagen.'

'Oh how I have tales that would steal the breath from your lungs and make your hearts bleed with love and loss,' Teller added, his eyes closed in their seemingly untarnished memory.

'Not now, not now,' Incantus said. 'They have enough to process today without your tired stories, old man. These Elementals have just finished their training with our Akili.'

'Ah, Akili. He was more fun before he became a monk.' Teller grinned. 'More entertaining. Remember, Ian?'

'Entertaining wouldn't be the word I'd use,' Incantus replied, answering to the name that Akili had also called him, the name of the older boy written on the back of the photograph. The boy in Alexis's dreams.

'Mr Sagen —' Caeli began, before Teller interrupted her.

'Teller,' he corrected. 'Mr Sagen makes me sound old.'

'Teller. What are your powers?'

'Memory. Infinite memory,' said Teller, his green eyes gleaming. Met with a pause, he elaborated. 'Not only can I remember every event I have ever witnessed, but also those experienced by anyone else, exploring the origins of their memories even if they have been long forgotten.'

Alexis took a moment to process all that he could do with such power. What would that mean if Teller could search through his mind? Maybe he could reveal things Alexis himself had forgotten, exposing all that had been lost to him following his amnesia. Before he was adopted . . .

But would it be wise to ask? To let a stranger poke about in

123

the innermost depths of his brain, allowing him access to things Alexis had kept hidden and buried? The hallucinations he used to experience. The *Shadow Man*'s voice that had finally fallen silent. Maybe there was a reason why his brain had chosen to forget such things. Maybe it was its only way of coping.

Alexis felt Teller's eyes on him, stirring him from his introspection. It was a similar curious scrutiny that Incantus and Akili had shown when he first met them, a study that didn't extend to the rest of the Children of the Elements.

'No offence, but isn't that a bit boring?' Blaise asked, causing Teller to look away from Alexis. 'I'm sure it's great to remember if you locked the front door or to remember a girl's name on a date, but other than that, what use is it?'

'Ignore him,' said Demi, glaring at Blaise, but Teller didn't appear to be the type of person who got offended easily.

'Handsome boy,' he said, reaching for Blaise's hand. 'I can learn and memorise anything from a single exposure to it. I can make you forget something you thought you'd always remember, implant memories you're convinced you really experienced. I used my power to construct the department of Erasers in the High Order who maintain the secrecy of our world by wiping the memories of any mortal exposed to it. In my eyes, dear boy, learning and memory are the greatest gifts of all. Without it, we would be nothing.'

For the remainder of their lunch break, the Children of the Elements tested Teller on his abilities, entertaining themselves by asking him what was the name of their first crush or what colour their childhood play toy had been, things they themselves no longer remembered. The old soldier was highly entertaining company, even if Incantus had to occasionally scold him.

'Keep it clean, Teller,' he warned. 'They're only kids.'

'Old enough to go on a trecherous quest to save our world, but too young to hear a crude joke and a harmless swear?'

Incantus had shrugged and waved for him to go on.

At one point, through the crowd, Alexis spotted Ezra Alastor gawking at them, nose still inflamed and darkened with dried blood. He slipped past relatively unnoticed, a shadow within the crowd. Alexis met his eye and didn't look away until he was out of sight.

The young Elementals had barely finished eating by the time Raeve dispersed the crowd, walking to its centre, weaving between the Elementals as if she were smoke. Without a word, she took off in the direction of the Haven, the sunlight shimmering against the silver of her Elemental suit.

'I'm afraid that is your signal,' said Incantus.

'Do make sure you come and pay me a visit in the Elder Sanctuary on the fourth floor,' Teller said as they drew to their feet, holding onto Incantus's hand for support. 'I have plenty more stories to tell.'

'It is always a struggle to keep you quiet,' said Akili Pierce, coming to stand beside Incantus and Teller. Together, the three men looked like a completed trio whose friendship had stood the test of eternities.

'Ah, my favourite hermit,' Teller teased, reaching up to try to slap Akili's bald head. Akili dodged, predicting the attack even if he hadn't have the power to read minds. 'How is the life of worship treating you? Bored yet?'

'Not quite,' Akili replied calmly. 'And you? How is the life of arthritis and daytime naps?'

Teller chuckled good-heartedly, pointing to Akili with his thumb whilst he looked at the five young Elementals. 'I've always been able to steal the man away from the monk. Besides, it's time to let another group save the world. I cannot wait for Serena to be with us again. She is going to love them.' He paused briefly. 'As would have Darcy.'

At the mention of the name, Incantus's smile faltered.

'Indeed she would have,' Akili added quietly, his eyes falling to his own feet.

Incantus clapped his hands. 'Time to go, children,' he said, gesturing for them to get up, his smile back in an instant. 'Ziya, if you wouldn't mind escorting them. I shall join you shortly.'

Bidding goodbye to Teller, Ziya hurried them back through the great stone archway, re-entering the Haven. From a distance, Alexis could see Raeve already crossing the upper passageway of the hive, disappearing through the corridor.

'I'll leave you here,' Ziya said, ushering them on. 'Good luck!'

Raeve didn't turn to check that they were following her. Only once back inside the Training Academy room did she address them, spinning perfectly on her heel to face them.

'Each of you will go into your own quarter of the arena for this part of the training. But first, you have to choose your weapon. Gravitate towards that which attracts you and suits your fighting style. You have a couple of minutes, otherwise, I'll assume you intend to fight with your fists.'

A bulging case appeared before her in a wave of purple cloud, revealing an array of gleaming weapons.

'Might be a dumb question, but why don't we just use guns? I know it looks cooler, but this isn't 100 BCE,' said Blaise whilst running his finger along the blade of an axe.

Raeve showed little sympathy when he cut it and cursed. 'The aura of an Elemental can act as a shield,' she replied. 'A protective armour. The stronger the Elemental, the greater the aura. Mortal guns and bullets would be of little use, especially with your suits. I made sure of that when Taranis and I designed them.'

A metal sword caught Alexis's eye. It looked as though it were made up of two halves of different swords, equal parts bronze and steel, conjoined in the middle of the blade and hilt. He lifted it. In his grip it felt easy, the weight surprisingly light. Pulling the two cross-guards apart, the sword split into two smaller halves. He envisaged himself swinging it, slashing at the air. The movement of the swords were fluid, acting as extensions of his arms rather than something he held.

'Interesting choice,' said Raeve, taking them from him. 'Forged by twin Elementals who used to attend here; Aes and Adamas.' She examined the blades, turning them over before re-joining them and handing it back to him. 'Strong, swift, sharp.'

Without warning, she unsheathed the sword at her hip and swung at Alexis. Instinctively, he parried the blow, his body working faster than his brain, relying on the years of playfighting he had done with his brother. At least with Jason they had used wooden sticks or blunt plastic lightsabres.

'Woah!'

The others turned round, each still holding whatever weapon they had initially picked up.

Raeve leapt again, their swords meeting in the middle, the clanging sound of metal ringing out. A familiar warming sensation flooded Alexis's body as he sensed Incantus had entered the room. Wanting to prove himself to his mentor even more so than to his peers, he stepped forward in response, catching Raeve slightly by surprise. She regained her balance, sending a high kick upward to push Alexis's blade away. An impressed smile crept across her face, her eyes brightening at the prospect of a challenge.

She lunged again, fast. Despite her lean frame, she was incredibly strong, and Alexis struggled to maintain a grip on his sword every time they clashed. Spinning him around, she kicked at the back of his knee, sending him to the ground.

'Protect your weak spots,' she said calmly. She had barely broken a sweat. 'You need to be aware all the time of the other person's powers and skillset. You might well have more than one assailant. Quick reactions. Up again, sweetheart.'

Using the sword to help him stand, Alexis got to his feet.

'You aren't going to let them heal before training?' asked Incantus, drawing closer.

Raeve slapped the blunt edge of her sword against Alexis's stomach. The suit absorbed most of the impact, but his skin underneath still stung.

'There will be little recovery time during the quest, sir,' she replied, shoving Alexis over with a light kick. 'Comfort breeds softness. It is success that qualifies the pain of hard work. They may hate me now, but when the quest is over and the Darkness destroyed, they will be grateful.'

Raeve hadn't taken her eyes off Alexis since they started duelling, the sword flipping between her hands, unparalleled confidence in her abilities.

'When you are defending yourself,' she said, loudly enough for the others to hear, 'you need to not only block these attacks, but simultaneously think of all your options. How to escape if the enemy is better than you, or how to catch them off guard. The first thing that happens when a warrior is on the attack is their lack of caution. Use this to your advantage.'

She advanced again. The sword spun in her hands, creating a silver outline of the tip of the blade. 'Look at my stance and predict my attack.'

Already Alexis was covered in a light sheen of sweat and was panting slightly, his dark curls sticking to his forehead. But he was not willing to give up so easily. He pushed past his tiredness and focused on Raeve's movements. Each time Raeve attacked, it had been when her right leg was back, moving with the blade as she brought it forwards, her momentum adding to the strength.

Now, when she swung her sword, he blocked it with his own, his muscles taut beneath the blow before forcing it down to the side. With her body exposed, he went to strike at it with his fist. Then, all of a sudden, he stopped. He had caught her eyes – her large, open, entrancing eyes. The longer he looked at them, the more transfixed he became, trying to decide what colour they were. Purple? Indigo? Violet?

Even as she moved, Alexis couldn't look away from her. It

was only when she slid behind him, holding his own sword against his throat, that he realised he had fallen prey to her Concilium charm.

'But that's not fair!' Demi shouted. 'She used her powers.'

Incantus answered for her. 'Elementals are whom you may be up against, some with powers you won't be aware of until revealed in battle.'

Raeve had tricked Alexis into defeat, that much he knew. But he hadn't surrendered just yet.

Without warning, Alexis pushed the blade away from his neck with one hand. The sword cut into his skin and instantly drew blood, but he ignored the searing pain. He snaked his leg behind Raeve's and flipped her over his hip.

She landed on the ground heavily, both swords still in her grip, looking up. He heard the others exclaim from the sides. Even Incantus was silent, watchful. Did he sense a spark of a smile?

'I'm so sorry, Raeve,' Alexis began, worried that in response to getting his pride hurt, he had just maddened one of his teachers. He was cut short by the sound of her laughing.

'Brilliant, Alexis. Amazing.' She got to her feet, handing him back his bronze-steel forged sword, her face split with a proud smile. 'Weapons are merely a means to channel your strength. Useful but not necessary. Your real strength comes from your powers – it comes from you. The best fighters find their opponent's power and use it against them.'

From her pocket, she pulled free a small jagged crystal, its colour a pale yellow. She held Alexis's bleeding hand in her own and pressed the stone against his skin. The healing crystal instantly began to illuminate, and within seconds Alexis felt the odd sensation of his skin repairing itself, stitching the deep wound closed.

By the time she had let him go, his palm was undamaged, slightly pinkish where it had been cut. The healing went beyond his hand. The glow spread up his arm to the rest of his body, rebuilding the torn muscles and relaxing the tension that ached them.

'That's incredible,' Demi gasped. Raeve passed the crystal to her where she marvelled at the magic up close as she pressed it against her chest. 'Make sure we pack our bags with these.'

'The healing crystals are re-charged by those in the Healing Sanctuary,' Incantus informed them. 'They can repair almost any physical damage on an Elemental's body, so long as they were not cut by a poison blade. But they are in short supply and should not be used to replace proper training and precaution.' He smiled. 'I'll leave you to it, Raeve.'

'So are witches a specific type of Elemental?' Alexis asked as Incantus exited the room.

'Our powers are our magic which we conduct using spells or potions,' Raeve replied. 'We attend the Coven Academy to learn our branch of magic, but I didn't appreciate the politics for it as I grew older. It suited my cousin to operate in chaotic freedom, but I prefer order and purpose. It has long been a dream of mine to open a Coven here for those Elemental magic-wielders who wish to stay in the Haven . . . but the High Order refused, too scared to incur the wrath of the High Coven.' She shook her head.

'So your cousin is an Elemental as well? A witch?'

Raeve looked at him, her expression concealed. 'A *witch* amongst other words which rhyme.'

With a snap of Raeve's fingers, the projectors on each of the four stages buzzed, a hologram developing. 'On me,' she instructed once standing alone at the centre podium. Slowly, the hologram projections morphed into model copies of Raeve's figure, solidifying when complete, each facing a Child of the Element. As she moved, the faceless statues mirrored her.

'The bots are set to mimic my actions, enabling you to closely follow exactly what I do and, at a later date, to be used as training partners.' She glanced round at them all. Blaise was holding a powerful-looking double-sided axe, the blades thick and heavy, requiring strength to be wielded. Caeli had gone for a long simple-looking spear, a sharp blade protruding from the hilt at each end. She toyed with it, throwing it up in the air and catching it, admiring its reach. And lastly, Demi had found herself clutching a short, curved dagger, holding it so the metal edge ran parallel to her forearm.

'I see that you have all picked your weapons, excellent choices. As you go on, by all means, change it up and use what you see fit. But for now, sweethearts, eyes on your opponents.'

The bots reflected Raeve as she pulled out her sword, and Alexis knew that the rest of the session would be just as demanding as the last.

13

MERAKI

Meraki (v.) *Greek origin*
The soul, creativity or love put into something;
the essence of yourself in your work

Taranis joined them half an hour early, saying he was unable to wait any longer. He bounced about, his energy infectious, giving the four tired Elementals the spur they needed as they learnt how to use the tools that would aid them on their quest, notably the portalling device that would transport them as close as possible to the location of each Elemental Gem, and broad survival techniques that would keep them safe.

'You've done well,' Taranis said at last with a rapid applause. 'I think you can finish early.'

'In that case, Taranis,' Raeve said from the doorway, her cat-like eyes trained on him, 'perhaps you could give me a hand with something before dinner.'

Taranis flushed and hurried off, his body cackling with excited yellow sparks, pausing for barely a second to bow at Incantus who had just returned.

Incantus laughed, watching them go. 'You wouldn't believe how much they hated each other when they first met,' he told the exhausted Elementals. 'I am exceptionally proud of the four of you,' he said, his strong hands clasped in front of him. 'You have earned the right to have the evening to yourselves. Eat, explore and enjoy the company of each other.'

They parted from their mentor and headed to their rooms to wash before dinner.

'Al,' called Blaise. He stood with his hands in his pockets, rocking back and forth on his heel, unable to keep still. 'Want to chill in my room for a bit?'

Over Blaise's broad shoulder, Alexis saw Demi give him an encouraging thumbs up.

'Sure,' said Alexis with a crooked smile. He choked down a laugh when he saw Demi punch the air in victory and then stumble up the stairs to disappear to her room.

'I thought you said to chill in your room!' Alexis choked when Blaise opened his bedroom door. He fanned his face as a stifling wave of hot air enveloped him and made his eyes water. 'Your room is a sauna!'

Blaise threw his head back to laugh. 'Just how I like it.'

Alexis took a brief sweep of Blaise's room; it had the same two-tiered layout as his, but it was decorated in reds and yellows and oranges, with a wall-length fireplace in the place where his swimming pool would be

Alexis perched on the coal-black sofa and Blaise sat awkwardly opposite.

'I just wanted to say . . .' Blaise cleared his throat again. 'Cheers for helping me earlier. You know, back when we were swimming.'

'*Drowning*,' Alexis corrected. Blaise gave a rueful grin. 'And you're welcome. If we're going to be together every day for the foreseeable future, we might as well help each other out.'

Blaise nodded. 'You're right.' He lounged in his chair and crossed his hands behind the back of his head. In the firelight, the clips of his short braids looked like gleaming cinders. 'I don't have many guy mates. I try making them, but for some reason it never lasts. We get competitive, argue. Guess I must burn them.'

What Alexis wanted to say in reply was, *I don't know how to be a friend. Please don't reject me. I promise I'll try if you do.*

But his voice would never betray him to admit that. Instead, he said, 'Good thing water doesn't burn then.'

Maybe Alexis had been wrong about him. Maybe Blaise hadn't intentionally tried to outshine him; maybe that was just who he was. A bold, bright character who naturally caught the attention of the people around him, just like the sun in the sky or a bonfire in the woods.

Alexis couldn't blame Blaise for being different from him, for not finding comfort in the darkness or at the outskirts. Blaise was who Alexis had always wanted to be.

Perhaps it was best to keep someone like that around.

Blaise jutted his chin to the door. 'So what's the deal with you and Dee? You can't tell me that nothing's ever happened between the two of you. I see how you two look at each other.'

Alexis shook his head probably more vigorously than necessary, for he caught Blaise's eyes narrowing in scepticism. 'No, we've just been really good friends for a really long time and our families are close. She would n— We're just close.'

Blaise grinned to himself. Alexis wasn't sure if he believed him. He wasn't sure if he believed himself. 'So you wouldn't mind if *I* tried to get to know her better?'

The steam of Blaise's room was becoming overpowering, making it effortful for Alexis to do anything other than sit there and sweat. The idea of Blaise and Demi made his stomach churn, but there was no way Alexis could say no without Blaise probing him for more questions.

'Do what you want,' Alexis said nonchalantly, swallowing even though his mouth was dry.

Blaise let out a low chuckle. 'Nah, not my type,' he said. 'She's stunning and all, but too much of a good girl for me.'

Alexis couldn't fathom a sane person on Earth who would take one look at Demi or be the subject of her smile and not want to spend their life pining over her.

'What about you and Caeli?' he asked, turning it on him.

Blaise let out a little hum. 'Friends, just like you and Dee,' was all he said.

They sat in silence for a while, staring into the fire that danced before them, licking at the air. Blaise clutched his stomach. 'I'm starving. I can't wait to see what the big guy cooks up for dinner.'

'I don't know if I want to go to the Garden tonight,' Alexis admitted, receiving a perplexed look from Blaise. 'I don't like being the centre of attention. I feel like half of them there are waiting for me to prove something to them. To prove that I deserve to be the one that's got these powers.'

'Who cares what others think?' said Blaise with a wave. When he spoke again, his voice came out quieter than it had before. 'It doesn't matter what people think of you. The only thing that matters is what you think of yourself."

Blaise shook his head. 'If we spend our whole lives obsessed with what other people think of us, we'll be too scared to do anything. I'm not living like that. I'll burn brightly, whether they are there to see it or not.'

Alexis placed his arm round his new friend and repeated what he had just told him. 'The only thing that matters is what you think of yourself.'

'*I* think I'm pretty great.'

'There you go, then,' Alexis replied. 'And if anyone ever says anything . . .'

'I don't need your protection,' said Blaise, playfully throwing his arm off. His mouth curved in a smile. 'But I'll take your friendship. Something tells me that you're cutthroat. I'd rather you as an ally than a rival.'

14

GEZELLIGHEID

Gezelligheid (n.) *Dutch origin*
The cosiness, warmth and comfort of being
at home or being with friends or loved ones

A gentle knock at the door shook Alexis from his slumber. After showering and changing into a pair of shorts and a loose black jumper, Alexis had fallen asleep to questions and theories of what would've happened if his coach hadn't stopped by Stonehenge or if his parents hadn't agreed to let him go on the trip. Would the Prophecy still come to into play? Would his parents notice any difference with his proxy? Would he ever meet Mortem in person?

Sleep was the only forthcoming answer.

Demi Nikolas was there when Alexis opened the door, leaning against the door frame in a honey brown sundress.

'And you say girls take longer than boys.' Her dark hair came down in unruly damp curls, with two braids tied together at the back. Alexis noticed there was a faint shimmering glitter around her eyes, making the green in them stand out. He glanced behind her, wondering where the others were.

'I told them to save us a seat. I realised I haven't shown you my room yet.'

She took him by the hand and led him to her bedroom. He was welcomed with the rich scent of soil and flowers as if he had stumbled into a greenhouse. Her room was far more decorated than his. The walls were coated in curling vine branches and leaves of all shades, leaving barely an inch spare of the natural, growing life. Even the bedposts of the magnificent mahogany bedframe were ornate, hand carved with spiralling patterns of thorns and flowers.

Most startling of all was the single, great oak tree protruding from the centre of the room, the base of the trunk nearly two metres wide, the top of its branches folding against the high ceiling, stunting the potential for its true growth.

'You have a *tree* in your room?'

'That Elemental eyesight seems to be working,' Demi replied with a grin.

Alexis ran his hand round the width of the trunk, his palm feeling the roughness of the thick bark. He didn't think he'd ever seen one so old.

'Apparently it's based on the Tree of Life which really did exist somewhere in the world.' Demi placed her hand against its side next to Alexis's. She then lowered herself to sit, her back resting against it, her head tilted up towards the high leaves.

'So, talk to me,' she said, nudging him as he took a seat beside her. 'Something's bothering you – and I don't just mean the whole saving-the-world thing. Something else. Every time I looked at you today, when you thought no one was looking, you had on that face you pull. Like you're trying to hide what you're really thinking. You were . . . I can't think of the word in English.'

'Distracted?' Alexis offered. Demi nodded.

Demi's eyes were fixed on his, looking at him the way she always did. As though she knew everything about him. As though she accepted everything about him. Of course, she didn't, for there were things that Alexis had never and would never tell her. He didn't want to risk losing that look, that faith.

But was it fair to only showed her a side to him he thought she wanted to see? Was it fair to himself? Surely he deserved to have company in the darkness of his revelation, to be alongside a person that would be his torch? Maybe there was an innate strength in exposing one's own vulnerability.

Against every instinct that told him to keep it to himself, Alexis decided to confide in the only person he knew for certain would never judge him. 'I *was* distracted. I still am. And this is why.' With his fingers tapping his thumbs, encouraging him on, Alexis took a deep breath and said, 'I think Mortem is my birth father.'

He told her of the photograph of the two boys, and the resemblance between himself at that age and the younger boy. How it would make sense, that Alexis was born with the water element, the power Mortem used to possess. How Alexis had dreamed of two people he had never met.

'But what does that mean?' he went on, filling the silence with more rambling as Demi just sat and listened. 'Did my parents know about the Elemental world when they adopted me? And does this mean that Incantus is my uncle? Does he know? And who was my mother?'

Demi placed her hand on his. She squeezed it firmly to stop him. 'We don't know enough yet to say. Mortem may be your birth father. He may not be. You're basing this all off a dream and a photo taken a century ago of a boy who looked a bit like you did when you were younger.'

Alexis looked away, failing to put any authenticity into his laugh. 'Can't deny I've got a good imagination, huh?'

Demi tutted. 'Deep down, you know who your real parents are. The ones who raised you and taught you everything you know. You can speculate all you want, but the only person who might be able to tell you the truth is Incantus.'

Alexis picked away at the leaves on the branch just to give him something to do. 'The way everyone talks about Mortem . . . the things he's done and intends to do. I don't know if I want to know. I . . . I don't want to be the odd one out again.'

Demi didn't blink when she replied. 'What makes you different is what makes you special, Lexi. I wouldn't change you for the world.' Her eyes were kind but sure.

Alexis smiled before pulling her into a hug, her head resting against his shoulder. He didn't believe her, but he thanked her nonetheless.

'I know it sounds childish, but I'm missing my family so much,' Demi muttered into his chest. 'But, more than anything, I'm really struggling with the idea of hurting or killing someone. It goes against everything I believe in, against the person I am at my core.'

Alexis let out a slight sigh, not quite knowing what to say. 'Dem, if what Incantus says about Mortem is true . . . we have to do whatever it takes to stop him and anyone else who gets in the way of our quest.'

'I know that,' she said. 'I get that he's awful and a murderer and needs to be stopped, but who's to say we should be the ones that take his life? I can't kill, Lexi. I won't be able to live with myself.'

Alexis took Demi's hand, holding it for longer than he should have. He admired her commitment to her values in the face of all that could go against them. 'Then don't. We'll go on the quest, we'll get the Gems, and we'll come home without anyone getting hurt.'

She let out a faint sigh. It seemed she was far more believing than he was. 'I hope so.'

'We've got this, me and you,' Alexis promised, kissing her fingertips once. With that kiss, he made a promise to himself, too, that he would do whatever it took to keep her safe. 'We're in this together. Until the seas settles and the Earth stops turning.'

That he knew with certainty to be true.

When Demi and Alexis arrived at the Garden, passing through the glowing ancient stone archway, they were greeted by a horde of Elementals who had been eagerly awaiting them. Caeli and Blaise were in the mix, telling the story of how they all met to a rapt audience, including Ziya who gave them a cheerful wave. Before they could get a word in, Libero appeared, forcing full plates of food into their hands where they ate until Alexis's oversized white jumper fitted comfortably.

Stories, jokes and laughter carried on for hours into the night as the moon rose high into the sky, shining as though it was there just for them. At one point, Raeve and Taranis joined, fascinated to hear of the early lives of the Children of the Elements.

Alexis couldn't help but smile after seeing Blaise flirting with Ziya's friend, Althea Orenda, who was telling him she had left her Coven Academy to learn under Raeve. Alexis also noticed Caeli staring at them, and the brief flash of disappointment on her face.

It didn't last for long, however. Caeli quickly found herself sitting next to a handsome young man with floppy blond hair called Joe Coin, laughing loudly enough to catch Blaise's attention.

Alexis just sat back and sipped his drink as he observed what was certainly going to be an interesting and reliable source of entertainment for the next month.

It was approaching midnight before Akili Pierce appeared, telling the entire forest clearing it was time for bed without his lips ever parting.

As the Leaders began to usher the Elemental students inside, mumbling that the Alpha team had better be ready for another day's training, Alexis caught a glimpse of Gibbous strolling through the woods in the direction of the canyon, the moonlight making it look like his fur coat was glowing. He wondered where he could be going at this hour. To hunt? But he had seen Ziya feed him from her plate only half an hour earlier.

Or perhaps the dire wolf was seeking his master. This might be a rare chance for Alexis to speak to Incantus alone. To see if he could get answers to some of his questions.

Alexis silently slipped away from his friends, disappearing through the crowd after Gibbous.

Free from the shelter of the sea of trees, Alexis felt the bite of the brisk, evening air as he walked down the winding lantern-lit trail, guided by the scattered starlight and the distant sound of rushing water. He was about to turn back when he noticed that up ahead, Gibbous had stopped in his tracks, his ears pricking up.

Would Gibbous attack him now that there was no one around? Alexis held his breath, readying himself, but the great white wolf eventually continued, slowing his pace as he led him towards the canyon cliffside.

There sat Incantus, his legs dangling over the edge, the moonlight illuminating his ashen hair. Gibbous's tail wagged softly as he approached him, nudging into the hand that extended towards him as he took his place by his right side.

'Not many people can sneak up on me,' said Incantus lightly without turning around. Alexis freed himself from the shadow of the treeline. He drew closer to his mentor, looking at the view beyond the cliff edge. The river at the bottom of the canyon washed on peacefully by, its dark waters like a black canvas, concealing what lay hidden beneath the current's surface.

Incantus didn't look like he wanted to be disturbed. A brown patterned blanket was cloaked round his shoulders like a shawl, the weaving of the fabric loose and worn. It was the first time Alexis had seen Incantus in normal clothes; a baggy-fitting T-shirt and a pair of old jeans.

'I'm sorry to disturb you,' Alexis said. 'I'll go.'

Incantus gestured with a glowing hand for Alexis to sit beside him. 'I knew you would come at some point, Mr Michaels. Join me. I would love to have your company.'

15

KAWAAKARI

Kawaakari (n.) *Japanese origin*
'River light'; the gleam of last light on a river's surface at
dusk; the flow of a river in darkness

Gibbous's snowy eyes were watchful as Alexis sat on the other side of Incantus.

'How did you find your first day of training? Was it anything like you expected?'

'Harder,' Alexis admitted, hearing his voice echo across the canyon as he buried his hands beneath his armpits.

'Your whole world has changed drastically within a couple of days. If it's any consolation, you have handled it much better than most new Elementals who discover the true reality.'

'I've always been pretty good at riding the wave,' Alexis said, making Incantus chuckle. 'And you're an incredible teacher. You all are. The way you speak to us . . . it makes me feel like I'm capable of anything. I've never had that from a teacher before.'

Incantus offered Alexis the tattered blanket when he noticed him shivering, spreading it across the both of them. His gaze returned to a distant point on the river, light eyes thoughtful beneath dark eyebrows. 'I aim to teach differently from my mentor. I respect him, but I do not wish to be like him. That was a conscious decision I made many years ago, to be a leader and not a ruler. I'm glad it's paid off. How are you getting along with your new friends?'

Friends. Alexis had never had those before. He had to swallow an unexpectant lump in his throat before answering. 'Good. Really good. It's only been me and Demi before now.'

'People like her are rare,' said Incantus. 'Hold them close and pray they never leave or get taken from you.'

Incantus looked more human than Alexis had ever seen him; strong, angelic, but mortal. With an immortal life, there must have been people he had outlived, people he had watched die. It was difficult to reconcile this person with the one who had trained him all day, how he could be simultaneously brimming with light yet harbouring a sadness that weighed him down.

'I know how lucky I am to have someone like her in my life,' said Alexis, his mind's eye flashing with the dying scream of the *Shadow Man* as it vanished the first time he met Demi and their amulets ignited. He looked at Incantus. 'I guess the Prophecy was just behind all of that though.'

'You were destined to meet each other. Becoming friends, becoming family – that was your decision.'

Gibbous had stirred at the sound of their conversation, huffing that he had been awoken. With Incantus beside him for protection should he need it, Alexis reached out his hand to stroke Gibbous's head. The white wolf flinched at first, but after moment, he settled and eased into his touch.

'I'm not sure he likes me,' Alexis said.

Incantus smiled at his companion. 'It may be because you

147

resemble someone. The master of his brother. The person who used to have the powers now surging through you.'

Alexis internally swore. 'Mortem.'

Incantus's smile faded slightly. 'What do you wish to ask me, Mr Michaels?' He resumed gazing upon the view, the starlight illuminating his face, revealing the years of a lifetime in his eyes. 'Your head has been swimming with thoughts all day and you don't strike me as a person who often silences their opinion.'

Alexis mirrored his mentor, looking outward whilst playing with the weaving of the blanket. He thought of the photograph of the two boys, of how it had made its way into his room. 'We share similarities?'

'As is expected being born to the same element. It is what connects you two, more so than he with your friends.'

Could that be all there was to it? Could the relation be that of their powers and nothing else?

'My birth parents. Did you know them?' Much to his surprise, Alexis's voice caught in his throat. It wasn't often that he thought of where he came from, but ever since stepping foot into the Elemental world, where inheritance was instrumental to his power and purpose, he couldn't help but wonder.

Gibbous adjusted himself on Incantus's lap as the Elemental delicately brushed the fur between his sleepy eyes. 'I didn't sense your presence until the day of that mega-tsunami where you washed up.'

'The day my adopted parents found me?'

'Yes,' Incantus said, his reply slow, thoughtful. 'I had searched for you, wondering who the Child of the Water could be. But I couldn't find you. When I finally did, your parents were in the middle of the adoption process. Aadya Parashakti and I performed your Elemental inhibition without their knowledge.'

'Why didn't you just take me?'

Alexis thought briefly how different his life would be had he been raised by Incantus Arcangelo, growing up within the Elemental world. Another person entirely. Would he have suffered the demons that had tormented him during his childhood? The *Shadow Man*?

But then he wouldn't have his family. An upbringing without his parents and brother would be no life at all. Alexis would rather have the agonising company of the *Shadow Man* than lose them.

'You had to come to *us* when fate determined it was ready,' was all Incantus replied. He smiled, a sad smile. 'Get some rest. There will be time for more questions. For now, it is enough.'

Walking uphill towards the forest clearing, back to the Haven, Alexis was lost away in his thoughts. So much so that he hardly noticed Ezra Alastor at all.

The pale young man stood underneath the glowing archway, his hands running along the white chalk line that connected the Haven to the Garden, the sharp edge of his jawline gleaming against the canopy-covered moonlight. Alexis silently moved behind a tree, squinting through the darkness as he tried to make out what he was doing so late.

Ezra was carefully examining the teleportation lines, his fingers passing between the threshold as if testing its power.

Alexis recalled Ziya saying that he had helped create the devices that constructed them. But why was he doing it in the dead of night?

As Alexis shifted his weight, a twig snapped underneath. The sound echoed throughout the enchanted woods like a signal. Ezra shot to his feet as Alexis pressed himself against the tree, hoping that the shadows would obscure him.

He had no such luck. A whooshing sound, a flash of bronze light, and suddenly Alexis was shoved against the tree trunk, his head rocking against the hard surface.

'The darkness won't hide you,' said Ezra, his lips pressed into a snarl. He lashed a vicious kick into Alexis's side, knocking the wind out of him, and teleported further back, out of range. 'How about I portal you somewhere Incantus won't find you?'

Alexis spat blood at Ezra as he drew to his feet. 'Try it, Eczema. At least people will care if I go missing.'

The look of anger cast across Ezra's face dropped, and for a short moment, there was a glimpse of something else. Alexis's words had resonated, striking him where it hurt. The corners of his mouth dipped and his gaze dropped.

'I'm sorry,' Alexis started. 'I didn't mean—'

Ezra flung his hand in his direction. A shimmering bronze portal sparked from his fingertips and shot towards Alexis, too fast for him to dive or dodge.

Just before it enveloped him and teleported him somewhere far away, probably in pieces, Gibbous came bounding through the clearing. He knocked Ezra aside, cutting off the portal. The great wolf stood on his hind legs, towering over the wiry teen as he growled, forcing him back towards the Haven.

Whilst Incantus was nowhere to be seen, it was clear that Ezra was unwilling to challenge Alexis again in Gibbous's presence.

'You don't deserve any of this,' Ezra hissed, as Alexis moved to Gibbous's side. '"*Children of the Prophecy of Light and Darkness.*" What have you done to deserve your powers? To deserve respect? To be seen?'

'Jealousy, really?' Alexis rolled his eyes as he made sense of Ezra's immediate disdain towards them. He feigned a yawn. 'Such a cliché, Eczema. It's inconsiderate to be both boring and breathing. Pick a struggle or I'll pick for you.'

Ezra's nostrils flared as he glared daggers at Alexis. 'You think you're so smart and funny—'

'Are you flirting with me?'

Ezra's jaw tightened, his chest rising and falling, fury exuding from him in crashing waves of repressed anger. His voice turned cold as he spoke his next words. 'I always get my revenge. I'll start with your little girlfriend. Let's see if we can get blood from a stone.'

Alexis hurled over Gibbous at Ezra, his smile gone. Violence had dethroned his humour. Every cell of his body beat as one in a single, murderous chorus, a blind rage he could not and did not want to pacify. He wanted Ezra to suffer for what he'd said. And he didn't want to use his powers – he wanted to use his hands. He wanted to feel the bones break beneath the skin. Karma took too long. He wanted revenge now.

But he wasn't fast enough to catch the teleporter. Ezra vanished before Alexis could tear him apart.

'Touch her and I'll drown you in your own blood,' was all Alexis managed to utter as Gibbous brushed up beside him, nuzzling his nose into his hand, forcing it to unclench. 'There won't be a place you can teleport to where I won't find you.'

Ezra's let out an empty laugh that echoed throughout the dark clearing. Before he disappeared in a wormhole of bronze, he turned to Alexis.

'You will be dead before you get the chance. You all will. And then everyone will know my name.'

PART II

CAELI
Foretold to fly
'I am more than my insecurities'

16

HALCYON

Halcyon (adj.) *Greek origin*
'Kingfishers'; denoting a period of time that
was idyllically happy, tranquil, peaceful

Almost four weeks later

The days became a blur; one task merging with the next, the training sessions overlapping, the weeks mounting. The anticipation and trepidation in the Haven beneath Stonehenge seemed to rise with each passing day.

There hadn't been a single day where the Children of the Elements hadn't trained, and towards the middle of June – with the summer solstice less than a week away – not many nights either.

On the eve before the quest, Alexis found himself in the Elder Sanctuary with Teller Sagen, listening to his stories. He knew he should be putting in some training on his last day. It was what his friends were doing. But he couldn't tear himself away from Teller, even if he wanted to. Besides, his mind was far too distracted to risk picking up a sword.

'And that was how Incantus, Serena, Akili, Darcy and I defeated Apex, the greatest dark Elemental of our generation,' said Teller in his proud Nordic accent, taking Incantus's hand as he stood beside the seated older storyteller.

'That . . . was incredible!' said Alexis, his mouth pulled into the widest smile.

'Novelty wears off after you've heard it for the billionth time,' mumbled a nearby lady from her chair, getting up to shuffle away.

Incantus erupted into laughter, much to Teller's frustration, who swatted at his lower back, surprisingly fast.

'Always was your blind spot,' Teller said with a wink.

'Because I always had you to defend it,' Incantus replied, cradling the old man's face. 'Alexis, I will summon you shortly for the final stage of training.'

With a flash of white light, Incantus light-jumped away, the afterimage of his body imprinted in Alexis's vision. In his absence, a period of quietness settled between the two remaining Elementals as they sat by the Elder Sanctuary's fountain centrepiece. Alexis let his hand play with the water that poured from its stone design, manipulating the stream around the lilac-coloured quarters, doing his best to make sure it didn't jitter. He tried to conceal it, as he did with most of his emotions, but the temperament of the water was restless and, like anything else, Teller saw through it.

'You wish for me to look into your past?'

Alexis nearly dropped the flow of water. 'How – what makes you think that?'

'Akili may be the one that can read minds, but I can never forget. I know the look of someone when they are desperate to ask a question but are afraid to know the answer.'

Alexis slowly returned the water to the fountain, watching

as it poured over the stone angel statue whose wings formed the tiers. He still wondered, constantly, who his birth parents were, where he came from, if he had been the one to cause the tsunami that may have killed them and hundreds of others. Teller could unlock his past, and with it, the truth.

Teller sat patiently waiting, letting Alexis decide what to do. Eventually, the young Elemental spoke. 'I have no memory from before I was adopted. Nothing. I know childhood amnesia can happen, but I have no memories until I was about six years old. The only thing I have is a nightmare that repeats every night and I don't even think it's me in the dream.'

'The brain cannot configure new faces, not for most people at least,' Teller informed him, leaning forward in his seat. 'You can only dream of people you have seen before, however fleeting. What is it you are looking for?'

'I don't know. Anything. *Something*, at least. To see what my birth parents looked like. Or what happened to them. How can I move on with my life without knowing who I was before and where I came from? I feel like a boat out at sea with no anchor and no memory of how I got there.'

He didn't say anything about Mortem being his father. He was sure that when Teller looked into his memories, he would see whatever was there. Until then, he would keep his theories to himself. Besides, the disdain in Teller's voice whenever he spoke of Mortem was palpable, alive and violent. It was clear that even when they had been on the same side, Teller had never trusted him.

Teller stretched and groaned. Through old age, his body had crippled, years of battles and injury finally catching up to him. He placed a stiff hand on Alexis's bouncing knee. 'I have no future,' he said, his green eyes unblinking, 'only endless memories. When you reach the point in your life where your past becomes more important to you than your future, then you know you have truly lived. You are not yet at this junction, Alexis. You cannot walk ahead with your head turned back, trust me. To cling to the past is a disservice to yourself and your future.'

But Teller's wisdom was lost on Alexis and his insatiable desire to know everything. After a long pause, Teller spoke again. 'Are you sure this is what you want? Memory can be a curse, and sometimes it is better to live your life simply not knowing some things. Ignorance can be a great thing. The truth cannot hurt you that way.'

Alexis didn't think much before he replied. He tried to give himself time to deliberate, but he thought seventeen years was long enough. 'I think I would rather know than not—'

Before he had the chance to finish his sentence, a deep, lyrical voice resounded in his head. It felt as if a communication line had opened between him and another, like a frequency shared by two radios.

Thankfully, however, it was Akili's voice that came through, sounding somewhat urgent. 'Sorry, Alexis. I apologise for shouting in your ear – rather, your head.' The sound transferred from Alexis's head to the whole room, projected by a seemingly invisible speaker. 'Can you make your way to the Training Academy now? It is time for you to complete the final stage of your formal training, The Elemental Armageddon. Leave the fragile Elemental to have his rest; you know how much they need it at that age.'

'That's not very monk-like and humble from you, baldy,' Teller's voice called, light with humour. 'Perhaps I should tell Mr Michaels of our brief time together as lovers.'

Akili's reply boomed throughout the Sanctuary so loudly that Alexis had to clamp his hands over his ears. 'As if I would ever stoop so low!' Hearing nothing but Teller's cackle in response, Akili swore under his breath and the telepathic voiceover abruptly ended.

Teller chuckled to himself before smiling earnestly at Alexis. 'Go to your training, dear boy. I have a meeting with the High Order tonight so I don't know if I can make it to the feast; much to everyone's dismay, I am sure. But if this is what you *really* want, come and find me here. I promise to tell you everything.'

17

WALDEINSAMKEIT

Waldeinsamkeit (n.) *German origin*
Forest solitude; the feeling of being alone in the woods

The Elemental Armageddon was a simulation that lasted close to three hours. The Training Academy had been converted, through the use of the projectors, into a treacherous mountain range, with their objective being to find a hidden glowing stone before the opposing team of Elementals, consisting of five of their new friends including Joe Coin and Althea Orenda – and Ezra Alastor.

Holographic training bots set to a dark graphite colour, the highest difficulty level, dotted the arena, guarding the stone alongside the power of the elements. Floods, earthquakes, walls of fire and even the realistic simulation of a windstorm swept the mountain, all serving to disrupt the Alpha team of their mission. Incantus and the Leaders watched from a floating platform, looking down on the battle like spectators viewing Gladiators in a colosseum. But with the combined powers of the primal elements, the Children of the Elements came out victorious. Bloodied, bruised, beaten, but victorious.

As Ezra teleported away, his absence as unnoticed as his

presence, Incantus, the Leaders and their friends congratulated the Alpha team on their graduation from training. To celebrate the Children of the Elements before their quest, the Leaders told them a feast was planned for that evening in the Garden, set to begin in less than an hour.

With that, Caeli rang out a string of curses before dragging Demi with her to rush to get ready. Raeve, never the one to compromise her femininity in the presence of the male Leaders, went with them to help them pick out outfits. Caeli practically squealed with excitement.

After Alexis retired to his room, showering off the sweat and dirt of his final training session, he made his way through the quiet, Hellenic-inspired Haven towards the entrance of the Garden. He wore a tailored black shirt that complimented his tan and brought out his eyes, leaving the top few buttons undone to reveal the blue-stone amulet that sat in the centre of his defined chest. It was the first time in weeks he felt like he looked nice, handsome even, without the semi-permanent shine of sweat that covered his exhausted body and stuck his dark hair to his forehead in messy waves.

The Garden had been transformed. Decorations hung from the trees surrounding the clearing, orbs and ribbons glowing in the colours of the Children of the Elements' amulets, creating a network of floating lanterns and fairy lights. Within the glade, row upon row of wooden benches seated the hundreds of Elementals, their combined aura illuminating the forest with vitality. In the far distance, the crescent moon was slowly revealing itself amongst the pastel coral evening sky, its reflection glistening against the river of the canyon.

A long ash-marble table sat at the head of the clearing, closest to the tree line. Incantus Arcangelo sat in the centre, the Leaders to one side, and Caeli, Blaise and Demi to the other. It was odd, how the sight of them made Alexis's breath catch in his throat. His eyes fell on the empty chair that awaited him, his name inscribed on it. A gap only he could fill.

Alexis stopped briefly by Ziya's table. She was cloaked in a beautiful orange silk sari, her black hair loose from its bun for the first time and falling nearly to her elbows, an intricate henna mehndi curling round her hand. Alexis half-knelt against her wooden bench as he answered each of her many questions about the Elemental Armageddon, smiling as she grew increasingly animated when she told him Taranis had live-streamed it for her and Teller.

Then he caught sight of Demi, and all else fell away. Demi was laughing at something Blaise had said. She looked ethereal in the forest, surrounded by her element, the golden glow of the setting sun illuminating her face. Her hair had been straightened for the evening, tied back from her neck which only accented the warm bronze of her skin. She wore a sage green satin dress that revealed the horizontal cross at her neck and her amulet hanging just below.

Raeve must have transferred her magical charm to her somehow, for even the dryads, formed from the petals and twigs of the trees they inhabited, came to admire her also, hanging from the branches to watch the Elementals and feel their power. Demi noticed Alexis approach. A wide smile grew on her face as she threw her hands up in exclamation.

'About time, Al!' called Blaise who wore an incredibly tight burgundy silk shirt. 'Last night of freedom.'

'You look beautiful,' Alexis said, his eyes meeting Demi's. Flushing, he added, 'All of you, I mean.'

Caeli answered with a simple, 'I know.' Her long platinum blonde hair was curled, her butterfly fringe parted down the middle of her face. Dark winged eyeliner contrasted against her snowy complexion, bringing out the greyness of her eyes. The light breeze around her had been stilled at her command – presumably to ensure her hair didn't move more than anything.

Blaise put his arm round Alexis's shoulders. As Althea had warned, the golden clasps of Blaise's braids had melted after he accidentally set his head on fire. The braids were unsalvageable, but she managed to shape it up so he now sported short waves. 'How do I look?'

'Even more beautiful than usual,' Alexis replied, grinning. 'But I can *feel* that shirt cutting off your blood circulation. If you pass out, I'm not doing mouth-to-mouth.'

The Children of the Elementals dug into their feast, talking and joking alongside Incantus and the Leaders who had also dressed for the occasion. After their meal, Caeli parted from the group to join Joe, and Blaise soon left too to join Althea who coincidentally sat at the same table. Demi pointed out Caeli's irritated reaction despite her arm being linked with Joe's, forcing Alexis to conceal his laugh so that they wouldn't hear.

With the others out of earshot, Demi moved into the seat next to Alexis. The two of them again. In spite of everything,

Alexis felt most comfortable this way. He drew a long inhale as he breathed in the scent of her: rich jasmine, a hint of her lavender shampoo and . . .

'Sorry, I ate my body weight in garlic bread,' Demi said with her hand covering her mouth. She then nodded to Incantus. 'Did you ever get around to asking him about your birth parents or the kids in the photo?'

Alexis smiled past her at the sight of the Leaders, hoping that he too would grow to live his life surrounded by his friends. After much encouragement from Taranis, Incantus had permitted one of the Elementals use their powers of intoxication on him. His cheeks were rosy, and for the first time in a long time, he looked completely carefree, unbound by his responsibilities as he tossed a leg of roast chicken up for Gibbous to devour.

'He's got enough on his mind,' said Alexis. 'I asked Teller to look into it instead – my mind, my memories. After the feast, I'm going to meet him.'

Demi's golden-hooped earrings dangled as she sat back. 'I never thought of that. Do you want me to come with you? Or ask Blaise to?'

He took her hand, finding comfort in its warmth. She squeezed it back as he replied, 'Thank you, but it's okay. It's something I want to find out for myself first, you know?'

Their conversation was cut short. Incantus cleared his throat as he stood up, gesturing for Caeli and Blaise to return to the table. The forest fell silent until the only noise came from Gibbous's heavy paws each time he leapt in the air at the glowing fireflies. Incantus had a glass raised, his other hand resting on the table to support his weight.

'I would like to make a toast,' he announced, half-spilling his drink on his white linen shirt. Akili held him steady by the elbow after that, but he didn't seem to mind. 'I would like to congratulate and thank you all for your encouragement and support of the four Children of the Elements. You have been everything I had hoped for and more.' He turned to the young Elementals at his table, beaming down on them. With the five of them together, the table practically glowed.

'I'm going to cry,' Demi whispered, her eyes welling.

Caeli nudged her arm and muttered, 'Don't. You'll ruin your makeup.'

'And, of course, to the rest of you,' Incantus continued. 'To my Haven, my children. And lastly to my fellow Leaders who have been by my side all these decades, helping me run the Haven and teach you all. I am nothing but grateful for your love and your loyalty.'

The Elementals of the Haven applauded deafeningly, whistling and calling cheers into the sky that had darkened to a rich blue as they entered nightfall. Alexis knew he wouldn't be able to, but he still tried to take it all in. He imprinted the details of the scene into his memory, the swell of happiness in his chest. He had seen so much – more than he had ever thought was possible for a boy who had never before been beyond his hometown.

Incantus opened his mouth to conclude his speech, but he never got the chance.

Gibbous howled and bounded over to him. The hairs on his back stood straight, his nose in the air. The remnants of Incantus's smile vanished, his eyebrows drawing together as he looked at something in the distance – at the archway that tethered the forest to their home. The white chalk teleportation marking that lined the stone doorway was flickering, its colour dimming.

Alexis squinted to make out the shape of the person stood beside it. Emerging from his hands came his distinctive bronze glow, its colour intensifying as he merged his portalling powers with the white teleportation line.

'Ezra!' Incantus bellowed, striding towards him, Gibbous at his side.

Ezra turned, his eyes wild and jaw clenched tight. His dark hair was wet with sweat, plastered to his forehead. The bronze colour that poured from his hands continued to infect the line, running round the entirety of the archway. He didn't look Incantus in the eyes, speaking to the ground between them instead, his voice trembling. 'You had your chance. And you failed. It's his turn now.'

Incantus's body flashed white, and in less than a second, he had crossed the entire distance of the clearing, too fast for the eye to follow. He cast his hand over Ezra, and from it came an intense flash that threw the Elemental far from the teleportation line. The young man's body crumpled to the earth and he stayed down.

Yet the teleportation line continued to change in colour, only now, from the opposite side of the portal, it was deepening into a deep blood red. The redness completed its connection with Ezra's bronze portal, the two colours mixing into a black glow that encircled the huge archway between the Haven and Garden.

'There's a portal connecting them from both sides!' Incantus called, stepping away from the Haven. 'Get them back!'

The Leaders reacted immediately, jumping to their feet to marshal Elementals away. Never before had they displayed that look – the look of urgency and fear. Raeve grabbed Alexis by the collar, pulling him back. 'Come on. We have to get you guys to safety!'

Alexis and his friends hurried without hesitation. They ran alongside the other Elementals, deeper into the forest behind the treeline, closer towards the canyon. When had it suddenly got so dark? Even the tree nymphs had disappeared.

Alexis found himself at the front of the Elementals, overlooking the deserted glade, his heart in his throat. Raeve had gone to join the other Leaders who stood guarding the treeline before them.

In the distance, the portal had begun to seep a tar-like substance that bled across the archaic archway. Incantus threw beam after beam of light energy into it, but the portal absorbed it easily, shutting off the rest of the Haven. When the seal was complete, Incantus let out an anguished scream and dropped to his knees. Gibbous growled, moving to stand protectively over him as he cradled his head in his glowing hands.

'What's happening?' Caeli called out, wrapping her arms across her chest.

Taranis spoke, not taking his eyes away from Incantus. 'Someone's trying to break in. Ezra's made a portal from this side and it's joining with another portal at the other threshold, where the forest exists in the real world in Iraq. Incantus is trying to prevent it, but it's tearing his mind apart.'

The portal rippled. From it, a tidal wave of dark shadow exploded, barrelling towards the forest. Incantus scrambled to his feet to meet it, spreading his arms wide. The full force of the blow tossed him far away from the archway. He didn't move once he landed.

Bounding from the black portal emerged a huge animal, a shadowy four-legged creature. It was a dire wolf, almost identical to Gibbous except for its midnight-coated fur. Incantus had said Gibbous had a brother.

The person he belonged to, Alexis recalled instantly.

The other wolf snarled, leaping towards Incantus, but Gibbous immediately intercepted him, gnashing at its side. He threw the black wolf back, blood tipping his sharp teeth, a growl rumbling deep in his throat in warning.

The two great wolves stood their ground, not yet attacking each other, but not backing down either. The black wolf only flinched when a second being emerged from the portal, his ears flattening in fear of his own master.

The tall, broad-shouldered man marched forwards. His black wolf bowed as he passed, tail tucked between hind legs. Before Gibbous could lunge at him, the man threw a wall of jagged shadow his way, sending him crashing into a nearby tree which splintered apart upon impact. The night wolf looked over to where Gibbous lay, his tail relaxing only when he saw the white wolf stir. Meanwhile, the man had moved to stand over Incantus and removed his helmet.

'Hello, brother,' said Mortem Arcangelo, grinning as he devoured the sight before him. 'Did you miss me?'

18

SÚTON

Súton (n.) *Croatian origin*
Twilight; the approach of death or the end of something

Stifled screams. Muffled cries. And then silence.

Each came in waves, sweeping across the forest, burrowing terror into the Elementals hidden within. Without a spoken word, the Elementals of the Haven drew together, concealed within the shadows.

Only the darkness was not their protector – it was their reckoning.

Mortem Arcangelo stood like a beautiful creature of sin, an unspoiled demon of the night. The devil incarnated as an angel, or possibly the other way around. His muscular frame was swathed in a suit of blackened armour, its cuffs sharpened into daggered points. Atop it lay a robe that seemed to be stitched by darkness itself, its body morphing with a mind of its own, twisting to form angered spikes. When he finally turned his focus towards the forest, Alexis saw his face, and heard Demi gasp beside him.

Catching the last of the flickering light from the blazing torches was the edge of an old ragged scar, faded with time.

It started at the corner of Mortem's strong jaw and tore down the side of his neck before ending somewhere behind his back. The only fracture in his handsome face.

The most startling thing about Mortem, however, was not his clothing nor even his scar; it was his eyes. The colours of them. A ring of blue, encircled by an outer ring of black. The resemblance between them was so clear that Alexis had to look away when he blinked.

Mortem scanned the tree line of the forest. At his feet, Incantus strained to get up, beams of light beginning to glow at his fists. The light was extinguished the moment Mortem cracked his knee against his brother's chin, sprawling him on the ground. As Mortem extended a hand towards his brother and curled his fingers, Incantus let out a scream, writhing in excruciating torture as whisps of darkness ripped open his skin. Even Mortem's wolf flinched at the sight, with Gibbous, his body still broken, howling in distress from afar. All the while, Mortem hadn't taken his eyes off the forest where the Elementals stood in hiding.

Spoken without moving his lips, Akili inclined his head to the Children of the Elements behind him.

'Stay here.'

His words cemented them to the spot, paralysing their bodies so that they couldn't move even if they tried. With Raeve and Taranis at his side, he stepped forward to help their Leader and friend.

The rolling torrent of darkness reluctantly withdrew as Mortem turned to face the Leaders. Beneath him, Incantus rolled to his side, his clothes in tatters, soaked with blood.

'Crescent, take him away,' Mortem ordered.

The black wolf warily approached a motionless Incantus. He hesitated when Gibbous growled from the edge of the forest, unable to get up. Before Crescent sunk his teeth into Incantus's leg, a ray of purple energy flew across the clearing, hitting him square in the chest. Crescent staggered for a moment before Raeve's sleep charm took hold and he collapsed.

Mortem shook his head. 'Stupid dog,' he muttered through clenched teeth, kicking him free from the battlefield. Even though she couldn't move, Alexis felt Demi wince beside him.

'Akili Pierce,' said Mortem, his eyes widening. 'It has been a long time, old friend.'

Mortem received no answer. Instead, Akili removed the robes to free his arms. Beside him, Taranis curled his hands and electricity crackled around him, the night sky instantly exploding into a network of lightning. To his other side, Raeve opened her palms, her outline glowing violet as she hovered off the ground, her tattoos gleaming the same colour as her aura.

Shadows bled from beneath Mortem's armour in response, turning sharp. From behind his shoulders, a single curved blade rose, blackening as it absorbed the light from around it like a black hole stealing starlight. Mortem flipped the scythe between his hands, his mouth curving into a smile as his eyes lit up. He tossed his helmet in the direction of Ezra who lay still not far from the portal.

'The famous Leaders of the Haven,' he said, beckoning them towards him. 'This ought to be *fun*.'

Alexis felt the floor of his stomach drop, his torso suddenly

171

feeling hollow. He was unable to do anything other than watch the horror that unfolded before his eyes.

Akili roared. Taranis turned his hand towards Mortem and the lightning flew, but a wall of shadows rose impossibly fast to protect him against the hot blue and yellow strikes. Raeve soared into the sky, her eyes glowing with furious passion.

Akili reached him first, just as Mortem's shield of darkness faded away. His fist crashed into Mortem's chest piece, forcing him off his feet. As Mortem got up, a purple hex thudded into the side of his face, throwing him into a nearby tree. Without giving him a spare second to recover, a thunderous streak of lightning struck the ground behind Mortem.

Emerging from the sparks came Taranis. He took Mortem from behind, wrapping his arm round his neck and pulling him backwards with all his might. The shadows of Mortem's robe slashed viciously, cutting into Taranis's arm, but he didn't let go, sending further shockwaves down the intruder's body.

At the same time, an undulating soundwave rippled towards Mortem, pouring from Akili. It forced Mortem to his knees, and Alexis could hear the faint repeated order to feel pain beyond anything he could imagine.

Mortem roared and sent a sharp elbow crunching into Taranis's side. When the hold round his neck loosened, Mortem used his momentum to flip Taranis over his hip onto the ground with a heavy thud. Before he could impale him with a pike of shadow, a purple shield coated Taranis's body, hauling him in Raeve's direction just as the dagger cracked into the earth where he once lay.

The Leaders reformed, standing in line with one another,

looking unstoppable as a trio. Sparks danced at Taranis's fingertips.

Alexis's eyes shot back to Mortem as he regained his composure, dusting the dirt off his charred robes, the action somewhat casual. He rolled his shoulders back as though he had just been on a leisurely jog, his expression free from fear.

'Incantus taught you well,' Mortem admitted. He inclined his head in a short bow and tucked his scythe by his side. To Alexis's horror, he could see moon-cast shadows gathering on the ground behind the Leaders. 'But didn't he tell you?' A cruel grin spread across his face. 'I was his best student.'

The shadows of the forest pulled together, transforming into a spear. Before Taranis could react, it launched in his direction, rocketing across the glade like a javelin and impaling him to the ground by his thigh. Taranis let out a cry, shockwaves erupting from his body as a blackish poison began to seep into his skin.

When Raeve screamed, a surge of purple energy swept from her. Her magic wrapped around one of the trees of the forest, ripping it from the earth in one mighty pull, its shredded roots narrowly flying over the Elementals stood closest to it. With a grunt, Raeve threw her arms forward, and the uprooted tree spun towards Mortem.

By the time Mortem had fashioned a huge blade of darkness to sever it into splinters, Raeve was already upon him. She dodged a tendril of shadow that stabbed at her, ducking beneath it as she grabbed at the hilt of Mortem's scythe, desperate to get her hands on a weapon to make it a fair fight.

But Mortem was somehow faster than her. His hand closed

around hers as he pulled her into him, throwing his head forward and cracking against hers. She staggered back, trying to regain her balance, but she was unable to shield herself from the wall of darkness that slammed her to the ground. It pinned her down, only an arm's distance from Taranis who had fallen quiet, black veins spreading over his face like rivulets of liquid shadow.

'He's *imprinting* him!' Raeve screamed, her voice breaking at the fate worse than death. Before Raeve could cry again, a black mist forced itself into her mouth, silencing her as it had Taranis.

'*Mortem!*'

The name rang out across the entire clearing, bellowed by the eldest Leader. It struck Mortem like a blow to the chest, an invisible hurricane, a verbal projection stronger than any physical assault.

Mortem pushed himself up with both hands, raising his head to look at Akili across the battlefield. Blood stained his teeth, dripping from the corners of his mouth where he grinned. Akili charged at him again and punched his head so hard it should have ripped it from his neck.

Battered, Mortem still replied, 'Akili, have you lost all your love for me? I want to see the old you. The ruthless one. The fighter.'

Mortem attempted to swing the scythe in a great arc, but Akili caught his hand first. He snapped it at an awkward angle, causing Mortem to grunt. When Mortem curled a whip of darkness at Akili's feet, he jumped just in time and ducked underneath the next attack. The Leader was reading his enemy's mind, predicting his attacks.

'You and Teller always trying to get into my head,' Mortem said between breaths, no longer smiling.

Whilst Mortem stood his ground, the darkness from beneath his robes spread out from him in a dense fog, obscuring much of the fight from sight. Thick tentacles surged from the bodiless shadow, lashing out at Akili in a series of cracking whips, almost too many for him to predict or dodge.

And then Mortem stopped and Alexis saw why.

Incantus had woken and was crawling towards them, pulsing with a pale glow. Mortem smiled, preparing to turn and strike.

Through the cloud of fog, Akili must have seen Mortem or have read his thoughts. He must have known what was about to happen. Beating away the last of the darkness whips that tried to restrain him, Akili launched himself into the space between Mortem's scythe and Incantus.

Only the blade never struck, for it had never been thrown.

Instead, rising from behind Akili like coiling snakes of shadow, two daggers of darkness appeared. Akili had been misled; Mortem had managed to trick the man who could read his mind. With nothing more than a gasp, the black blades stabbed straight through Akili's shoulders, sinking all the way through until they protruded through his front.

The force that had been incapacitating the Elementals of the Haven was suddenly relinquished. Without it there to keep them silent, to keep them on their feet, the forest erupted into a chorus of screams, screams that grew only louder as Akili was lifted higher off his feet by the darkness blades.

Alexis had to use both of his hands to catch Blaise as he

nearly collapsed into him, his knees going out from under him. Alexis knew that he should be reassuring his friends or fleeing to safety, but some part of him still felt paralysed.

Shackles of darkness latched themselves to Incantus's hands, forcing his arms above his head. Small stabs of blackness tore at his arms and legs, preventing the white protective glow from forming. In the meantime, Mortem finally had the opportunity to collect himself. He licked the blood from his lips and surveyed the motionless battleground around him. Satisfied in his victory, he stood before Incantus, inclining his head up at his brother, waiting for him to meet his eyes.

Beside the black-glowing portal that had once connected the Garden to the Haven, Ezra Alastor had awoken. He rose to unsteady feet, but kept his head low, unable to look at the carnage before him. Alexis thought him too much of a coward when he didn't bring himself to meet the eyes of his teachers, unable to watch their lives slowly draw to an end.

'Incredible fighters,' was the first thing that Mortem said, stroking the chains that pulled tighter around Incantus's body. 'Great heart, yet no match for me. Now, because of your failure, their life slips away from them. But I, ever generous, will do them a favour.' He nodded at Incantus with a knowing smile. 'I will imprint darkness into their souls like I've done with so many of your friends. Their powers will be *great* additions to my army.'

There was a blinding white flash that lit up the entire forest. With a violent bellow, Incantus broke free from the chains that bound him, his powers erupting like an exploding star, wings of light sweeping outward. Mortem staggered. His mouth fell open as he barely kept to his feet. Half-turning back, he swung his arm outwards, and from the centre of his palm shot forth three serpents of shadow.

The coiling tendrils slithered towards the scattered Leaders, prising open their mouths and forcing themselves inside. The poisoned veins of their bodies pulsed once with a blackish finish.

All the while, Incantus had got the upper hand. Arms ablaze in a white fire, he countered Mortem's attacks, beating him down and pushing him further back towards the molten black portal. Alexis had never seen Incantus so desperate, utterly taken aback by the raw potential of his powers. Even in the darkness of the night, Mortem looked scared, eyes wide in panic.

The Leaders stood, their wounds healing as though being sewn together by threads of darkness. But something was wrong, Alexis thought. It wasn't until he noticed their shadows had disappeared that he realised they were no longer the Leaders.

'Incantus, look out!' Alexis shouted.

Raeve shot a blast of magic that sent Incantus away from Mortem, and the Elementals in the forest gasped in disbelief.

'What did she just do?' Caeli whispered, turning from Joe to wrap her hands round Blaise's arm.

The Leaders took a stand beside Mortem, moving to surround Incantus. Lightning, purple magic and reverberating waves of pain manipulation flew from their hands towards Incantus. When the onslaught ended, Incantus Arcangelo lay crumpled on the ground, his shirt torn to shreds, chained in thick ropes of blackness.

Alexis caught a glimpse of Akili's face and instantly recognised the change. The imprinting had been successful. The Leaders' eyes now shone utterly black like glowing obsidian orbs. They stood there, expressionless remnants of the people they once were.

Raeve devoid of her charm, Taranis unnervingly still and Akili's calming presence dissolved. They were now under Mortem's unwavering control.

19

CAIM

Caim (n.) *Gaelic origin*
'Sanctuary'; an invisible circle of protection, drawn around
the body with the hand, that reminds you that you are safe
and loved, even in the darkest time; spear

Alexis looked over to the canyon. If they stayed silent, he was sure that a few of them could go by unnoticed, concealed by the forest. If they stayed away from the clearing, whilst Mortem and the Leaders were distracted, then he could get to the river. He could use it to defend Incantus. He could use it to swim away.

With the Haven cut off by the black portal, there was no way the Elementals could contact anyone inside. They were alone in the woods, defenceless.

Mortem bent down to look into the pained eyes of his brother, his hand tightening round the lower half of his face, digging in his nails. Over the sound of the wind whistling through the trees, over the sound of his own heartbeat drumming in his ears, Alexis heard Mortem speak.

'Clever trick. Took me years to find a way to break in. A portal connecting the inside and outside of the Haven. I found another portaller, much more powerful than this one.' He gestured to Ezra. 'At least this one didn't need imprinting. He knew which side to fight for.'

Incantus let out a sigh and Mortem turned away, bored with the lack of reaction. The lights that had kept the forest bright had long faded. Only the moonlight and a couple of fire torches provided any glow. It was enough to illuminate Mortem's stage.

'Alexis Michaels is thinking of forming a surprise attack,' said Akili, pointing towards the forest. 'He's trying to manipulate the river.'

Alexis swore under his breath. He tried shutting off the connection between them, straining to close the line that allowed Akili access.

'Keep out of his mind,' Mortem ordered curtly.

Immediately, the buzz in Alexis's head shut off, the surveillance of his thoughts disappearing. Did Mortem not consider him worthy of defending himself against? Alexis looked at Incantus on the ground and the Leaders with black eyes and no shadows. Of course he didn't, he thought.

Mortem didn't so much as look at the Leaders of the Haven when he said, 'Go through. I don't need you now. I will be with you shortly.'

Ezra went through the blackened archway first, wary of the empty look of the Leaders' eyes trained on his feet. Raeve and Taranis followed, deaf to Incantus's muzzled protests. Only Akili hesitated, glancing back towards Incantus.

Alexis couldn't make out Incantus's expression, but he could imagine the pleading of his eyes, imploring his friend to recognise him, to fight against the darkness that played at the strings of his mind.

Akili dropped to his knees, hands pressed against either side of his head with enough pressure that it looked as though he would crush it. As he did, tides of telepathic messages poured from him in shockwaves, a series of overlapping emotions too jumbled to be coherent, his astral projection thrashing as it tried to break free from his corporal body.

But with a wave of Mortem's hand, the portal face lurched from the archway. Limb-like arms took hold of Akili, wrapping round his now-healed shoulders. He was dragged into the portal and disappeared without a word.

Mortem let out a long breath, then turned his attention towards the forest, his arms extended in welcome.

'Elementals.' He didn't have to raise his voice in order for it to carry through the darkness. 'You have been brainwashed by my brother who had been brainwashed by those who had taught him. "*A duty to protect those who cannot protect themselves.*" Is that what they have forced upon you? To make yourselves smaller, to hide in the darkness and protect the mortals that don't know we exist? Who would seek to destroy us if they did, out of fear of our powers?'

Mortem shook his head, his lip curling with distaste. 'I do not wish to cause this bloodshed between we who are superior. I do not wish to kill our kind – I wish to *lead* them. To overcome the light that blinds us, that forces us to take refuge in the shadows.'

Alexis felt a coldness against the back of his neck, one that casued a ripple to crawl down his very spine. It was a sensation that made him feel as if he was being watched, a sensation that made him flinch involuntarily, something he hadn't done for a long time.

'Children of the Prophecy of Light and Darkness,' said Mortem, causing all motion and murmur to cease at once, bar the incessant grunts of a bound Incantus. '*Alexis.*' The way he said his name, it was as if the word was unnatural on his lips. 'Reveal yourselves. I can sense you . . . My, my, so powerful already.'

The four friends exchanged looks with one another, but none of them dared make a move. Even if they tried, the hands of the Elementals of the Haven were gripping tightly to their arms and clothing, preventing them from exposing themselves. Mortem's eyes gleamed at the apparent lack of challenge.

Meanwhile, Crescent had stirred, returning to Mortem's side, his eyes similarly transfixed on Alexis through the darkness. 'I've heard that your plan is to bring home the lost Elemental Gems,' Mortem continued, slapping Incantus's chest as if they were old friends sharing a joke. 'Based on what, not even a month's worth of training? My brother has set you up for certain failure. You will die screaming at the power of the Creatures – you can't want that. Join me instead. With your primal powers, you could lead by my side.'

He looked in the direction of Alexis at the last line, smirking as he did. The black portal rumbled, shimmering wisps of bronze and red dripping from its frame. It detached itself from the huge archway. Beyond it, the old teleportation line remained connected to the Haven, intact as if it had never been corrupted.

Any hope that an army was waiting on the other side of the archway vanished like a flame in the wind. They were alone.

Beside it, Alexis noticed how the intensity of Ezra's portal was fading, its opaqueness lessening, losing power without Ezra there to sustain it. Already it was beginning to shrink. How much longer would it stay open for – a few minutes at most? That was all the time they had left to stop Mortem.

Alexis took a step forwards.

'What are you *doing*?' said Blaise, grabbing his arm and yanking him back

'He knows we're here. We can't hide forever. He's going to kill Incantus.'

'He's going to kill us too,' Caeli hissed, her face drained of colour.

Alexis took her hand and placed it just over her amulet. The grey stone lightly glowed at her touch. Too scared to say anything more, even with Akili gone, Alexis only motioned his eyes to the canyon once, then, after looking at Blaise, to the few fire torches that remained around the glade.

Demi nodded. 'The first lesson Incantus taught us.'

Use our surroundings, draw on our elements. Together, we are stronger.

As one, the four friends stepped into the clearing before Mortem. Incantus lashed out at the chains that restrained him, but he was silenced by a hard backhand.

Mortem's eyes found Alexis, staring at him as if he was some sort of prize that he had long been waiting for. It chilled him to the bone, the feeling that his enemy could see right through the brave exterior he was trying so hard to wear. It crushed any hope he had that they would get out unscathed.

'Look at you,' said Mortem with a veracious sigh. For a split second, his pupils dilated, his focus finding their amulets, but the look of authority returned a moment later with the lift of his chin. 'Done are our days of darkness. We deserve to be revered as gods, the five of us. You belong with me.'

Mortem smiled a beautiful smile, but the expression failed to reach his eyes. It was the same rehearsed smile of assurance Alexis had spent his childhood perfecting. After years deciphering between what was truth and what was fantasy, Alexis could spot a lie when he came across it, no matter how convincing it first appeared.

'Why wait until now?' said Alexis, finding his voice, surprised at how confidently it came out. Mortem didn't deserve the satisfaction of seeing his fear. He ignored Incantus's wide-eyed look of warning. He had to keep talking. He had to mask the sound of rushing water in the distance. 'You could've revealed Elemental-kind at any point to the real world. In the right way, it would be too much for even the Erasers to clean up.'

Mortem shifted in his stance, his smile faltering.

'You don't want us out of the shadows, you just want us in yours.' Alexis's hand was trembling by his side, his fingers pressing to his thumbs so hard that the bones nearly broke. 'You want a world to rule where no one can stop you. And you fear those you can't control, those that are a threat to you. Incantus . . . and us.'

Mortem noticed all too late the tidal wave that had risen from the river of the canyon.

Alexis pitched it with both arms and flooded it across the clearing towards Mortem. Its mass overwhelmed him, crushing him to the ground. As the dark Elemental attempted to shield himself from the onslaught, a quaking tremor tore through the earth and the ground cracked apart at his feet, forcing him to lose his balance and succumb to the tide. At the same time, Caeli launched a gust of wind at Crescent, sending the black wolf back through the portal with a fleeting yelp. Manipulating the gales, she swept Incantus towards them, narrowly escaping the weight of the flood.

With Incantus back by their side, Alexis tried his hardest to keep Mortem enveloped within the ball of water, but he was no match for the fallen angel. Mortem broke free in an explosion of vicious, thrashing shadows, his face a mask of fury. Blazing fireballs shot out from the torches, charring Mortem's sleeves, forcing him to retreat before he could retaliate.

Behind the treeline, dozens of glowing powers began to ignite as the Elementals of the Haven joined the Children of the Elements in their fight. Beams and rays of colour soared overhead, colliding with Mortem, forcing him to his knees. Alexis saw Mortem's face contort through the mirage of power, the blueness of his eyes drowned by a spreading blackness. Before Alexis could hope to shove his friends behind him, Mortem let out a roar, and an explosion of black blades erupted from his body, shooting in the direction of the forest.

Yet the blades did not cut, they did not sever, they did not impale.

Alexis opened his eyes and saw Incantus Arcangelo standing before them, his hands now free, his body glimmering with a blinding white light. Spreading from his hands came a veil of light, one which expanded to shield the entirety of the forest front, absorbing the onslaught of shadow.

'How dare you!' Mortem thundered, his eyes glaring like

two black holes. One after another, he hurled spears of shadow toward the treeline, each hit almost too much for Incantus to counter. Weak from torture, sweat stained with blood gushed from Incantus's face as his shield cracked further from each impact, its glow dimming.

'You're not the Children of the Elements. You're the horsemen of the apocalypse. You signal the dying of the light!' Mortem screamed, striding towards them, a continuous wave of darkness now pouring from his body, crashing against the shield. Through the translucent barrier, Alexis saw Ezra's portal behind Mortem fading. Too consumed with rage, he didn't seem to notice. 'You have won *nothing*! I'll turn your bones to dust, tear the skin from your body, and I'll make *you* watch,' he whispered, pausing to point at Alexis, his whole body pulsing black, 'as the world you know plunges into darkness.'

Alexis's breath hitched in his throat. He suddenly forgot how to breathe. Tightness gripped his chest, paralysing him still. Even with his friends by his side, and the Elementals of the forest coming forth to form ranks behind Incantus's shield, he could not move.

For in that moment, Alexis had seen something worse than a ghost, something he never thought he would see again. The thing that had tormented him for his whole childhood. What he had thought was a figment of his imagination, the contaminated, corrupted, sick part of him.

The *Shadow Man* stood in the place where Mortem had once been.

Alexis's knees buckled from beneath him, and only the combined strength of Blaise, Caeli and Demi could support him.

What if, after all this time, he had never really been ill, but had been afflicted with visions of the Elemental world years before entering it? Or, worse, what if the stress of it all had made him relapse?

'Please stop.' Alexis's chest threatened to collapse with the weight of the discovery. He couldn't feel his fingers as they tapped his thumbs. He couldn't feel the wetness on his cheeks that must have come from rain or river or tears. He could only feel the memory of the icy hand round his neck from the vice that had tortured him in his youth. Whispers left his quivering lips as he begged over and over again to no one and to everyone, *'Please stop, please stop, please stop.'*

And then it did.

The assault came to a sudden, abrupt halt.

In the distance, there was a faint strangling noise, the sound of a man gasping and another grunting. With half-open eyes, Alexis looked through the cracks of the shattered semi-transparent veil to see the *Shadow Man* was gone, its faceless pitch black figure pulled back into Mortem's body as he was being restrained. Someone was dragging Mortem away.

Incantus swore, his hand pressing against the barrier as the view of their defender became clear.

Teller.

The old man's grip around Mortem's neck was unyielding as he hauled him towards Ezra's portal with shocking speed. The unretired, undying power of a warrior.

'Always. Wanted. To do this,' Teller grumbled in between breaths. 'For the Quinate.'

Teller's hands ignited with a pale yellow colour. He was using his powers on Mortem, searching his memories, something he said he'd never been able to do in all the years that he knew him. They were an arm's distance from the portal now, the black–glowing threshold ebbing with only a few moments left.

In one swift motion, gleaming daggers of shadow burst from Mortem's chest and sliced at Teller's hands, tearing them apart into limbless shreds. Teller staggered backwards, mangled tissue and bone hanging from what was once his hands, face aghast.

Incantus's fist smashed against his fractured shield, breaking it apart like a huge shattered window pane. But before Incantus could take off to protect his old friend, Mortem had got to his feet and stepped towards Teller.

So this is it. This is where it ends. My final moment to be made a memory.

After a lifetime of looking back on my past, this instant here would become my last.

Mortem swung the scythe from his back and plunged the curved blade through my chest, stealing the air from my lungs in a single blow.

He had always been an intolerable prick.

The icy blade slid further into my body. With the last of my energy, I took a step closer to Mortem and pushed him back with what remained of my hands. He vanished into the black portal, swallowed whole by the threshold. Moments later, it sealed over, shrinking in on itself until it disappeared, no trace that it had ever been here. No trace that Mortem had ever been here, bar the destruction in his wake.

Incantus caught me as I fell. I smiled at him, but I was too cold and too tired to speak.

'I know, I know,' was all Incantus said, tears filling his eyes as he cradled my broken body. 'A hero's death. What you always wanted.'

The muscles that tugged at the corners of my mouth withered until I was no longer able to smile. My senses were fading. I could no longer feel the cold. I could no longer feel the pain.

The Elementals from the forest gathered around us, unable to do anything other than stand and watch. Somewhere behind us, Ziya appeared from inside the Haven. When she saw me on the ground, she sagged against the archway, her hands rising to cover her mouth. There was much I needed to tell her, but time was not in my favour, and there were greater truths that needed to be revealed before I went.

'Alexis,' said Incantus, his voice broken, rushed.

The boy looked to see me staring at him. My mouth moved slightly, but no words came out. I tried to sound it out again, desperately trying to share what I now knew. 'N . . .'

I couldn't muster the strength to say it.

Incantus's hands began to light up, but I shook my head. I was too far gone. It would be a waste of his, and her*, precious power to use on me, to heal me when my time making memories had passed. Now, it was I who would remain the memory.*

I looked at Incantus until eventually my gaze went blank, the last breath leaving my chest as I heard his far away voice saying the words, 'For the Quinate.'

A soft light glowed from Incantus as he sat cradling the old Elemental.

Beneath Incantus's eyelids, his eyes darted from side to side as though watching something the others couldn't see. What Alexis and his friends would later be told was that it was

Teller Sagen's life flashing before Incantus's eyes. The most significant events of his life. The most powerful memories that had the greatest impact on him, shown in a rapid sequence. Almost like a film. That was what Incantus experienced when close by to someone who had just died: the light of their life as it left their body.

When the glowing died down, and Incantus drew still, the story of Teller's life reached its end, and Gibbous howled dolefully into the night.

20

KENOPSIA

Kenopsia (n.) *Greek origin*
The eerie, forlorn atmosphere of a place that is usually
bustling with people but is now abandoned and quiet

Incantus stayed by Teller's cold body for a few minutes, and
whilst he did, no one moved. Gibbous licked Teller's unsmiling
face just once before lowering his head over where the blade
had gone in, almost as if he was trying to stop it from bleeding.

Only when Incantus eventually stood, his eyes red with
unshed tears, did time seem to resume.

'All of you,' he said, 'go back inside. Mortem will not return
tonight.'

Then he stooped and, despite his injuries, he carried Teller's
limp body away into the Haven. The older students escorted
the younger ones to their rooms, muttering assurances of
safety. With the moon rising higher in the sky, and the air
growing colder, they all wanted to get away from the darkness
and into the Haven as quickly as they could.

When Alexis and his friends reached their rooms, Ziya was
waiting. 'Incantus asked me if you wouldn't mind coming to
his office,' she said.

They nodded and, without a word, began to follow her.

'It's my fault Teller is dead,' Ziya whispered, finally shattering the oppressive silence.

'What do you mean?' Alexis reached to put his hand on her shoulder.

'I left the feast briefly to go to the toilet. On my way back, I noticed the portal had been corrupted. I tried everything I could to close it, but the teleportation lines were never something I understood too well. Then I heard Akili cry out from the other side and I knew I needed to get help. Most of the students were at the feast, so I went to the Elder Sanctuary. Akili had already contacted Teller. Only he was brave enough to help.' She wiped her eyes, smearing her makeup. 'If only I had tried harder to befriend Ezra, or at least learned how the teleportation lines operated, I could've fixed it sooner . . .'

Surprisingly, it was Blaise who spoke. 'He's a sad, whiny traitor. He didn't deserve anything from anyone, least of all you, Zee.' It was probably one of the few times the two of them had spoken directly to each other. Unable to meet his eyes, Ziya smiled once.

'Teller would've come to help, no matter what,' Demi added, her eyes filling as she spoke. 'You helped him save us. You did more to keep us safe than most of the Elementals out there with us, powers or otherwise.'

The vision of the darkness slithering inside the Leaders replayed itself over and over in Alexis's mind. How their shadows had vanished, the darkness pulled back into their bodies, eyes blackened and devoid of humanity. Empty vessels, now instruments of Mortem's power. The look on Teller's dying face as he tried to speak. He had seen into Mortem's past, and with his final breath had tried to tell Alexis something.

And now Alexis would never know what it was. Or what his past contained, the secrets locked in a part of his memory too fragile for his consciousness to recall.

'How is Incantus?' he asked abruptly, getting the words out as soon as he could before the image of the *Shadow Man* swathed his mind, arresting him in its ice-cold capture.

'I've never seen him like this, not in all the years I've lived here,' Ziya answered, slowing her pace as they approached his office. 'With the Leaders gone and the High Order challenging his authority over the Haven, he's fighting a battle before the real one has even started.'

As her hand rose to knock on the door, there was an unlocking sound, followed by its gentle opening. Inside, Incantus sat at his desk impossibly still, staring blankly at his hands. He hadn't changed since Mortem's attack, and the blood-soaked white shirt barely clung to his healing body. Obscured by the dried blood, Alexis couldn't make out how many of the scars that laced Incantus's shoulders and back had been made that night and how many had been inflicted long before.

Ziya nodded to them. 'Be kind to him. He needs a friend,' she said before departing.

The Alpha team entered, finding themselves standing awkwardly in the warm-toned, library-like office. It seemed as though they had just walked into the middle of a virtual conference. Two Haven command tablets sat in front of Incantus. Holographs projected from them displayed separate audio bars which fluctuated every time a person spoke or, for better a word, shouted.

A man's voice boomed from one tablet. 'Incantus, you promised us that the Haven was impenetrable! You said there were protective measures. And not only did Mortem break in, but he also killed an important asset and took the minds of your Leaders. Least of all, some of our council members' children were there.'

'Don't you dare refer to Teller as just an "asset!"' shouted a woman in a thick Scottish accent from the second tablet that Incantus had closest to him. It glowed fiercely when she spoke, shuddering on the table. The woman's voice dripped with audible aversion. 'And it's good to see where your children fall on the High Order's list of priorities.'

'Serena, that was not what—' began another voice from the first tablet in response. It was curtly interrupted.

'We are not friends. We are barely comrades. It is Miss Aevum to you,' the woman, Serena, replied. For the first time since the invasion, Incantus smiled. 'And it is your indifference and negligence of Mortem's desire to lead in a new Dark Age that has strengthened him, in addition to your failure to prosecute him properly for his crimes. This lies at your door.'

'That's Serena Aevum,' Alexis whispered to his friends, remembering her from Teller's stories of the Quinate. 'She's the Leader of the other Haven on Easter Island, you know, the place with the huge stone heads. She's the eldest daughter of Sapientis Aevum.'

'Why does that name ring a bell?' Blaise said, gazing into the white fire in the corner. Gibbous's absence was obvious; the wolf was still being treated in the Healing Sanctuary.

'Sapientis was Incantus's mentor,' Demi answered, looking

194

at her own. 'The Elemental who foretold the Prophecy of Light and Darkness.'

'Shh,' hissed Caeli. 'I want to hear the drama.'

For the first time since the Alpha team had arrived, Incantus raised his voice to speak.

'The *Haven* is impenetrable. No one can enter without my authority. Mortem knew that so instead he invaded the Garden through the teleportation lines with the help of two portallers, one from the outside . . . and another from the inside. Ezra Alastor betrayed us. I should have foreseen him becoming radicalised, that was my mistake. That was my failure. However, whoever opened the gateway from the outside was the failed responsibility of the High Order to monitor.'

'Sing it, Ian,' praised Serena Aevum.

'We are yet to identify the individual who opened the portal on the other side,' came a strained reply from the first tablet.

'The point of the matter is that you were not prepared,' said another from the High Order.

'An institute built for training students and for those who wish to retire was not ever planned to be prepared for this kind of attack,' Incantus retorted, rising to his feet. 'On your orders, many of *my* Elementals were sent to positions across the globe in a vain attempt to suppress Mortem's influence. All these years, you refused to stand up to him, arguing you had no role in this. So how about you do your duty and prosecute Mortem whilst the Children of the Elementals protect your spineless, prying backs.'

A laughing cackle burst from Serena's tablet. The energy that came from her was so strong that the tablet exploded into flames. No sooner had Blaise put out the fire, Incantus ended the call with the High Order.

Caeli looked at Incantus with new-found awe. 'That was probably the coolest thing you've done.'

Incantus's chest deflated and he had to catch himself by placing both hands on the desk. 'I am sorry, my children, for allowing you to witness that. The High Order . . . they have done many good things for our people, but they are flawed too. Many sympathise with Mortem's "aims" – for Elementals to retain dominion over the world, as we did aeons ago. We didn't understand why Teller went to work for them at the beginning, but it turned out that whilst he did he provided us with an insight we otherwise wouldn't have had. He showed us that the only people we could count on were ourselves. He was a powerful ally and a fierce friend.'

The memory of the night returned to him. Alexis could almost see it washing over their mentor. He ran his fingers through his dirt-ridden hair that now looked more silver than white. 'In light of what's happened to the Leaders, I have no other choice but to remain at the Haven. It is as I feared and as I hoped to evade: the Children of the Elements must go on the quest alone to recover the Elemental Gems, as the Prophecy inferred.'

Alexis wasn't surprised, but that didn't take the sting out of panic that came at the prospect of venturing out without Incantus. Without his counsel and guidance and protection.

Blaise, though, clearly hadn't seen this coming. 'How are we supposed to do this by ourselves?'

'Do we have any other choice?' Caeli muttered defeatedly.

She nudged Demi awake beside her, sweeping loose strands of hair from her weary face with a soft blow of air.

'Of course you do,' said Incantus.

'No, we don't,' Alexis snapped.

He hadn't mean to be abrupt, but he knew the inevitable outcome and he was too tired to dance around it. Mortem's arrival had only solidified his decision to go on the quest. Even though fear crippled his body and exhausted his mind, he would not let it shackle him further.

'This is the only way he stop him,' Alexis added, more softly this time.

He couldn't let Teller's death be in vain or the Leaders' capture be for nothing. He wanted revenge on the man who had haunted him long before he came to the Elemental world. He wanted to destroy the chance of ever seeing the *Shadow Man* again. It may not be for as virtuous a reason as he initially had, but if anything, this was stronger. Simpler.

He knew that didn't make him a hero, but the world didn't need a hero. They just needed someone powerful enough to do what needed to be done.

'We agreed to do this and we will stick to our vows,' said Demi firmly. She stifled a yawn. 'If you don't mind, can we continue this conversation tomorrow morning? Mum always said that news at night sounds worse than news at light.'

'That's a good idea,' agreed Incantus. He gave them a tired smile. 'Right now, nothing is more important than getting a good night's sleep. It's going to be an early start, I'm afraid.'

Blaise mumbled out of the side of his mouth, 'I'm expecting heavy reimbursement for this trip.' Both he and Caeli turned

197

to leave. Just before they were out of earshot, Alexis could've sworn he heard Caeli ask if she was the only one who thought Mortem was kind of . . .

Meanwhile, Demi lingered by Alexis in the doorway, blinking hard as though to wake herself up. 'You okay?'

'Yeah, I'm fine.'

She sighed, smiling sadly. 'You're always *fine*. You know, it's okay to not be fine all the time. After what happened tonight, it would be weirder if you were fine than if you weren't.' Her gaze dropped to her feet. 'It broke my heart to see you like that earlier.'

Exhaustion and embarrassment made his voice bitter. 'I said I'm fine.'

'Don't displace your anger on me,' she snapped, crossing her arms. 'I'm only trying to help.'

Alexis took a breath and palmed the back of his neck. 'I'm sorry. I'm just . . . trying to process everything. I guess I'm not really good at it.'

Demi nodded and her gaze softened. 'I get it. I know this sounds odd, but have you tried crying?'

'I can't say I have,' he said slowly.

They were less than a foot away from each other, so she need only speak softly for him to hear her. 'I cry at least three times a week. If I don't then I feel like I haven't got my emotions out. This morning I cried because I realised I won't see my family until after our quest, the other day I cried because Caeli brought me a coffee without me asking. You're an Elemental and a man – but you're a human being before all of that, Lexi. It isn't selfish to prioritise your emotions.'

Alexis smiled with her, for the first time in hours feeling as though his head didn't weigh a hundred pounds, that his chest was wide enough to take a full breath. 'I wish I was as brave as you,' he said as she unclipped her golden-hooped earrings. 'I learn so much from you.'

Demi pulled him into a hug. She tightened her arms round his waist, pressing the side of her face against his neck. With his chin resting on the top of her head, Alexis held her, forgetting about Incantus sitting behind him probably watching them, forgetting about the quest, forgetting about Mortem and death and darkness. He didn't know how long they were standing there in each other's embrace before she let out a faint yawn.

Reluctantly, Alexis released her. 'I'll let you get some sleep.' Then, unable to stop himself, he leant forwards and placed his lips against the centre of her forehead in a brief, fleeting kiss.

He could've sworn he heard her sigh in contentment.

Demi looked up at him with her deep green eyes. 'I'm sorry you never got to find out the truth tonight.'

Alexis shrugged. In a way, he felt as if he had.

21

MÅNGATA

Mångata (n.) *Swedish origin*
'Moon road'; the reflection of the moon on water

Incantus had changed into a loose grey sweatshirt by the time Alexis turned back to his office. With the worn, brown-woven blanket tucked under his arm, he placed his hand on Alexis's shoulder and gave him a knowing nod.

'We're getting Gibbous first,' he said.

At his touch, Alexis was absorbed into what he could only describe as a soundless vacuum of light energy; by the time he had blinked, he was in the Healing Sanctuary of the Haven. He stumbled, rubbing his ears to get rid of the loud popping. It was as if he had just been sucked into a black hole.

Perhaps 'white hole' would be more fitting, he thought.

Incantus continued walking as though he hadn't just moved at a fraction of the speed of light, forcing Alexis to jog after him. Alexis could already feel the power of the healing crystals in each room ebbing a low, reassuring wave of recovery across the pale-yellow stone Sanctuary.

Towards the end of the corridor lay Gibbous, the bed lowered nearly to the ground beneath his weight. His tail

200

wagged gently as Incantus reached him, and he slowly got up on bandaged legs. Asleep in the chair beside him was Ziya, her frizzy dark hair sprawled over her face, moving every time she breathed.

Silently, Gibbous jumped down from the large bed and started licking Incantus's hand.

'Let's walk,' Incantus suggested softly. Together they exited the Healing Sanctuary, descending the stairs that ran in a spiral round the hive. The teleportation line to the Garden had been sealed off, but at Incantus's touch, the vacant stone archway became relit.

Abandoned, the rows of benches in the forest were staggered in an uneven pattern. The fire torches had been extinguished, the only light coming from the pale moon. Alexis noticed Incantus staring at the pool of dried blood just beyond the entrance to the Haven. The image of Teller lying there, mouth moving silently as his voice failed him, made Alexis avert his eyes.

There was something Alexis had admired so deeply about Teller, and it took him until his death to realise what it had been. It had been how he lived his life, rich and momentous and unapologetic until the very end. Alexis wished he could ask him how he did it. How he had lived day in, day out, coping with the bad times and cherishing the good. Meeting people, losing people, first times and last times, a lifetime of nostalgia. Alexis had lived a fraction of his life and he already felt overwhelmed on most days, uncertain how long he could endure it.

Was that what it felt like to grow up? Alexis thought he had been forced to do all of that already, his childhood exchanged with premature scepticism and wisdom. But did he have much more growing up to go? In his darkest moments, did he even want to?

Alexis placed a hand on Gibbous to steady himself. After a long time spent in silence, he and Incantus took a seat by the cliffside overlooking the canyon. The quiet stillness of the river below allowed Alexis to finally ask himself the questions he had been ignoring.

Was he really cut out for this? He had worked so hard to move on from the darkness of his life. Should he not be doing everything he could to get himself away from any glimpse of the *Shadow Man*, whatever it may be, hallucination or otherwise?

'*I didn't come this far just to come this far.*'

That had always been the mantra for his slow and turbulent recovery. Was he condemning himself to relapse by staying in this world?

He spoke before he spiralled further. 'I'm sorry for your loss,' he said tentatively as Incantus draped the blanket over his shoulders. 'It seems as though there won't be much time for you to grieve.'

'There never usually is,' Incantus said dully.

Alexis turned to him. 'We don't have to talk about all of that if you don't want. It's okay if you take a moment to stop being the head of the Haven and just be a man that's grieving the loss of his friends.'

'Such a perceptive boy,' Incantus said, his eyes slowly closing.

Alexis wrapped his arms round himself. 'My dad always said

that there is so much more to a person than what they show you. I guess his view of people was shaped by his job . . . or maybe his upbringing. His mum has been in a care home ever since he was born, with early-onset dementia or some kind of mental paralysis. And he never knew anything about his dad. Either way, he had to make his own way. His weird quotes always stuck, you know.'

Gibbous lowered himself to the ground between them, laying on his belly, his front paws hanging over the edge of the cliffside as he looked up at the crescent moon.

'You father sounds like a very decent man,' Incantus said, voice faraway. 'I would have loved to have met him and your mother.'

Alexis meant every word when he said, 'He's the best dad I ever could have hoped for. And mum. Speaking about them now makes me realise just how much I miss them. Even Jace.'

Relief washed over Incantus's face, soothing the tautness of his expression. It made Alexis wonder.

He thought of Mortem, the way his gaze had singled Alexis out. The look of recognition on his face.

As crazy as it sounded, Alexis found himself wishing to see Mortem again.

'You seek to know more about Mortem.' Incantus had been watching him, noticing how his fingers tapped his thumbs without him even being aware of it.

'I do. But I want to know who he was before.'

Incantus considered him. The thing Alexis feared was that Incantus would say that they were similar. That Mortem was once a man with the power of water that had turned.

Something that would make the link between them clear.

'My oldest friend,' Incantus eventually replied. The photograph of the two young brothers came to Alexis's mind, their arms tossed round one another as if it was the most normal, casual action. How had one gone on to create the Haven and the other to commit murder?

'Mortem and I both had one thing in common all our lives: putting him first. Where the light gives, the darkness takes. Mortem claims it is time for Elementals to step into their power and rule mortals – bold aims, but I believe behind them is one, simple, true motivator: fear. Fear of the Prophecy of Light and Darkness that foretold his demise, and fear that once again he may become powerless to those who seek to harm him. Covering the world in darkness is his way to ensure that neither ever happens.'

Alexis chewed the inside of his cheek as he stared at the moon's reflection on the water's surface. The flow of the river disturbed its crescent shape, altering its image into one of ever-moving shards. 'What happened to him? Surely there must have been something that turned him. I can't believe in a world where you are born either good or evil.'

Incantus sat still, hands clasped. If there had been a pleading note in Alexis's voice, a quiet desperation, Incantus didn't mention it. The air was silent except for the low sound of Gibbous breathing and the faint rush of the distant river. Although there was no wind, Alexis felt colder still, pulling the blanket tighter around him.

'In truth, perhaps it was the Quinate and I who made him Mortem.' Alexis didn't know what he meant by this, but Incantus continued without much pause between his sentences, the truth spilling from him as if he could no longer hold it back. 'Mortem allowed his past, much of which I shared with him, to dictate his future. There is a fine line between all opposites. Light and dark. Good and evil. Life and death. Mortem used the pain and abuse we suffered to justify his decisions and drive his hatred for others. To shape his desire to ensure he would never again be a victim, and to inflict a fraction of the suffering he experienced onto the rest of the world.'

He turned to look at Alexis. When they locked eyes, Alexis felt both vulnerable and at ease beside his mentor. The angel whose wings had long been broken and yet still tried to fly.

'We are not a product of our biology, or our environment, for that matter,' said Incantus. 'Rather, the accumulation of our decisions, our choices, our actions. I want you to promise me, that no matter how dark the day gets, you will remember that the greatest and most powerful light is the light of life. The light that is in friendship, in family, the light that transcends death. Light will always find a way through the darkness, and if you can't find it, *become* it.'

Alexis had left his mentor not long after. Incantus told him he would return shortly, but when Alexis looked back from the archway between the Haven and the Garden, he saw him sitting there still, the ugly, worn blanket hugged within his arms, his head buried into Gibbous's side.

When Incantus had spoken, he had looked reminiscent, his eyes wet with the memory of his life and of all those he held dear who had died along the way. It was on his return to bed that Alexis vowed that he would fight not just for himself and the people he cared for, but also for Incantus, and for the people he had loved and lost in the battle against the darkness.

22

RESFEBER

Resfeber (n.) *Swedish origin*
The restless race of the traveller's heart before the journey
begins, when anxiety and anticipation are tangled together

Flesh tearing. Vision blurring. Mind splitting.

The nightmare. Only this time, it felt all the more real.

Alexis shot awake moments before the boy smacked into the water. Gasping for air, he told himself that the nightmare wasn't real, that he was safe and in bed. It took him a few minutes of tapping his fingers to his thumbs before he realised that the vividness of the dream had coincided with meeting Mortem for the first time. He guessed that seeing him in real life had triggered the more intense nightmare of a memory that was never his own.

Alexis's hopes of getting a couple of hours of more restful sleep were extinguished by the knocking on his door. He padded over, opened the door and found himself standing before Ziya. Her cheeks flushed deeply at the sight of him in just boxers and a baggy t-shirt.

'I'm starting to think you only knock on my door when I'm half-naked,' he said, wiping the sleep from his eyes.

Ziya made a noise somewhere between a laugh and scoff.

She was wearing the same clothes as last night. Her large, dark eyes were puffy from crying, her wiry hair tied back in a bun.

'I swear I'm not! It's just . . . bad timing. I promise!'

'I know, Ziya,' he replied with a small chuckle. 'I was just playing around.'

'Oh.' Ziya's smile faltered. 'I'm afraid your quest has to start now. Incantus is waiting to give you all a debrief as soon as you're ready. I'll tell the others.'

And just like that, the time for jokes was over.

After showering, Alexis took a moment to look at himself, remarking on the transformation he had made since arriving at the Haven. Muscles now built his frame, strong and defined. His chest was fuller, his shoulders wider, narrowing to a lean waist.

Silver lining, he thought – if he were to die, at least he would die in shape.

Alexis changed into his black all-in-one, and stuffed whatever he thought was important into an enchanted rucksack, its capacity infinite. As he was leaving his room, he paused for a moment, standing in the doorway, one hand pressed against the heavy wooden door, still crooked from the first time Demi had used her powers. He realised it might be the last time he was there.

He took it in, the smell of the water of the pool, the dozens of books he had stayed up late to read, even the little area he had cleared in the centre of the room to practise with his sword. Running back to his bedside, Alexis grabbed the photograph of Ian and Nero from the bedside table and tucked it into the bag. He didn't know why he would need it but, with it, he was able to close the door and finally leave.

Caeli and Demi stood at the bottom of the stairs, both dressed in their black Haven suits, each with the corresponding grey and green colour detail.

'Sleep well?' Demi asked, the top of her cheeks rosy, probably from her last hot shower for a while. As he nodded, he checked on Caeli. Her head was buried in her phone, her fingers typing away rapidly.

'Who's she arguing with now?' he asked Demi.

'Just dumped Joe,' Caeli replied, pocketing her phone. Her long, straight hair was down as always, but without her usual face of makeup, she looked younger, her skin paler and eyes smaller.

'What? Did he get into bed with his outside clothes still on?' Alexis joked, knowing how fickle Caeli could be sometimes.

Caeli wrapped her arms round herself. Her chin dropped slightly. This was one of the few times that Alexis thought she seemed genuinely upset, the façade of a brazen, independent young woman having faded.

He realised that was the biggest difference in how Caeli and Demi held themselves. Caeli's confidence was apparent at first glance, with her head held high and her seeming disregard for others' opinions. Only it wasn't real. The slight breeze of doubt would cause it to come tumbling down if only one was looking closely enough, revealing the vulnerability beneath – the girl that had been forced to grow up too quickly, not out of choice, but of obligation.

They hadn't spoken much about her being an only child, abandoned by her father before she was even born, but Alexis knew in the way that she carried herself that Caeli had been the responsible adult of the house long before she should have.

Alexis wrapped his arm round her shoulder. 'I'm sorry.' For a brief moment, she allowed him to hold her, her thin frame resting against his side.

'Joe's great,' she said, standing up straighter at the opening of Blaise's door. 'And he really didn't want me to end this. But, to be honest, I knew from the beginning it wouldn't last.' She fixed her hair and added quietly, 'There was just no . . . *fire*.'

Ziya nudged Blaise out of his room. 'No, you don't need your passport,' she said, sounding equally amused and exasperated. 'Now come on, you're already late.'

The Haven was quiet in the early hours of the morning, a little before five am. It was only when at the doorway to Incantus's laboratory, the white walls forever glowing brightly, that Ziya suddenly turned and enveloped the Alpha team into a group hug, ducking her head between them.

'We'll see you soon, Ziya,' said Demi. 'We promise to keep in contact as much as we can.'

'It's weird – I haven't even known you that long, but I know I'm going to miss you all so much,' Ziya mumbled.

Caeli wasn't tactile at the best of times, but she reached out to pat Ziya's arm. 'Look after this place whilst we're gone.'

Ziya nodded sincerely, wiping her nose with her sleeve before accepting Blaise's fist bump. 'The Haven was my sanctuary, you know? It was my home. Even when I was alone and scared, it was always where I felt safe. And it's not the same anymore. So please – do this for me. Do it for all of us who have nowhere else to go if you fail.'

210

Alexis took both of her hands in his own. 'The next time you see us will be when we're holding all four Elemental Gems. And we will tell you *every* detail of the quest.'

The Children of the Elements parted from Ziya and went through the door to the laboratory. Incantus sat in his chair in the middle of the room, staring at the huge overhead board that displayed the interactive world map.

'Around the world in a weekend,' Alexis muttered, gesturing for his friends to look at the display. 'I hope we don't get jet-lagged.'

Despite looking like he didn't get a wink of sleep all night, Incantus broke a slight smile.

Alexis hadn't been in the laboratory since they first arrived at the Haven. He peered at the wall that had once opened to reveal the doorway he and his friends had come through, leading straight from beneath Stonehenge. He felt so close to his old life, which seemed like a lifetime ago – when his biggest concern was whether he needed to take a jacket to the beach to avoid getting cold.

'Got everything?' Incantus asked, drawing to his feet. Gibbous rose beside him, attentive to his master's movements. The four friends rustled their bags in the air in response, thankful for the spell which made them weightless despite having been filled to the brim.

Incantus rounded the tall, white tabletop, leaning with one hand against its surface. Lines of worry ran across his forehead, his dark eyebrows half-obscuring the lightness of his eyes. Their intensity, however, could not be masked. 'Utilising the unique auras of your amulets, we have managed to approximately locate the Elemental Gems' whereabouts across the globe,' he continued as he packed containers of food into their bags.

'The Gems lie on the four axes of the Earth. Europe, Asia, Africa and South America. Earth, air, fire and water. The *precise* location is unclear, but your amulets should be drawn to the Gems they were cut from. They will likely be found near great natural sights; mountains, volcanoes, waterfalls.'

'And the Creatures?' Blaise asked hesitantly.

Incantus gestured for Gibbous to bid goodbye to the Elementals. 'Neither they nor the Gems have ever been seen by someone who survived. But from what we know of old scriptures and stories, we know that the Creatures will take a form associated with their element.'

'Fantastic,' muttered Caeli. 'I'm praying for a pigeon and not a dragon.'

'I'm not,' Blaise replied with a shudder. 'Pigeons freak me out.'

Incantus reached into a drawer from the desk opposite and pulled out a flat, silver disk. Alexis recognised it as one of the Haven's communication devices. Taranis taught them how to use it just last week. It was only the size of Alexis's palm as he took it, weightless, fitting easily into his backpack.

'This is if you need to contact me,' said Incantus. 'When you have possession of a Gem or are in trouble, place your thumb onto the centre and I shall answer. Now – and this is vital – do not let *anyone* see you using your powers,' he emphasised, looking at Blaise in particular, knowing his propensity to draw attention. 'The Maya force should conceal the Elemental world from most mortal eyes, as it has done for aeons, but we still

212

cannot risk the chance of being revealed. Be cautious.'

'How will we be travelling around the world?' Demi asked. 'Obviously, Ezra portalling us is no longer an option.'

Incantus walked over to one wall of the laboratory and placed his hands flat against it. It hummed in response to his touch, a whirring noise starting up as his palms began to illuminate. Emanating from his hands, a thin, white substance latched itself onto the wall, spreading out to meet the edges of the teleportation lines that ran at its borders.

'An old pathway, intermixed with the power of light to travel you there,' said Incantus, stepping away from the great opaque wall. 'Ezra was the only Elemental of the Haven to be a teleporter or portaller in decades. The communication device in your bag has been infused with the ability to create portals, but I'm not sure of its strength, particularly over such large distances. It is likely that I will have to send a portaller from the High Order at some point. As for now, this portal will take you to Greece, close to where the Earth Gem resides.'

'And we find it just by trusting our amulets?' Demi asked.

With the portal open in front of them, the reality of the impending quest could no longer be ignored or side-lined. This was it. There was no turning back now.

'The silver disk will also indicate its direction by reading its energy output,' Incantus assured them, standing before them. 'Together, it should be enough to lead you to them, just as you were led to Stonehenge.'

'*Dragged*,' Caeli coughed. 'This better not be a suicide mission. Dying would be so inconvenient.'

Blaise squinted at her in disbelief. 'Did you really just say "dying would be *inconvenient*?"'

Incantus smiled, the wrinkles of his forehead softening. He lowered his hand to the side, and Gibbous slowly came towards him. 'For the Gem of the Earth, Miss Nikolas, as far as I know, it is close to the sanctuary of Athena Pronaia in Delphi, mainland Greece.'

He gestured them forwards, another step closer to the portal. Alexis wasn't sure if he was mistaken, but he could almost feel the heat beyond the white veil.

Incantus lowered his head and clasped his hands in front of his chest. 'I'm so sorry I cannot go with you.'

'We've got this, Incantus,' Alexis replied, hoping to instil in his friends the confidence they so desperately needed. Hoping to instil it within himself. 'It's what we were born for.'

The Children of the Elements linked arms with one another, stepping into a line before the portal. As they did, Incantus Arcangelo moved behind them, placing a hand on each of their shoulders for a second, his grip strong, motivating, but far too brief.

'Call me whenever you need me,' he said, his deep voice heavy with emotion. 'This is a timed mission. There is no space for errors, but *come back* together and alive. I am not losing any of you. Good luck . . . Children of the Prophecy of Light and Darkness.'

'Now's a really bad time to need the toilet, isn't it?' Demi muttered.

'Yes, it is,' Caeli replied, blinking slowly.

Demi shook her head. 'I knew I shouldn't have had that coffee.'

Together, sharing a look with each other, the four strangers turned friends stepped through the glowing white portal, and their quest began.

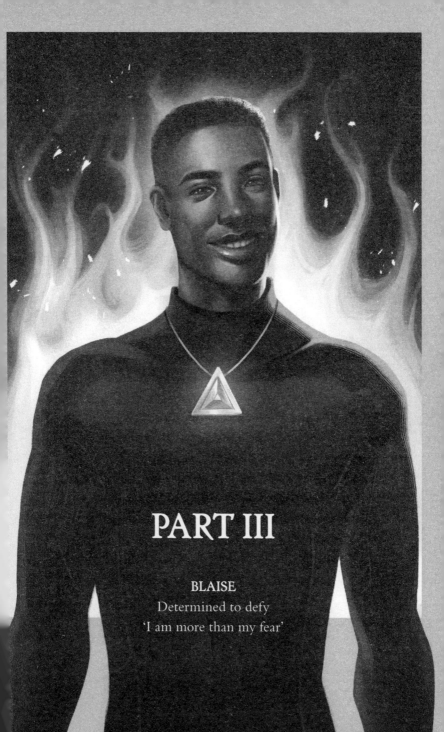

PART III

BLAISE
Determined to defy
'I am more than my fear'

23

DÉRIVE

Dérive (n.) *French origin*
'Drift'; a spontaneous journey where the traveller
leaves their life behind to let the spirit of
the landscape guide them

The first thing Alexis noticed when he emerged from the portal was the unyielding Mediterranean summer sunshine, warming his body to the very centre in a way the artificial lights of the underground Haven couldn't mimic.

The earth rose into mountains and dipped into valleys all around him like a treacherous sea of green and brown, decorated with yellow-coloured flora. In the early hours of the morning, the air was clear, reserved for them alone. It wouldn't stay that way for long, but Alexis took a moment to take in the smell, the sound of nature, the beauty that couldn't be encapsulated in a picture or with words.

To his disappointment, the experience was ruined by the sound of Caeli complaining.

'I forgot my sun-tan lotion!' Caeli threw her hands up. 'I knew I'd forget something. I can already feel my skin burning. This whole thing is a mistake.'

'It's been six seconds, Cae,' drawled Blaise, his face turned to the sky. 'R-e-l-a-x.'

The portal blinked closed behind them. There was now no way back to the Haven. They were alone, with no Incantus and no Leaders to come to their aid should they need it.

Demi turned slowly in a circle as she took in her surroundings. 'It looks like an ancient Greek theatre.'

Rows of staggered stone steps climbed before them in a wide semi-circle, half-buried into the slanted hillside. Between the cracks and fissures of the limestone slabs flourished tall grass and wildflowers, splashes of bright green fighting for sunlight and prevailing. It was as if the Earth itself was slowly claiming back its land.

Demi moved towards the centre of the stage. She was almost shining, although in Alexis's eyes, she always was. With the grass beneath her boots and a sea of pine and olive and cypress trees growing in every direction she turned; she closed her eyes and drew on the proximity of her earth element.

'They used to do plays here, didn't they?' said Blaise, jumping from the stone slabs until he found himself a patch of soft grass to sit. 'You look like you could be the main character, Dee.'

Alexis pulled his eyes away from Demi. 'Hopefully my story won't be a Greek tragedy,' she said with a laugh.

Caeli held out her hand to Alexis. 'Pass me the disk thing.' She didn't seem to be in the mood to waste time. She powered up the silver disk and examined it. 'It's saying the sanctuary is up ahead, only a couple of kilometres away. Wait . . . it's this way'

'Great, we're lost already,' said Blaise. He reluctantly turned his face away from the sunshine. 'Can't we just stay here for a bit?'

'The roads and the temple will probably get busy soon,'

Caeli said, her watch readjusting to the new time zone two hours ahead. 'This isn't a holiday.'

Demi took Blaise's arm and pulled him along. 'It is beautiful though, isn't it?'

Alexis peered at the Haven device in Caeli's manicured hands. On a basic infrared map of the mountainside, they were heading towards a strong, consistent glow in the distance. They passed flasks of water between them from their bags as they walked, and darted out of sight whenever the occasional car drove past until Caeli figured out how to manipulate the air to obscure them from sight.

Alexis filled the silence with what he had read in one of the ancient hardbacks on the dusted bookshelf in his room. 'The Ancient Greeks believed Delphi was the centre of the Earth. The sanctuary here contains the Tholos of Delphi, a temple home to the Oracle who would speak prophecies. Apparently, it was also home to a great monster of the Earth.'

'It's a bit sad how much reading you did after training all day, Al,' Blaise stated.

'It's a bit sad how the only books you read are ones with big pictures that take up half the page,' Alexis replied sweetly.

'Do you think the Oracle might have been the Woman of the Earth?' asked Demi, racing ahead in her eagerness to get there.

Alexis shrugged. The book hadn't mentioned anything about the Elemental Gems.

Eventually, the Elementals reached a stone-paved pathway that led away from the roadside and trailed further down the mountainside. Beside it read a sign, in Greek and English: 'Athena Pronaia Sanctuary.'

'This is it,' said Alexis. The four friends cautiously made their way down the sloped pathway. 'Surroundings,' he reminded them, gesturing to the security camera attached to the wall above. Blaise pointed his hand towards it, and a small flame sparked as the electric wires burned out, the red light switching off.

As they took another turn, the slope began to level out, the dry bushes and trees becoming more sparse as the pathway widened. Just as they were about to enter what remained of the sanctuary, Caeli drew to a stop. She extended her hands in the direction they had just come. Her fingers moved slowly in the air, reading it with caution.

'Someone's just come off the road behind us. Judging by their breathing, they're probably a hiker or just really excited to see some fallen rocks. We don't want anyone seeing us – I'll go take care of it.'

'The dryads of the Garden taught me how to create these powdered herbs that can make someone go unconscious,' Demi suggested, taking her hand. 'I'll go with you. Wait here until we're back,' she added to the boys as they retreated up the pathway.

The moment they disappeared from view, without a spoken word between them, Alexis and Blaise continued ahead.

The hillside of Mount Parnassus towered over the site to one side, but with the sun rising from the east, it provided no shade. Oak trees bordered the perimeter of the huge rectangular-shaped sanctuary of fallen temples, a series of once-great structures reduced to ruins. Small marble boulders sat on the dry ground, grass sprouting atop them, arranged in rows unmoved from when they first fell.

In the maze of debris, one structure stood more prominent than the rest; a circular temple, with most of the columns reduced to small stumps. The Tholos of Delphi. Alexis made a beeline towards it.

Blaise caught up to him. 'What's up with Cae?' He made a face. 'She's quiet and not taking the piss out of me . . . it's weird.'

'She broke up with Joe,' Alexis replied, watching closely to see his reaction.

Blaise's eyes widened. He then started picking at the skin-tight sleeves of his charcoal suit, suddenly fascinated by them. 'Didn't I call it? I said she's too much for him to handle.'

Alexis grinned. 'What?' Blaise asked. Alexis only raised a suggestive eyebrow in response. 'Oh, please,' said Blaise. 'Whatever you're thinking, you're wrong—'

He broke off as Caeli and Demi returned.

'That is some strong stuff,' Caeli told them, her eyes watering. 'Anyway, he's out for the count. Having a nice snooze under a bush . . .'

She trailed off as they all took in the only semi-standing structure within the ruins, the temple situated near the centre of the sanctuary.

Elevated on a podium, it somewhat resembled Stonehenge. An outer rim of broken columns, mostly stumps, ran round the circular podium. Only three pillars now stood tall, barely supporting the remains of a horizontal frieze between them. A smaller circular stone wall lay in the centre of the structure, surrounding a patch of grass growing within. As with the pillars, only part of the inner rock wall remained, arranged in a pyramidal shape just beyond the grass. Even in ruins, the temple was beautiful.

'To think this structure was built before Jesus Christ ever walked this Earth,' Demi said under her breath, so quietly that Alexis barely heard her. She edged closer, not turning back when she asked, 'What does the disk show?'

Alexis wrestled Caeli for it. The lights indicating their auras were on top of a greater glowing mass. The Gem of the Earth should be . . . at their feet.

Demi climbed over the fence that flanked the temple, hesitantly taking a step onto the circular podium. The moment her foot made contact with the dais, her amulet flickered alight with a bold emerald glow.

'Oh God,' she whispered, freezing on the spot as her amulet lifted from her chest in the direction of the temple.

Alexis, Blaise and Caeli quickly joined her on the elevated stone dais, although there was no such change to their amulets. As Demi walked further into the centre, the entire temple illuminated with a steady low glow, the light shining a wild bright green against the sun's yellow.

Demi's voice startled Alexis when she spoke. 'Look! Can you see that?'

Following her line of sight, Alexis noticed a small emblem glinting brightly against the stone pyramid before her. It was the same symbol as the one carved into her door at the Haven, the same as her amulet. A downwards-pointing triangle with a line cutting across it.

Demi lifted the chain above her head. She lined up the edges of her amulet and pressed it against the engraving.

A blinding green light burst from the Tholos of Delphi, erupting through the air like a wave of pure energy, so bright that it lit up the whole mountain range. Before the Elementals could hope to react, the temple jolted and a loud rumble echoed throughout the valley.

At first, Alexis thought Demi had triggered an earthquake. The trees trembled in the distance and the stone ruins shuddered around them. It wasn't until he noticed the sea of mountains growing taller that he realised the Tholos of Delphi was slowly sinking into the ground, taking them with it.

'Do we get off?' Blaise shouted.

'No!' Demi called back, reaching out to link hands with the others. The podium continued to descend, falling below the surface of the hillside, carrying the Elementals down.

Walls of mud and dirt encased the edges of the circular temple as they were lowered so deep that not even the summit of Mount Parnassus could be seen. Eventually, after what felt like minutes, the platform ground to a halt, possibly a hundred metres deep. The surface had already sealed above them, trapping them underground where the limited air was heavy with moisture and the rich smell of dirt. When the green glow of the temple dimmed, they were once again submerged in darkness.

The snapping of Blaise's fingers echoed against the walls of earth that encased them. A spark caught, ignited into a flame over his hand where it grew in size and illumination. Not that there was much to see.

Before Alexis could ask where the Gem and the Creature may be, the grass that covered the centre of the podium hummed to life and flickered alight blade by blade. The Elementals jumped back from it, pressing themselves to the mud wall as they pulled out their weapons from their bags.

'What's happening?' Caeli shouted.

The blades of grass began to rise from the ground, each one glowing and swirling in the air as if manipulated by its own current. Thousands rose upwards, floating into a spinning column of glowing jade, so bright that Blaise extinguished his fireball, its light no longer needed. As the grass spun faster and faster, the blades started to blend and morph into something larger. Something solid. Something real.

Before Alexis's eyes, a woman's figure took shape, earth-coloured hair falling down past her waist, a gown of the green blades knitting over her body, sweeping the ground. She stood tall and broad, delicate yet strong, her hands folded behind her back.

Her eyes remained closed as a network of tree-like roots sprouted behind her, snaking up the pillars of the temple. They thickened with age in an instant, growing browner, stronger as they twisted round the peaks of the temples' columns for support. The body of the trunk elongated and engorged, sprouting branches that budded leaves, one growing from the other like an interconnected web of fruition.

In no more than a few seconds, a magnificent oak tree had grown completely underground, its base roofing the temple, hundreds of feet tall. Demi tugged on his sleeve, but Alexis didn't need her to tell him what it was.

The ancient Tree of Life had just materialised before them, the most sacred tree of existence.

With a lasting flash of light from the Woman of the Earth's body, she opened her glowing emerald eyes. They instantly fell upon Demi and the amulet she was wearing, glimmering in recognition of it, and of what it meant.

She removed her hands from behind her back and presented the Child of her Element with the gift she had been searching for. The first of the lost Elemental Gems of creation.

In her hands, shining eternally, lay the Gem of the Earth.

It was about the size of a clenched fist, surprisingly small despite the immense power it contained. It wasn't similar to any stone or emerald Alexis had ever seen before, the colour and clarity ethereal, unnatural almost. Bearing no cracks or fissures, only one edge had been chipped away, cutting a piece for Demi's amulet which now shone in its presence, thrumming with power. Demi's eyes had never been so bright.

Demi swallowed before speaking. 'The Woman of the Earth.' She bowed awkwardly, the others following suit. How were they supposed to address an omnipotent force that had created the world, a being they weren't even certain was real? Now seemed as good a time to bow as any.

'My child,' the Woman answered, her voice gravelly, resonant and regal.

The Woman stood still, frozen in time, the magnificent oak tree thriving above her like a halo or the antlers of a stag. She looked upon the Children of the Elements and surveyed them, taking in the sight of their amulets.

Alexis couldn't help but feel intimidated when her eyes found him and narrowed.

'The Darkness has returned,' said the Woman, nodding to herself in regretful understanding.

For some reason, Alexis found it his responsibility to respond. 'An Elemental with its power wishes to use it for destruction and control. We have to stop him before he has the chance to cover the world in shadow.'

The Woman continued to stare at him. He wasn't sure if she knew anything that he was saying; her time in creation was eternities before Mortem. He let out a sigh of relief when she eventually looked away.

'The peoples of this world have been polluting and destroying my Earth ever since the beginning of their time.' The Gem in her hands hadn't wavered once. 'But, yes, the Darkness will attempt to cover it again, to destroy me and my sisters.'

Caeli finally found her voice. 'Sorry, but are you human? Or Elemental?' Her double-tipped spear was still in her hand, faintly shaking where she held it tightly.

'I am taking this form for your benefit. Every single thing born from earth or solid, whether it be a grain of sand or a whole forest, is me.'

'And the Creature of the Earth?' asked Blaise, looking her up and down. 'Is that you too?'

The Woman shook her head gently, the roots of hair that ran down her exposed back swaying as she did. 'My sisters and I are the holders of the Gems that built this world and all else. With our powers we can only create, we cannot destroy. It is why we made the First Borns, your Elemental ancestors, to fight the Darkness.'

'But the First Borns' sacrifice didn't work,' said Alexis. 'The Darkness survived somehow.'

'Indeed it did,' was all the Woman replied, her gaze lingering.

'So about this Creature . . .' Blaise repeated.

'We birthed the Creatures to protect the Gems. It will only be called once the Gem is out of my possession.'

'And how do we defeat it?' Demi asked.

For the first time, the Woman smiled. It was a faint smile, a faint, beautiful smile that transformed her whole face, like that of spring's first flower, nature's first song of the season. Her response was a simple one. 'With your powers, of course.' She gestured to her forehead, pointing to the very centre. 'We once planned for the Gems to sit above the centre of the Creatures' heads. Now it remains the only part of their bodies that is vulnerable.'

Demi took a step back, pressing herself against the wall of dry earth behind her. 'I don't know if I can bring myself to do it,' she whispered. 'Any of it. All of it.'

'Raise your head and look at me,' said the Woman, the order spoken softly. 'A single weed does not ruin a flower bed, daughter of my element, just as a single sin does not darken the purity of your soul. Do your duty and protect our earth.' Although the Woman didn't lean forward, she extended her arms towards Demi, the glow of the Gem shining brighter against her face. 'The ground beneath you will continue to support you, as it always has.'

Demi's hands shook as she raised them, but she raised them nonetheless. When she placed them round the Woman's, her muscles tensed, electrified with energy. With Demi's eyes on the Earth Gem, she didn't notice how the Woman's face slowly changed. How her smile withered before slipping away.

'In return for your bravery, my sisters and I will offer you each an insight into your future. A glimpse of what there is to come, in the hopes that it brings you peace. I shall tell you yours, child of my element.' When the Woman spoke again, her voice was distant, almost remorseful.

'With water washing your roots, you will finally rest.'

The Woman passed the Gem into Demi's hands before she could ask what she meant. With the Gem no longer in her hold, the Woman's face softened. Gradually, the glow of her skin diminished, and with it, the great Tree of Life that had grown wilted into nothingness, its colour reabsorbed into the Gem.

The Woman's lasting words faded as she did, her body returning to the individual blades of grass that had formed it. 'Your Prophecy is following its course. I hope you succeed in what you are destined to accomplish. Good luck, my child, this will not be the last time we meet.'

She then said something in what Alexis assumed to be Greek, something he didn't understand. Something he desperately wished he could, especially when the Woman's eyes had flicked to him.

'Το να αγαπάς αυτό το αγόρι θα είναι ο θάνατός σου.'

One by one, the grass blades came away, drifting towards the floor of the temple. The glowing aura that was once the Woman returned to the Gem, illuminating its power ever more. With the shadowy underground barely lit by the Gem, Demi clutched onto it tightly.

'Dem, what did she mean?' Caeli asked, moving to stand beside her. Demi flinched when she placed a hand on her shoulder. '"*With water washing your roots, you will finally rest.*" She doesn't mean "rest" as in *die*, does she?'

'I – I don't know,' Demi stuttered, her chest rising and falling sharply.

From the moment the Woman had spoken Demi's prophecy, Alexis hadn't taken a breath. He hadn't even moved. His body was frozen in overwhelming, paralysing fear. It wasn't from the knowledge that the Creature of the Earth would be soon coming for them, its sole purpose to destroy any that sought the Gem in their possession. It was from the thought that there might be a day when he would have to live in a world without Demi. He didn't care about his own life if it meant she wasn't in it.

With water washing your roots.

The thing that scared him most of all was how it was by his element that her demise had been prophesied. What had she said in Greek that was preventing Demi from meeting his eyes? He tried to repeat how it sounded, but already the words were becoming lost to him, falling out of his mind like water between his fingers.

'You're not going to die,' he said, pushing past the others to stand before her. Demi was still staring at the Gem of the Earth in her trembling hands. Alexis tilted her chin until she was looking into his eyes. 'Not anytime soon. None of us will let that happen, you hear me?'

'Yeah, we got you, Dee,' Blaise added. 'We won't let that Creature near you. But first, we have to find out where the hell it's hiding.'

A deafening thundering answered in reply. A series of tremors rippled through the earth so violently that it shook the pillars of the temple and cast dirt up into the air. It took Alexis a moment, through the ringing of his ears, to realise that it hadn't been an earthquake that had shaken them. It had been the roar of an animal. The roar of the Creature.

And it was being signalled by the Gem of the Earth.

24

TAKANE NO HANA

Takane no hana (n.) *Japanese origin*
'Flower on a high peak'; someone or something
one desires but is far away or unattainable

Shockwaves thundered through the earth, casting broken clusters of marble onto the temple's dais. Caeli threw her hands up, manipulating the little air that remained to create a windshield to protect them from the falling debris. It would be only a matter of time before they were truly buried alive.

'Get us out of here!' she shouted.

Demi closed her eyes, extending her free hand to face the ground. Splaying her fingers, she yelled, *'Rise!'*

The base of the temple quivered before shooting upwards, the force so great that it pinned the other Elementals to the ground. It raced past the walls of earth that entrapped them, breaking free from the underground chamber in seconds. As sunlight struck Alexis's face, the temple shuddered to a halt back at the ground level, dry soil raining down upon them.

The Elementals jumped free from the temple as the Gem pulsed again, making a shrieking noise that echoed throughout the forest valley and called the Creature to them.

Just like they were taught in training, the four friends

formed a tight square facing out, weapons gripped tightly in their hands. Alexis flung his rucksack to the side and raised his bronze and steel bi-sword as he checked on the others.

Caeli was twisting her long double-edged spear in her grip, fastening a quiver of arrows to her back – no need for a bow to fire them. At her side, Demi had untied her specially crafted vine whip, its tail snaking across the ground, Gem in the other hand. In a single striking motion, Blaise beat his forearms together which sent sparks racing up his heavy axe, igniting the blade and the four detachable throwing knives that it held in coiling scarlet flames.

They were as ready as they'd ever be.

A brilliant green light burst from the Gem as it exploded with power. Alexis had no time to shield himself from the blast. The force swept outwards in an instant, flinging the Elementals apart.

Alexis crashed into the remains of a nearby temple, smashing the thousands-year-old marble to dust. Panting for air, he brushed the debris from his face, grateful for the Haven suit for absorbing most of the impact, saving his spine from shattering. It still took him a moment to find his feet and stagger over to Demi.

'Look!' shouted Alexis. The Gem lay on the ground where it had been dropped, a network of fractures cracking out around it. Its surface was untouched, but there was something from within that was breaking its radiating beams of light, something slipping in and out of view.

'What is that?' Demi leant forwards. 'It looks like it's . . . hatching.' She gasped when a green slitted eye rose to the surface of the stone. 'Oh my God,' she whispered, pulling

Alexis back with her. 'The Creature isn't being summoned by the Gem. It's *inside* it.'

As the words left her lips, a claw bled from the shell of the Earth Gem and planted itself on the ground of the mountainside. It swelled in size once free from the stone, growing as long as a human arm. Three more claws emerged, curving downwards into the ground, splitting the earth beneath its pointed edge. Following the claws came a single wide foot, plated in a scaled armour.

The Elementals stood there as the scene unfolded, another leg squeezing free from the Gem's surface, thickening once in contact with the earth, turning from a two-dimensional image reflected on the Gem's surface into a three-dimensional limb. Two huge, curved tusks made of some kind of greenish ivory protruded from either side of its temples as its face fought to emerge. A third, smaller horn appeared between them on its nose, forming an inverted triangle that mirrored Demi's amulet, the tips of the horns curving over its forehead.

As lizard-like, acid-green eyes materialised, its jagged mouth following, another thunderous roar escaped it. The Children of the Elements were hurled aside, rolling down the foothill of the mountain, colliding with the forest of trees and bushes that snapped under impact. Through half-open eyes, Alexis saw them falling further apart from one another, dispersing like sand in the wind. He eventually came to a stop, spitting dust and dirt, his mind still spinning. He felt two hands grip him tightly, pulling him to his feet.

'Are you hurt?' came Demi's voice, her face whirling in and out of view.

'I'm fine.' He used his sword to keep him upright, steadying himself against a tree trunk. He glanced around the dense forest valley, searching for Caeli and Blaise. 'Go find the others.'

Demi hadn't heard him. She was no longer looking at him. Following her gaze, Alexis's eyes traced back up the mountain peak to where the temple remains were. But he could no longer see the sanctuary. The only thing he saw was the Earth Beast.

The Creature was a mammoth to the trees surrounding it. The length of its body was even greater, its belly low to the ground, tipped with a huge tail that split into two downward-clawed spikes. Its whole body was plated in hard, brown armour, its spine and the sides of its back bursting with dozens of piercing spikes jaggedly pointed upwards.

Even from where he stood, the warm breath of the prehistoric monster was pungent, sickly, pouring out between its rows of yellowed teeth. Behind it, underneath its curling tail, sat the Gem, the light from it glowing lowly again.

A string of curses followed as Blaise re-joined them, Caeli by his side.

'I'm going to kill Incantus,' Blaise muttered.

'Not if this dinosaur kills you first,' Caeli answered. She ran her fingers through her hair, ripping out equal clumps of dirt and silver-blonde streaks. 'Ideas on how to beat this thing?'

Alexis searched for the blind spot, remembering what the Woman had said about their foreheads being their only vulnerability. A small area, no bigger than the size of the Gem, lay flat and free from the armoured skin. It sat in the centre of the inverted triangle of horns, just above its reptilian eyes. He gestured to it with his sword. 'Aim for that.'

Caeli gasped. 'We've got no chance! Even with my accuracy, I don't know if I could hit that, especially if it's moving.'

'It's the only way,' said Demi, unsheathing her curved dagger.

The Creature growled again. Its glowing jade eyes bore into them, watching their every move, waiting.

'We have to try. We need to distract it while Demi goes for the Gem,' Alexis decided. 'Once she has its unlimited powers, maybe it'll disappear. Keep an eye on its tail,' he added, tracking the two-pronged daggers as they whipped from side to side, cracking apart earth and stone.

As if sensing that they had formed a plan, the Beast roared again. The ground quaked at its feet. As the Elementals tried to keep their balance, the Creature charged at them, thundering towards the valley, trees splintering as it burrowed through without hesitation.

Within an instant, the adrenaline and memory of Alexis's training took hold. With superhuman speed, the Elementals broke apart, Alexis and Blaise diving either side of the Beast whilst Caeli flew into the air over its head. Demi rolled under its legs, narrowly dodging its great tail.

Alexis got to his feet just in time to see the Beast's spear-tipped tail burrow into the earth, dislocating a huge chunk of soil beneath a nearby oak tree. With a sudden flick, the tree was unearthed, breaking free and sent hurling in Blaise's direction, too fast for him to outrun.

Seconds before it would have struck, the tree trunk exploded apart from within into nothing more than wood shavings and splinters. The Beast turned to see Demi crouched beneath its hind, her hand extended in Blaise's direction.

She was too close to it, Alexis thought.

The Beast raised its clawed leg over Demi, its shadow great enough to block out the sunlight. She stood there, dagger in hand, frozen. Not even the series of spitting fireballs Blaise threw at it had any impact, merely bounding off its plated armour, leaving only charred scorch marks.

The air suddenly shifted around Demi and a swift gale carried her away from the Beast. At the same moment that Demi joined Caeli's side, Alexis bolted past them.

He leapt into the sky using the water vapour to propel him, higher than any human could jump, as tall as some of the remaining trees nearby. The Creature's head loomed towards him as he crashed into its side, his hand managing to get a hold of one of its upper tusks. Alexis grunted as the Creature tried to shake him off, struggling to maintain his hold as he swung dangerously just in front of one of its great eyes.

'Just. Let. Me. Kill. You. *Please*.'

With each word, Alexis slashed with his sword at the centre of the Beast's face, hoping to make a dent in the small unprotected area before his shoulder dislocated. Somewhere far below, he heard the clanging of metal upon stone as Blaise swung his burning axe repeatedly against the Beast's underbelly.

'Get the Gem!' Caeli shouted to Demi, gesturing to the glittering stone that lay far away, back up the mountainside. She hesitated before nodding, tearing away from the battle as Caeli flew into the air, joining Alexis.

Manipulating the wind, Caeli pulled arrows one by one from her quiver, spinning them to form a circle round her.

She hurled them at the Beast, slicing through the air toward its chest and neck. They barely missed Alexis as he clung on with one hand, his grip slipping as he continued to stab at its face, his arms burning.

'Caeli, here!' Alexis called. He was swung to the side just before the tip of his sword could puncture the centre of its forehead. 'Stop moving!' he added to the Beast, slapping it with his sword.

'I'm scared I'll hit you!'

His voice climbed an octave or two. 'Then don't hit me!'

Caeli's full attention turned to the Beast's face, biting into her lip so hard that she drew blood. She hovered back and forth, spear in her hand, forced to retreat every time she got too close to its triad of curved tusks. Whilst she occupied it, Alexis checked on Demi. In the direction of the mountain, he made out her small figure as she raced up its side, the Gem of the Earth only metres away.

Looking away was Alexis's mistake. The Creature's slitted eyes followed Alexis's, noticing the absence of the Elemental that possessed the power of its creator. That was when it roared.

The sound rippled outwards, colliding against the bodies of all things solid; the ground, the trees, the Elementals. As it furiously shook its body, Alexis was rocked forwards. His cheekbone cracked against its plated face. Losing his grip, stunned, he fell backwards off the mountain-sized Beast. He crashed into one of the upturned spikes that edged its spine, his breath escaping him as he felt his ribs snap, unable to even scream.

Blinking away the searing hot pain, he focussed on his own

element, the liquid around him. He clenched his hand into a fist and called on whatever fluid remained in the soil and the trees as the ground rushed closer and closer.

Bursting free from the earth, thin trails of water dashed to meet him, catching him like a falling leaf in a river stream. It barely held his weight, but it was enough to carry him away, just in time for the earthquakes to begin.

Seismic waves shook the entire forest mountain range, so great that even the ruined temples from the sanctuary came crashing down the valley. A gaping fissure cracked open from where the Beast stood and snaked impossibly fast towards the Gem, tearing the earth apart as though it held no greater resistance than paper.

Moments before the Gem would have been in Demi's grasp, she was forced to dive aside to save herself from falling into the broken crevice.

Alexis planted his sword into the ground and forced himself to stay conscious. He had to get to his knees and, after that, to his feet. The ground trembled with every footstep the Creature took as it bounded towards the Gem of the Earth. Nothing would slow it down, not Blaise's firewalls, not Caeli's wind torrents, not even the trees that Demi was toppling against it to block its path as it advanced on her.

Demi glanced round, and her jaw clenched in concentration. The ground seemed to part beneath her feet, pulling her underground, not a moment before the Creature would've trampled her. It lashed its spiked tail into the ground where Demi had just disappeared, tearing deep beyond the surface of the soil.

'*Demi!*' Caeli screamed, throwing her spear towards the Creature. It cut through the air in seconds but was easily deflected by one of the Creature's great ivory tusks.

Deeper in the forest valley, Blaise rushed to Alexis's side, helping him to his feet. Together, arm in arm, they staggered up the hillside.

'We keep fighting,' Alexis said between breaths, shaking away the pain that stabbed into his side with every footstep.

'We can't beat it,' Blaise said hopelessly, hauling him along. 'We don't even know where Demi is. If she's even a—'

Alexis cut him off. 'If we get to the Gem and find her, maybe it could heal her if she's hurt.' He couldn't consider the alternative. He wiped blood from his lips and swept dark hair from his eyes. 'I'll go right, you go left. Unless you'd rather tell Incantus you're the weakest of the group?'

Blaise ignited both of his hands into balls of yellow-burning flames. It kindled his swinging axe, the flaming blade licking at the side of his face, evaporating his sweat.

'We don't stop until it's dead, or we're all dead,' said Blaise, nodding to Caeli in the air. Weapons in hand, they charged again.

The Creature lunged towards Caeli, its daggered tusks ripping through her suit by her thigh. She cried out, then cast her hands to the sky.

'Now you're starting to piss me off!'

With that, she threw her arms down. Sweeping from around her, a tempest of whipping gales followed her command, rushing against the top of the Creature's head with such power that it forced it to the ground. Not a moment later, Blaise dashed forwards, hacking his flaming axe at its fallen face, tearing through the flesh and nearly shattering the smaller tusk.

Alexis sprinted around the Beast, hiking as fast as he could towards the edge of the sanctuary where the Gem lay. The Creature must have felt his footsteps on the earth. Before his very eyes, the Creature's spiked tail lunged towards his chest.

Over the sound of his own pulse in his throat, over the sound of Blaise's cry of warning, Alexis heard the cracking of a whip. He felt something tight lasso itself round his waist, hurling him backwards, the tip of the spike missing him by a hair's breadth.

Standing behind him, holding the other end, was Demi. Dirt clung to her face, the tunnel she had burrowed to escape the Beast's wrath exiting just beside her.

'Thank me later,' was all she said before unfurling her whip and lunging again for the Gem.

The Creature's venomous gaze returned to Demi just as she reached the Gem of the Earth. She shook the glowing stone frantically, clutching it to her chest as she prayed for something to happen, for her full powers to be released. With a spare hand, she forced aside the section of ground where Alexis was standing, throwing him out of the way as the Creature advanced on her, the earth trembling under its thunderous footsteps.

'*Come on, come on, come on!*' Demi shook the Gem again, but, still, nothing happened.

Alexis looked back at the Beast watching as thick tree roots burst through the earth, wrapping round its legs as Demi tried everything she could to slow it down. But the Creature was unstoppable in its charge, drawing closer and closer. Nothing would stop it from reaching her and the Gem from where her amulet had been cut –

Wait.

'Demi!' Alexis shouted, crawling towards her. 'Press it to your amulet!'

Demi beat the surface of the Gem against her amulet without question, and everything changed in an instant.

In a silent blast, she erupted with a wave of green light. Power surged free from the Gem of the Earth and flooded into Demi. The energy of the ancient stone became absorbed by her skin, seeping through the veins and tissues and bones of her body, amplifying them with colour.

When she opened her eyes, they shone with a powerful emerald. She dropped the colourless, dull Gem behind her and extended both hands towards the Creature that was only metres in front of her.

'*My turn,*' she said, her voice reverberating throughout the forest valley.

With a wave of her hand, the ground beneath the Earth Beast split apart with a seismic pulse. The Creature fought to outrun the earthquake, but the fissure grew too wide for it to escape. It flailed helplessly as it fell beneath the ground and the earth reclosed over its body, trapping its scorpion-like tail and leaving exposed only its anguished face.

Demi curled her fingers, cracking apart the earth by her feet. With the thrust of her palm, the ground propelled her into the air, soaring straight towards the writhing, buried Creature. The blade of her curved dagger glinted against the sunlight as she raised it above her head with both hands. She landed in between the triad of horns that guarded the Creature's face.

Although he couldn't hear her, Alexis saw Demi mouth, 'Please forgive me.'

The last thing Alexis saw before the flying dust and dirt obscured his vision was the Creature's slitted eyes slowly closing as Demi brought down her dagger towards the Gem-sized space of the Earth Beast's forehead.

Through the clouds of rubble came Caeli and Blaise, linked arm in arm, their weapons out as they searched blindly.

'Where is she?' asked Caeli, her voice barely a murmur, swallowing back a cough.

Alexis couldn't bring himself to call her name, petrified at the prospect that it would be met with silence. The dust finally settled and he saw something moving.

Materialising atop the huge head of the Earth Creature's carcass appeared Demi Nikolas, resting against one of its curved tusks. She grinned brilliantly as she turned to look at them, her eyes twinkling with power beyond their wildest imagination.

'*Now* you can thank me,' she said.

25

EXULANSIS

Exulansis (n.) *English origin*
The tendency to give up trying to talk about an experience
because people are unable to relate to it

Demi jumped free from the Earth Creature's head and Alexis, Blaise and Caeli rushed forth to meet her. They drew to a stop only centimetres away. An unfamiliar aura surrounded her – an aura so great that it reminded Alexis of the Arcangelo brothers. He didn't want to get accidentally incinerated by getting too close – how embarrassing would that be?

'Can I . . .' he began, struggling to find the right words. 'Can we touch you?'

Demi nodded, looking between the three of them.

Alexis placed his hand on her shoulder. His muscles tensed and he felt the hum of eternal energy that coursed through her body. 'Don't ever do that again,' he said to her.

'What?' Demi smiled. Even her voice sounded stronger, deeper. 'Protect you?'

'Not if it's with your life.'

With the dust settling around them and the prospect of danger wilting away, Alexis could no longer ignore the pain in his chest. He was sure he had broken a rib or two, for he felt a sharp stabbing every time he inhaled. He peered down and noticed his Haven suit was glowing around the injured area, the superficial healing properties working to repair it.

'Dee, is that you?' Blaise gawked, shifting to look at her from different angles. 'You've never looked hotter.' Caeli glanced at Blaise out of the corner of her eyes, her expression masked. Only Alexis noticed. There wasn't much he didn't notice; it was exhausting sometimes. 'How do you feel?'

Demi exhaled slowly, examining her hands. 'I – I can't even describe it. I don't even know which words to use. I feel . . . I feel how the Woman looked. Just . . . powerful. But still me. Like it's me . . . but stronger.'

For the first time, she saw the pained expression on Alexis's face. 'Let me try this.' She pressed her warm hands to his mid-section, and Alexis forced himself to remain still at her touch, at her closeness. 'Relax,' she said softly, her fingers lightly stroking the lines of hard muscle that patterned his abdomen.

Alexis heard a slight cracking sound. He blinked away the yellow spots that clouded his vision, and through the initial pain, he was able to stand up straighter and breathe comfortably again, for he was sure she had somehow just repaired his broken bones.

'It's not just the earth power I feel now, but all solid matter,' Demi explained, smiling gleefully as she stood back. 'I can feel it all, the ground beneath us, the Earth slowly rotating. And it's not just manipulation any more, I can *create* it. Just like Incantus said we would be able to.'

'Talking of Incantus, we should probably tell him we found the Gem,' Caeli interjected.

Alexis wasn't sure what she was most envious of, Demi's

powers or the way Blaise was looking at her. Either way, she was doing an unusually bad job at hiding it.

Demi bent down to pick up the now dull Gem. 'It looks empty.'

Behind them, there was a faint rustling sound. Whilst they had been talking, they hadn't noticed that the Creature had begun to disintegrate. Green dust, similar to what the Woman had returned to, was all that remained of the great Beast as its body fell apart. Instead of its essence drifting away in the warm breeze, it travelled to Demi's amulet where it was absorbed with an emerald glow, signalling the end of the first quarter of their quest.

'The temples!' Demi gasped once they walked back up the mountain, returning to the ancient Sanctuary of Athena Pronaia. From the series of earthquakes, the remains of the structures had been reduced to broken marble fragments. It looked like the site of a building demolition.

'As if they weren't ruins before,' Blaise said. He received a stern glare from Demi that withered the shrubbery around her.

Alexis pulled the flat, silver communication disk out and pressed his thumb against the centre. The surface of the tablet flickered and a live image shimmered into view. It showed the ceiling of the Haven's laboratory, the continuous white panels lined with a faint blue hue. In the background, he could hear two voices in deep discussion.

'Incantus?'

The image shifted as the disk was picked up. Holding it was Ziya, her black hair tied away from her face. At the sight of them, she cried out.

'Holy First Borns . . . *Demi.*'

Incantus dashed into view, taking the tablet with both hands. As he tilted the screen, Alexis glimpsed the dozens of papers and tablets scattered across the high tables of the laboratory.

'Show me everyone!' Incantus demanded. 'Are you all well? Are you hurt? Do you need healing? Do you need me?'

'We're all okay,' Alexis answered, passing the pale-yellow crystals from his bag to Caeli and Blaise. 'We've got the healing crystals for that. And now Demi,' he added.

'Tell me everything,' Incantus ordered. 'And Miss Nikolas, my goodness. You look . . . transcendent. I can almost feel your power from here!'

Demi blushed as the four Elementals began tripping over each other to explain what had happened.

'So the Creatures of the Elements really exist? After all this time. Hiding in the Elemental Gems!' The questions poured out of Ziya's mouth, each one louder than the one that came before.

'Yeah, and they were bigger than you led us to believe, boss,' Blaise said, wiping away the sweat at his hairline.

'Nothing my best and brightest couldn't handle,' Incantus replied proudly. 'But the most important thing is that you are all safe and you've managed to retrieve the first of the Elemental Gems.'

He smiled as the four teenagers passed around congratulations to one another. And yet, Incantus's expression didn't last. Alexis noticed it withdrawing soon after, replaced with a tight-lipped look.

'What is it?' Alexis asked.

'Demi, I'm awfully sorry, but I have to ask you to return the powers to the Earth Gem and then give it to us.'

Demi's grip tightened around the precious stone. 'Why?'

'We need to ensure its power is safe for you to use. Extremely high seismic activity has been recorded across the whole of Greece, including a shift in the tectonic plates. I need to study it and ensure that such dangers to the rest of the world do not occur during the solar eclipse. This will also prevent Mortem from stealing it should the Shadowless find you.' Incantus tilted his head and pressed his hand over his heart. 'My dear, I know it feels intoxicating, having all this power and energy. But power becomes dangerous when one doesn't learn how to use it properly. With so much of the quest laying ahead, we can't risk it.'

Demi hesitated. For a moment, Alexis wondered if she would hand the Gem over. He wondered whether *he* would hand it over. Unlimited power – surely that would be useful in the fight against the other Creatures?

Yet, Demi had always been better than himself. She pressed the dull Earth Gem against her glowing amulet and the colour drained back into the stone, its power returning. Without so much as a second thought, she pushed the fist-sized Gem against the silver disk. At its touch, the communication device screen shimmered and the Gem sunk through.

Incantus held it on the other side, using his powers to keep it floating in the air, cautious to touch it. If Ziya leaned any further away from it, she would fall off her chair.

'Thank you, Demetria,' Incantus said, to which she only nodded. There was a deep sadness in her eyes, as though she were experiencing loss.

Ziya pointed to one of the computer screens in the laboratory and said something incoherent to Incantus, who nodded.

He turned back to face them. 'As wonderful a job you four have done already, I am afraid you have no time to celebrate yet. Our readings detect a group of Elementals rapidly approaching your location. It could be the High Order. They have promised to send the Erasers to each location you visit in case of any human sightings, but not to get involved beyond that. But it may also be the Shadowless. You have to get a move on.'

'The next destination is in China,' said Ziya, pressing buttons on the side of the device.

'Of course, we know the four Elemental Tribes reside close to each Gem's approximate location, with the central Air Tribe being hidden in the skies of Mount Everest,' Incantus added.

'Of course,' Alexis repeated under his breath, as though it was common knowledge that a secluded cult of Elementals who worshipped the air element lived at the peak of the world's tallest mountain. A tribe, which, according to Taranis, Caeli's ancestors had been a part of, just as Alexis and the others had been descendants of the other respective Elemental Tribes. Taranis had only mentioned it in passing, but it made Alexis wonder that if the Gem of the Water was in South America, did that mean that was where he was from? Would he be going to the continent or even the country of his birth?

Incantus continued, 'After matching the energy tracing across the globe against Caeli's amulet, the Air Gem appears to be located in the famous Zhangjiajie National Forest Park in the Hunan Province. The Woman of the Air—'

He broke off. Blaise was rustling noisily around in his backpack, his hand reappearing with a protein bar that he waved in the air. Receiving a glare from Alexis, Caeli, Demi and Ziya through the screen, he slowly lowered his hand. 'Bad timing. Bad timing, I know, but I got hungry. Go ahead, Incantus.'

'Thank you for your permission, Mr Ademola,' Incantus replied with a slow blink. 'As I was saying, the Woman of the Air will have sensed the Dark Prophecy unravelling and will be aware her sister has passed. As you know, stay vigilant. Use your training, your trust in one another. Get Caeli to her Gem immediately. It is your best, if not your only chance of success. And ensure you preserve the site where you can.'

'Yeah, because we did such a good job of that here,' Alexis mumbled, too quietly for Incantus to hear.

'Right,' said Ziya cheerfully. 'So if China is five hours ahead of Greece . . . it should be early afternoon. You are doing amazing for time.'

'Incantus, I think I sense people not too far away,' Caeli said, her arm stretched in the direction of the road further up the hillside.

'Yeah, we need to hurry,' added Blaise. He scrunched up his chocolate bar wrapper and dropped it on the ground. Demi gasped, and without a word, she pointed to the wrapper as it scuttled in the breeze. With a sigh, Blaise bent down to pick it up. As he shuffled over to the dustbin not a few metres away, he called aloud, 'I don't want to get blamed for destroying the temples.'

Through the communication disk came the sound of a chair

tipping over. 'You – you destroyed the sanctuary?' Incantus sputtered.

'Didn't you say we had to hurry?' Demi asked, crumbling beneath Incantus's stare.

Caeli took the tablet from Alexis's hand and faced it against the ground.

The white substance latched itself onto the earth, thickening as it grew with every passing second. Its colour wasn't as bright as before. Alexis wondered whether it would even make the next portal to Africa, let alone onward to South America.

'The portal should take you close to the Gem of the Air, somewhere along the mountain tops. All you have to do is jump through,' Incantus told them through gritted teeth, audibly mad still.

'Al, go first,' Blaise said, standing just behind him.

'Why me? Is it even stable?'

'About as stable as your mental state,' said Caeli.

Alexis shrugged. 'That doesn't fill me with much confidence.'

He put the disk in his pocket, drew a deep breath, then felt three hands on his back shove him forward. He extended his arms to catch his fall, but, instead, he disappeared straight through the face of the white portal.

When he opened his eyes, he wasn't on the ground. He was hundreds of metres up in the sky, freefalling fast, as if he had jumped straight out of a plane.

Without a parachute.

26

ATYCHIPHOBIA

Atychiphobia (n.) *Greek origin*
Fear of failure; fear of not being good enough

As Alexis looked down, far down, he spared a moment to wonder if he was still on Earth.

The sight was dreamlike, as if he was flying towards an enchanted forest of another world. A great valley of towering pillar-like rock columns spanned out from the ground below him, poking through the clouds. With the mist obscuring the land below, the mountain peaks almost looked as if they were floating in the sky. It was magical.

Alexis ruined it by screaming and swearing at the top of his voice as he plummeted, the sound swept away by the wind – the list of curse words wasn't exhaustive, but he made up for it with passion.

He could just about hear the distant sound of Incantus calling his name over the wind rushing past his ears. Within moments, he reached terminal velocity, a bullet shooting downwards with no way to stop, moving so fast that his breath was snatched away.

Far above him, he could hear a girl's petrified screams.

Barely able to turn his head, he saw Demi flailing behind him, her hair whipping in her face. Within seconds Demi had shot past Alexis, an arm's reach away from him. Even when facing the Creature of the Earth, she hadn't looked as terrified as she did when he failed to catch her hand.

They weren't far from the ground, less than a few hundred metres. Alexis made his body more streamlined, cutting through the sky like a diver. He felt the moisture in the clouds, the water within the fog. He pointed his hand at Demi, and the network of water molecules became denser, thicker. As Demi passed through them, instead of parting around her, they collated to meet her, cushioning her fall and slowing her descent. Demi's screams fell silent when Alexis reached her, his arms wrapping round her waist, securing himself to her like skydivers in tandem.

But they were still falling too fast. The ground was approaching too quickly.

With the top of Demi's head pressed hard against his neck, Alexis turned to see Caeli and Blaise approach them in the sky, Caeli's free hand extended outwards for him to cling onto. The mountain peaks shot by past them. Within fifty metres of the ground, Caeli still had her eyes closed in concentration.

Their plummet started to slow, but the unfamiliar act of carrying four times her weight wasn't something Caeli had practised, and they landed far harsher than intended.

Alexis slammed into the ground, snapping the branches of what felt like every single tree in the forest . The air escaped his lungs like a punch to the gut. A fall that high, at such a speed, should've shattered their bodies, but with their superhuman aura and Haven suits to absorb most of the impact, the four Elementals rolled apart from each other alive and wheezing.

The muffled sounds from the other end of the tablet in Alexis's pocket drew his attention. Groaning in pain, he pulled the disk out and let it sit in the space between them.

'You couldn't put the portal on the ground?' Demi shouted, her voice unusually high-pitched, echoing throughout the forest.

'Sorry, team!' The hologram of Incantus's face peered through the surface of the upturned screen to assess them. 'With the differences in the Earth's surface level, particularly in the mountain range, I wanted to avoid any accidental teleportation in the middle of one of the mountains.'

'I think I would have preferred that,' Blaise mumbled, his chest heaving as he lay on his back.

'Miss Doran, how did you do?'

'Yeah, she saved us all,' said Alexis.

'Barely,' Caeli moaned, combing leaves and dirt from her hair with little mercy. 'I lost my concentration . . . I should have been ready.'

'It's fine,' Demi said, sitting up. 'We're all alive. Oh, for goodness's sake, stop moaning, Blaise. You could have tried flying with fire like you nearly did that time in training.'

'I couldn't focus over the sound of you screaming,' he countered, lightly kicking her leg before getting up.

The image in the disk screen flickered once, the colour dimming.

'The power is fading,' said Incantus, cursing under his breath. 'It's not used to such great jumps. I'll ensure the National Park closes in twenty minutes so there won't be anyone around, so use whatever transport you can now whilst it is operating. Contact me when you get the second Gem or if you need help—'

He barely had time to finish his sentence before the line went flat and the infrared map display returned. The strongest light on the map came from the peak of the tallest mountain column.

'It's in that direction,' Caeli stated. She pointed to where she must be able to hear the greatest number of human voices, even over the chaotic wildlife of the forest. Without waiting for the others, she started walking.

Blaise ducked underneath the trunk of a fallen tree as he matched his strides with Caeli's. 'Could've landed us a bit closer, Cae. I haven't got the stamina for all this running and climbing.'

Without turning round, Caeli retorted, 'You haven't got the stamina for a lot of things, *Bee*.'

Taken aback by her reply, but more so by her snide tone, Blaise tilted his head at Alexis and Demi. 'Someone's in a bad mood.'

'I'm not in a bad mood. I'm in a hurry.'

'Don't take it out on me just because you had a barney with your little boyfriend of the month,' Blaise muttered. 'It's not my fault you can't use your powers properly—'

Caeli turned on him, almost knocking over Demi. 'Always talking large, but what have you done to protect any of us?' snapped Caeli, facing up to Blaise, grey eyes cold. 'Alexis stood in the way of the Creature when it was going for Demi. Demi

256

saved us all. I got us here alive. What did *you* do back there, exactly?'

Blaise huffed and pushed past her. 'I was distracting the Creature. You've probably forgotten how to work as a team after ditching us all summer for your boyfriend. I mean your ex – what number is that now?'

A gust of wind torrented into the back of Blaise, shoving him onto the jungle floor hard.

'Let's get one thing straight,' said Caeli, now hovering in the air. Her hair flew wildly. 'I'd rather die than apologise. And I certainly have never and will never apologise for who I do and don't decide to date. Don't you dare try to shame me when you do the exact same.'

'It doesn't matter who did what back there,' said Demi, standing between them as Blaise's fists started smoking. The fog and sun were relentless, and the restless journey and lack of sleep and food was slowly getting to them. Only she seemed at ease, surrounded by her element and rejuvenated by the fleeting full powers of the Earth Gem.

Alexis took Blaise's hand to extinguish the kindling flame. 'Calm down, Blaise. We're okay, that's all that matters.'

Telling Blaise to calm down was like pouring gasoline on a bonfire. Blaise snatched his hand back. 'Don't tell me what to do, Al. Stop thinking you're the leader of the group just because you and Incantus have some weird special friendship.'

'You are such a child,' Alexis replied through gritted teeth, trying to keep his cool. 'Stop burning those around you whenever you get pulled up on something you've done wrong.'

A long moment passed before Blaise spoke again. He always

had to have the last word. 'Whatever. *She* puts the "mental" in Elemental.' He lazily pointed at Caeli who had continued up ahead, using her powers to lift herself off the ground to avoid walking over the uneven shrubbery.

For the next twenty minutes, they walked in uncomfortable silence, spaced out from one another, focussing on their own paths. Few words were exchanged, and that was only when Alexis offered Blaise a swig of water which he took with a mumble of thanks.

After a while, Alexis was joined by Demi who hiked beside him, clearing the path ahead with her powers. 'We're not about to fight another Creature of the Element with everyone at each other's throats,' Demi said curtly. 'Go and make up with Blaise properly.'

'I already offered him water,' Alexis argued back, keeping his voice low.

'I don't care.' Her green eyes were luminous in the forest as she glared at him. She had tied her hair up and was using her hand to fan the back of her neck. 'Be the bigger person. *I* always am and I'm barely five foot. Don't make me tell you twice.'

If anyone else had spoken to him like that, Alexis wouldn't have been able to bite his tongue. It surprised him when he found himself smiling. 'You won't stop till I do, will you? Stubborn.'

Despite trying, she failed to keep a straight face. 'Stubborn as a rock,' she said and then pushed him towards Blaise.

'So,' said Alexis tentatively as he joined Blaise. 'What do you think a Creature of the Air is going to be?'

Blaise smirked. 'Anything but a pigeon.'

Without an apology, Alexis knew that they were back to normal just like that. Meanwhile, he eavesdropped in on Caeli and Demi's conversation as they flew metres above the boys at Caeli's command.

'I hope you're okay, Cae,' Demi said, placing her hand against her arm, her other hand clearing hanging branches out of their way.

'He got under my skin,' she said, continuing to stare straight ahead. Alexis had to strain to hear what she said next. 'But it's not just that. After Ziya told us about the Elemental Tribes earlier this week, I've not been able to stop thinking about my dad. If he was or is a member of it. If my mum was. If that means I'm half-Chinese. If my dad will somehow sense that I'm here.' Her chest deflated as she let out a deep sigh of frustration. 'What's annoying me more than anything, though, is that I've been needing to change my tampon for the last hour. This suit does a lot of things, but it isn't period-proof.'

She glanced sideways at Demi before admitting, 'I'm nervous. I just hope I can do it, you know? The way you did. It'll be a way of proving myself.'

Demi turned to face her. 'Oh, honey, you don't need to prove yourself to anyone. Least of all to us. You've got this. I know you do. Look at where we started and how far we have come. Look at you now! Flying.' She squeezed her hand. 'Don't doubt yourself now or let Blaise's frustration get the better of you. You know how much he needs you, even if picking arguments is the way he shows it.'

'You always see the best in others,' said Caeli, voicing Alexis's exact same thought.

Demi smiled as she rubbed her back in slow circles. 'With you, there is only the best to see.'

Faces glistening with sweat, neck and hands riddled with insect bites, Alexis and his friends eventually heard the excited rumble of a crowd in the distance. They approached the edge of the forest and saw thousands of tourists lined up in a huge queue before the base of a steep towering stone mountain. Built into the giant, quartz-sandstone pillars, tracing up and down its vertical cliff edge, were three huge glass elevators.

'Look,' Caeli whispered, tugging on Alexis's sleeve. She gestured to her amulet. The grey triangular stone was slightly elevated, its tip pointing in the direction of the mountain summit.

'I'm not waiting in that queue,' Blaise stated. He nudged Caeli's arm. 'Cae, can you sneak us onto one of them?'

Caeli nodded. It was the only indication that they were back to being civil. A shimmering wave rippled in the air surrounding the four Elementals as Caeli shielded them from view. They kept in a tight group, walking out from the forest and through to the noisy queue to cut in at the front.

'Bailong Elevator; hundred dragons sky lift,' one of the signs read. Alexis pointed to it, chuckling at the irony. 'Three guesses what your Creature is.'

Caeli paled.

Soon enough, the huge glass elevator emptied. A pair of park operators stood on either side, checking the visitor's passes. As the four invisible Elementals snuck through, Alexis noticed Caeli lingering. One of the park operators was staring straight at her. The woman didn't say anything. In fact, she didn't move for a while, holding up the tourists who began to wave their tickets at her impatiently. After a brief moment, she gave a knowing sort of nod. Slowly, as though giving them enough time to continue, she soon resumed checking other people's tickets.

'Was she Elemental?' Alexis asked Caeli as they found themselves in a corner of the glass elevator.

'I think so. She saw right through it.'

'Incantus should be calling to shut down and clear the Park soon.' Alexis made his way to the window so that he would have a good viewpoint of the forest through the heavy ring of mist. 'Let's hope this is the last one that goes up.'

With a great shudder, the double glass doors closed and there was a loud reeling noise of metal pulling metal. The heavy elevator began to rise into the sky, scaling the rough vertical edge of the cliffside.

'It's not that high, it's not that high,' Demi muttered to herself, squeezing her eyes shut.

'Oh my god, we're up so high!' Blaise exhaled, his hands pressed up against the glass sides.

Demi *almost* swore under her breath.

The view was spectacular as the elevator rose over a thousand feet into the sky, revealing a view of the valley of hundreds of pillared stone mountains, each jutting out from the ground.

Alexis couldn't spare a look away – nothing in Protegere could come close to this. He grabbed Demi's hand, urging her to steal a look. She must've opened her eyes, for he heard her gasp beside him before she soon shut them again as they continued into the clouds. The ride lasted less than a couple of minutes, until they drew to a halt at the peak of the mountain.

'See-through,' Demi mumbled, clinging to the sides of the railing as she stepped off the elevator. She practically jumped onto the solid earth of the mountaintop. 'They had to make the whole thing fricking see-through.'

Caeli released the shield of invisibility from round them once they were safely away from the tourists. 'Even the air up here is cleaner,' she said, sighing deeply. 'I know this is going to sound weird, but my body feels like it belongs here. My horoscope's always telling me that Libras belong somewhere in the mountains.'

Caeli's amulet had lifted higher from her chest, the metal chain round her neck tugging her along the tourist-created pathway. They followed its lead, darting between the groups of startled visitors as a siren started to ring out across the mountaintop, telling tourists to follow the Park operators down the designated hike paths.

It was coming close to an hour later when Alexis was fairly confident that most, if not all, the people on the mountain peak had at least started their descent. During that time, the Alpha team took the opportunity to go to the toilet, wash their hands and faces and, most importantly, eat.

Once satiated and hydrated, Caeli led them to the viewing deck that adjoined one edge of the steep stone cliffside. It overlooked a single prominent mountain pillar that stood alone, punching upwards through the clouds as if it was protesting for air against the surrounding sea of green. Although almost the same height, the second pillar was far narrower than theirs, its uneven top densely covered in an array of light and dark flora.

The sign from the viewing deck read: 'The South Sky Pillar; the Pillar between Heaven and Earth.'

'There,' Caeli said, pointing towards it. 'My Gem is there.'

'How do we get over to it?' Alexis asked. There was no bridge connecting the two mountaintops across the deep valley below. He took his backpack off and rested it against the wooden wall of the viewing deck, his back wet with sweat. It was frustratingly humid, so much so that he couldn't distinguish between his own sweat and the salty fog that swathed them.

'No one make any sudden movements,' Caeli ordered, shutting her eyes. 'You know what, no one even speak for a minute.'

Carefully controlling the air surrounding them, Caeli gently lifted the four teenagers into the sky. The whole time, Alexis held his breath, worried that even the slightest change in the air would distract Caeli and send them free-falling down the space between the mountains.

They jostled slightly in the winds, but Caeli held them steady, focussing to keep their trajectory as they approached the South Sky Pillar, her amulet glowing grey the moment she set foot on its peak. Demi clung to the huge trunk of the nearest tree on the mountain, hugging it with so much force that the dark bark cracked beneath her grip.

Caeli followed the pull of her amulet. The others watched her as she knelt, the ends of her silvery-blonde hair sweeping against the moist earth. In front of her, carved into a rock that lay in the centremost point of the mountain, appeared a glowing engraving identical to the symbol of her amulet.

263

'Should I do it?' she called back to her friends, not daring to look away from it. Met with silence, she swallowed hard. With a delicate touch, she pressed her amulet against the symbol.

Blinding grey light rustled the treetops of the South Sky Pillar, exploding outwards with a great gust of wind and rolling down in a ring over the edges of the mountaintop. Swift gales whirled around the peak, swirling and pulling at the sky above where Caeli stood.

It almost looked like a trick of the light at first, but the winds began to create a silhouette in the sky. The edges of its shape became clearer, carving its figure distinctively, the colour darkening into grey similar to the formation of a tornado funnel.

Her face started to take form, the detail of her gown, simple and long, identical to that of the Woman of the Earth. With a great flash of grey light, the Elementals were once again momentarily blinded.

As Alexis opened his eyes, peering through his fingers, he saw what floated in the sky in front of them. In the hands of the Woman of the Air was the second Elemental Gem.

27

NUBIVAGANT

Nubivagant (adj.) *Latin origin*
Wandering in the clouds; moving through the air

The Gem of the Air was similar to the Earth Gem; a clear, perfect stone, untarnished by time. An alluring, subtle grey, like cloud swirling within the ancient rock, mirroring the eyes of the Woman.

When she spoke, her voice was soft and airy, like the gentle breeze of early autumn. 'Daughter of my element. Here for our power.'

Caeli didn't respond. For someone who always had a comment to make, an opinion to give, Alexis found her silence unsettling.

'The Earth has been given already,' the Woman observed, nodding to Demi. 'I sense her presence has left its corporal state. And so the time has come.' The Woman swept her gaze across the forest of mountains in the clouds. Her body glowed as she inhaled the air around her, almost as if she was savouring its taste. 'My life force contains the Creature. When I pass my Gem onto you, it will be freed.'

Alexis couldn't see Caeli's face. He could only see the

downward angle of her head, her chin lowered to her chest. With that alone, he knew what she was thinking, because out of them all, she was the one most similar to him. She was doubting herself.

'Your emotions are fleeting my child,' the Woman said, raising Caeli's head with her powers. 'Yet they are still your emotions. Feel them freely in the open air – do not bury them. Order and control is not our way.'

She touched her translucent hand against Caeli's cheek, infusing it with streaks of energy that made her long hair come apart in the wind.

'*When you find that which you seek, the sky will grow dark, and your demons will come to find you.*'

Her prophecy, spoken just like the Woman of the Earth's.

Caeli finally found her voice. 'What do I seek?'

As Caeli waited for the reply they knew would never come, the Elementals felt a disturbance in the air. There was a whistling sound of something cutting through the wind, severing the stillness.

Centimentres from Caeli's face, a single black arrow whizzed past, its point shooting into the Woman's chest. Instead of impaling her, the arrow simply passed through her body, puncturing the tree trunk behind her. Caeli screamed and staggered back as the Alpha team turned to face the larger mountain they had flown from.

Standing on the viewing deck, arriving one by one, came a group of at least half a dozen people. Not people – Elementals. And they weren't there to help them.

Even from the distance, Alexis could somehow sense the

darkness within the soldiers, a shadow controlling their minds. It was a brittle iciness, one that drew the warmth from the air around it. He could sense it as easily as he could water, long before he noticed the absence of their shadows.

There remained few that seemed uninfected, having chosen their path – the path to support Mortem. Their eyes were clear, their souls uninfected but dark nonetheless.

The Shadowless had found them.

The four friends came together immediately as a thunderous chorus of arrows and bullets began firing. Demi manipulated the body of the treetops to block them from view, the bark and branches forming a protective barrier before the summit of the South Sky Pillar.

'Are they after the Gem?' Blaise shouted, pulling his axe free.

'Or us,' Alexis replied. 'We have to get off here and fight them *and* the Creature when it arrives.'

He felt the eyes of the Woman upon him and instantly felt small. Her head was angled curiously as if trying to read something on his face. It wasn't too dissimilar to how the Woman of the Earth had looked at him. There was no time for him to question why. The trees were already beginning to splinter apart under the assault. They wouldn't last long.

Caeli stomped her foot. She flipped the spear in her hand, blades protruding wickedly from either end. 'Why couldn't I just . . . be . . . normal?'

No longer light and airy, the Woman's voice rumbled with the force of a hurricane. 'I can help you. I can delay the awakening of the Creature to provide you some time to get away. Fighting it, and these opponents, however, is still a task of your own.'

The grey-glowing Woman raised the Gem to her lips and placed a kiss against its surface. Upon her touch, a thin pale layer sealed its exterior, muting the Gem's aura. She floated in front of Caeli and passed the Gem into her hands before she could deliberate whether to accept it. The stone looked masked, its powers hidden as though she needed to scratch through the surface to access it, but the hum of its energy within whirred on steadily.

As the force that kept her body together began to dissipate, the Woman of the Air looked once more at Caeli. 'Good luck, free spirit. This will not be the last time we meet.'

Her lasting words echoed as whispers as her body blew away. Her essence, a glowing grey, was pulled back into the Gem, seeping inside with a final flash in the afternoon sky.

The onslaught continued to strike the wall of trees that protected them, shattering the wood and snapping the branches. Intermixed were beams of energy, projectiles blasting the stone mountain and shaking the peak.

Blaise darted to Caeli's side and shook her out of her trance as she stared at the Gem. The thin layer was beginning to abate, unprotected breaks already appearing. Within the stone, the Creature was moving.

'The seal won't last long. We have to hurry!'

Alexis's mind raced to figure out a plan. Their location could hardly be worse – it was dangerous enough being suspended hundreds of metres up, let alone when fighting an eternal Wind Creature and the Shadowless.

'We've got to get somewhere safer to fight the Creature!'

As the treeline finally shredded apart, the broken trunks tumbling down the side of the mountain, Caeli erected a forcefield. The onslaught thudded into its side, but it held true for now. With only the shimmering wind barrier separating them from the Shadowless, Alexis squinted to get a better look at who they were up against.

Of all the Shadowless, there was one who stood out larger than the rest. A beastly man. His slanted forehead led into a large nose, and his eyes were sunken in their sockets. The bones of his chin and cranium bulged unnaturally. With one huge hand, he commanded the Shadowless to attack, and in the other, he held a cage of sorts, its contents obscured. Across the canyon, he grinned at the sight of the Elementals in peril.

'The portal device,' Demi said, her eyes darting across the South Sky Pillar. 'Where is it?'

Alexis swore, only now noticing the absence of his backpack. 'I left the bag on the viewing deck.' The rucksack had been pushed against the edge of the cliffside of the main pillar by the Shadowless. A chipped wooden fence was all that prevented it from being lost to them.

'I can't hold it much longer,' Caeli grunted. As she spoke, cracks snaked across her forcefield like a window pane about to shatter.

Demi stood in front of Caeli. 'Cover me,' she ordered.

Blaise ran to her, striking his forearms together and igniting his hands with red and yellow flames at the ready.

'What are you doing?' Alexis asked as she edged toward the uneven cliffside.

She didn't answer him. Instead, she extended her hands to the thousand feet tall canyon between the two pillars. The quartz-sandstone mountain began to shudder beneath their feet, reverberating as she squeezed her eyes shut.

Free from the protection of the dying forcefield, the huge commander barked an order to the other Shadowless. At once, they focused their assault in Demi's direction, but before any arrow or projectile came close, Blaise was there, scorching and discarding them with fireballs.

'Hurry up, whatever you're doing,' Blaise called, glancing back at Caeli to see that she had dropped her forcefield entirely. Alexis stood beside her, sword in hand, cutting through any arrow that shot their way as she caught her breath.

Suddenly, Demi's hands erupted with a wave of power. Ground and dirt, mud and soil rolled outwards in a continuous stream, clumping together in the air. They moulded into a long shape, stretching out to bridge the open expanse between the smaller pillar and the main mountaintop, a makeshift suspended walkway.

Demi was creating her element for the first time, with not even the unlimited powers of her Gem at hand.

'The other side,' said Caeli, pointing to the viewing deck.

Alexis was forced to look away from Demi to see the Shadowless rushing towards the other end of the earth-bridge, going to strike it down from where it connected to the mountain edge. Without hesitating, he pulled an arrow free from the sheath fixed to Caeli's back. Hearing Taranis's energetic voice in his head telling him to *aim through the target*, Alexis launched it across the canyon, watching as it soared through the air.

The arrowhead found one of the Shadowless, stabbing deep into his shoulder with such a force that he flew back. Alexis spared no second thought as to whether he had just killed someone for the first time, for it didn't matter. Not if his victim had sided with Mortem. Not if it was to protect his friends.

As Caeli recovered her strength and created a second shield beyond the front of the bridge, Blaise joined Alexis in throwing continuous balls of their elements towards the attackers. Only the commander with the cage did not flinch, laughing as wicked flames licked the side of his face and pellets of ice skidded past him. Impossibly, he appeared impervious to any of their Elemental attacks.

In less than a few seconds, Demi's bridge had soon fully formed, an enormous, sturdy walkway connecting the two mountain peaks. Sweat stuck her hair to her neck and her amulet ebbed with power. She briefly turned back at her friends, her foot rising to take her first step.

'Catch me if I fall,' she said to Alexis as she shifted her full weight onto her creation.

It did not break. She took another step and another, but the bridge held steady.

Alexis shrugged. 'Might as well.' With that, he joined her, pulling Blaise along with him, Caeli following. All four Elementals ran across the passage in the sky. 'You can create your own element?' Alexis called to Demi.

'I guess so,' she replied between breaths, not looking down. 'A leftover ability of the Gem.'

'Big move from you,' said Caeli.

'Huge,' added Blaise.

Once they reached the other end, Alexis swung his hands together in a single clap. The water vapour from the mist and haze around him rushed forwards, forcing back the Shadowless to allow the Alpha team space to return to the viewing deck.

'The bag's not here,' Caeli whispered.

Behind them, the earth-bridge crumbled apart, cascading through the sky towards the forest floor far below. Alexis scanned the mountaintop, but the bag with the teleportation device was no longer there.

'Don't be stupid,' growled the beastly Shadowless commander. He jostled their bag in the air, a self-satisfied, amused expression contorting his face. 'You are surrounded. Trade the Gem or I'll kill you one by one and pry it from your pretty little hand.'

Alexis glanced at the cage he was still holding. There was a vigorous scratching coming from it, the sound of claws on metal. Were there no dog-sitters in Mortem's castle? The man didn't pay it any attention, relishing in the young Elementals' fear.

'Dr Sinner,' said one of the Shadowless, approaching the general hesitantly, his head bowed. 'What of the Creature . . . has it come?'

The general didn't respond, only glared at him until he withdrew.

'The protection is wearing off,' Caeli muttered. She held the Gem delicately, as though it could bite her hand off if she squeezed too tightly.

Without warning, Blaise lashed forwards, his axe ignited in roaring flames. The blade struck the chest of the opponent facing him, sending him tumbling away. The others had no choice but to follow suit.

Alexis focussed on the water in the barrel of the bag Sinner was holding. He exploded it outwards with such a force that it should have torn the skin from the general's face. Instead, he only stumbled backwards as the rucksack struck his chin and fell from his hand. Behind him, Alexis heard the slumps of two more bodies on the ground and turned to see Caeli's spear tipped in blood, and Demi releasing her vine whip from the neck of the unconscious opponent before her.

Caeli splayed her fingers and a gust of wind swept the backpack off the floor and into her hands. She passed it to Demi who pressed her thumb against the cool, silver centre of the communication device. It flickered to life, barely having the power to open the communication line to Incantus.

Dr Sinner, defenceless besides the cage in his hand, was all that opposed them.

A wide smirk crept across his twisted face and a barking laugh escaped him. He reached down and tore off the metal padlock that secured the hatch of the cage.

From within shimmered some kind of animal, its scaly surface refracting the low-lying sunlight. It was a snake-like creature, a king cobra, but with a ratty, pointed face, and four legs that had been haphazardly stitched onto its underbelly, the skin welted and infected. It peered venomously at the young Elementals before flinching away from Sinner as he grabbed it by its neck.

Sinner pulled a vial out from his pocket and poured a green viscous liquid into its mouth, forcing it to swallow. The crossbreed creature dropped from his grasp, retching on the ground as though its insides were burning.

Demi shuddered at the sight of the animal recoiling in pain. 'You sick freak.'

From one of Sinner's flared nostrils came a trail of phlegm, dripping into his mouth as he growled. He licked it away before spitting on the ground at Demi's feet.

'You children are no match for me or my Hybrids.' He straightened, gesturing to the rat-snake still writhing in anguish in front of him. It looked like it was shedding its skin, slowly growing. From beside him, Alexis heard the muffled sound of Incantus's voice, broken in connection.

Caeli shrugged off Blaise's arm and took a step towards Dr Sinner. 'You do not scare me,' she said, eyes narrowing. 'It's me you should fear.'

With her words, a single shockwave thundered from her body. The wind rolled against the top of the stone mountain, pulling the tiles of the footpath free. The Hybrid was flung away, disappearing from view. Dr Sinner stood his ground for much of the force until the ground itself ripped away, taking him with it.

Before Sinner would have collided with the double glass doors of the Bailong Elevator, a huge blood-red portal exploded out of thin air. Sinner flew through its two-dimensional threshold and vanished in a blink. A moment later and the portal also winked out with no trace of it ever having been there.

'Who did that?' Blaise asked, spinning around.

'Not Ezra – his powers are bronze,' Alexis replied. 'But they could still be here.'

'Children!' Incantus's voice came clearly through the communication device in Demi's hand. On the ground, the white portal had been made, far smaller than the previous one. It was less stable, its edges uneven and already shrinking. 'Who was that?'

'A Dr Sinner?' Caeli said, returning to the group. 'Caveman-looking troglodyte.'

'Bigger than Akili,' Blaise added.

'He wasn't affected by our powers,' said Alexis. 'For a doctor, he clearly isn't a fan of the Hippocratic Oath. And he had this weird rat-snake creature that he poisoned in front of us – it was a weird power move, I've got to say.'

Through broken audio and buffered video on the disk's silver surface, Alexis still saw the concern on Incantus's face, and heard the panic in his voice. '*Sinner*. Is he still there?'

'No, he disappeared into a portal,' Demi said with a shiver. 'Thank goodness you told me to give you the Earth Gem when you did, otherwise Mortem would have it by now.'

'He's dangerous,' Incantus warned. 'Extremely dangerous. After his twin brother, Plague, disappeared years ago, he has operated as Mortem's second-in-command. He specialises, and relishes, in experimenting with animals, creating vile amalgamations of creatures he calls Hybrids.'

'Nice that he's got a side hustle,' Blaise murmured.

Incantus tutted. 'He took out five senior High Order operatives at Delphi barely a few minutes after you left – he is not to be joked about. Where is the beast he released?'

'Probably thrown off the mountain, or dead,' Alexis answered. 'Anyway, this won't survive another portal to get us from the Fire Gem to the Water Gem. How are we going to make it?'

'I'll either come myself or send someone from the High Order. But are you not still yet to fight the—'

Caeli's scream interrupted him, answering it in turn. 'The Gem!'

The protective shield the Woman had placed on the grey stone had faded. The Gem of the Air reverberated violently in Caeli's hands as she struggled to hold on.

There was a silent explosion, following which came an ear-piercing screech that burst from the translucent Gem. The sound was so loud it cleared the fog free from the sky, shattered the silver communication disk, and flung the Elementals back with an unbelievable force. The Gem dropped, cracking the ground where it fell just metres in front of the portal, its perimeter already withdrawing.

A loud ringing echoed in Alexis's ears, paining his unfocused mind. He looked to see that his friends had all landed somewhere across the mountaintop. Caeli had been thrown as far as the edge, barely visible over the foliage that decorated it.

The Wind Dragon burst from the Gem of the Air, crying an almighty screech that tore across the mountainous valley. It flew into the sky, flapping its humongous wings before crashing back atop the summit where they were. The entire peak shuddered beneath its weight.

Then, snarling, it turned its head toward the Elementals.

28

L'APPEL DU VIDE

L'appel du vide (n.) *French origin*
'Call of the void'; the unexplainable urge to
jump when on the edge of a cliff

First an earthquake-creating dinosaur, now a commercial plane-sized Chinese dragon.

'Thanks, Incantus,' Alexis muttered as he inched away from the Creature of the Air, not daring to take his eyes away.

Ash-coloured scales plated its serpentine body, darkening to a metallic grey towards its webbed claw-tipped wings. Thick spikes sprouted from the end of its beak and arched over its eyebrows. Much like the Earth Creature, there was a single Gem-sized unprotected area that sat in the centre of its forehead, guarded by a vertical triad of spikes. It shifted its weight on eagle-like talons, tearing through the foliage that coated the narrow mountains.

With a single beat of its wings, the unconscious bodies of the Shadowless were hurled from the stone mountaintop, disappearing over its edge. Only the Gem of the Air resisted, sitting just as still as when it had first been dropped. The Dragon's tail, tipped into a fragmented spike, curled round it as if it were its egg. Beside it, the white portal remained, growing smaller by the minute.

Demi climbed through the dense trees that lined the edges of the mountain walkway, joining Alexis and Blaise as they took shelter. In the distance, they made eye contact with Caeli who nodded.

'Distract it long enough for Caeli to get the Gem,' Alexis said in a low voice as the Dragon raised its head. 'But, Blaise, if the portal looks like it's going to close, you *have* to go through.'

'Why just me?' He asked, igniting his throwing blades. 'I'm stronger than you.'

Alexis gritted his teeth. 'Because, genius, you're the only one who can retrieve the Fire Gem from the next location.'

'Oh.'

'I saw a natural bridge connecting two peaks a little bit further down,' Demi said, wrapping up the tail of the vine whip so it wouldn't get snagged. 'It's a good vantage point to distract it. Cover me while I get there; I might be able to move the earth to get the Gem closer to Cae.'

Silently, with a squeeze of Alexis's hand, she parted from the boys.

'Ready to cause havoc?' Alexis said, turning to Blaise. The Dragon rose taller, sensing an imposing battle.

'Might as well have been my middle name,' said Blaise, setting his arms alight.

'Except it's Oluwamuyiwa.'

Blaise groaned. 'I really regret telling you that.'

The two Elementals emerged from the shelter to face the great Creature of the Air. Conducting the water from the humid sky, Alexis manipulated the streams to encircle him. The gushing blue hissed where it met the red and yellow of Blaise's fire. In unison, they hurled their elements against the Dragon.

Continuous torrents of fire poured against the Dragon's shielded underbelly, forcing its long tail to unwrap from the Gem. With faultless precision, Blaise aimed blazing throwing knives at its wings which tore through the webbing that connected them and charred at its long silvered hair.

Before the Dragon could release a scream of vicious gales, Alexis lashed the streams of water against its pointed jaw, rocking it shut.

'Dream team, baby!' Blaise shouted, his amulet burning brighter against his chest.

Just as the Dragon was about to beat its enormous wings, thick roots from the trees on the mountainside burst free from the earth. They rose taller than the trees themselves and latched onto its clawed wings, restraining it at its sides. With the Creature chained, Caeli sprinted past, taking flight to avoid the whipping tail on the way to the Gem.

The connection between the Creature and the Gem was stronger than they anticipated, however. It must have felt the amulet beating against Caeli's chest or heard the rushed sound of her breathing as she approached. With a strength far greater than the Elementals, the Dragon ferociously twisted its body in the sky, breaking free from the tree roots. Its tail thudded into Caeli's side, hurling her away where she vanished from view. With a great leap that shook the mountain summit, the Dragon rose high into the sky. Its small eyes grew colder as it hovered over the Air Gem, locating the Elementals who threatened it.

The Dragon threw its wings forwards and a rolling sound of thunder erupted across the valley of stone mountains. Alexis clung to the sturdiest-looking tree trunk beside him, but it was no use. The water dispersed and Blaise's fire extinguished like a blow to a candle as both he and Alexis were flung into the sky. Knocked semi-conscious, Alexis couldn't stop spinning, falling. Unable to do anything but wait for the impact to steal his final breath.

Alexis jolted to a halt. He reached out, but his hands caught nothing but air. When he opened his eyes, he saw that he was suspended in the sky between two mountains, floating beside Blaise.

Caeli was kneeling on the mountain peak below them, her silver-blonde hair billowing in the wind, hands outstretched in his and Blaise's direction. The muscles of her neck were taut as she strained to keep them afloat against the Creature's powers. Alexis felt the air shift around him as Caeli joined them in the sky. A whipping gale then launched them forwards.

'What are you doing?' Blaise shouted, twisting in the air, trying to escape the wind tunnel as they soared beneath the flying Wind Dragon. Its tail narrowly swept past them as it went to guard the Air Gem, but that wasn't what they were aiming for.

The portal, their only chance of escape, was narrower than a single door frame. Caeli was sending them towards it. She had lost hope; she had given up. And she would rather flee than fight.

'Caeli, don't!' Alexis called, only his voice was silenced by the thunderstorm that came from above. Whether they were headed for the Gem or the portal, the Dragon wouldn't let them get away.

With a lightning-fast swoop, it crashed back onto the mountain, shuddering the land just as Caeli, Alexis and Blaise reached the portal. A great gust of wind sent them skidding backwards, crashing on top of Demi as she raced to meet them. Alexis fought to disentangle himself, watching as the Dragon's bulk fell, about to crush them all.

With a cry, Caeli was on her feet, arms thrust upwards, stopping the Dragon from smashing into them. She nearly collapsed under the several-tonne weight, her knees shuddering.

'Get through the portal,' she screamed.

'Not without you,' said Demi, guarding Caeli's injured side. She raised her hands, attempting to push at the air as though she could form a forcefield herself.

Desperately, Alexis looked for some way out. He thought of the Woman's Prophecy – *'When you find that which you seek, the sky will grow dark, and your demons will come to find you.'*

Had this been what the Woman of the Air had meant – that when they found the Air Gem, the sky would come dark, and the Creature would come for Caeli?

With a powerful blow from its mouth, the Dragon shattered what remained of Caeli's barrier. Caeli slumped to the ground, exhausted from carrying the impossible weight. The Dragon rose once more, ready to crash down on them with the weight of a collapsing building.

'I'm sorry,' Caeli whispered, tears in her eyes. Blaise took her hand, still trying to find a way for them to escape. He hadn't given up yet. Neither had Alexis or Demi. With their weapons raised, they stood over their fallen friend and prayed that when the Dragon came down again, the metal of their blades would be strong enough to fend it off before it crushed them.

As the jaws of the Wind Dragon came to meet the Elementals, a hissing screech erupted into the sky. There was a flash of colour as a huge snaked creature flung itself towards the Dragon's neck, forcing it off-balance just seconds before it would have crushed the Elementals.

The Hybrid.

Only the potion had engorged its size, great enough to wrap its body round the Dragon's throat. It sunk its teeth into the Creature's collar and regurgitated a venomous green acid into the lesion. The Hybrid flailed as the Dragon let out a thundering shriek and took to the skies, barely keeping hold.

'Now's our chance!' Alexis shouted, scrambling away, dragging Caeli with him. He glanced back when he heard an anguished cry and saw the Dragon's clawed talons clamp down on the Hybrid's body, tearing it away from its neck.

Blaise grabbed Caeli's other arm. Between the two of them, they lifted her off the ground, half-carrying her away. As the Dragon ripped apart the Hybrid, blackish-green blood spilt over the ground where the Elementals had just been, scorching through the stones.

Alexis felt Demi's hand against his back as she pushed him on. The portal's white light was almost completely dimmed, its glow nearly transparent.

Above them, the Dragon began to lurch in the air. Whatever poison was in its system from the Hybrid's attack was starting to take effect. It was disorientated, distracted.

Alexis saw Caeli look at the Gem of the Air just as he did. It was finally unguarded, glowing fiercely only a few metres from the portal.

'Don't!'

But Caeli Doran had never been one to follow orders.

She wriggled free from his grip, tearing herself away from the portal's side. She somersaulted over the Dragon's thrashing tail and, with both hands, she took hold of the ancient grey stone and pressed it hard against her amulet.

In a surge of pure energy, the unlimited powers of the skies washed into her, making her whole body tremble. Alexis barely saw her through the torrenting winds, but he felt her presence. Her eternal presence. Her unstoppable, unlimited power.

The Dragon let out a roar. From its mouth shot huge undulating soundwaves which rolled out in piercing, circular beats. Caeli ran to intercept it before it reached her friends, sweeping her arms wide to meet the winds. She sent it hurling back towards the Dragon, forcing it to raise its wings to shield itself from the attack.

With a brief look at her friends, Caeli shot into the sky. She flew from the mountaintop at such a speed that a sonic boom exploded like a thunderclap. The Dragon followed her, dispersing the clouds with one great beat of its wings. It rose to meet her, its size dwarfing her in the open air, like a plane to a human in comparison. Only she wasn't human.

Alexis couldn't make out Caeli's face. He could only see her slender frame. Her hands became a blur, spinning torrenting gales around the Dragon, drawing the air into a tight, forceful tornado, so powerful that the Creature of the Air could barely resist twisting in the sky, using its fading might to stay level with the Elemental. She was the only thing still in the motion of the storm.

The Dragon shrieked again, but the sound was swept away by the thundering. It was confined within the vortex.

It was then when Caeli could see that it couldn't move, that it was frozen in the sky, that she hurtled her spear towards its face. Slicing through the wind, unperturbed by the storm, it found its way into the vulnerable spot of the Dragon's forehead, driving deep past the rows of protective horns.

With a silent exhale, the Wind Dragon's face fell slack, its grey eyes rolling to the back of its head. The coiling gales that formed the whirlwind dispersed and, for a moment, the Dragon stayed afloat. But when the air that suspended it scattered apart, the Creature began to fall, shot out of the sky like a bird. With every metre it picked up speed, drawing closer and closer.

Alexis shouldered Demi through the narrow portal, hearing her scream Caeli's name as she vanished. Blaise dived in straight after her, screaming even louder. Alexis cried for Caeli once more as he saw her appear, racing against the Dragon's body towards the mountain summit. She barely overtook the crashing speed at which its disintegrating corpse fell, using a lasting burst of her powers to hurtle past the Creature and snatch her spear from its head.

Alexis couldn't wait any longer for her, not before the

284

perimeter of the portal's threshold would shrink too narrow for his body to make it through. Poised to leap, Alexis stretched out his hand towards hers and jumped.

He landed on the soft ground of a rainforest floor

'Where's Caeli?' Demi asked.

In his hand, he had caught nothing but air.

Blaise scrambled to his feet, standing beneath what was left of the portal. 'Caeli!'

The portal blinked closed, and as it did, Caeli nosedived through its threshold. It closed at her feet, sealing over seconds before the Dragon's corpse would've smashed into them. She collapsed hard into Blaise, knocking him down to the ground where he caught her.

For a moment, they lay with their eyes shut, recovering. When the four friends opened their eyes again, they found themselves no longer in the mountains of China.

They were in the deep jungles of Africa.

29

TEULU

Teulu (n.) *Welsh origin*
A lifelong blessing; a family, or household; a clan, or tribe.

'Cae!' Demi cried.

She pulled Caeli towards her in a single swoop, hugging her tight. Blaise slowly sat upright, his hand pressing against the side of his head which took the brunt of Caeli's fall. Blinking hard, he joined the girls, shortly followed by Alexis, who wrapped his arms round them all.

Alexis did a head count over and over again, reassuring himself that they were all there, all together. They had made it through. Suddenly, in each other's safe embrace, the strangeness of it hit him. He wasn't alone anymore. He had friends, friends he would do anything to protect, friends he considered family.

His parents. Alexis's hadn't thought of his own family in too long a time. He had spent more time obsessing over his potential birth father than he had his actual parents who may never see him again.

The realisation of it, the sinking guilt and the shame, weighed Alexis down from within, snatching away the moment of shared relief just as swiftly as it had blossomed. What kind of son and brother was he?

Slowly, not wanting to ruin the moment, Alexis pulled away from his friends.

'You did good, Cae,' said Blaise, keeping her hand in his even after the others broke apart. 'I wasn't expecting it to be this jungle-y, especially on a mountain,' he added, scanning the environment. 'Must be somewhere in central Africa.'

The luscious sea of green vegetation surprised Alexis too. The midday African sun shone brightly through the dense, misty rainforest, its tall canopy protecting their faces from the sunlight. Through the gaps in the treeline, the vague mountaintop wasn't yet visible, its huge snow-capped peak obscured by the clouds.

'Tanzania,' Demi noted, pocketing her dagger and rolling up her vine whip. 'The mountain's got different ecosystems and climates as you go up. It looks like the portal landed us halfway through the rainforest zone. Next is moorland desert, and, at the peak, it's mostly ice glaciers.' Blaise snorted and she looked sideways at him, feigning offence. 'What? I watched a documentary with Ziya on Mount Kilimanjaro the other week. Love me a documentary,' she added quietly to herself.

Caeli attached her spear to her back. The empty Air Gem was still in her hand, her fingertips illuminating the surface where she held it. When she spoke, her voice travelled clearly through the air. 'How long would it take to climb?'

'Depending on the route, on average seven days I think,' Demi answered.

The heat and suffocating humidity was taking its toll on

287

Alexis. He struggled to follow the conversation. Tiredness coupled with anxiety in a chaotic marriage that drugged his overworked and hyperactive mind.

'Seven days?' Blaise repeated, flopping onto the soft jungle floor. 'The solstice is in two days and Incantus said we can't win without all four Gems.'

'Experienced climbers have done it in less than six hours,' Demi added, stifling a yawn. 'Not that I'm an athlete by any stretch.'

Caeli's lips curved into a slight smile. 'But you *are* an Elemental.' She tilted her head to the side in challenge. It was enough to make a weary Demi grin.

From his backpack, Alexis passed out the small healing crystals, handing one each to Demi and Blaise. Caeli, with the full powers of the Gem of the Air, had no need to re-energise.

'With the time difference from China, it's just after midday here. We could try to reach the summit by nightfall,' Alexis suggested. Although he knew it couldn't heal homesickness, he pressed the crystal to his chest, so he could feel its warmth and imagine it was his mother's embrace.

'How do we even know the Fire Gem is up there?' asked Demi. She stretched her neck to take in her surroundings, smiling at the jungle alive with life, flora and fauna alike. 'The communication device is destroyed and we can't contact the Haven.'

Blaise spoke with certainty. 'It's up there.'

Caeli nodded. 'I don't know how to describe it, but I feel like my Gem is drawn to the other one. Plus, the mountain's a volcano, and when is it ever easy?'

Blaise chuckled emptily, groaning as he got up. 'We should've taken out travel insurance for this bloody trip.'

For a long time, it didn't feel like they were scaling the tallest free-standing mountain in the world. After a while, though, Alexis noticed the change in the air. It was becoming thinner, the shift in altitude beginning to make him nauseous even with his Elemental adaptions and extensive training.

Soon enough, a dry rocky trail replaced the land underfoot, moss-covered trees traded in for great heather shrubs and tall grasses. Alexis felt little to no moisture to draw from, not the sky nor the earth. Although his Haven suit was designed to prevent them from overheating, it felt tight and uncomfortable, the dry air now hurting his throat. From the look of his friends, they weren't faring much better.

'We should break for a bit – to eat and rest,' he suggested, the first spoken words in over an hour. 'We'd be useless fighting another Creature of the Element like this.'

Demi nodded, loosening the headscarf she had fashioned to protect her scalp from burning. She lay on the slanted mountainside and pressed her hands against the surface to draw from the earth's strength. Around her budded a ring of tiny white Everlasting flowers.

When Caeli spoke, her suggestion caught Alexis so off guard he thought she was joking. 'I'll carry us up.'

The others turned to her.

'This direct sunlight is really drying out my skin,' she added, pointing to red blotches on her cheeks. 'With the Gem's power, I feel like I've got an unlimited amount of energy. And I know what Incantus said about giving it to him for safekeeping so I don't unconsciously cause any natural disasters elsewhere in the world, blah blah blah . . . but there's no way for us to contact him. Its powers are safest with me using it. Might as well get us to the top with it.'

'I'm in,' Blaise called. He slung his arm round Caeli's waist and pulled her into a hug. 'Wish you'd suggested it earlier.'

'If you're up for it Cae, then sure,' said Alexis. He extended an arm towards Demi. She dusted her hands on her suit before taking it. 'I mean, if you can make a tornado, you can fly us up a mountain.'

Caeli smirked, creases forming at the edges of her mouth. 'I'd be lying if I said I didn't want to try my powers out. It's fun being the undisputed powerhouse of the group, even though, to be honest, I already was.'

All three of them began arguing with her, but she entertained none of it, stilling the air between them so the sound of their voices failed to reach her ears.

Demi let her actions speak louder than her words. Using her powers, she tugged a wide slab of earth from the mountainside, large enough to seat them all. Through haggard breaths, she curtsied sardonically.

Once Caeli appeared confident with flying the rock platform, tracing the odd plateaus and steep inclines, she took a seat beside her resting friends. It wasn't exactly comfortable, but it was better than walking, and no one complained, not even Caeli.

Despite his tiredness, however, Alexis couldn't sleep. Behind him, he could just about make out the faint whispered conversation between Caeli and Blaise as they lay next to one another. He was glad they were on speaking terms again.

For the first time, now more than ten thousand feet elevated into the sky, the snowy white peak of Mount Kilimanjaro finally emerged, breaking through the cloud line. It stood impossibly far away, and yet Alexis knew that they would likely reach it within the half hour, just in time for nightfall.

Peering over the edge of the floating platform, he could make out the great rainforest below that enclosed the first zone of the mountain, the huge setting sun level with them on the horizon. It set the sky ablaze with colour, a canvas of pastel blue and pink and peach. Alexis breathed it in with a slight smile on his face, and admired the primal, natural beauty of the world beyond Protegere, a sight more encapsulating than anything he thought could be possible.

Until Demi arrived.

'Incredible, isn't it?' came her soft voice.

She took a seat beside him, the side of her leg brushing against his. Alexis expected her to move it away, but she never did. As she closed her eyes to feel the last of the sun's heat, Alexis couldn't help but sneak a look at her. The curl of her long eyelashes, the radiant glow of her skin, the line of her jaw. *She was more captivating than a thousand sunsets*, he thought, sleep in her eyes and hair a mess nonetheless. The greatest proof thus far that there was a God.

'I wish I saw the world the way you did,' said Demi, watching as the clouds rolled overhead, their underside glowing burnt orange, their top an outline of shadow. 'The way you take it all in like it's the first time you're truly seeing it.'

Alexis made a low humming noise, neither agreeing or disagreeing. If she knew how he truly saw the world, she would not wish for it. Demi didn't look out for shadows at every corner nor was she forced to contemplate if what she experienced was even real. The purity with which she saw the world was something he envied more than words could express. So, instead, he said something he did know how to say.

'Every night, from as young as I could remember, I would stay up to watch the sunset.' He ran his palm across the edge of the slab of earth, crumbling dry pieces of dirt between his fingers. 'I'd pray for it to last longer, hoping for the day to never end – hoping for the night to never come.'

It was a half-truth. He didn't want to reveal that after a lifetime of living in the dark, he was worried that the light of day had become blinding. That there was comfort in sadness, in darkness, for it was constant, unlike the fleeting nature of hope.

Demi untied her hair from its ponytail. From sweat and humidity, her unruly curls had returned, coming down in thick brown waves over her shoulders. 'Ziya once mentioned that all Elementals are born with the innate fear of the dark. For some reason, when she told me that, my mind went to you. I didn't think you would be. To be honest, I wonder if you're scared of anything.'

She was looking at him, but Alexis was unable to meet her eyes. What she had said was so far from being true. He was scared of everything. He was scared to sleep out of fear of the nightmare. He was scared to wake out of fear that his whole life and everyone he held dear would turn out to be nothing more than a hallucination. He was scared to love out of fear that he would destroy it, that it wouldn't last. Most of all, he was scared of the darkness because of how familiar he felt with it.

'What we fear about the dark is not being alone in it,' he found himself saying, his eyes on the distant trees of the rainforest, their silhouettes standing black with the setting sun behind them. 'It is the very opposite.'

The memory of the *Shadow Man* hung before him, as it had that night in the Haven, the night Mortem had come. Just like the trees before the sunlight, it stood out, clearer than anything.

Was it real? Had his visions as a child been a manifestation of an illness – or had he been afflicted by Mortem's shadow, something his mortal parents were blind to? Now that he was a part of this world, would the *Shadow Man* come back?

Demi took his hand, and as she did, she pulled him out of his memories, grounding him the way she always did.

'Then we'll have to make sure we spend forever chasing sunsets, Lexi,' she said, looking from his amulet to his eyes. To his lips.

Despite the sun dipping past the horizon, a rush of heat spread across Alexis's cheeks. He forced himself to swallow, fearing his voice would betray him if he didn't. 'What did the Woman of the Earth say to you in Greek? I recognised two words: *Agape* and *Thanatos*. Love and death.'

Demi smiled to herself. 'Nothing I plan on listening to.'

They were sitting so close to each other, close enough for Alexis to feel her breath, to see her pulse thrumming in her neck. Close enough to question why she hadn't yet moved away.

Demi blinked slowly, and asked gently, 'Why won't you kiss me?'

Alexis thought his heart would explode if it beat any faster. He reached out to tuck a loose curl behind her ear, and then slid his calloused hand against the curve of her neck. She leaned into his touch. His voice dropped so low that he wasn't sure she could even hear him. 'Because once I start, I fear I won't ever be able to stop.'

Demi looked into his ocean eyes with an intensity that set his body electric, that made him think, *If this is a dream, please don't wake me.* Alexis didn't know how long they stayed like that, but he wished that just like the sunset, the moment wouldn't ever end.

'I won't ask you to,' she said eventually.

She leant in, or maybe he drew her towards him – he wasn't sure. But inches away from each other, they heard a gasp from behind. It broke the moment, shattering it into a thousand shards that each made its way to Alexis's heart as Demi pulled away.

'Shit!' Caeli gasped again, scrambling to an upright position as she turned to face Alexis and Demi. Her eyes darted between them. 'Sorry,' she said, a guilty look passing across her face. 'Sorry. I just thought of something we hadn't considered. You know how Mortem used to have your powers, Alexis?'

Alexis cleared his throat, steeling himself as Demi shuffled away from him. 'Yeah. Incantus said he gave them up to unleash his dormant darkness powers.'

Caeli nodded, her eyebrows lowered in thought, her fingers playing with the ends of her hair. 'Does that mean he'd still be able to use Water Gem's power? If he finds it before we do, would he be able to use it?'

Alexis frowned. 'I hadn't considered that,' he admitted. 'Maybe he could.'

'I still don't get it,' said Blaise with a weary shake of his head, joining them. 'There should have only been *one each* of the Children of the Elements. How could Mortem have been born a hundred years before the rest of us? And how do *you* have the same power he used to?' Blaise scratched his jaw where tight dark hairs were starting to grow in patches. 'If I'm being honest, Al, I'm surprised you don't have more questions about it all.'

Demi kept her gaze on the ground, sweeping her palm against its rough surface in circles. Alexis knew she wouldn't ever pressure him to reveal his secret, to tell the others what he had told her beneath the old oak tree in her room weeks ago about his potential father.

Alexis thought that was what he wanted. He hated sharing anything about himself that might make him look strange, an outcast, especially not in this world where he felt more than ever that he at last fit in. Just like the ocean, most of its depths remained concealed, hidden in darkness. He preferred it that way.

Or at least he used to.

During the quest, he felt closer to his new companions than any another person outside of his family. The threat of death and danger had drawn the bonds that tied them even tighter. Maybe if he told them, it might lighten the heaviness inside him.

'There's something I have to tell you guys.' Alexis's hands shook so much that he could barely tap his fingers to his thumbs. He wasn't sure if it was the altitude or nerves, but he felt as if he was breathing with just one lung. 'Please promise me you won't hate me for it . . .'

He unzipped his bag and pulled free the old photograph that had been left in his bedroom at the Haven.

He then handed it to his friends and spilled his secret.

30

TROUVAILLE

Trouvaille (n.) *French origin*
A valuable discovery; a lucky find

A great expanse of desolate rocky desert was passing beneath them, the penultimate zone of the mountain. Huge volcanic rocks and boulders spewed from previous eruptions lay along its steep mountainside, frozen by the approaching sub-zero temperatures as they drew closer to the summit. As the sky fell swiftly under a blanket of darkness, thousands of white stars dotting the sky, Blaise ignited a small fire in the centre of the rock platform to keep them warm.

'So Mortem is your dad?' Blaise said, the first person to break the long silence.

'I – I think so,' Alexis said.

'It would explain a lot,' Caeli admitted. She took the photograph from him to inspect it. The floating rock trembled for a moment before she steadied it again. 'How you look similar, where you got your powers from, the reason why he called you out personally when he met us. It also explains why you've avoided mentioning his name since last night.'

Alexis hadn't noticed. Mortem occupied his thoughts so

much, why couldn't he bring himself to say his name?

'Mortem's eyes are identical to yours too,' said Demi, her voice rather quiet as though she didn't want to say it aloud. She began to tidy up the disposable food containers, packing them away as she added, 'Same pattern of blue and black.'

Alexis took the photo back and carefully returned it to his bag. 'If it was Incantus who left the photo for me to find, he must be waiting for me to come to him.'

Caeli leant back from the group slightly, the sunset casting shadows from her prominent cheekbones. 'I asked Incantus to look for my dad too,' she said hesitantly. 'To see if there was a reason why he took off before I was born. He said to ask my mum.'

Alexis hadn't even asked Caeli about her father, that she too might have wondered who and where he was.

'Looks like we've both got deadbeat dads,' he said, extending his palm to her. Caeli wiped her nose with her sleeve and reluctantly high-fived him.

'Incantus plans on putting him down for ever – you okay with this?' Blaise asked. He tried to make his question sound casual, as though there was anything casual about it.

Alexis thought back to how Mortem had first vowed to let him lead by his side. How easily he had lied before they had overpowered him. His final promise to plunge them into darkness forever. He wasn't a man that deserved redemption, father or not. There was nothing Mortem could give him that he didn't already have, except answers, right?

'I stand by Incantus,' Alexis stated. He had hoped that saying it aloud would validate it and convince himself that it was truly what he wanted, but his reply left him more undecided than ever.

The four friends split into pairs soon after for the remaining few thousand feet as they passed into the final arctic zone, the temperature falling far beneath freezing. The only warmth came from the crackling bonfire in the centre of the rock stage.

'What is it, Blaise?' Alexis asked lightly, noting the jittering of his legs.

Blaise closed his eyes in a long blink before he answered, almost whispering it so the others wouldn't overhear him. 'Why didn't you tell me? I thought – I thought you would've told me.'

'I didn't want to tell anyone. I wasn't even sure I could admit it to myself.'

'Yeah, I understand – I just . . . I know I make a lot of jokes about being the strongest and the toughest. I also know that you see through that most of the time.' Blaise shrugged, unable to sit still. 'I know you've already got a brother, and that you may only be friends with me because you have to, but . . . I guess I'm saying that if you wanted, I could be your brother too.'

Blaise didn't turn to him fully, so Alexis met him halfway. Alexis clasped his hand, the Elementals of water and fire, each element's natural weakness, and they drew from one another only strength and power. Alexis almost felt their amulets humming as one.

'Wait.' He pointed to Blaise's amulet as the red stone flickered alight. *'Look.'*

The triangle-shaped amulet levitated from Blaise's chest, pointing towards the volcano summit. The peak flattened out, an uneven horizontal plain. In the distance, kilometres away on the opposite side of the crater rim were the glaciers, a magnificent wall of ice and snow barely visible in the darkness. Blaise's amulet was pointing down, however, towards the centre of the ashen, smoking crater.

Caeli steered them in the direction of Blaise's amulet, barely holding it steady in the turbulent gales. Despite the insulating properties of his Haven suit, Alexis found himself shivering once they jumped free from the hovering rock dais, fresh snow crunching beneath his boots, the smell of sulphur swathing the summit in a suffocating fog. Blaise used the last of the dying firepit to ignite his hands into flames, casting light onto the centre of the crater before them.

The ash pit was huge, a few hundred metres wide, ending in a sunken tip. Coiling fumes rose from its base and trailed into the black skies. Alexis shuffled as close to the rim as possible to get a better look, doing his best to hold his breath and taking each step with caution as the combination of loose sand and ice threatened to scatter beneath him.

'You've got to be kidding me,' Alexis heard Blaise say.

His face was illuminated by the fire that burned at his fingertips. His amulet, still raised above his chest, pulled at the chain fastened round his neck. Its tip pointed downwards, towards the bottom of the ashpit, into the heart of the volcano.

31

ZUGZWANG

Zugzwang (n.) *German origin*
'Compulsion to move'; a situation where every
possible move or decision is a bad one, or one that
will result in damage or loss

'"Go on a quest, find the lost Elemental Gems, retrieve your full powers,"' mocked Caeli in Incantus's voice. 'And I can't even put "saving the world" on my uni applications so honestly what's the point?'

'I'll go first,' Blaise offered, much to everyone's surprise.

'Have you been imprinted or something?' Alexis asked in disbelief.

Blaise blinked a couple of times. 'That's literally "dark humour." I'm the only one resistant to fire, and it's my Gem anyway. And –' he grinned – 'I'm the strongest of the group.'

Blaise bunched his fists, rolled back his shoulders and trudged into the sunken ash pit. He soon reached the base, standing over the vent from which the fumes rose.

'I'll lower you through the vent and you can tell us what you see,' said Caeli, her lips pinched together with worry. 'We wouldn't want you to fall and damage the volcano with your head, would we?'

Blaise blew her a kiss.

She slowly lifted the air beneath him. Blaise hovered into the sky, unsteady at first, his arms wavering. As Caeli lowered her hands, Blaise simultaneously dropped, passing through the steaming vent of the volcano and disappearing from view.

Alexis couldn't bear to wait for a response. He skidded down the sides of the ash pit closer to where he had last seen Blaise, wishing he had gone first to make sure it was safe.

'Blaise!' he shouted.

'I'm all right!' came Blaise's voice, a series of fading echoes following it. 'Cae, you can let me go – there's a pathway just below me!'

'Are you sure?' she called, floating herself and Demi down beside Alexis.

'Well I wouldn't want you to drop me if there was lava, would I?'

'It's actually magma when it's underground,' Alexis muttered.

There was a faint thudding sound, like that of a weight landing on something hard, solid. 'It's safe for you to come down,' he called.

One by one, Caeli carried the rest of the Elementals through the vent and into the volcano. Once inside, Alexis immediately felt the little breath in his lungs snatched away. The claustrophobic, scorching heat was a drain on his powers and energy.

'Over here.'

He turned to see Blaise standing on some sort of ledge made out of hardened rock. It extended from the edges of the sloped wall, curling downwards in a huge spiral round the interior of the volcano's hollow chamber.

'You look like you're going to throw up,' said Blaise, helping Alexis onto the rocky platform. They both moved away from the exposed edge, keeping flat against the moist, rugged wall.

'Fire is water's opposite,' Alexis gasped. 'Not my ideal holiday destination, but I'll be fine.'

Unable to satiate his curiosity, Alexis peered over the side and looked down over the empty cavern. The base of the volcano was too far down to be seen, its faint orange glow darkened by the rising columns of smoke that Caeli had to blow away to prevent asphyxiation. Daggered stalactites lined the insides of the cave's wall, hanging from its sides like giant arrows pointing down.

'The earth we're standing on is weak,' Demi said, tying her bushy hair from her neck. 'I'll go first to make sure it can hold our weight. Follow me *exactly*.'

It was a painfully slow descent, but at least it was safe – as safe as things could be when travelling through the inside of a volcano. The further down they walked, the more the heat intensified, growing to an almost sweltering level. Alexis felt weaker with every step. Caeli stayed beside him, steadying him so he wouldn't faint or fall, though she was also clearly affected by the enclosed space. Their adaptive Elemental lifeforce was barely protecting them. In fact, once the sight of bubbling red and yellow molten rock came into view, only Blaise didn't seem close to collapsing.

After what felt like hours, the pathway widened, flattening to a plateau. The scorched rocky trail bled onto a huge platform that sat in the centre of the magma chamber, surrounded by a moat of raging, bright orange. Thick streams of gas rose around the rim of the podium, enclosing the Elementals in a hazy stage of burning steam. Riddled across the base of the earth stage snaked worm-like cracks of liquid fire, decorating its surface with glowing lines of yellow. If he wasn't so exhausted, Alexis would have marvelled at a view he was certain he would never see again.

Dozens of stalagmites protruded from the ground in an array of miniature pyramids, jagged and disfigured from the blistering heat. One stood apart, taller than the rest, in the heart of the stage. It was the very one that Blaise's amulet desperately pulled towards.

Blaise held the hot stone tightly in his fist as he raced towards the rock, dodging the thin magma rivulets, unfazed by the soaring temperature.

'I think this is it,' he said, not looking back. 'Don't worry, guys, we'll get out of here as soon as I get it.'

Through clouds of smoke, Alexis could make out the faintly glowing engraving that appeared on the front of the stalagmite before Blaise. It matched perfectly with the back of Blaise's amulet, lining up with its triangular shape as he pressed it down.

A violent ripple beat against the underside of the platform, throwing the Elementals to the ground, trapping them as though they were on a life raft in the centre of a whirlpool. Another detonation came from below. From where he lay, Alexis saw a thick tendril of magma burst from the sea of fire from the far side of the stage. It swirled in a blistering column, growing hotter and brighter as it approached the huge stalagmite.

Fire poured over the stone, casting a blinding flash of vermillion light. Barely blinking away the brightness, Alexis's vision finally focussed to see what now stood before them. The column of magma had been transformed.

In its place stood the Woman of the Fire.

She bore a resemblance to her sisters. An eternal presence, an overwhelming aura. A loose gown was draped over her shimmering body, its colour flickering between scarlet and gold. Wisps of burning embers drifted from her. Like a fiery inferno, there wasn't a moment of stillness about her. She was beautiful. She was dangerous.

The Woman channelled her gaze to Blaise, her eyes a deep shade of swirling crimson, just like the glinting Gem in her hands and amulet in his. She then glanced over at the others.

Alexis thought her gaze lingered on him, just as the other two Women had, with a look of almost . . . confusion. And this time, he wasn't the only one that had noticed. Demi followed the Fire Woman's eyes, and too looked at Alexis curiously.

The Woman's smoky voice reverberated against the walls of the great volcano. 'You are over halfway through your journey in retrieving our powers; *your* powers. It is now that I bestow the Gem of the Fire to you, my child.'

Blaise looked up at the flaming statue of the Woman, his head slightly shaking. He barely managed, 'C-can I beat the Creature?'

On the Woman's face, a smile slowly caught, illuminating the area. 'All it takes is a spark to start a fire. Let yours burn brightly, my child. Without fear, without restraint, without concern for those in your path who cannot bear the heat.'

Blaise could only nod in response. Behind him, Alexis was struggling to stay conscious. The heat and fumes were overwhelming his senses. His knees buckled and he hardly caught himself, keeping to his feet with the help of Demi and Caeli.

'After this, only the Gem of the Water remains.' Once again, the Woman's eyes found Alexis. 'Always be careful with the water, for it can be shrouded in shadows. No one truly knows what remains hidden within the dark depths of the seas.'

Despite the prospect of being burned alive, Alexis was unable to bite his tongue. 'What's that supposed to mean?'

Demi tugged on his arm but he ignored her, holding the Woman's fiery stare.

The redness of the Woman's aura deepened to a rich magenta. 'We were born from darkness, my sisters and I. The eldest of us feared it would attempt to destroy us and the light we created by corrupting us from within. She feared it would come for me, for fire holds no shadow. Instead of paying so much attention to my element, she should have focussed on her own.'

Demi asked something, but her voice sounded too far away for Alexis to register. Instead, his mind fought to comprehend what the Woman was saying.

Corrupting us from within.

There was only one person it made Alexis think of. Mortem. The Elemental who possessed the power over both water *and* darkness.

Was it possible that Alexis shared the same vulnerability as his father, the same affliction? He forced out the words. 'Is

306

there an inherent link between the darkness and water?'

'That is a question for my sister, not for me,' the Woman replied bluntly. Her chin jutted away from him with notable distaste and the tone of finality was clear in her voice.

Blaise had half-turned to Alexis, his head tilted in question, dark eyebrows knitted together. He didn't see the Woman reaching out until she had passed the glowing Fire Gem into his hands. He jolted with surprise, her searing hands on top of his, their colour shining brighter at his contact.

She leant into him, her eyes burning with passion. 'Your friends may have mellowed you, but always keep your spark alight. You were never meant to be contained.'

She then lowered her voice and revealed the words of his prophecy.

'Beware, for your fire will be the first to go dark.'

'What do you mean "go dark?"' Blaise asked, his voice broken, unsteady.

The Woman took a step back and smiled once more as her skin turned to ash, smoke rising from the glowing embers that remained of her body. Fire took hold of her gown, the heat so great that the rock underneath began to melt and smoulder.

'What do you mean "go dark?"' Blaise repeated, staggering toward the blaze.

'It will not be long before we are reunited,' the Woman said, the sound no longer coming from her mouth, but spoken as if coming from the fire itself. With a lasting flash, her body returned to the column of spinning red magma, its essence flooding into the Fire Gem within Blaise's hands.

In her absence, the light from the chamber withdrew to

gloomy darkness, the only illumination coming from the Gem of Fire and the magma surrounding the podium.

Blaise turned to his friends. The surface of his dark skin was coated in a sheen of sweat and his eyes were wide and glistening. Panic soaked his voice as he shouted once more, 'What did she mean the first to "*go dark*?"'

He took a step towards his friends, and they towards him. But before he could take a hold of Alexis's extended hand, the Fire Gem furiously pulled him away. It thrust Blaise with a force greater than he could resist, like he was nothing more than an ember in the wind, weak and weightless. The Fire Gem soared over the rock podium and hurled itself – and Blaise – into the red sea of molten magma.

Blaise Ademola disappeared into the heart of the volcano before he could say another word, his body vanishing without a trace.

There was a scream. It was an ear-splitting, heart-breaking cry that filled the cavern, shattering the field of stalagmites across the podium. Alexis only heard its echo, some part of him registering that it came from Caeli.

And then came another deafening screech that erupted from the heart of the volcano. It came from the Gem submerged beneath, from the Creature that no longer lay asleep within.

32

ANASTASIS

Anastasis (n.) *Greek origin*
Resurrection

'*The first to go dark.*'

Alexis thought it to be too cruel for Blaise's prophecy to come to light just moments after the Woman spoke it. For the Fire Gem to be responsible for the death of the person he had bled and fought and laughed with. The person who had started out as his rival but who had quickly become his friend, possibly even his best friend.

It wasn't a physical pain as such that Alexis felt, but rather a gaping hopelessness that spread across his body, a feeling worse than the horror the world or his mind could show him.

Caeli had broken from his side to run to where Blaise once stood, falling to her knees. 'We have to do something!' she cried.

Demi's voice came out dull, heavy with shock. 'I don't think anyone could have survived that,' she said, her eyes fixed on the bubbling molten magma beneath the earth's edge as she joined Caeli. 'Not even Bee.'

As Alexis stood beside them, Caeli looked up at him once,

her eyes filled to the brim with tears. He sunk to his knees beside her before pulling her into a tight hug. A ragged, breathless cry escaped from her as he held her whilst Demi stroked her trembling hands through her silver hair.

'Stupid powers,' Caeli muttered, shaking her head against his shoulder. 'This whole thing was a mistake. We should've just gone *home*.'

Near the three friends, over the cliffside where the magma lay beneath, arose the sound of something swirling, something bubbling. Alexis caught a glimpse of what was happening before the heat of the steam scolded his face, making him jerk away. The moat around them was stirring as if it was being manipulated.

'*Blaise?*' Caeli shouted, freeing herself from Demi and Alexis so she could see over the edge of the uneven earth stage. She was caught short just centimetres away from reaching it. 'He's not dead, I know he isn't—'

Exploding from the surface of the magma broke free a magnificent Fire Phoenix.

Its body dripped with liquid flames as it flew into the hollow volcano chamber. Before Caeli could cast a protective shield, a droplet of magma splashed onto her upper thigh. She cried out, falling back in shock as it seeped through the weaving of her suit, burning her flesh.

With the earth platform shaking from the rippling luminescent sea, fissures snaking out, Demi struck her palms against its surface to keep it intact. 'The volcano's become active!' she screamed, gasping as another surge nearly rocked her off her feet.

The Fire Phoenix continued to ascend and dive, circling the inside of the volcano, dipping in and out of the billowing fumes as they wafted through the air. Feathers, burning as individual flames, layered its pointed wings, painted deep orange with wisps of black smoke rising from its tips. Its torso was shaded crimson, so hot that it appeared to be shimmering.

The huge Fire Bird squawked, spitting fire against the inside of the volcano, splitting its side. Alexis shielded Demi from the debris and molten showers, praying that his aura would protect her.

The Phoenix had turned its head to them. Long, dark feathers lined its brow line, creating the base of a burning triangle on its forehead. There, like the Earth Beast and Wind Dragon, lay a small, Gem-sized area, free from shield and fire. Alexis knew there was no way he would be able to get close enough, Haven suit or otherwise, without burning to a crisp.

The Phoenix locked its crimson eyes on an injured Caeli before squawking once more, flames shooting skywards from its beak. With a great swoop, it began to dive, moving so fast that trails of fire were left hanging in the air like the fading remnants of a firework in the night.

The platform trembled again from the rousing volcano, active after thousands of years of dormancy. The disturbance threw Alexis down before he could reach Caeli. He crawled forwards with the last of his energy, biting back a scream as his muscles burned, as though they were on fire with a heat as great as the magma itself.

'Caeli! You have the Gem's powers!'

She was not weak; she had only forgotten just how powerful she really was.

Caeli screamed, and her amulet exploded with limitless power.

In a huge wave of celestial energy, the Phoenix was thrown away faster than the speed of sound. It crashed into the side of the volcano, colliding with it so hard that the mountain trembled, almost cracking upon impact.

With a dying look into Caeli's gleaming grey eyes, the body of the Phoenix erupted into a bright blue flame, and disintegrated into a cloud of burning ash.

The glowing cinders drifted down, floating to the rock platform and the magma pool, flickering out one by one. As Alexis drew to unsteady feet, Demi by his side, he saw a shimmering Caeli glide down to their level.

'Did you do it?' Demi asked, looking around wildly. She examined the scarring on Caeli's leg which was already starting to heal itself. 'Has it been destroyed?'

Alexis watched, frowning, as the ashes slowly took to the air, collating together in a large burning cloud, almost as though it were being picked up by the wind.

'Are you doing this, Cae?' Demi asked.

'No,' Caeli said, shuffling backwards, expression uneasy. 'Maybe it's Blaise!'

The colour of the ashes changed. Lines of red embers reignited, twisting across the surface.

Alexis grabbed at Caeli's arm to pull her back, but she shook him off. 'He's still alive,' she protested. 'I can *feel* it. I can sense he's still with me!'

The cloud behind her exploded into purple and red flame, striking the Elementals onto the jagged rock surface.

'The Phoenix,' Alexis coughed, spluttering blood and vomit. 'It can be reborn.'

Emerging from the cloud of ashes in front of them, the fully-fledged Phoenix once again took flight. Caeli and Demi gasped as the resurrected Creature landed on the platform before them, its talons cracking the earth beneath.

It looked stronger, more fierce. The fire of its body scorched hotter than before, a burning magenta, scorching the walls of the volcano.

'Go,' Caeli whispered, nudging them back, not breaking eye contact with the Fire Creature. 'You're no help down here. Get to the crater while I hold it off and help from there.'

'Don't get all selfless now,' Demi replied through gritted teeth, unsheathing the curved dagger by her side. Alexis followed suit, the coolness of his bronze and steel sword comforting in his grip no matter how frail he felt. He closed his eyes, trying to feel for the coldness of the glaciers that sat at the crater so far above. He begged his element to obey his command, to come forth to him . . .

The Phoenix roared skywards. Fumes charred the rock walls, melting the stalactites and thinning the hollow inner mountainside. With a fire that hot, like that of a contained supernova, there would be no way they could survive a direct blast. Not even Caeli's powers could protect them from it. Their luck had expired.

The Phoenix flexed its immense wings, the purple of its torso spreading across its wingspan. With a great scream from

313

its beak and a flap of its ablaze wings, a mirage of shimmering fire shot toward the Elementals. Alexis closed his eyes as he felt the heat approach.

Only the fire never met them and the pain never came.

Alexis waited, holding Demi's hand so tightly that he was sure he had broken her bones. Slowly, he opened his eyes to see through the rising smoke.

Hovering in the air, his back to them, was Blaise.

His arms were spread wide, containing the impossible temperature of the Phoenix's fire. Beside him, resting against the earth, lay the Fire Gem, its power disconnected and transferred.

'My fire was never meant to be contained,' Blaise muttered, absorbing the onslaught, a shield protecting his friends. The Woman of his Element's words echoed around the volcano.

Caeli squeezed Alexis's arm in disbelief. Somehow, she had known all along that he hadn't left her. That Blaise would return, baptised by fire.

Rising. Like a phoenix from the ashes.

33

INCALESCENT

Incalescent (adj.) *Latin origin*
Growing hotter or more ardent; set ablaze

The Phoenix's fire gradually withdrew, leaving embers dancing in the air, fading remnants of crimson flame. Its small, burning eyes turned almost cold as it stared at the Elemental who wore the red-stone amulet.

'You can't handle the heat!' Blaise's laughter filled the cavern and rebounded against the walls in a chorus of pride and power.

With the Phoenix distracted, it didn't seem to notice the giant slab of ice plunging through the air from the volcano's summit. Alexis was teetering on the border of unconsciousness, but the hard work of breaking the glacier apart was done. All he had to do was aim.

Alexis shifted its trajectory at the last second, and the glacier crushed the Fire Bird to the ground with a sickening thud, extinguishing its flames.

The Creature fell silent without so much as a squawk.

'Blaise!' Caeli screamed, scrambling to her feet. She leapt into his open arms, her aura smothering the fire that encapsulated his body just in time. He picked her up, swinging her around with ease before allowing her to stand back on the ground. Her hands found either side of his face, searching his eyes. Just as Caeli and Demi had, Blaise brimmed with an incalescent glow with the Gem's powers, his amulet shining valiantly.

Demi ran forth and hugged them both tightly, too overwhelmed to contain her joy any longer. Blaise's eyes then met Alexis's across the rocky platform, and both girls stepped aside to allow the two to embrace.

'I was worried that you—' Alexis started, his voice catching in his throat. He placed his hand on the back of Blaise's head, pressing against it hard, making sure he was real. 'We thought you were dead. Except for Caeli. Miss Optimistic just knew you were alive.'

They slowly broke apart. Blaise and Caeli exchanged a look that was oddly shy.

'It'll take more than being thrown into volcano lava to kill me,' Blaise boasted.

'It's actually magma,' Alexis repeated quietly.

Blaise took a breath as he went to reply, but he was silenced with a screech before he had the chance. The glacier cracked apart in a steaming explosion, revealing the Phoenix just as it dipped its tail into the magma below. The soaring heat travelled up its body, reigniting its feathers into burning red and blue flame. Already its broken body was healing, supported by its element.

Alexis had to shout to be heard over the rumbling volcano. 'We have to get it back into the Gem somehow!'

'Either way, we can't fight it down here,' Demi added

before crouching to the ground. She flattened her palms against the platform, digging her nails into the rock. A crack formed between the standing Elementals and the furious Fire Creature. Gasping as though she had been kicked in the chest, she uttered, 'Get ready to fly us out of here.'

The platform beneath them shot into the air. The Elementals fell flat against its surface from the force. Caeli recovered immediately and leapt into action, soaring it skyward. The Phoenix raced after them, drawing closer with each beat of its blazing wings. Behind it, the magma level was rising.

'It's catching up!' Alexis called, ducking away from the rock's edge, narrowly avoiding a blast of fire.

Above them, the volcano walls were narrowing as they approached the summit, the night sky now visible through the small jagged crater.

'We're not gonna make it!' Caeli screamed. With her spare hand, she blew the crater's ash pit out, widening the funnel that was now only metres away.

The edges of the flying rock scraped against the crater, splintering into dust. The Elementals were hurled into the air, shooting through the cylinder funnel. As Alexis fell freely through the sky, his face was hit with the harsh coldness of the air after hours within the smoke-filled firepit. He felt his strength return. The snow and the glaciers supported him, restoring his energy.

Then the Fire Phoenix burst through the crater, and the volcano erupted.

Rolling clouds of volcanic ash sputtered upwards, billowing fumes that rose high into the sky and blocked out the array of white-dotted stars. Bubbling molten lava spilled from the crater rim like an overflowing tap of luminescent paint against a black canvas. As the toxic debris rained down across the flat mountain peak, Caeli caught the Elementals and landed them far from the ash pit.

'There's magma everywhere!' Blaise shouted, redirecting streams of liquid fire away from them as Caeli erected a forcefield around the foursome to protect them.

Alexis might have been choking on fumes but couldn't help himself. 'It's actually lava now—' he started, but Blaise silenced him with a fiery glare.

'I don't know how we'll defeat this one,' said Demi, her gaze tracking the Phoenix as it encircled the mountain peak, swooping in and out of the ash cloud. Its colour, purple in the centre of its body and red at its wings, illuminated the night sky, burning brightly despite the cold.

Alexis sighed and said to no one in particular. 'I want to give up, but I am far too stubborn. Alas, I must go on.' He paused before turning to Blaise. 'You're the only one who can get close to it. Try to press the Gem against its forehead and hope for it to be absorbed? That's all I've got as far as suggestions go. In the meantime, we'll try to put out its fire.'

Blaise nodded, sparing a glance at Caeli before he departed. He disappeared into the swirling cloud of falling blackness.

Caeli splayed her fingers and her forcefield exploded, blowing the ash and smoke away from the remaining Elementals. Her power caught the Phoenix's attention. It flapped its wings indignantly and landed on the mountaintop in front of them, rivers of molten lava washing its claw-tipped feet.

'Keep your distance,' Demi warned. Her lips were trembling blue in the cold, her dark hair plastered to her skin with sweat.

In unison, Alexis, Caeli and Demi broke apart to surround the Creature that eagerly awaited their attack. In the distance, Alexis sensed his element within the ice glaciers that fenced the volcano summit. Its coolness. Its power. Despite everything, Alexis couldn't help but smile.

With a striking motion, he cracked apart the thousand-year-old ice walls and threw his arms forwards. Rushing above him, blistering comets of jagged ice soared across the mountaintop towards the Phoenix. The Fire Creature met the assault with a burst of magenta flame, splitting the speeding icebergs apart.

With the Phoenix distracted, Caeli cast her hands to the sky. Gales swept across the volcano peak, beating against the Creature and shoving it off balance, snatching the flames away just as it reignited, leaving wisps dwindling in the air.

'We've got to put it out!' Demi called. She swept her arms wide, collating dust and debris from the summit, before hurling it atop the Creature to smother its flames.

Alexis felt for the snow in the skies, pulling it free from the clouds high above and raining it onto the struggling Phoenix.

The Fire Creature and the rivulets of lava hissed from every cold stab of rainfall. Without its burning feathered flames, the Phoenix looked naked in the night, only its red eyes still gleaming.

In a violent shake, the wings of the Phoenix broke free from the ice and earth sheath. A ring of purple flames burst from them, rolling over the mountain summit, scorching all in its path. Caeli took to the sky, but she wasn't quick enough. The heatwave struck her down just as it flung Demi away before she could sink beneath the earth's surface. Alexis hardly had time to manipulate the water around him to create a shield that held.

The great Phoenix headed towards him, now the only one standing.

He was alone on the battlefield, one wrong move away from death.

The Phoenix reeled its head back and hurled a blazing firebolt straight at him. Alexis instinctively pulled his hands together to shield his face from the hellfire, screaming for any water that remained.

His arms shuddered as a column of water rippled from his palms.

Alexis gasped. He hadn't manipulated the water, he had *created* it. For the very first time, without ever having borrowed his Gem's powers. With continuous streams of water matching the Phoenix's fire, he looked beyond the mirage of heat and steam to see a subdued Demi staring at him in amazement. It was a feat not even Incantus had expected them to achieve.

Water fought fire in an incessant battle. Yet, despite his best efforts, Alexis wasn't sure how much longer he could hold up. Supported by the Gem, the Phoenix's fire grew more ardent, red flames turning violet as it towered over him. Flames swathed him. His hands were burning, blackening – he couldn't withstand it any longer.

Thankfully, he didn't have to.

Blaise soared into the air. The sky was cast into an explosion of bright light, illuminating the scene of the Elemental against the Creature. What happened next, Alexis only saw in blurred flashes.

Blaise allowed the fire to consume him. He rocketed forwards, burning hotter than ever.

The Woman was right. His fire was never meant to be contained.

Reaching the face of the Phoenix, Blaise pulled the Gem free from his pocket. With a bellow, he pushed through the flames and breathed in the fumes as he sunk the Fire Gem deep into the Phoenix's forehead, silencing its fire for good.

34

BRONTIDE

Brontide (n.) *English origin*
The low rumble of distant thunder

The Phoenix screamed. The shrill noise rang over the mountain range, splitting apart the blanket of silence that had fallen atop the summit.

Alexis jolted awake just as the familiar cold darkness of his nightmare crept into his resting mind. Through the lack of sleep and portalling between time zones, it was the longest time that had ever passed where he hadn't experienced the nightmare. He never thought he would feel incomplete without it, but even pain was a welcome associate when its company was so familiar.

His eyes adjusted past the falling black smoke to see the writhing Phoenix. The Gem, now half-stuck in its forehead, seemed to be draining its power, sucking the lifeforce from it. Eventually, the Phoenix faded away into glowing ash, pouring back into the amulet on Blaise's chest that now housed its powers.

Blaise came running over to Alexis, spirited by success, Demi and Caeli just behind him. Despite the cold, Alexis's hands felt like they were being bitten by a hundred tiny fire ants. He dug his fingernails into his palms to distract him from the agony. He didn't want to take away Blaise's moment. 'Well done, bro, that was big from you.'

Blaise bowed deeply. 'Thank you, thank you. And don't think I didn't notice you creating your element for the first time. Huge move.'

'How are your hands?' Demi asked him. She gently took a hold of them, examining the deep scorching that blistered apart the layers of skin, forcing them to tremble uncontrollably.

'Nothing the healing crystals can't fix,' Alexis told her.

'Don't you worry,' she said. Her touch lingered, tracing the veins snaking down his hands. 'We'll get the crystals on it right away and the herbal pastes I've made.'

'So where do we go from here?' Blaise asked. 'We can't portal and I don't feel like waiting around on an active volcano.'

Alexis forced himself to look away from Demi as she rummaged through her bag. 'The next destination is over in South America, but I have no idea how we'll get there.'

'Incantus said we should wait for him,' Demi said, straightening up. She wrapped the scented herbal-soaked bandages round Alexis's shaking hands with a delicate but firm grip, folding in the healing crystals. She only nodded after Alexis's hands began to glow with a pale yellow colour, relieving his pain immediately to nothing more than a dull, distant ache.

Caeli stroked her fingers through her hair and pulled a face of disgust. 'I *so* need to wash my hair. Sweat, ash and dirt have completely ruined it.' She caught her friends' collective stares and threw her hands up. 'What? We just killed another mythical Elemental monster and you want to get going straight away? Can't we have a single normal conversation anymore?' She was once again met with nothing but silence. 'You've all become boring. If you're so desperate to get to the Water Gem, maybe I could fly us there.'

Blaise pressed his hand to his abdomen as he laughed. 'Trust your sense of direction? No, thanks. I've seen your driving.'

Caeli kicked at the ground. 'What's *your* big plan, then? Send Incantus a smoke signal? Or dig your way there? Or swim?'

'Not bad ideas, Cae,' Alexis muttered, trying to conceal his grin. 'Probably safer travelling with the Shadowless than—'

Realisation slapped Alexis across the face.

'What is it, Al?' Blaise asked.

'Mortem's sent the Shadowless to each phase of our quest so far.' He pulled his sword from his backpack. He couldn't explain it, but even as he spoke, he felt his chest constrict, his body turning numb as if an icy gust had struck his insides. 'The Leaders would've told him everything they knew. Who's to say Mortem didn't send anyone here? Who's to say they aren't *already* here and were just waiting for us to kill the Creature before taking the Gem from us?'

His question was answered by a huge streak of lightning which bolted across the dark sky, splitting apart the ash clouds. Seconds later came a thunderous booming, so loud that Alexis had to cover his ears.

Thousands of feet in the air, the Children of the Elements were open and exposed in the night, at the mercy of whatever and whoever was coming. It was just as Alexis had said to Demi earlier.

What we fear about the dark is not being alone in it. It is the very opposite.

The end of Demi's whip uncurled at her feet. 'Please don't tell me that's—'

She was interrupted by another crack of lightning, forcing a yelp from her. In the sky, a spiderweb of hot streaks illuminated a silhouette in the clouds. The Elementals didn't need to wait for another flash to know who it was.

Taranis.

A line of blue-and-yellow light zigzagged towards the crater, cracking at its side, exploding rock and molten lava. Only metres away from where it had struck, Alexis could feel its searing temperature, the bright afterimage of its colour obscuring his vision as he blinked it away.

Blaise ignited his hands into coiling flames, turning to the sky. 'Do you think we could take him?'

'We're more powerful and it's four to one,' said Caeli. When she spoke, however, her voice shook.

Demi swallowed hard. 'He'll recognise us. He won't hurt us, right?'

Alexis recalled the look on Taranis's face as Mortem imprinted him the night before in the Garden. Another streak of lightning snaked out across the sky. Through clenched teeth he said, 'You can show him all the restraint you want, but don't expect any back.'

A streak of blistering lightning rushed towards the Alpha team, striking the earth between them, too fast for them to dodge. The blast forced the Elementals to the ground, causing shards of stone and ice to rain over them. As they scrambled to their feet, Alexis caught sight of a darker shape in the shadows just below them.

Tall and lean, purple hair pulling in the wind.

'Hello, sweethearts,' said Raeve, her black eyes gleaming in the moonlight.

Lightning struck the ground beside Raeve, and emerging from it came Taranis. In all that Alexis had witnessed in the last few days, the sight of the two Leaders who had trained them, their eyes dark and blank, was the most unnerving.

Otherwise, they looked untouched, still clothed in the same outfits they had been wearing during the feast: Raeve in a beautiful violet gown that revealed her patchwork of tattoos and Taranis flashing a luminescent gold suit jacket. The injuries they had sustained in their battle with Mortem had been healed without a trace, barely a scar remaining in the place where the spear had impaled Taranis's leg.

Aside from their black eyes, there was only one other giveaway that they were corrupted. Their bodies cast no shadow in the faint glow of the amulets.

'Alpha team,' Taranis said, his voice devoid of its distinctive playfulness. 'We've missed you so much. Come closer, it's been too long since we've all been together.'

The young Elementals stayed where they were, frozen in place. Alexis was as scared now as he had been when fighting the Creature of the Fire, his muscles stiff in anticipation. At least with the Phoenix, he knew that it was only doing its duty to protect the Gem; with Raeve and Taranis, he had no idea what they wanted and what they would be forced to do to get it.

'Amazing job you have done,' Raeve continued, advancing

up the steep mountainside towards them. 'Three-quarters through your quest! I knew we trained you well. *Incantus* must be so proud.'

Incantus's name was the only word Raeve said that held any sort of emotion. Mortem's hatred for his brother seeped through his control of their minds. Nothing could mask it.

'He'll be here soon,' Alexis said. He tilted the bi-sword in his hand, intentionally reflecting the red glow from Blaise's amulet to glint at their black eyes for no other reason than to irritate them. 'He'll be able to save you, the real you.'

Taranis's face folded into a scowl, the outline of his figure flashing yellow.

'He won't,' Raeve whispered. 'Come with us now before we will be forced to kill you. Mortem's offer still stands to spare you. All of you.' Her eyes rolled over Blaise, Caeli and Demi. She grimaced as she spoke, almost as though a part of her didn't want to say it. 'Are you going to allow *Alexis* to speak for you all? Did he tell you the connection he shares with Mortem? How do you know he hasn't already sided with him in secret?'

Demi snapped her liana whip in the air. 'You can't turn us against each other,' she said, breathing heavily through her flared nostrils. 'If you want to beat us, you'll have to do it yourselves.'

'You won't be able to kill us,' Taranis retorted, sparks flickering at his fingertips. 'We trained you. You would be nothing without us.'

Alexis knew it to be true. But he had two powers the Leaders didn't; the element of water and the element of surprise.

327

Alexis blasted a stream of water from his hand at Taranis, hoping to catch him off-guard with his newfound powers. Reacting impossibly fast, Taranis flashed away in a ripple of electricity, reappearing high in the sky. Not even the shadow of the night could conceal the Leader's surprise.

Raeve pulled free two blades from behind her back. Mortem must have given them to her, for she had been unarmed at the Haven. Had she been, the Leaders' fight with Mortem might have gone differently.

Raeve's outline shimmered its distinctive purple as she floated to meet their eyeline. Before she could cast a hex, muttering its incantation under her breath, Blaise hurled a fireball her way. She erected a shield just in time, but it still shuddered under the force of the inferno.

Alexis knew they would have to split up to fight them both. It made sense to have one Gem-powered Elemental in each pair. 'Cae, with me,' he ordered, sheathing his sword.

Together, he and Caeli ran back up the mountainside, focussing their attention on the sky. Caeli's eyes turned stormy as she raised her hands, her amulet glowing fiercely against her chest.

Even from where he stood, Alexis felt the pull of the winds far away, picking up speed until gales and torrents rained down on Taranis. Through the occasional flashes of blue and yellow light, Taranis's face was illuminated, contorted in anguish.

'Make it rain,' Caeli muttered.

Alexis flooded the sky with rainclouds, holding his breath as he forced the temperature to plummet. With a gasp as his lungs screamed for air, Alexis unleashed the tide from the skies.

A flood of ice and rain crashed down, taken up by the spinning winds, striking Taranis in the centre of the storm, hiding him from view. Only the distant sound of thunder and the faint cracking of his lightning still rang out. Allowing himself a second to catch his breath, Alexis turned to see how Demi and Blaise were holding up.

Collision upon collision came with Blaise throwing an unrelenting tirade of rockets at Raeve, keeping her at bay. She absorbed or dodged most of the attacks, but it was clear she wouldn't hold out for long, not if she were unable to conjure a spell of her own. Still her swords were raised; she kept coming.

Then came Taranis's pained cry from the sky.

The sound made her freeze. The colour of her eyes flickered and the blackness disappeared for a moment.

'Raeve, please fight it!' Demi urged, moving towards her, her empty hand outstretched.

Blaise snatched Demi away. 'Are you stupid? She'll kill you! She'll—'

Blaise fell still. His gaze must have met Raeve's, leaving his body paralysed under her Concilium charm, inflicted with a curse like that of the Gorgon, Medusa.

Just before Raeve went to strike through Blaise with one of her short swords, Alexis rushed to intercept, their swords clanging violently. Raeve's eyes were wide in Alexis's face, but her charm didn't take hold, for he didn't dare sneak a peek.

'*He's* waiting for you, sweetheart' she whispered, her lips brushing his ear. 'You'll never be able to escape his shadow.'

Alexis's eyes shot to hers, realising all too late that she had managed to get the best of him, that his curiosity would be responsible for his demise. Frozen in place, he could only watch as she raised her sword –

There was a harsh cracking sound. A thick brown vine lassoed round Raeve's neck. With a grunt, Demi desperately tugged back with her whole body weight, sending Raeve hurtling away from Alexis and into the darkness far down the mountainside.

'Thank me later,' Demi said, her breathing ragged as she shook Blaise from his trance.

In an ear-splitting eruption from above, hundreds of lightning bolts burst from Taranis. The strikes cracked across the sky like nothing Alexis had ever seen before, raining down and crashing into the mountain so violently that it shook its side.

'Let's end this!' Blaise shouted, his arm intertwined with Caeli's. Stepping free from Alexis and Demi, the two omnipotent Elementals threw their hands to the to the heavens. A thunderous wave of wind and fire swept across the sky, blasting into Taranis with a force too fast and too great for him to avoid. In the distance, Alexis saw his smoking body soaring in the direction Raeve had been thrown, incapacitated for now.

'They'll be back,' Alexis warned, signalling to his friends to stay vigilant in a protective circle.

'And what do we do when they come back?' Caeli demanded.

'Are we going to have to kill them?' Blaise asked uneasily.

Demi turned on him. 'We can't kill them! The real them is inside somewhere, didn't you see it?'

'She's right. It's not them – it's Mortem controlling them,' Alexis protested.

'At this point, it doesn't matter,' Blaise argued, igniting his axe into flames. 'If it's between us or them, even they would say to pick us.'

Alexis's voice came out loud and clear. 'We are not killing our Leaders.'

What Raeve had said still echoed in his mind, making his body feel cold all over. In the quest to fight the Creatures of the Elements, he had forgotten who the real enemy was. He had forgotten that all of this was to stop the man who had given him life, and who so viciously wanted to end it.

Alexis knew what it was like to have something in his head telling him to say and do things he didn't want to. Although the *Shadow Man* had fallen silent for a long time, he still remembered everything it had made him do. He couldn't ever forget.

'Imagine if it were us,' he said, urging his friends to listen. 'Imagine if one of us had been infected. Would you want us to just kill you or would you want us to help you fight it?'

'Depends if I was trying to kill you,' Blaise muttered.

'And countless others,' Caeli added quietly. She let out a frustrated sigh. 'So do we just wait until Incantus arrives to exorcise them? My plan of flying there doesn't sound so bad after all.'

Over the howling winds, Alexis heard a faint *pop*.

Only a few metres away, on the mountain slope above, the sky began to shimmer. It started out as a faint circular mirage, like the rippling seen on the disturbed surface of water, distorting its reflection. As the rest of his friends turned to follow his gaze, a huge red ring, just short of the size of a train

331

tunnel, started to bleed out of nowhere.

'This you, Blaise?' Demi asked, glancing at his amulet. 'Or Raeve's magic?'

'Hers is purple,' Caeli said, eyeing the glowing red circle. The colour started to fill in, seeping across the large two-dimensional surface.

It was a portal, one far more powerful than any conjured by the teleportation device.

'Get ready,' Blaise said, gripping his burning axe with both hands, pulled back and ready to swing.

The portal face shimmered as a person Alexis didn't recognise appeared. The wind whipped the long jet-black hair from her pale face. She was sickly thin, almost fragile in the unshapely rags she wore, yet she stood upright, dignified and important.

'Do not worry, Children,' said the young woman who emerged. She smiled, but with it came no warmth. 'I am here to save you.'

35

ASCIAN

Ascian (n.) *Latin and Greek origin*
A person who has no shadow

Alexis liked to think of himself as a good judge of character.

For years, he had stayed quiet and just observed the world around him, analysing the intentions people displayed through their actions and mannerisms, and those they tried hard to conceal. The art of reading people, Jackson Michaels had always said, was one few people mastered, but once you did, it would change your entire outlook on people.

If his dad were here with him now, he wondered whether he too would pick up on something off about this woman. A guarded quality. Despite her dramatic entrance and the way she addressed them, Alexis couldn't help but feel as if it were all a façade. He recognised it because he often wore it too.

'I'm a book written in a language you will not be able to understand, darling,' said the young Chinese woman, breaking the burdensome silence and matching Alexis's critical stare. She eventually averted her eyes away, however, and stroked the long dark hair that fell almost to her hips.

Caeli's tone was accusatory when she asked, 'Who are you?'

'Valentina,' said the woman.

'Valentina . . . ?'

The woman replied without a pause. 'Just Valentina, for now.'

'Did Incantus send you?' Blaise asked, looking her up and down. 'Are you the portaller from the High Order?'

Caeli struck his arm in scolding. 'Blaise, shut up, we don't even know this girl.'

Through thin, cracked lips that curved upwards at the corners, Valentina replied. 'Ignore her, *Blaise*. She doesn't know what she's talking about. You are right, beautiful boy of flames. The High Order did send me, and just in time by the looks of it.'

Caeli scowled. 'Hun, you've got a lot of attitude for someone who looks like they've just escaped prison. Don't you think you should be a little more humble speaking to the Children of the Elements when dressed like that?'

'I *have* just escaped prison,' Valentina replied calmly. She regarded the ripped clothing hanging off her thin frame. There weren't many people who could look elegant dressed like that, Alexis thought, but she managed it. 'Mortem's. And yet, despite all of your powers, I am still the one coming to your rescue.'

Caeli went to take a step forward, but Demi caught her arm, tugging her back.

Valentina did a poor job at stifling a laugh. 'I'm not going to give you the attention you so desperately crave, *Doran*. I want to talk to the one who makes the decisions. Assuming by the way everyone keeps looking at him, I'm guessing it is Alexis.'

She jutted her chin towards him. It rattled him that she knew their names.

Alexis held Caeli back and narrowed his eyes at Valentina. 'You escaped Mortem's castle? How? And how did you find us?'

'Pure intelligence and charm.'

Caeli scoffed. 'The audacity of this girl,' she muttered.

'I couldn't exactly portal out,' Valentina continued. She inclined her head to the steadily red-glowing threshold behind her. Whilst the sub-zero winds played with her hair, ruffling her clothes, she hadn't appeared to shiver once. 'In his castle, our powers are robbed from us. No one really knows how. During a cell transfer last night, I managed to escape, even past his new psychic henchman.'

'Are you talking about Akili Pierce?' Demi asked, almost whispering his name.

'I slipped right past him. After I got out, I portalled to the High Order where they told me about your quest. I came here at their behest.'

'There's no way you would have escaped past Akili if he didn't want you to,' Alexis stated, shaking his head. 'Maybe Mortem's hold on him is loosening?'

Blaise nodded towards the portal. 'Whatever it is, are we going to go? Raeve and Taranis are still out there, evil and murderous. Time's running out and she can get us to the Water Gem. The more time we waste here, the more time Mortem has to send Sinner or whoever else after us.'

Behind him, Valentina stood composed. The glowing redness of the portal behind her continued to illuminate her silhouette, but even so, it was not bright enough to cast a shadow.

Caeli failed to keep the bitterness from her voice as she gawked at Blaise. 'Why are you so eager to join her? Is an empty compliment all it takes to forfeit any critical thinking?'

'Sorry that I'm beautiful,' said Blaise, holding up his hands in mock defence. 'Besides, princess, I am a betting man and her plan beats your one of flying.'

'Where did the High Order tell you to portal us to?' Alexis queried, interrupting them.

Valentina replied confidently. 'Iguazu Falls, the waterfall in between the borders of Brazil and Argentina. Home of the hidden Gem of the Water.'

Demi shrugged beside Alexis. She lowered her voice so Valentina couldn't hear. 'Incantus must have told the High Order where it was; there's no way they would know its location so specifically.'

'I don't like her,' Caeli said unhelpfully, not attempting to be quiet. 'The story adds up, but there's something about her that is just . . . *odd*.'

Alexis agreed. There was a haunted depth to her eyes that put him on edge. 'Blaise's addiction to gambling is actually helpful in this case,' he finally decided. 'The odds with her are better than being stuck here.'

'Made up your minds yet?' Valentina called, folding her hands behind her back in waiting. 'It's not safe to hold a portal open for too long. As you are travelling over such a great distance, a tunnel stretches out between both ends – kind of like a wormhole between two points in space. I can't keep it open all night.'

Caeli stormed forwards until she was level with Valentina. 'Just to let you know, this whole "princess in rags" look really isn't working out for you.'

With a gust of wind, Caeli shoved Valentina aside before stepping through the portal. Blaise crouched to help Valentina up, but whatever interest she had initially shown in him had vanished. She stood by herself and waited for Blaise to follow Caeli. She exhaled a short sigh of relief once he disappeared, leaving only Alexis and Demi remaining on the mountain.

'She should be grateful I arrived when I did,' Valentina muttered. 'Trust a Doran to not think about the consequences of their actions.'

'Join us,' said Alexis pointedly. 'We don't know where we're going. We don't have much experience with portals, especially as you said this one acts like a tunnel. Please show us the way.'

'As you wish.' Valentina simply exhaled and passed through the portal, disappearing into the two-dimensional threshold.

Alexis caught Demi's arm as she went to follow. In the portal's glowing light, her shadow fell on the ground beneath her, the dark silhouette joined at her feet where her body obstructed the light. As had Blaise's. As had Caeli's.

'Stay vigilant,' was all Alexis said to her. She nodded and moved her hand to the hilt of her dagger. She kept it there as she passed through the barrier.

Standing on the mountainside alone, Alexis did not want to take a look behind him, too afraid to see what could be there – or rather, what wouldn't be there. It would be confirmation of a growing fear he had developed ever since Mortem invaded the Garden; something the Woman of the Fire had aroused once again. Something that could be identified not only by the blackness of one's eyes, but also by the absence of their shadow, for when the body contains darkness, it hides from any light that seeks to blind it.

The Leaders no longer projected a shadow, not since their encounter with Mortem. And neither did Valentina.

Alexis didn't look back before crossing the threshold of the portal. If he had, he would have seen that he too cast no shadow.

PART IV

ALEXIS

Destined to destroy

'I am more than my shadow'

36

ELEUTHEROMANIA

Eleutheromania (n.) *Greek origin*
A manic yearning for freedom; an intense
and irresistible desire to escape

As soon as Alexis passed through the mouth of the portal, the view of Mount Kilimanjaro was snatched away. The experience was unlike any other portal he had travelled through. Surrounding the bridge where he and his friends stood lay an endless sea of swirling carmine light that formed a tunnel without an end in sight, a never-ending abyss.

Valentina seemed to know exactly where to direct the bridge, moving past Blaise and Caeli, careful to not touch either of them. With her back to the group, Alexis rushed to catch up with his friends, tracing Valentina's exact footsteps. As usual, Blaise and Caeli were bickering.

'I told you, you're being paranoid,' Blaise denied. 'Anyway, why do you care if she was flirting with me?'

Alexis interrupted before Caeli could reply. 'Do you believe she escaped Mortem's castle?'

'She looks like she has,' sneered Caeli. 'The High Order could have at least let her shower and change before coming to get us. Quite frankly, it's disrespectful. And it really pissed me off the way she said my surname like that. What does she know about me?'

'Even if she is lying, two of us have our unlimited powers,' said Blaise. 'Rather her than Raeve and Taranis.'

Demi hadn't said much since entering the portal, her hand still on the hilt of the dagger following Alexis's warning. The only thing she said was, 'I feel so sorry for her.'

Alexis couldn't satiate his curiosity, not even at the risk of his own safety. 'Keep your guard up,' he said to his friends before he jogged to catch up with Valentina.

Matching her long strides, Alexis attempted to catch her eyes. She held her chin high, only giving him a fleeting look of acknowledgement. With her dark hair falling to her waist, trailing behind her as she strode, she looked graceful, like someone who had been taught how to hold herself.

'Have a question for me, blue-eyed boy? I know you can't be admiring my outfit.'

'Thank you for helping us,' he said, catching her by surprise. 'I don't think any of us could have survived had you not arrived when you did.' She waved her hand dismissively. Her gaze remained ahead, concentrated. 'You really did save us, Valentina – thank you. I mean it. So the only question I have for you is, how are you? After everything you must have gone through, I think that's the only question that matters.'

Valentina stumbled to a halt, falling still as if the batteries had been ripped from her. 'How am I?' It didn't appear to be a question she was often asked, one she was not accustomed to answering. One she didn't know how to. She blinked harshly, so much so that wrinkles formed each time she pressed her eyelids shut. She stammered when she spoke. 'Fine. I'm fine. I just need to get you there.'

She walked on, as though she couldn't get away from him fast enough.

'Did you see how she responded to a few kind words?' Alexis murmured once his friends caught up to him. 'She must be around our age. We can't imagine the torture she's endured. She might have no one.'

Demi instantly went to head towards to Valentina, but Alexis pulled her back. When she went to protest, Alexis tilted his head to Caeli.

'She called me stupid,' Caeli began, shaking her head. 'No way. Why should I be nice to her? Why not brilliant, *beautiful* Blaise?'

'Cae, please,' Alexis insisted. 'I think I'm on to something. Just try to touch her.'

'Imagine if it was you,' Demi added in support. 'Imagine if the same day you escaped your abductor, you were forced to go on a mission where you put yourself at risk of crossing him again.'

'But be careful. I don't trust her yet.'

Unable to hide her confusion at whatever plan Alexis said he had, Caeli grudgingly nodded. He let water trickle to his hands at the ready, as Caeli approached Valentina.

'Here it is,' said Valentina without inflection, drawing to a halt and gesturing to the flat wall.

'Look,' Caeli started, not exactly well-practised in being forgiving. 'It's clear I don't like you. I'm happy to never see you again.' Valentina scoffed, but Caeli persevered. 'But . . .

343

I am sorry for what you must have gone through. No one should have to experience what you have, and I respect that you managed to come out again for us.'

Caeli extended her hand in offering. Before Valentina could pull away, it grazed against the bare skin of her arm.

At her touch, Valentina flung herself back. A strained, strangled scream escaped her as she collapsed to the ground.

'What happened?' Caeli gasped, whirling around to her friends. 'I didn't do anything!'

'Fight it, Valentina!' Alexis shouted, crouching before her. 'Fight the darkness!'

'*Darkness?*' asked Blaise. His hands erupted into coiling flames. He pointed them at the imprinted woman as she spasmed on the ground before them. 'How do you know she's been infected?'

Not turning back, doing his best to engage a writhing Valentina, Alexis said, 'The portal. It's the same red as the one that joined with Ezra's and allowed Mortem to break into the Garden. The one that took away Dr Sinner. Did Mortem send you?'

Through bloodshot eyes, Alexis watched as a blackness spread across them. At each blink, it was forced back, but the darkness inside fought hard to maintain its control.

'H-he made me,' Valentina said through haggard sobs. She twisted on the ground as though someone was digging a knife into her chest, looking unrecognisable from the graceful, composed woman who had greeted them. 'It's a t-trap . . . an army on the other s-side.'

The Alpha team instantly regrouped. The endless red

tunnel retracted as Valentina convulsed, the length of the bridge they had just walked shrinking in on itself. It was as if she had stretched the portal's distance to prolong the amount of time she spent in there, away from Mortem's influence, long enough to try to warn them.

Demi's hands were clenched into shuddering fists. 'How can we help you?' she pleaded, searching the walls of the swirling portal as its colour darkened with currents of midnight.

So quietly that it was almost a whisper, Valentina said, 'J-just hide and go. P-please. I don't want to hurt you. Please go before I do . . .'

Reluctantly, against every urge in his body that told him to stay, Alexis nodded. He knew she was right. They could not face an army, not yet.

He had never felt like more of a coward.

'Thank you, Valentina. Incantus will come for us and we'll explain. He can save you . . .'

Valentina pointed once more. Her lasting words followed the Elementals as they took a step beyond the portal. 'I'm sorry.'

37

EPHIALTES

Ephialtes (n.) *Greek origin*
A nightmare

Alexis clamped his hand over Demi's mouth to silence her scream as an army of Shadowless appeared before their very eyes. Caeli's invisibility shield held, ensuring they were not seen, but the unnerving awareness of his every heartbeat was enough for him to feel exposed.

Thankfully, the South American rainforest was abundant with noise, enough to mask them: birds twittering in the trees, insects buzzing in the soil and a low roaring of rushing water in the distance. A light mist seeped from the latter, coating the space in a foggy haze. Alexis physically longed to reunite with his element. To bathe himself in the late afternoon and wash off the remnants of the ashen and desolate mountain summit they had travelled from, thanks to Valentina.

Valentina. The image of her contorting in pain was vivid in Alexis's mind. Would she be punished for warning them of the ambush? A shiver ran down his spine as he wondered whether the stranger had just exchanged her life for theirs.

Dr Sinner made his way through the rows of awaiting

soldiers, his huge frame far taller than any other around him. Held firmly in his hand was a single obsidian-tipped arrow, its head gleaming in a way that most metals did not, absorbing the light from around it. He drew dangerously close, close enough to impale any one of the Alpha team quicker than they could blink.

A second man with an unsteady voice spoke. 'Dr Sinner.' Another Shadowless slipped through the ranks, approaching Sinner as if he was a beast that couldn't be trusted. 'Surely the Lì girl should have sent them through by now? Unless, perhaps, she managed to resist our Sire's powers . . .'

Sinner remained crouched for a moment longer, staring straight at the shielded Alpha team, a line of thick mucus seeping from one nostril. Alexis could barely breathe, gripping his sword so tightly his hand felt numb. Then, to his horror, Sinner moved.

Only he didn't turn on them. Instead, he spun round to the Shadowless soldier who had spoken and stabbed the arrow deep into the man's chest in one swift, effortless movement. It drove through him with as much resistance as a sheet of paper against a sharpened pen. Blood splattered the slackened faces of the imprinted Shadowless behind him, yet they remained motionless, unflinching.

The Shadowless man dropped to his knees. Sinner yanked the red-dripping arrow from his chest and stood over him as he gargled on blood. Within seconds, he had stopped moving, stopped resisting, and lay still. Alexis sensed his heart pumping out the last of his blood at the very moment he died.

Alexis felt Demi violently trembling beside him, her eyes

welling with tears, her breathing hitching in her throat. Alexis reached for her hand and squeezed. The slightest noise could betray them.

Without realising he was doing it at first, Alexis started pinching her fingertips one by one, applying pressure, forcing her to follow his slow, steady pace. Demi tore her eyes away from the dead Shadowless and stared at what Alexis was doing, eyes narrowed in focus. Soon enough, her panting started to settle, falling quiet and regular once again.

Alexis went to let her hand go, but she clung on with a fierce grip. Instead, he intertwined his fingers with hers and let her press it to her chest as if to savour it to her heart.

'I never want to hear anyone challenge our Sire's powers,' said Dr Sinner, wiping the arrow clean on the shirt of an imprinted soldier. 'No one can resist his omnipotent authority – least of all a peasant girl. We wait as ordered.'

Slowly, steadily, Alexis felt the wind lift his feet from the ground. Caeli carried them far above the Shadowless, careful to ensure not a single leaf or twig fluttered. Now at a bird's eye view, Alexis was able to fully grasp how large the army was. There were hundreds of Shadowless crammed together in lines in amongst the rainforest, each dressed in blackened armour or rags, weapons in hand. In the centre of the ordered rows stood the motionless, emotionless victims of Mortem's imprinting, bordered by those who had chosen to follow him freely.

Then came the Hybrids. The grotesque, unnatural amalgamations of creatures were held at the rear of the Shadowless army: hairy spiders with abdomens fragmented with spikes, mutated panthers with featherless vulture wings stitched to their backs. Just like the rat-snake in China, they were fully grown, greater even than Sinner.

Demi gagged and whispered, 'They're the most disgusting things I've ever seen.'

With the army fading into the distance behind them, the Children of the Elements flew towards the edge of the jungle. The treeline parted to display the open view ahead. Blinking to make sure he wasn't dreaming, to check that he was still somewhere on Earth, Alexis took in the sight below him and somehow managed to forget all about Sinner and the Hybrids.

Before him wasn't just the peak of a single waterfall, but rather a collection of hundreds of drops and cataracts submersed within the rainforest, spanning miles wide, far further than his eyes could see. Dozens of rocky islands protruded along the cliffside, dividing the flow from the river into finger-like streams which splayed over the edge like a frothing curtain. The water plunged into a great U-shaped gorge hundreds of feet below, casting a cloud of white mist into the air that refracted the early evening sunlight.

There was something about this place that felt right to Alexis, a synchronicity or familiarity with the air itself. As though he was finally home.

Near the brink of the waterfall was a huge wooden viewing deck, constructed atop a wide columnar rock. It was positioned perfectly to provide a view of the entire waterfall system. Caeli flew the Elementals across the waterfall before setting them down on it, dissolving her invisibility shield and exposing them to the fresh spray of the crashing water. There was a large sign that Alexis read aloud.

'"Iguazu Falls, the largest waterfall system in the world." And that bit there is called the Devil's Throat.' He pointed to the huge horseshoe-shaped canyon that channelled the majority of the river until it collapsed into the waterfall. 'Of course it's called Devil's Throat.'

'Luckily, the National Park closed at five pm,' Demi said, reading the sign alongside Alexis.

Over the roar of the surging river, Blaise called the Elementals together. 'So Valentina – if that's even her real name – tricked us.'

'She was under Mortem's control,' Alexis replied. He removed his amulet from his neck, allowing it to be pulled freely in whatever direction. 'The fact she was able to fight against it long enough to betray him was incredible. More than what Raeve or Taranis was capable of.'

'Her eyes weren't back until the end though.'

'Maybe the darkness was hiding from us.'

'I felt it when I touched her,' said Caeli, examining her hands. 'I felt cold all over. I think I might have helped her . . . a bit, at least. I don't know why you asked me. Out of us all, I'm the least compassionate – there's no denying it.'

Alexis rubbed the tiredness from his eyes as he allowed the river's spray to refresh his face. 'An act of kindness is most significant when it comes from the person we least expect it from. Sorry for not letting you in on my suspicions, but I wanted it to be genuine.'

'I hope she manages to escape,' Demi prayed, stroking the length of her cross. 'I can't imagine what they'll do to her if they find out she helped us. Hopefully, Incantus will figure out where we are and will be able to find her and save her.'

The group fell quiet when they noticed a faint blue glow coming from Alexis's amulet. 'It's close,' he said, moving to the edge of the viewing deck. His amulet pointed over the waterfall cliff edge, down towards the mist-filled abyss. 'Looks like it's near the base of the waterfall.'

He fell back in line beside Caeli and Blaise as Demi took a look herself. She climbed the wooden barrier, careful to not fall over the edge, and inhaled a long breath of the warm, wet air with her eyes closed. In the centre of her palm, a single small leaf grew, no bigger than the shape of her amulet. She allowed the wind to take it up and watched as it floated over to the river's surface before it disappeared in the frothing white, falling over the edge.

Alexis tore his eyes from her to secure his rucksack. 'This is it, guys. We're home after this.' He received excited grins from both Caeli and Blaise. 'You ready, Dem?'

'Yeah,' Demi said from behind him. 'I was just enjoying the v—'

A whistling noise cut through the air, followed by a thud.

Alexis jolted.

. . . And time

staggered

to a

stop.

Only then, as a single second stretched out into what felt like an eternity, did he feel the sinking sensation that something was wrong. Horrifyingly wrong. It was Caeli's scream, her anguished, petrified scream that forced Alexis to follow her and Blaise's gaze towards the waterfall edge.

With blood dripping from the corner of her mouth and the trace of a smile fading from her face, Demi looked down to see the obsidian-tipped arrow that had pierced her chest.

She swayed where she stood, her eyes finding Alexis.

Alexis felt his heart drop into his stomach. No matter how hard he tried to will his body to move, his legs disobeyed him. It had to be a hallucination.

Please be a hallucination.

Unable to keep her balance, Demi's feet slipped from the wooden fence. Without a word nor a breath, she toppled over the side, falling into the thunderous river.

Dr Sinner stood at the far end of the viewing deck, waving his now-empty hand. The portalled army of Shadowless then surged past him towards the remaining Children of the Elements.

Blaise roared in fury, his entire body erupting into an inferno. Without hesitation, he tore straight into the Shadowless. Caeli took off immediately after him, her spear dropping to the ground, freeing her hands which burst with silver light.

'*Save her!*' she called to Alexis as she collided with the first of the imprinted soldiers, ripping their bodies to shreds in a single swipe.

Alexis watched in horror as Demi's small body tipped over the brink of the waterfall.

This time, unlike in his dreams, he didn't fight to stay away from the cliff edge. Without thinking, without considering his own safety, his own life, Alexis jumped off its edge and dived into the waterfall after her.

38

MORIBUND

Moribund (adj.) *Latin origin*
Dying; at the point of death

*The pain in my chest had gone from white-hot agony to a dull numbness
that spread across my body. The arrow's poison was already thickening
my blood, stifling my heart. With the waterfall crashing around me, I
remembered Incantus saying that falling into water from a high enough
height would feel like concrete when I landed.*

*Strange, how Alexis was the one I felt most at peace with, and yet
it would be by his element that I died.*

*It hurt too much to move or scream as the current swept me down.
All I could do as I fell was think of my life. Oh God, I'm not ready to
leave it. I'm not ready to leave the ones I love; Mum, Dad, Kallisto.
Caeli. Blaise. Incantus. Alexis.*

Alexis. If only he was here to hold me.

*He must have known how I felt about him. How can he know
everything and guess everyone's intentions except for mine? Or maybe
he did and he ignored it. Maybe he did and he wasn't ready for it.
Maybe I waited too long for him. Maybe I should've waited longer.
Either way, it was too late.*

Oh Lord, did my time have to come so soon?

Why did you take my life before I lived it?

Strong arms wrapped round my body. I would recognise them anywhere, but I did not trust my mind. I had to see for myself.

It was my Alexis. He took my limp body into his arms as we fell down the violent waterfall, and whispered over and over in my ear, 'It's okay, it's okay; it's going to be okay. Just hold onto me, just stay with me.'

As best as I could, I clung to his trembling body. I saw his face, contorted in fear and desperation. It was a look I had never seen before on him. Usually so controlled, so powerful and reassuring. It was hard to believe someone like him could feel such things.

The cold had found its way to my heart. I shivered as I said, 'Lexi, I'm sorry . . .'

He pulled me even closer in response, his lips praying against my forehead.

It took me by surprise when I realised I would die in his arms.

"Το να αγαπάς αυτό το αγόρι θα είναι ο θάνατος σου."

"Loving him will be the death of you."

I had been warned, but it was already far too late to turn back. There was no way to stop loving him, and so the punishment for my failure was death. Better me than him, though.

It was becoming harder to stay awake. My lungs struggled to inhale, my breathing staggered. How much time did I have left here on Earth with him? I stared into his eyes that looked past me, wide and focussed on the approaching plunge pool. I don't think I've ever been so close to be able to look at them this deeply, uninterrupted. They really were beautiful, the way the blue reflected the light.

In my final moments, time gave me the grace of slowing. It allowed me to see something in Alexis's eyes that stirred a hazy memory. The dark outer ring encircled the blue like it was . . . infecting it.

I'd seen eyes like this before. The Leaders and Valentina had looked like this when the darkness had bled into their eyes as they had been imprinted. This was as though Alexis had been caught halfway through the process.

It couldn't be. Alexis and Mortem had never met before the other night in the Garden, when he had been surrounded by us. Mortem couldn't have imprinted him then.

Unless . . . it had happened before?

Unless there was a time, before Alexis was adopted, when Mortem had tried to imprint his own son? But why? Was it because he feared his powers? The powers they shared? Mortem had been born to both water and darkness, and he had chosen the darkness.

I tried to not ask myself the question. As my vision went dark, I tried to focus on the beauty of the nature around me one last time — but even that was not enough to silence my mind.

As I closed my eyes, I couldn't help but wonder if Alexis was subject to the same choice as well.

'Hold on to me,' Alexis said, squeezing Demi awake once her eyelids fluttered closed.

Just before they hit the water's surface, Alexis outstretched his hand. The water parted, sweeping them both underneath the current, softening their fall. He propelled them upwards, breaking free from the plunge pool.

Sunlight struck their faces as Alexis solidified the water beneath them. With each breath, more blood came from the lodged arrow in Demi's chest. Alexis swept her off her buckling legs and into his arms. She didn't have the strength to hold on to him. Her head fell back, soaking wet hair brushing against the water level. No longer submerged and diluted, the bright red of her blood pooled at the front of her suit, trickling down.

Alexis carried her to the edge of the jungle, away from the waterfall's spray, and lay her gently on her side on the earth, hoping contact with her element might help. It didn't.

Alexis crouched over her, wiping the water from his dripping face. His jaw clamped shut at the sight of the arrow burrowed in her chest.

'You are going to be okay.' Her eyes opened weakly when he cupped her face, first finding the green treetops and then searching for his face. His throat threatened to close, but he wouldn't be silenced. 'You're going to be fine, Demi. Don't you dare bail on me. I still need you. We all need you. You stay awake and stay with me. We're so nearly home, my love.'

My love. He couldn't stop himself from saying it any longer. He didn't know if she had heard him, but her body had stilled, no longer writhing. After a moment, she pressed the side of her face harder against the palm of his shaking hand. He felt her hot tears.

With his free arm, Alexis ripped off his backpack and searched through it until he found the healing crystals. He placed them on top of the wound, waiting for the faint yellow glow to illuminate.

Behind him, over the crashing sound of the waterfall, came cries.

From the distant brink of the waterfall, Alexis saw bodies soar over the edge. Some flailed as they fell, but as soon as they collided with the water at the base with a sickening *smack,* they fell still and were pulled beneath the surface.

'I bet you my powers that's Caeli and Blaise's work,' Alexis said, trying to get a response from her.

With all her effort, Demi reached to touch the side of his face, stroking his cheek just once.

Why weren't they working? He shook the crystals again. Even the healing powers of the suit had failed.

'Lexi,' she said breathlessly. Her voice cracked as she whispered, 'I don't want to die.'

A single choking sob escaped Alexis's lips as he clawed onto his sanity with everything he had left. Through gritted teeth, he swore, 'You're not going to. You're not, do you hear me? If you can create an earthquake and survive three Creatures of the Elements, you can survive this, okay? We – we still have a lifetime of sunsets to chase together.'

Demi nodded, her eyes searching for the truth in what he said.

In his head, all he could hear was the Woman of the Earth's prophecy.

'*With water washing your roots, you will finally rest.*'

Somewhere far away, someone called his name. 'Al!'

Caeli and Blaise appeared over the cliff's edge, descending towards them. Both were bleeding, but the injuries looked minor and already healing. They soared through the air, landing heavily on the ground beside their friends.

'There were hundreds,' Blaise wheezed. His eyes fell on Demi as she lay silently on her side, curled into a ball. 'We had to leave when the Hybrids came.'

Caeli dropped by Demi's side and held her bloodied hand.

'Use the healing crystals,' she ordered.

357

'I am,' said Alexis. 'They're not working.'

'Then make them work!'

'I'm trying!'

'Wait!' Blaise shouted. 'She's trying to say something.' Soundless words were coming from Demi's quivering lips. 'The arrow! She wants you to pull it out.'

Alexis turned back to Demi's ashen, tired face. She nodded once, using the hand Caeli was holding to gesture to her blood-soaked chest.

'Okay,' he said. 'Okay, Dem. Okay.'

'No, it could kill her!' Caeli protested, shoving his hand away. 'It's keeping her from bleeding out.'

'It's also poisoning her and preventing her body from healing,' Alexis snapped back.

'I can . . . handle it,' Demi sputtered. 'Please, Lexi.'

Alexis hastily held her face in his hands, smearing blood across her jaw. 'Just hold on. Our story's not done yet, Demi. Just hold on until it works, okay?'

Demi gave him one last smile, her teeth now painted red.

With his Elemental senses, Alexis could feel her depleting heart rate, the staggering of the blood flow, but he was not yet powerful enough to stop it.

Blaise crouched on her other side, resting Demi's head against his lap. 'Just hit me or something if you need to,' he said to her, not knowing what else to say.

Her hands, usually so warm, were cold in Alexis's grasp. He slipped out of her weak grip and he held the arrowhead with both hands.

Alexis shared one look with his friends, blinking the tears

out of his eyes, forcing himself to stay focussed for Demi.

It had to work. It just had to. Without giving a countdown, he pulled the bloody black-tipped arrow from Demi's chest in one rapid motion.

Her back arched, but no scream came.

Tossing it away, Alexis pressed the healing crystals against the hole in Demi's chest.

'It's not working!' Blaise shouted as he massaged Demi's head. 'Why's it not working?'

'I said not to do it!' Caeli cried, shaking her friend's limp arm. 'No,' she wept. 'Please!'

Her eyes had fallen closed. The jungle was silent, the animals living within stopping to watch the girl whose powers had birthed them take her last breath.

No matter how many times Alexis called her name, Demi Nikolas no longer answered.

Somehow, even though my eyes were closed, I saw an image appear before me.

It sketched out on the back of my eyelids, illuminating the darkness. It was a simple scene, one I didn't recognise, one I hadn't seen before. Even so, it was as clear as the view that had once been of Alexis.

As the seconds drew out, the light of the image grew brighter, and soon enough, it became the only thing I saw. The last thing I saw.

'Don't leave me, Demi, please don't leave me,' Alexis begged over and over again, his voice nothing more than a whisper.

He couldn't imagine a life without her. It would cease to be a life worth living. He had seen the wonders of the world but it all meant nothing if he couldn't share it with her, if he couldn't go home with her. To her. He would take all hallucinations and delusions and arrows to the chest if it meant he could exchange his life for hers.

Alexis left the dull healing crystals against her wound and placed both of his hands on either side of Demi's still, unsmiling face.

When he did, a spasm rocked his body and stole the breath from his lungs.

A surge of energy erupted from the four friends. Evanescent white lights spilled out and swept between them, synchronising and infusing and pouring together, beaming into the sky as though Demi was calling to the very laws of nature to undo death and bring her back.

It was just as Incantus had said. They were stronger together. Nearly unstoppable together. Alexis's touch completed the nexus between the Children of the Elements. It completed the final link between the four primal elements that birthed all of creation.

The light they created flooded into Demi's wound and destroyed the darkness that poisoned her, and, before the Elementals' stunned eyes, the healing crystals stitched her chest closed.

I gasped as the light of life returned to me, my heart beginning to restart, my soul snatched back from the clutches of death.

The image in my mind faded away into nothingness, and my eyelids fluttered open again.

39

NYCTOPHOBIA

Nyctophobia (n.) *Greek origin*
Extreme fear of the night or darkness

Demi lay still for a moment. Her bloodshot eyes darted left to right as if to figure out where she was. They finally settled on Alexis.

He was leaning over her, the crease between his eyebrows dissipating, the corners of his mouth turning up into an incredulous smile. Caeli said something about giving Demi air, but Alexis batted her hand away, not daring to leave until the last of the yellow glow of the healing crystals had seeped into the wound in her chest.

Demi clenched her jaw in discomfort as she tried to sit up with Alexis's help. Her hold on him was weak, but it was there. Her voice was hoarse when she spoke, huskier than it had been before. 'You – you saved me?'

She had come back to him.

Alexis felt his chest deflate. 'Thank us later,' was all he could manage.

At her touch, at the return of the warmth of her hand on his neck, at the sound of her voice, and the smell of her hair over the heavy copper of her spilled blood, every wall of restraint Alexis had carefully constructed and maintained for years came tumbling down.

His heart erupted in a crescendo of emotion. He reached for her as if she was the air he had been deprived of his whole life. He held her as though she was a lifeboat and without her he would sink and drown. And he kissed her as though he had loved her for his whole life, which he had.

She had come back to him.

Alexis couldn't hear anything over the rush of blood in his ears. He could only think of his arms thrown round her. Of his smiling lips on hers.

And then, of her tears on his cheeks.

Reality rushed back into focus like the crashing flood of a tsunami. The muscles of Demi's face tensed in pain, the realisation that she wasn't kissing him back, Caeli and Blaise's stunned silence, the lingering aura of death between them.

She wasn't kissing him back.

In that moment, Alexis felt like Icarus who had soared too close to the sun, relishing in his newfound liberation, only to be struck down by the very thing he had spent his whole life hoping to reach; the incalescent embrace of light.

He pulled away, embarrassed. No, more than embarrassed. He was mortified beyond belief.

Demi's eyes looked into his searchingly as though she was desperate to tell him something, but no words came to her lips as he pulled away. She only winced in pain as she sucked in a breath and steadied herself into a seated position.

The other two must have realised, because they rushed in.

362

'I thought we lost you,' said Caeli as she gently held Demi and tucked the hair behind her ear. 'I was sure that was it. That you were gone for ever.'

Demi's head dipped as Blaise joined their embrace. Alexis felt her look at him, but he couldn't bring himself to join them.

'I thought I did too,' said Demi breathlessly, rubbing her eyes.

'How are you, Dee?' Blaise asked, unsure of where to look.

'Sore,' Demi decided. 'I feel like I've woken up from a really deep dream.' She examined the small hole in the centre of her chest. The arrow had cut through her suit, stabbing through the space between where her crucifix and her amulet lay. Although the crystals had healed her, a thin scar was visible. Alexis didn't know if it would ever fade. She sounded distant when she asked, 'Where's the arrow?'

The midnight arrow glinted on the ground beside them. Demi leant over and scooped it up, inspecting the way it absorbed the light instead of reflecting it. Then, with Caeli and Blaise on either side of her, she ignored their protests and forced herself onto unsteady feet.

'Do you think all the ammo is poisoned with darkness?' Blaise asked. He glanced at the brink of the waterfall high above. The bulk of the Shadowless army still remained at its peak, Alexis noted.

'Unlikely,' Demi replied. 'Dr Si–' She stuttered, unable to say his name. 'He's Mortem's right hand. They're probably reserved for the lead people.' She flicked the arrow free from her blood, staining the green jungle floor, before tucking it down the heel of her boot.

'Are you going to return the gift?' Caeli asked.

Demi's voice was unusually monotone. 'Something like that.'

Alexis finally turned to look at her. He didn't recognise this Demi; stony, emotionless, unsmiling. She had come back, but she was not the same person who had left.

The girl she once was had been murdered, and Alexis had to make the man who killed her pay for his sins.

He let rage consume his mind as his body drummed with the familiar prickling sensation. It wasn't hot fury that spread across every cell of his body, but instead something cold, bitter and spiteful and destructive. He unsheathed his sword from his side, his mind on one thing alone: revenge.

'Send me up there, Cae.' The oppressive weight of shame was no more. Someone had hurt the person he loved most in the world. It didn't matter that she didn't reciprocate his feelings. It only mattered that she should be safe from ever being hurt again. 'Send me up there so I can kill him. I'll freeze his heart to ice, I'll drain the blood from his body, I'll make sure that he stays like that forever, frozen in agony for what he did.'

The words came to him all too easily. In that moment, Alexis came to the realisation that despite trying everything he could, it was not Incantus Arcangelo who he resembled. It was Mortem.

Demi put her hand on his shoulder and forced him to face her. If she thought the same thing, she didn't mention it. 'Getting the Water Gem is more important, especially before nightfall. The sooner we have it, the sooner we can go *home*.' She tiptoed

364

to remove the amulet from his neck and placed it in his palm.

Were they just to pretend the kiss had never happened? That he had never called her *my love*?

Was he able to do that?

He had to. It felt like an arrow in his own chest keeping his silence, but an even worse agony was the thought of making Demi uncomfortable and risk losing her.

Alexis moved to the land's edge and bathed his amulet in the rushing water until the blue stone glowed. It pointed towards the thunderous bulk of the frothing waterfall. Alexis wasted no time. He took a step onto the water's surface, not falling beneath.

'For God's sake, man,' Blaise complained, shaking his head. 'You look like Jesus doing that.'

Alexis increased the cohesion of the moving liquid's surface to support their weight and they cautiously walked across. The waterfall parted like a curtain opening, splitting apart under Alexis's influence, revealing the entrance to a dark cave hidden behind it.

'Speaking of Jesus,' Caeli said Demi, working overtime to fill the strange void hanging between them all. 'When you . . . when you stopped breathing, did you see anything? Any light or darkness?'

Demi hesitated for a long moment before replying, twisting her crucifix between her fingertips. 'To be honest, I'm not exactly sure what I saw.'

The Elementals reached the cavern floor, wet stone slick underfoot. Alexis allowed the waterfall to resume its natural flow behind them, shielding the cave entrance from view or pursuit.

Demi crouched with difficulty and flattened her hand

against the rock floor. 'Someone's trodden this path. Within the last couple of hours, I'd say.'

Caeli's head tilted to the side. 'I can sense about half of the Shadowless still breathing. They're making their way down.'

'Let's hurry up, then,' said Blaise.

Alexis took a lasting look at the sunlit waterfall before leading the way into the darkness. Soon enough, the damp tunnel bottlenecked and the walls began pressing inwards. They were soon forced to walk in single file, their bodies brushing past the rough edges.

'Lexi,' came a whisper from behind him. Demi.

'Sorry about earlier,' he mumbled, not looking back, struggling to keep his voice casual. 'I – I was just so happy you were okay. I'm sorry, it won't happen again.'

He focussed on tracing the bluish glow that was reflecting against the shimmering rockface, the intensity of its shine growing with each footstep.

'Lexi,' Demi said again, softer this time. 'That's not—'

She never got to finish her sentence, for the underpass finally ended. Alexis moved hesitantly, listening out for anything other than the echo of their footsteps as the passageway opened up into an empty, elliptical-shaped cavern.

At its centre, showering from the cracks in the ceiling, rained a thin, circular waterfall. It stood as tall as the cave, leaving only a small area of rock in the centre free from its trace.

'Very feng shui,' Caeli muttered.

There was an unspoken tranquillity about the cool cave, the steady flow of timelessness, something that had evaded them

366

since the start of their training for their quest. Even if only for a few hours, Alexis wished he could stay, comforted by its seclusion from the world beyond.

But that was a child's dream, and after everything they had endured, none of them were children any more.

Alexis approached the glistening waterfall alone. It washed over his skin, the sensation of its touch refreshing in a way the polluted Iguazu River hadn't been, clean and purified. He held out his pendant, the stone catching the glowing water's light. The outline of the inverted triangle-cut stone matched the silhouette that had been inscribed on the rock at his feet. Alexis kneeled and pressed his amulet into place, the last piece of a jigsaw puzzle.

A kaleidoscope of blue light burst from Alexis's amulet and beat against the walls of the dark cave, refracting rays of azure, cerulean, and sapphire back at him. Each shade washed over him with a different sensation, some warm, some cool, some cold as ice.

Finally, it was his turn to experience what his friends had. The Water Gem, the unlimited powers of the seven seas. Immortality.

And yet, for some reason, despite all of the things he knew he should be excited about, it was the Woman of the Water herself that he was most eager to meet.

'Instead of paying so much attention to my element, she should have focussed on her own.'

The Woman of the Fire had spoken as though the water was contaminated. Dirty. As though Alexis was too. He desperately wanted to hear his prophecy, his fate. To a person who knew no past, the future was all he had. Without thinking, he had stepped away from the radiant waterfall, the weight of his amulet familiar back against his chest.

The trickling water glimmered as it started to pull together, collating into a figure. The long train of a gown fell from her body, a dazzling mixture of all shades of blue swirling around in a dangerous current. Hair tumbled down her back, dripping water between her shoulder blades. Eventually, a face formed too, eyes closed.

There was one final flash of light and then, standing where the waterfall had once been, was the Woman of the Water, her timeless crystalline blue eyes fixed upon Alexis.

'I have been expecting you,' she said. Her voice was melodic, like the soft motion of a tide against a beach. Glowing in her palms was the Gem of the Water. The ancient eternal stone glinted in the dark. 'I felt your presence and sensed the proximity of my sisters' Gems.' Her gaze fell on Alexis's amulet, raised from his chest, yearning for its reunion with the Gem. Without meaning to, Alexis felt for it, running his finger across the three-sided shape. 'The Children of the Prophecy of Light and Darkness, how far you have come. Only the Gem of the Water, my Gem, is left to be given . . . to fulfil the first part of your story.'

'Our *story*?'

'A prophecy to one is a story to another, of which there are countless.' She didn't elaborate any further.

In the distance, beyond the waterfall, human bellows and animalistic screeches resonated down the hollow cave. Dr Sinner and the remaining Shadowless were closing in, drowning themselves if it meant they would find the Elementals.

The shade of the Woman's gown darkened as if sensing death within the water. She spoke with a greater sense of urgency. 'Another came before you.' The illumination of her body alit the Elementals' faces as they drew closer. 'Only one was born with the power of the water. When the man arrived, I assumed it to be you. However, it came alone, without the other Children of the Elements, its aura cloaked in darkness.'

'By "it" do you mean Mortem?' Caeli asked.

'Knowing my sisters had already bequeathed their powers, I was the last to pass mine over,' the Woman continued.

Alexis inspected the Gem still glowing in her hands. 'You said his aura was cloaked in darkness – should that not have told you it wasn't me?'

Water fell freely down her gown into a ring by her bare feet. The Woman paused thoughtfully before choosing to speak. When she did, her voice almost mournful. 'As is yours.'

Three words was all it took for Alexis to feel like a child again, a helpless, naive, *doomed* child. He shook his head in disbelief, but deep down, he knew it to be true.

He thought of the first time he had used his powers, the night he arrived at the Haven. The initial dark feeling that had washed over him. The sensation of coldness, of loneliness.

He thought of his missing shadow, just like those whose minds Mortem had invaded and imprinted. Dark silhouettes that should've been cast out by the light now lay trapped within their souls, unable to escape.

Last of all, he thought of the *Shadow Man*. All these years, he had believed the *Shadow Man* to be a hallucination, part of his illness, something to be managed by medication and therapy years ago. But after seeing how Valentina had tried to resist the darkness, the torment she experienced as the power imprinted within her forced her to do something she desperately didn't want to, it only reminded him of how he had spent much of his childhood. Battling demons no one else could see, as real as anything in the world around him.

Alexis felt as if the walls of the cave were closing in, drawing closer with each panicked breath that hitched in his throat. It wasn't his mental health issues that had made him violent. They had made him a victim. It was his biology, his very DNA, a part of him as much as the beat of his heart or the colour of his eyes. Perhaps the *Shadow Man* was nothing more than a projection of his deepest impulses and darkest desires.

'I am sure you are aware of where your powers came from,' the Woman of the Water went on. 'That your elements were born from the Darkness at the start of time, exploding free into creation and birthing light. Yet, the Darkness remembered back to the beginning of creation. It knew that when the four elements come together, light would be created, too bright for it to survive in the shadows. It had to ensure its survival on this world somehow, and it did, by leaving its remnants within the oldest and strongest of the elements – mine. *Yours.* It imprinted the waters, hidden within the depths of the seas, tethering its existence to this world and allowing it once again to come free and be born alongside a Child of the Water when the Dark Prophecy came to be.'

Alexis's fingers hadn't stopped tapping his thumbs. It was the only thing distracting him from the hollowing realisation that his friends had all taken a step back from him. He heard his own voice waver as he spoke. 'So you're saying there is darkness inside of me? A power I can control? Just like my— Just like Mortem?'

The Woman of the Water nodded. 'If you choose it, yes. An unbreakable connection between the power that bore us and our own.'

Alexis fell silent, thinking and feeling only one thing. That no matter how far he had come from escaping the darkness of his mind, it would always be there waiting for him to give up and fall back into its clutches.

In that moment, more than anything, Alexis longed for his parents to wrap him in their arms and tell him it would all be okay, even if that was a lie.

'Why didn't you give Mortem the Water Gem, then?' asked Demi. She reached her hand out towards Alexis, but he pulled away. He was an infected man, a person whose touch would poison others. Demi was the last person he wanted to pollute.

'Its soul was empty,' the Woman replied, clasping her hands together over the sparkling Gem. 'It bared no amulet to its body like the Children of the Elements bare to theirs. I knew it was not the one, not deserving of my power. I could not bring myself to give the Gem away. So I deceived the darkness.' She paused, her chin lifting slightly. 'I gave it a replica, a clone.'

Alexis looked up at that.

Blaise shook his head in disbelief. 'You legend.' He didn't notice the Woman's look of confusion.

'And he didn't realise?' Caeli inquired.

'People often believe what they want to believe and see

what they want to see,' she replied, returning her level gaze to Alexis. 'I showed it what it desired, something it thought it was entitled to; an illusion of the mind in which it possessed the Gem of the Water. It didn't think twice that it would be misled. Surpassed in arrogance, it left thinking its power scared the Creature into silence. It deposited enough of an army in its wake to appear as though it was still searching for my Gem and to obstruct you in your quest – but despite its best intentions, it was a failed halting of the Prophecy. A prophecy it always believed it could escape.'

Blaise cleared his throat, tapping his axe against the cave floor, spitting sparks. 'But *we* still have to beat the Creature, right?'

'It is time,' said the Woman, approaching Alexis just as he wondered if he was also an '*it*.' As she placed the Gem of the Water into his hands, she spoke the words of his prophecy, her eyes closed as though she couldn't bear to see his reaction.

'By the blade of Darkness, you will fall, wielded by the one you expect the least.'

Alexis knew better than to ask her what she meant, yet he couldn't help but reach for her as she pulled away. His hands only fell through the liquid of her body as she started to disperse into a glowing shapeless column of water.

'I am afraid this will not be the last time we meet,' said the Woman. Shining a dazzling sea blue, smiling for the first and last time, her essence fell free before drifting into the Gem, flashing only once before resting.

The moment of silence that followed her passing felt far longer than it probably was.

Blaise nudged Alexis's shoulder. 'Come on, Al, she didn't

say you were going to die, just that you would fall. And we managed to stop Demi's, Cae's *and* my prophecies from coming true. We'll keep you safe from your dad, don't worry.'

Caeli leaned forwards to get a better look at Alexis. 'Are you thinking that if we destroy the darkness, it may destroy some part of you?'

'I didn't even think of that,' Blaise muttered.

'Yeah, me neither until now,' Alexis admitted. 'Cheers, Cae.' The vagueness of the Women's prophecy had infuriated him. He almost wished she hadn't said anything at all. 'I'm just scared to use my powers now. What if I accidentally use the darkness? What if I go dark like he did?'

Demi reared up in front of him, taking both of his hands in hers, forcing him to meet her eyes. 'You are nothing like him. We could waste time telling you how you aren't or we could get out of this cave before that thing erupts!'

She gestured to the Water Gem that was beginning to glow violently in his palms. His existential crisis had come at an inconvenient time. They had to go, and it had to be now. Demi led the way, followed by Caeli and Blaise. Alexis was the last one out. He didn't look back.

The waterfall was deafening as the Elementals reached the shuddering cave mouth. At the element's proximity, a thunderous growl rippled from the Water Gem, so forcefully that it slipped from Alexis's grasp. The ancient stone cracked the cavern floor before spilling over its edge, washed away by the frothing tide.

With the Gem submerged within its element, a blinding light splayed from underneath its surface, exploding apart

373

the water in all directions as though the stone had detonated. Through the vertical flood that obscured their view, Alexis could do nothing but watch in horror as the Water Serpent slowly emerged.

40

PSALM 22:1

Psalm 22:1 *Hebrew origin*
'My God, my God, why have you forsaken me?'

'Well done, butterfingers,' said Blaise, slapping Alexis's back.

Alexis's vision through the waterfall was as pristine as it was when looking through the air, and so he wasn't spared from seeing the Water Serpent as it escaped its prison. It looked like something between a dragon and a giant snake. Its body stretched greater than any of the other Creatures, curling round the rim of the waterfall's base. Midnight blue and sea-green scales gleamed in the twilight, patterning its body, an unbreakable chain of armour. Its tail ended as a trident of pointed daggers that thrust tidal waves at huddled groups of Shadowless and Hybrids. They stood no chance, either crushed under its weight or impaled by the Serpent's speared tail end.

'How does it look?' Caeli asked.

Had it not been so threatening, Alexis would have called its design a masterpiece, beautifully sculpted as a Creature to protect the Gem of the Water. The only area free from protection on the Creature was the single Gem-sized spot in the centre of its forehead, surrounded by an upturned triad of spikes. Its aqua-blue eyes searched the system of waterfalls, watchful for anything that approached the Gem encircled within its great body.

'Yeah, we're going to die,' Alexis said, making Blaise whimper. Then he shook himself. Emotions he didn't understand, but fighting and strategy he did. 'Same plan as always. I run for the Gem, you distract it.' Incantus's 'know your environment' mantra was drilled into his mind as he recalled what he had seen that could come to their advantage. 'There are those huge cliff overhangs at the brink of the waterfall – if you girls could somehow push it off, that might do some damage. Blaise get yourself clear and launch a long-range attack.'

Demi's vine whip uncoiled in one hand, her curved dagger held in the other. 'I don't like it. It leaves only you up close with it. I don't care what the Woman said, Lexi. You don't need to get yourself killed to prove you're not a villain.'

Her voice echoed within the cavern, the final sentence circling back to Alexis over and over. He tried to hold onto it for as long as he could. He wasn't sure if he believed her, but he desperately wanted to, and surely that was worth something.

'I'll be fine,' he said, gripping his sword.

Caeli whipped Demi into the air before she could argue. 'Be safe, boys,' she called as they soared away from the Serpent.

'It's just us, brother.' Alexis grimaced.

Alexis felt Blaise's hand close round his wrist. 'Dee's right,' said his best friend. 'You're not a bad person unless you want to be. So let's kill this thing and save the world, all right?'

With his heartbeat thundering in his chest and his pulse

surging in his throat, Alexis couldn't trust his voice. He could only nod back.

Alexis's hand fell from Blaise's grip. 'For the last time, let the fun begin,' Blaise said unenthusiastically. His body ignited into a roaring flame that would've scorched Alexis to the bone had his aura been any weaker.

Together, they walked through the parted waterfall. The Serpent's eyes bore into Alexis and the boy on fire beside him, its three-pronged tail twisting with anticipation, surrounded by a sea of floating Shadowless corpses.

'Circle round by the trees,' Alexis muttered. 'And please, when things go south, don't be shy to save me.'

'I've got you, Al, I've always got you.'

There was no time to hug or embrace. Blaise took off into the air like a rocket.

Alexis was alone with his Creature. Before he could take a step, the Serpent roared and bellowed a huge stream of water from its mouth, its mass so great that not even sun rays could penetrate it. Alexis threw his hands up, cutting the torrent apart just in time, his shoulders shuddering as it rushed past his sides.

The assault ended as abruptly as it had started. The Creature didn't finish its attack. It was surveying him. It was testing his strength. Whatever the result, the Serpent had made a decision.

The Creature slithered closer, halving the space between them and pushing Alexis up against the crashing waterfall behind him. As he struggled to keep his balance on the heaving liquid floor, he glimpsed the trident-pike tail as it broke through the water's surface. It lunged at him at lightning speed.

Alexis parried it aside with his sword just in time. He took the fleeting moment to retaliate, forcing a surge from the waterfall against the Serpent's body. It rocked the Creature backwards, freeing himself some space.

Not a few seconds later, the heat from a shooting star raced across the plunge pool. The thundering fireball crashed into the Serpent's hind, but rather than extinguishing upon impact, Blaise manipulated it to encircle its neck. So hot that it melted the plated spine, the Serpent lurched to douse the flame in the plunge pool, causing clouds of steam to hiss from its scorched body.

The Serpent whipped its tail like a huge sledgehammer, striking the area where Blaise had just been. Trees crunched beneath its weight, shuddering the water and sending waves rippling outwards in rings.

With the Serpent now focussed on searching for Blaise, Alexis dived into the surging plunge pool after the Water Gem, praying for the sake of his life and Blaise's that Caeli and Demi would come to their rescue before it was too late.

Demi Nikolas was back at the peak of the Devil's Throat.

Caeli had flown them to the brink of the waterfall and set them atop a towering columnar rock that split the cascading river. After creating a wind dome to shield them from the spray, she asked, 'You okay?'

Demi was doing her best not to look towards the viewing deck beside the river. Even though the arrow was gone, she could still feel the cold hardness lodged into her chest.

'No.' She squatted to feel the great basalt boulder beneath

her palms, the wet grass tickling her fingers. 'But now is not the time.'

Almost instantly, Demi could feel the strain under the force of what she was trying to achieve. She pushed down the impulse to vomit from the pressure as she crumbled apart the several-tonne rock tower, blinking away tears.

She focussed on what might be happening at the bottom, of Alexis who needed her. She couldn't let that kiss be their first and their last.

She had been in shock. Her soul had been in limbo and the pain in her chest was too fresh and too raw for her to ignore, no matter how hard she had tried.

The image of his face, of the twinkling hope leaving his eyes, the dimples fading and the crooked smile dying on his lips replayed itself in her head. She had so much to say and put right. She had to see him again.

Alexis alone was worth ripping apart the fresh wound in the centre of her chest.

'I see something!' Caeli called. A small red portal appeared on the viewing deck where they had once stood. Before they could ask each other whether the flat, swirling vortex was the entrance or exit, a corresponding portal blinked into existence metres beside them.

Crawling out of it came Valentina.

The bone-thin woman rolled onto her back, her body shuddering despite the setting South American sun still warm in the sky. 'I'm back,' she said scathingly through clenched teeth as the portal closed behind her.

Caeli was on top of her in seconds, pinning her down.

Caeli swung back and punched Valentina hard across the face, rocking her head back. She slapped her again with her other hand, shuffling her flailing body along, jostling it with unrestrained anger.

Demi rose to her feet. 'Cae, stop!'

'She created the portal that transported that freak doctor and the Shadowless to us,' Caeli grunted. 'She's the reason you nearly died!'

Valentina used the brief distraction to twist beneath Caeli's weight. Her fingers found Caeli's spear and she thrust the shaft against her nose. Free to escape, Valentina dashed towards the edge of the rock tower, the brink of the roaring waterfall thundering just behind her.

'I didn't mean to,' she said, sinking to her knees. At that moment, her eyes weren't black. They were bloodshot and weary, but they weren't black. 'I came back to try to help you the moment I thought I wouldn't be a danger anymore.' She shook her head, her long dark hair plastered against her face like careless streaks of ink on a page. 'I can't be trusted. You – you should just kill me.'

Valentina flipped the spear in her hand effortlessly, with such precision that it was clear she had years of Elemental training behind her. The tip was now pressing against her own neck, already drawing blood.

'Don't!' Demi cried, starting towards her. She halted once Valentina pushed the blade against herself harder. 'Don't, Valentina! It's not your fault, I know that. But we can help you. Please just put the spear down.'

'You can't help me,' she countered miserably, her eyes

380

darting to Caeli. The grey-eyed girl stared at her, bleeding and seething. 'You don't know what I've done. You don't know whether I deserve help. I will always be at the mercy of men who want to use me.'

Demi sheathed her dagger and raised both hands. 'You're right,' she said eventually. There was a shout from one of the boys below. Black fumes of Blaise's smoke drifted to their level. 'I don't know if we can help you. But right now, we need to help our friends. Please. Please let us help them!'

For a few seconds, Demi couldn't breathe, the pain in her chest so tight that she wondered if she had been stabbed again. Valentina slowly lowered the weapon, her trembling hands resting against her lap. Only then did Demi exhale.

Caeli sighed in contempt as she outstretched her hand towards the kneeled girl and dragged her to her feet until they were face-to-face, less than a few inches apart. 'If you try anything again, no amount of reasoning or tears will stop me from killing you.'

'Whatever,' was all Valentina said, tearing her eyes away from Caeli, her pale cheeks flushed undeniably red.

A distant, enraged bellow stole the three Elementals' attention. Following the noise, they spun round.

Dr Sinner strode through the rushing waves of the river, his gaze unbroken, wielding a black-tinted broadsword. Blood drenched his dark clothes, most likely not his own.

Valentina shifted into a defensive stance, holding Caeli's spear above her head like a scorpion tail, prepared to face off against the Goliath-looking man.

'Demi,' Caeli muttered out of the corner of her mouth.

But Demi hadn't moved, her body rigid, impossibly still. 'Demi,' she said again, panic creeping into her voice as Dr Sinner closed in, now halfway through the river on his journey towards them.

All of their Elemental training at the Haven, all of their practice and experience with their powers, now counted for nothing. This man was impervious to the elements, far more skilled in combat, and without an ounce of humanity. Sinner's sunken eyes were boring into her, pinning her to the spot, chasing away her innate reaction to fight or flee. She felt like a deer in headlights, a lamb cornered by a butcher.

Escape was impossible, slaughter was inevitable.

'Demi, get behind me!' Caeli shouted, her hands shimmering as she erected a forcefield that they all knew would count for nothing. Sinner smirked, his thin lips curling behind his bared yellow teeth, mucus dripping freely from his nose. Whipping the sword in a circular motion, he quickened his charge towards them.

'Valentina, get ready to portal us out of here,' Caeli ordered.

Valentina grimaced at the prospect of a retreat, but she nodded.

In theory, the choice Demi had to make was a simple one. Maintain the values of the religion and the God she lived by, condemning herself to certain death, or put them aside to protect herself and her best friend. To die or to murder.

If it had been just about her, she didn't know if she would have done it; if she would have brought herself to pull out the arrow tucked behind the heel of her boot and hold the cold, hard metal in her tight grip.

How could she live with herself knowing she had sacrificed her place in heaven to ensure he received his place in hell?

But Caeli needed her. Blaise did. And, most importantly, Alexis did.

In one swift movement, with everything she had, Demi hurled the arrow. It flew with perfect trajectory, soaring high over the deafening tide before sinking deep into Sinner's chest, stopping him in his tracks. The enraged expression on his face dissipated, dropping into shock at the sight of his own arrow embedded in his body.

With a final, vacant look at the small girl who had thrown it, the rushing river swept his body away and cast him over the brink of the waterfall.

No one came to dive in after him.

Demi's breathing caught up to her all too quickly, tears springing to her eyes, hot and uncontrollable – angry at him, angry at herself, angry at her God.

'I killed someone,' she whispered. *I'm no better than him.*

Valentina rounded on her. Her eyes found Demi's golden cross sitting inches above her amulet. Valentina gripped her tightly and said, 'Not now. You can't fall apart yet. That sick bastard deserved it. He took something from you and you took it back. You didn't kill him as much as you saved the lives of hundreds of people he would've taken without remorse or repent. You don't get to break down yet. Quite frankly, it was badass.'

Demi swallowed her gasps and fought to shut off the sinking sensation that made her feel like she was being buried alive. It was only when Caeli came into view that she truly returned. For her best friend knew better than anyone that Demi's

383

actions were not ones without consequences.

'The boys need us. Dem, they need us.'

There was a pause, and then Demi nodded. With that, the huge cliff edge they were standing on shuddered as several tonnes of earth broke free from the rest of the structure.

'Okay,' said Demi, her hands clenched into fists as she held the impossible weight of both the earth and her grief. 'Let's end this.'

41

CORSUCATE

Coruscate (v.) *Latin origin*
To give off or reflect light in bright beams
or flashes; to sparkle

Alexis swam through the heaving water, praying that Blaise could distract the Serpent long enough. He let his amulet pull him to where the Water Gem lay, finally locating the sapphire hue within the corpse-filled, blood-stained river. It floated just beneath the underbelly of the Creature, protected by its great weight.

Alexis wasted no time. He pulled the sword from between his teeth and plunged it deep between the chink of the Serpent's armoured tail.

The Creature screeched and, as it did, a tidal wave crashed into Blaise, extinguishing his flame and throwing him towards the jagged rocks.

Through the frothing waves, Alexis saw a flash of red just before Blaise hit the rocks – and then his friend was gone, vanished from sight, swallowed by the portal.

With Blaise gone, the Serpent turned on Alexis, thrashing furiously to create a whirlpool. Alexis had no time to recover his sword, but, in amongst the chaos, he caught a glimpse of the glowing Water Gem, frozen in the centre of the spiralling motion.

Alexis reached out, his fingers finding the ancient stone at the same moment as the trident-tipped tail wrapped round his body, pinning his arms down by his side.

Still clutching the Gem, Alexis found himself bound and lifted into the air, locked in its vice-like grip until he was level with its pointed, daggered face.

Alexis's vision dimmed in the dying sunset, air no longer able to enter his compressed chest. He couldn't get to his amulet to the Gem. He couldn't use it. He would die before he ever had the chance.

As the head of the Serpent raced towards him, its eyes transfixed on the Water Gem in his hold, it failed to notice what was coming from above. An enormous, several-tonne boulder of rock and earth was hurtling towards them, too fast for the Serpent to escape. It crashed into the back of the Serpent, shattering apart upon impact, sending the Creature careering to the ground.

The grip of the Serpent's tail loosened around him. As he fell through the air, a single raindrop from the sky, Alexis slammed the glowing Water Gem against his chest, connecting his amulet to the stone from where it was cut.

In an explosion of power that sent the Serpent soaring away, flailing into the crashing waterfall, Alexis was left floating in the air. Energy beyond that which he thought was possible surged through his body. It amplified his senses in a way that it felt like until then he had spent his life in a dream, disconnected from truly experiencing consciousness or power or *reality*.

He felt the liquid around him as though it were a part of him, the clouds, the water, even the blood and sweat of his body. He felt eternal. Unstoppable. This kind of power was intoxicating, maddeningly addictive. Alexis now understood why Mortem did what he did, why he craved power so insatiably.

It was for no other reason than because it felt good.

His amulet shone like a torch in twilight as he pocketed the empty Water Gem. The aura of his body rose to a steady, radiant beam.

Alexis smiled. '*Finally*. Let's not forget who this is all about.'

The Serpent locked eyes with him. Alexis drew a breath. Then he made Iguazu Falls explode.

A tsunami came, destructive in its path, its tide unstoppable. It sent the Serpent hurtling towards Alexis, ripping the spears from its spine. Too fast to dodge, a loose dagger tore through Alexis's Haven suit, searing his arm.

More from shock than pain, he collapsed on the surface of the plunge pool, his hand clasping over the wound at his bicep. By the time Alexis pulled his eyes away from the redness of his blood, the Serpent had already regained its balance, closing him in against the waterfall.

It didn't matter how many times it got hit or how hard the punches were, Alexis knew that the only chance of putting it down was to strike its weak spot. With his sword still lodged into its underbelly, he would have to find another weapon.

Alexis turned away from the Creature towards the thunderous waterfall. He remembered what Incantus had said, how he told him that to manipulate the water, he had to think of its fundamental properties; the way it moved, its cohesion, its energy. As the Serpent slithered closer, Alexis slammed both his hands against the surging vertical wall.

The flowing movement seized at his touch. The clear liquid was traded by the glare of white crystals as the entire waterfall froze over into a wall of ice, a snapshot in time of the once rushing stream.

As Alexis ran up the vertical side of the waterfall, he pressed his palms together and channelled the blood that soaked his arm. The red liquid obeyed his command, collating and freezing into a long, sharpened blade – a weapon made from blood, from pain.

A weapon forged from suffering, created with the intention to inflict it tenfold.

The jaws of the Serpent closed in below him, its cold breath biting at his feet, drawing closer faster than he could hope to escape. He had run out of time. It had to be now.

Alexis kicked hard off from the frozen waterfall. His vision spun as he flipped backwards through the air, the inescapable force of gravity forcing him down now that he had parted from his element. He was airborne for a brief moment before his legs met the top of the Serpent's writhing head. His knees buckled beneath him as the Serpent lurched to the side, threatening to throw him off, but not even the Creature of the Water was able to react in time.

With the blood-sword quivering in his hands, Alexis reared back and buried the blade deep into the centre of the Serpent's forehead.

The last cry of the Serpent froze on its mouth and faded into the evening. Its aqua-blue eyes remained fixed on Alexis, an unspoken look of finality passing between the victor and victim. The anger had left them. Glistening in the early night, they looked soft, almost sad.

Like the others, the Creature had only done what it had been created to do – protect the Gem of its element. He wasn't too dissimilar from it, he now understood, for he too had been born for a reason, to fulfil a prophecy.

What if he had been born to become the darkness, just as Mortem had? What if the man they had set out to destroy was just another creature born as a pawn in a game of something greater?

If that was the case, was his father really a bad person, or was he nothing more than the villain someone wrote him to be? It was a question that undid Alexis, unable to be shaken away, unable to be washed free.

The great body of the Serpent swayed as its strength abandoned it, collapsing in on itself. Alexis dove free from the carcass before it crashed into the plunge pool, its weight sending cracks running along the frozen waterfall to the brink, splintering the ice into great shards until it eventually returned to its chaotic, liquid state.

Only then, with the noise of rushing water, was the silence broken.

Alexis tugged free his impaled bronze-and-steel sword from the Serpent's tail. The blue of its scaled body was draining away, drawing dark and lifeless. It would soon dissolve and return to the Gem.

Alexis wasn't sure whether it was the absence of the sun as it set over the jungle's horizon or if it was his own savage act, but he felt cold all over. Up to that point, adrenaline had coursed through his blood, keeping him alert and energised. Now, with the danger gone, a frostiness had replaced it, a dark remnant of the act of violence. Despite his powers, he couldn't shake the feeling; the ice that had set underneath his skin.

He had no time to question why. His friends came running through the river bank to join him at the land's edge.

'Al!' Blaise called, grabbing him by the arm and shaking him. 'That was fire!'

'Actually, it was water,' Caeli corrected him, allowing Alexis to hug her.

'What can I say?' Alexis replied, trying to smile. 'Save the best till last.'

'Thank God you're all right,' Demi said. She wrapped one arm round him and the other round Blaise, her head dipping between them, eyes downcast. There was a change about her – Alexis noticed it instantly, despite her attempt to conceal it. He caught Caeli's eye as the four friends embraced. She simply shook her head.

'We did it,' Blaise said, his voice muffled from having his lips pressed against the side of Caeli's head. 'Guys, we actually did it.'

Caeli laughed in disbelief. She squeezed them tighter. 'The Quest is over.'

Although she was silent behind them, far enough away from the group to go by unnoticed, Alexis locked eyes with Valentina. Wet from the waterfall's spray, her dark hair covered most of her face, sticking to her temples and neck.

She held Alexis's look, smiling at his victory and his reunion with his friends. As good as she may be at concealing her feelings, Valentina's loneliness was as clear to Alexis as the water's reflection. He wondered if she had ever had a friend as true as his.

'You came back,' he said.

'I did.' She bowed her head in acknowledgement.

'Is the darkness gone?' he asked, watchful for any twitch of her fingers.

Valentina kept her distance. 'No. But its hold is not nearly as strong as before.'

'Could you portal us back to the Haven?' Demi asked. She was the first to approach Valentia as though she wasn't a wild animal that could turn frenzied at any moment. 'I know you must want to go home . . .'

'I do not have a home,' Valentina said simply. 'But, yes, I should be able to take you, especially if that's where Mr Arcangelo is to rid me of this poison. So long as you direct me properly, I can take you almost anywhere.'

'That would be wonderful, thank you.'

Caeli turned back to Alexis. 'How do you feel? It's like nothing else, isn't it?'

Alexis wanted to agree. He wanted to say he felt amplified, like an eternal god with the unlimited extent of his health and abilities. Yet even with the omnipotent energy coursing through his body, he now only really felt one thing. 'To be honest, I just feel . . . cold.'

'*Cold*?'

It was Valentina who had asked the question, eyes widening. Her fear was enough to kickstart Alexis's brain into wondering why she had spoken with recognition.

And then it clicked, the words the Woman of the Water had spoken breaking through the surface of his memory. He wasn't sure if he made a sound, but his friends swirled around to him as though he had gasped.

'What is it?' asked Demi, staring at his cheeks where the colour had all but left them.

'Water,' he said, his legs refusing to obey him. Behind him, he could feel the blood-stained water stirring, the air growing cooler. Growing darker. 'The Woman of the Water said I have access to the darkness. What if the Creature does too?'

Before Alexis had the time to look back at the water-filled gorge the Serpent had slumped into, it was too late. He could do nothing as a tidal wave of shadow and destruction crashed into the Elementals.

The impact hurled them across the huge system of waterfalls like stringless puppets. Spinning through his vision, Alexis saw the giant dark shape that had struck them.

The gleaming blue had faded from its scales, replaced by an obsidian charcoal that absorbed the fading sunlight.

The Darkness Serpent slithered towards them, its once blue-slitted eyes now a midnight black. Tearing a look away, Alexis dragged himself towards the slumped, scattered bodies of his friends. Caeli and Blaise lay either side of Valentina, amulets still bright with life. But Demi was the only Child of the Element to have returned her full powers, no longer protected by its omnipotent aura. Her body was battered and tired when Alexis reached her, but still breathing – for now.

The Serpent loomed above them like a small skyscraper in

the twilight, a surrounding mist of dark cloud rolling from its body. The blood-sword Alexis had impaled in its forehead had snapped free, the only vulnerable spot on the Creature no longer accessible. It was without weakness, and Alexis didn't know if there was any other way to defeat it.

They had come so far, he thought, his hand over Demi's, hoping she stayed unconscious so she wouldn't feel any pain. But in the end, he would always be victim to the darkness.

In the moment of hopeless, the words of Alexis's father came to him. It was the reason why he got to his feet. The reason why he always got to his feet. The mantra for his battle against the demons of his mind.

'I didn't come this far just to this far.'

With Stephanie and Jackson Michaels at the forefront of his mind, his true mother and father, Alexis stood against the Serpent alone. If he died, then so be it. Maybe death was his fate, just as the darkness had been Mortem's.

'By the blade of Darkness, you will fall, wielded by the one you expect the least.'

Alexis closed his eyes, waiting for it to be over.

It was strange – after spending so many years silently wishing for death, for an escape from the torment of his mind and the *Shadow Man* that plagued him, death had ultimately become a fate he did not desire. It had taken him years, but he now knew with certainty that he was more than his past and greater than his pain.

Odd, Alexis thought, how when he was alive, he wanted to die, and now that he was about to die, he desperately wanted to live to see just one more sunset.

Life had a cruel way of reserving its meaning at its conclusion.

Alexis closed his eyes. He felt the coldness of the daggered tail rush towards him so fast that even if he wanted to move, he wouldn't have the time. He held his breath for what he thought would be the last time.

A brilliant white light from the sky blinded the scene. Alexis threw up his arms to shield his eyes. Despite the magnitude of its power, Alexis felt no fear. The glow was warm, powerful and *bright*. It rid the dread and thawed the ice from his body.

Alexis blinked away the afterimage, rubbing his eyes with his knuckles as he tried to see the person who had saved them. The very person who had introduced him to the world of Elementals.

Incantus Arcangelo, glowing like an angel from the heavens.

The light shining from his palms held the Dark Serpent's tail rigid in the air, millimetres from Alexis. The Serpent shrieked frantically, trying to tear away with such force that black scales ripped apart at its lower body. Its screeches rang out, booming around the huge waterfall system, ripping shadows from where they were cast.

The Elementals stirred on the ground below, crawling together, arms finding one another to hold onto for support.

'Close your eyes,' Incantus commanded from the sky, glowing brighter than an exploding star, great wings of light flourishing from his back.

Bursting from his body came a blast that lit up the entire rainforest, a light that obliterated the Dark Serpent and shattered the night with the incalescent glow of day, leaving nothing but wisps of shadow which dispersed at the water's touch.

The aura that had once been the Serpent's glowed a vivid blue before flashing black. It trailed through the air before seeping into the water amulet, its lifeforce absorbed and returned. It hummed against Alexis's chest, signalling alongside its fading light that the danger was gone – truly gone.

The nightmare was over, and Alexis no longer needed to chase the sunsets, for the dawn of day had arrived to drive out the darkness.

In the place where the Serpent had been was Incantus, the evanescent shining aura of his angel wings fading as his feet touched the ground. He walked tall in his white Haven suit, gleaming in the early moonlight. He beamed a wide, joyful smile, and said, 'Children of the Elements. Oh, how I have missed you.'

42

ADVESPERASCIT

Advesperascit (v.) *Latin origin*
The approaching dark; the evening draws near

'Incantus,' Alexis said with whatever breath remained in his lungs. He scrambled to his feet, grasping at his mentor's outstretched hand. He wrapped both arms round him with the force of a child being reunited with a parent they never thought they would see again.

'Can you sense us?' Blaise asked, rushing over to join them. 'Can you sense our full powers?'

'I can indeed, my boy.'

Caeli squealed behind them and found a space beneath his arm. She didn't try to mask her happiness. 'How did you find us?'

'Your energy levels were off the charts. The High Order didn't have any available portallers, so I light-travelled to Tanzania, but you weren't there. Then I saw your combined powers, signalling in the sky, calling me to you. Just in time, as well.'

Alexis turned back to look at the area the great Serpent had just occupied, its absence flooding him with relief. Despite the dark and the cold, with Incantus there with him, he felt safe for the first time since leaving the Haven.

'Demetria?' Incantus asked.

Alexis's face dropped when turned back to Demi. Silent tears streamed down her face as she held herself, arms folded across her chest as though she was scared she would break apart if she let go. Her head dipped, tangled damp brown hair hanging over her face, shoulders finally slacking from sorrow. When she lifted her gaze and saw Incantus's face full of worry and concern, she let out an uncontrollable sob and dropped to her knees, no longer able to contain the weight of her grief.

Incantus swept her up in his arms. 'There, there, darling. I'm here. You're safe now.' Demi buried her face into Incantus's broad shoulder, hiding from her friends in shame.

'She killed Dr Sinner,' Caeli whispered to Alexis.

She didn't need to say anything further. Alexis knew exactly the toll it would take on her. The irreversible damage that had made her go from girl to survivor in an instant.

'How about we go home?' Incantus suggested softly. Demi pulled away from him, and turned to join her friends. Together, they held each other in a tight embrace.

The bittersweetness of what they had survived and how close they had all come to death finally sunk in for Alexis. In the face of all that sought to hurt them, the success of their quest, alongside their survival, was not something he thought they would achieve.

Intermixed with relief, however, was grief. Alexis mourned the people they had once been, the people they had evolved from. The teenagers who had perished alongside each death of the Creatures of the Elements.

'And who,' said Incantus, looking past them, 'is this?'

Valentina stepped forward and bowed at the famed Elemental with the power of light.

'Valentina, sir.'

'She helped us,' said Demi.

Caeli cleared her throat and tucked flyaway hairs behind her ears. 'She was the other portaller who helped Mortem break into the Haven. She was imprinted then, and is still holding the darkness at bay.'

Valentina did her best to remain calm as Incantus strode towards her, but Alexis could see the fear in her expression as her eyes darted to Incantus's hands as they began to glow white.

Black veins flashed beneath the surface of her skin as Incantus carefully extracted the darkness from her body, forcing from her a grunt as a swirling ball of blackness was exposed to the open air. With a flash of light, the shadows that had once tortured Valentina's mind disappeared into nothingness.

'It appears as though the combined presence of the Children of the Elements waylaid the hold the darkness had over you,' Incantus said, his shoulders sagging from exertion. 'The last of it is now gone. Pleased to meet you . . . Valentina. Thank you for your bravery.'

Incantus outstretched his hand. After a moment's hesitation, Valentina extended hers and shook it.

From where Alexis was standing, he noticed, at the same time as Incantus did, a mark on the underside of Valentina's wrist. At first he thought it was her shadow, free to be cast from her body, but under closer inspection, he realised it was a faint burn. It was too intricate to be incidental. It looked more like a brand than a scar, in the shape of a circular Chinese dragon with a flaming pearl just above its head.

Valentina noticed Incantus had seen the mark and snatched her hand back. She looked at him expectantly, waiting for him to say something. Only he didn't. Respectfully, he turned to the side to allow her to stand with the other young Elementals.

Together, the friends watched Incantus as he pulled a silver teleportation device from his pocket.

'I can portal us,' Valentina offered eagerly.

'It's okay, dear, easier to just use this,' Incantus replied as a thin, white glowing wall expanded from the air between two tree trunks. 'To enter the Haven, I have to mentally grant you sanction, which is easier for me to do when using one of our own portal devices.'

To the others, it sounded perfectly reasonable, but Alexis, watchful for the subtleties of human expression as ever, noticed Valentina's straight-faced façade return. It made him wonder: who really was she? What was her story? And what did the burned tattoo on her wrist mean?

'Come,' said Incantus with a smile. 'Let's go home.'

Incantus was the first to pass through the glimmering white portal. Demi took Valentina's arm in support. Caeli rolled her eyes with an exasperated sigh before reluctantly looping her arm with Demi's other, linking a chain with Valentina who sneered in response to her joining.

The three girls disappeared through just after.

'You go,' Alexis said to Blaise. 'I just need a minute.'

Alexis watched Blaise walk through, calling back as he

vanished, 'Don't take too long, Alexis. There aren't any buses that can take you to Stonehenge.'

The moment his friends were gone, Alexis exhaled a deep sigh of relief.

He did not follow them through the portal.

There was something he had to do first. Something he could only do now there was no one around to stop him.

Alexis turned away from the portal face and made his way back to the edge of the rainforest, following the riverbank downstream from the base of Iguazu Falls. The treacherous river had diluted the blood of the fallen Shadowless, but with the unlimited powers of the Water Gem, it didn't take long for Alexis to find what he was looking for.

Dr Sinner lay sprawled on his back near the river's edge. He had propped himself up against a jagged rock that broke free from the surface of the surging water flow. His huge chest heaved as he took painful breaths, trails of blood seeping from the arrow that remained still in him.

That's my girl, thought Alexis.

'Pathetic,' Sinner tutted, spitting blood and phlegm at Alexis as he approached. 'Waiting for the High Order to come and arrest me?' He strained to adjust his position. 'You are so weak. Had my Sire permitted me, I would have ended you first.'

'No one's coming to arrest you,' Alexis replied blankly, voice detached from emotion.

To speak to your oppressor, you had to speak in a language they understood. Sinner, like Mortem and the *Shadow Man*, understood only violence and threat and fear.

And Alexis understood that language too.

400

Alexis took a step closer, close enough to see his lips had turned blue in the cold, to notice his sunken eyes were hazel in colour, far from black.

This man had almost murdered the best person Alexis knew. He had nearly taken her away from Alexis forever, and with her would've gone his sanity. Thankfully, Alexis's sanity and his morality were two different things. Sinner would pay for his crimes, but to enact a penance from such an impure man, the cleansing element of water was not sufficient.

Alexis thought it would've been harder to tap into his dormant powers of darkness, but it came to him as easily as his power over water. The threshold lay within reach. It always had. All he had to do was call on it and let his intensions be known.

Oh, how the descent into darkness was paved with broken promises and abandoned oaths.

Alexis felt its coldness seep through his veins like adrenaline, spiralling out from inside his body to envelop him in a second skin of coiling shadows. He had never before felt so powerful.

Sinner stared at him in horror, with the same fear he had relished inflicting on so many. He looked from the amulet on Alexis's chest to the eyes beneath his wet hair, eyes that now saw through the dark of night as clearly as day.

Sinner shook his head slightly. 'You're just like him.'

A phantasmagoria of images flashed through Alexis's mind in quick succession. The shock on Demi's face as the arrow struck her. The limpness of her body in his arms. Her blood on his chest. The warmth of her tears on his hands. The brokenness of her voice as she told him she didn't want to die.

Her pain became his power.

The shadows turned sharp in Alexis's hand, hardening to a pike. 'No,' said Alexis, leaning in. As he did, he sunk the blade of darkness into Sinner's chest, centimetre by centimetre, extracting from him a silent scream. '*I am worse.*'

Sinner was dead before the tip of Alexis's sword reached the rock beneath him. Alexis pulled it free in one swift tug, splattering blood on his face. The motion of it was enough to cause Sinner's beastly body to slip back into the river's tide, sinking beneath the surface as it was swept away. Once he was gone, the blade of darkness in Alexis's hand shattered, dispersing into clouds of blackness.

Alexis staggered backwards against the current of the river, examining his hands. There were no traces of blackness. Even his amulet remained blue, glowing steadily with its full powers.

Alexis had wanted to do it; he had wanted revenge paid for in the currency of blood that now stained his cheeks.

Yet he felt filthy, unmistakably unclean. He felt suddenly *wrong*.

Alexis dove beneath the river's surface, hoping for it to bathe him clean of his sins, hoping for it to wash away the remorse that hadn't yet come. He tore back the way he had come through the rainforest where the portal remained. His friends would be waiting for him. Incantus would know he had been gone too long. What would he say to them?

But that wasn't his biggest concern.

He had wanted to kill him and he had liked *it. He had liked using the darkness.*

Alexis felt his shadow powers more strongly now, disturbed

and unsettled after being temporarily unleashed, like a restless caged beast who had briefly tasted freedom.

His prophecy from the Woman of the Water resurfaced in his mind. His fall by the blade of darkness. The fate of himself and of the darkness harboured within him.

Incantus had once said Mortem had decided who he was, that he had chosen the darkness, but how could Alexis be certain that his father wasn't a victim just like Valentina had been, that he wasn't the first in a long list of people who had been imprinted by the darkness? Another question dawned on Alexis. Would he be the next victim of its power? Or worse, would he be the one pulling the strings?

As Alexis raised a foot to step through the portal, he heard something – a twig snap. He spun round.

A man was standing there, staring at Alexis in utter disbelief, mouth gaping open in shock. Worst of all, a camera was trembling between his hands, the lens pointed directly at Alexis.

He had been sighted. By a mortal.

A mortal Alexis *recognised*.

Alexis couldn't forget him, despite it being years since he had seen him, even if they had only met once. How could he forget the man who had taught him the technique that had kept him sane and steady in his darkest moments? Even now, the only thing Alexis found himself able to do, was to tap his fingers to his thumbs.

Could it be true? Had the very first man he had attempted to murder just witnessed him finally commit the act.

Before Alexis could utter a word, the momentum of his

footstep carried him forward. His body passed through the opaque white portal. In the blink of an eye, Dr Dash was gone, the quest was over, and he was back in the Haven.

43

VACILANDO

Vacilando (v.) *Spanish origin*
To wander or travel with the knowledge that the journey is
more important than the destination

'Are you sure?' Alexis repeated for the third time, pacing up
and down with his hands in his hair, grasping it so tightly that
dark curls broke away.

The constant thundering of the waterfall had been replaced
by the reticence of the Haven's top-floor laboratory. Alexis
had burst in, still reeling from seeing Dr Dash. He had to
explain why he was so late, why he was so panicked. All he
told Incantus and his friends was that he had seen someone –
he never divulged who it was or anything about Sinner.

If Incantus sensed a change about him or his aura, surely he
would have mentioned it? Maybe his use of the darkness had
only been a one-time thing.

In truth, the prospect that his face would be plastered to
every news outlet in the world as the person who had exposed
Elemental-kind was still something that shook Alexis to the
core. What if his parents found out? He feared them as much
as any Creature of the Element.

'Whenever a portal from our teleportation device closes up,

a wave that harnesses the Erasers' powers is emitted, wiping away the last few hours of any mortal's memory in a mile radius,' Incantus assured him, sweeping between the dozens of computer screens and switching off their monitors.

Beside him, Alexis saw his friends relax, too tired from the two days of continuous wakefulness and fighting to stay vigilant any longer.

'That is if they even processed what they saw,' Incantus continued. 'The Maya force prevents most people without Elemental blood from seeing directly into our world. Nevertheless, I have informed the High Order of each location you have visited and, as we speak, a team of Erasers are . . . cleaning up any mess.'

He chose his words delicately, glancing at Demi. She hadn't said a word since they arrived, half-asleep as she hugged Gibbous round the neck.

Alexis felt the knot in his chest loosen somewhat; but he still couldn't shake the unnerving fear that Dr Dash might have taken a photograph of him fleeing after murdering Sinner.

Gibbous's ears perked up at the approaching sound of hurried footsteps. Ziya Parashakti burst through the door.

'You're back! How was it? How did it go? I want to hear *everything*.' She glanced at Valentina. 'Oh, hello.'

'Mission accomplished, Zee,' said Blaise, giving her a high-five.

The bright white lights of the laboratory guttered off before Ziya could ask another question. The Elementals were suddenly plunged into darkness, save for the coloured glow from the full-powered amulets.

'Power cut?' Caeli asked.

'Didn't think you got them here,' Alexis added, seeing Incantus's face drop in the dim light. The computer screens flashed uselessly, unresponsive when he madly clicked at them.

The white-haired man turned to Ziya. 'Something's wrong.'

Incantus let out a gasp as if he had just been gut-punched by an invisible force. He pressed his knuckles hard against his temples, the light from his hands displaying the shadows of his contorted expression across the room.

'What's going on?' Blaise demanded, searching the otherwise empty laboratory.

Incantus let out a cry, and the lights of the laboratory shattered. Thick shards of glass rained from the ceiling, breaking into a thousand smaller pieces against Caeli's instinctive forcefield.

Incantus stumbled, his eyes cast wide open and glowing white. He shoved the young Elementals behind him as Gibbous growled by his side, pounced and ready to attack.

Slowly, in the centre of the room, a shimmering telepathic projection emerged from nothingness. It hovered in the air, stretching wider until it was at least the size of a football, bleeding into existence and somehow breaking through the shields and barriers that warded the Haven.

'Is this you?' Caeli barked, seizing Valentina by the arm and digging her nails in so deeply that blood welled.

'No, no, I swear!' she protested.

Whether Caeli wanted to or not, she and Valentina ended up standing back to back, searching the room for any other intrusions.

The single shimmering sphere was beginning to morph into

407

something that resembled a human face. Brown, aged skin, strong set features, a hairless scalp and grey-bearded chin. It was a face Alexis recognised, one he hadn't expected to ever see again.

With a grunt, the astral projection finally settled. Holding steady, his coffee-coloured eyes shot open, and the face of Akili Pierce once again appeared in the Haven.

Incantus's hands flew up and a beam of light burst from them, colliding with the projection, sending it soaring away. 'I must terminate his brain waves,' Incantus muttered, placing his hands to his temples.

'That'll kill him!' Ziya protested.

He turned to his protégé. 'You think I want to do this? He's my oldest friend, but if he jeopardises your lives and all the others in the Haven then I have no other choice.'

'There has to be another way!' Demi pleaded, holding Gibbous by his neck so that he wouldn't go after the hologram. 'You managed to get rid of the darkness imprinted in Valentina.'

'That was different,' Incantus countered. 'He's still in Mortem's castle. The darkness extraction isn't as simple as you think. It's dangerous for us both. When it's so entwined with the person's mind . . . removing it can be worse than death.' His voice caught in his throat, almost as if he were in pain, causing him to grimace. 'For the Prophecy of Light and Darkness to come true, people had to be willing to sacrifice anything. Teller knew that. Akili knew that. Raeve and Taranis knew that. They would tell you that had they not been enslaved by the person they fought to stop.'

'Sir, his eyes are not black like they were in the castle,' said

Valentina urgently. 'When fighting the darkness . . . it's like fighting against a tide that will eventually drown you. If that is your friend and he has managed to contact you, then this may be his only chance.'

Valentina's words hung in the air. Until then, Alexis hadn't been sure whether he liked her much, whether she could be trusted and if he could forgive her for getting Demi so badly hurt. But now, he couldn't help but respect her strength, for he had always admired broken things that defied the ease to fall apart.

'Ian. Ziya. Children. I don't have much time.' Akili's voice sounded strangled.

Incantus swept his hand and the projection returned to them. Valentina had been right; his eyes were clear from darkness – for the moment. 'Are you well, my friend? Raeve and Taranis?'

'He has poured so much of his power into us . . . I–I cannot hold it for long. I have to tell you something.' Dark-glowing veins bulged at Akili's neck as though he was suffocating, his body fighting the will of his mind. A black glaze seeped into the corners of his eyes each time he blinked, kept barely at bay. 'Finding the Gems was not enough to thwart him. Stopping the Children from retrieving them was only ever part of his plan. His focus has always been the eclipse on the solstice, and he has been building an army to prepare for it.' He gasped and his astral projection wavered between solid and transparent. 'It is not as we thought, Ian. Mortem never intended to cover our world in shadow or expose our kind.'

Alexis felt the hairs on the back of his neck stand in fearful anticipation. Only then did he realise just how wrong they had been. How painfully naive he had been to think that there wasn't something else Mortem had been planning all along, a fate far worse than a world covered in shadow.

But what could be worse than that, a world without any light?

Akili's voice cut out. The hologram of his face sputtered before flatlining. Incantus's fist struck the tabletop in frustration – so hard that it splintered – into the ground. Through the flickering lights, the projection finally became animated with Akili's face again. He spoke the words that once said, changed everything.

'If Mortem is within Stonehenge during the eclipse on the solstice, his powers will be amplified, and every person with a drop of Elemental blood will become imprinted.'

44

MIZPAH

Mizpah (n.) *Hebrew origin*
'Watchtower'; the deep emotional bond between people,
especially those separated by distance or by death

Akili's sentence held in the air, his words so shocking that, for a long time, no one reacted – not even Incantus.

What Mortem had done to Valentina, to the Leaders, he now planned to do to every Elemental. Alexis couldn't fathom the devastation. The control he would have, an authority no one could fight.

For the only thing worse than a world covered in shadow was a world without one – a world where the light of life had all but flickered out.

'H–he is coming,' Akili stuttered.

'Akili!' Incantus grabbed at the transparent projection, but his fingers passed through as Akili's resistance depleted. 'His power will grow as mine weakens on the solstice so get to me as soon as you can! If his hold on you carries for much longer and I try to extract it . . . you know what could happen.'

'Goodbye, my dear friend. If the time comes, do what you m–must. I do not want to share the same f–fate as . . .'

A furious shout bellowed from somewhere beyond the

projection. As the display of Akili's face crashed out of focus, the last image to be shown before it blinked out was the outstretched blackened hand of Mortem.

The lights of the Haven rebooted. The Elementals were once again cast into the bright illumination of the laboratory. The four Children of the Elements were gathered in an unsettled silence, looking searchingly at their mentor. Slightly further back stood Ziya and Valentina. Two young women who had never met before yet were somehow drawn together, not by love or friendship, but by their shared suffering at the hands of Mortem.

Incantus broke the silence, his voice faraway, eyes vacant and unfixed. His body moved instinctively, busying himself as he tapped away at multiple silver command devices. Trauma response – Alexis detected it right away, the automatic function. He was exhausted just looking at him.

'Ziya, please get our newest companion settled in. I need to speak to these four alone.'

There was no disagreeing with him. With a reluctant wave, Ziya bid them goodnight before asking Valentina to follow her. As they parted from the group, Valentina cast one final longing glance behind her in the direction of Caeli and Blaise. For the first time, Alexis couldn't figure out who it had been meant for.

'Will Akili be okay?' Demi asked delicately.

As Alexis waited for Incantus to respond, he wondered who the person was that Akili had tried to name before he had disappeared. A person whose mention alone cast Incantus into a grief-stricken depression. He couldn't help himself from coming to the discouraging conclusion that despite how much time he had spent with his mentor, he didn't truly know him well at all.

'I hope so,' Incantus answered. 'Akili and his powers are indispensable to Mortem; he knows it's worthwhile to keep him alive. In light of what Akili told us, once the High Order receives this message, they will be forced to stand against Mortem in battle in two days' time. This is no longer just a fight for light or darkness, but a battle for the sovereignty of our souls, and I can't do it alone.'

Incantus glanced at the anxious, exhausted faces of the four teenagers. He then put the device down and turned his full attention to them.

'Now, I want you to listen to what I have to say. Really listen to me. What you have done, what you have achieved, is nothing short of legendary. You have fulfilled your roles as the Children of the Elements and have managed to find all four of the lost Elemental Gems. No matter what is coming, this victory, *your* victory, is something no one can ever take away from you. Your role in this story, if you wish for it to be, is over.'

Story. He had called the prophecy of their lives a story too, just as the Woman of the Water. All stories had an end, and Alexis wondered if this was his, whether he would be the one to put down the pen or if it would be snatched from his hand by Mortem whilst there was still ink left to write.

The Children of the Elements didn't stay for much longer after that. Once they'd returned their full powers to the Gems, the four friends walked through the empty corridors of the Haven in silence, crossing the white-and-gold marble bridges that overlapped the open expanse of the facility's core.

They soon reached the individual staircases that led them to their beds where they would be allowed to sleep for the first time in days. Standing there, Alexis looked at the people he cared for the most. The people he couldn't imagine living without, and yet had almost had to.

No words were spoken between them, for they had surpassed the need for them to understand each other. Instead, they just gave each other a tired, knowing smile, certain that whatever was coming their way, they would experience it together.

Darker days *did* lay ahead. Yet as the Children of the Elements finally parted from one another's side, Alexis realised, for the first time in his life, that even the darkness of his nightmare would be swept away by the rising light. That it always had, he had just failed to appreciate it.

Alexis bade his friends goodnight and went into his room. He shut the door behind him. And then, once he was finally alone, he broke down.

The dam shattered and he no longer had the strength to hold back the weight of the flood. He didn't even have the strength to stand. His legs failed him and he collapsed to the ground, his back slumped against the bent wooden door. Tears rolled down his face, a tide of pent-up emotion releasing from him without restraint or reprieve, emotion too great for him to pretend he was incapable of feeling it anymore, out of fear that it would drown him if he acknowledged it.

He cried for Demi, for the part of her that could never be healed and for the damage between them that may never be repaired. He cried for himself, grieving the brief time he had spent feeling safe and sane, knowing it had come to an end.

He cried for his parents and for Jason, for the world they didn't know they lived in, the harm they didn't know was coming for them. For Blaise and Caeli, for Incantus and Ziya, for their pain and loss and the fight they were unwilling to give up on. For the Leaders and Valentina, for the sea of darkness they had drowned in, and for Teller, for the memories he would no longer make, the stories he would no longer tell.

Lastly, Alexis cried for Mortem Arcangelo. With his chest shuddering, eyes stinging and throat aching, he cried for what Mortem had forced him to do.

No matter what fate had determined for Mortem, Alexis knew he needed to stop him for what he had done and what he intended to do. And if that meant ending himself too, then that was a sacrifice Alexis was prepared to make.

The memory of what Incantus had said to him on the eve of his quest, when they sat staring at the reflection of the moon on the river's surface in the Garden, came to the forefront of Alexis's mind as he dragged himself into bed. It wasn't their speak of his parents whom he missed, nor was it their discussion of how Mortem came to be the way he was.

It was what his mentor had made him promise to remember. That no matter how dark the day may fall, he should never forget the light of life, of friendship. The light that would free him even from the darkest depths of his own mind.

As his head hit the pillow and he fell asleep, Alexis decided that was something worth fighting for.

Even if that meant using his powers of darkness once again.

For only the grace of light was worth the descent into darkness.

EPILOGUE

Within Mortem's frozen fortress, Ezra Alastor knew something terrible had happened.

The blackened walls pulsed with a defiant glow. Guided by the unsteady illumination, Ezra made his way through the castle and did his best to block out the endless, penetrating screams of the starved prisoners. It was a noise he didn't think he would ever get used to.

In the few days he had been a resident of the fortress, he had come to notice how it vaguely mirrored the Haven in its beehive structure, only it was warped version of it. A darker version. It lacked the Haven's warmth and light. Most of all, what the castle lacked in contrast to the Haven was Incantus Arcangelo.

Trying not to get lost on his descent down the grand stone spiral staircase, Ezra thought back to his first memories of Incantus and the Haven from more than ten years ago. It had been a maze to him back then too. He had been given a room to stay for the first few times he had visited, when his mother and father would kiss him goodbye and tell him they would see him soon. Being teleporters, their abilities were invaluable to the Haven and the High Order. As much as he hated the idea of them leaving him, he couldn't blame them for going, for the whole point of the Haven was to produce Elementals willing to fight and protect the safety of their kind and the mortals.

Only the last time his parents had left, they hadn't returned, and Ezra needed someone to blame.

Ezra remembered Incantus and Akili Pierce sitting him down to tell him and he remembered how he had secretly charged them with his parents' murder. How he had blamed humankind for not being able to protect themselves. Oddly enough, he had never blamed the creatures whose hands his parents had died at, nor the Elemental who had sent them. He had never met Mortem. Incantus, he knew. He could hate him. He needed to hate him. If he didn't have that, he would have nothing.

And now Ezra was walking towards the person who he had been brought up to believe was the villain. Except Mortem was the only one who truly saw him. Mortem appreciated him and recognised his potential. Or at least he had in the beginning.

In the days since his invasion of the Haven, Mortem hadn't paid any attention to Ezra, too preoccupied with interfering with the quest of the Children of the Elements and with preparing for a battle Ezra never knew had been on the cards. Just like Incantus, Mortem seemed to have forgotten about everyone else to obsess over the four inexperienced and undeserving Elementals foretold in the Prophecy of Light and Darkness.

Ezra couldn't wait to prove Alexis Michaels wrong; to prove

that, soon enough, everyone would come to know his name.

He came to halt just beyond the sealed doors of Mortem's chambers, residing in the lowest, darkest part of the frozen castle. Ezra pushed it ajar just in time to see the final strike of Mortem's fist against Akili Pierce. His huge, muscular body slumped to the cold ground. He didn't attempt to get up.

'Take him away,' Mortem ordered.

The great doors of the chamber opened wide and out exited the Leaders of the Haven. Raeve and Taranis dragged Akili between them, the senior Elemental bruised and bloodied.

As they passed Ezra, he caught a glimpse of their eyes; black and unfeeling. Inside the chamber, Mortem was assiduously wiping the blood from his fists. He didn't look up to greet him.

With his heart thundering in chest, Ezra mentally prepared himself to be in Mortem's presence. He brushed his overgrown black hair from his face, the wisps falling to the edge of his angular jawline. Just as he was about to announce himself, Crescent appeared before him. The dire wolf growled at him, baring pointed yellow incisors.

'Let him in,' Mortem snapped. Crescent's ears lowered at the command and he took a step forward. Ezra cautiously stepped inside. He came to a stop in front of the bloody trail Akili had painted when he had been hauled away.

Mortem rolled up the blood-drenched cuffs of his shirt and he sunk into his imposing black-gleaming throne, his broad chest heaving with exertion. He barely glanced in Ezra's direction with his blue-and-black ringed eyes.

'Sire,' came a woman's voice. A tall woman, her body all

sharp points and edges, stalked past Ezra. She bowed before Mortem, sinking so low that her chin almost scraped the dark stone floor.

'What is it, Vultress?' Mortem clicked his fingers, ordering Crescent to return to his left side. 'In the last hour I have discovered that the Water Gem given to me was in fact a fake and my dear, deranged Akili somehow managed to inform my brother of our plans for the eclipse. The High Order's hands are now tied. They will be obligated to step in. So whatever it is that you are desperate to tell me, make it quick.'

Ezra saw her throat bob before she spoke. 'None of our people have returned from South America. Not even the Lì girl. I ask that you send me there to find Sinner.'

Over the top of the woman's bowed magenta-coloured buzz-cut, Ezra watched Mortem's expression harden.

'Your brother-in-law is dead, Vultress,' he said disappointedly, wiping away the last of the blood on his hand against Crescent's coat. 'Otherwise he would already be back. It is a shame, for I believed his abilities to be better than that of four barely trained children.'

Dr Sinner was dead? Ezra didn't know how that could be possible. An Elemental impervious to the elements; how could Alexis and his friends hope to beat someone like that?

'I have for you a more important mission, Vultress,' Mortem decided, inclining forward in his throne. 'A task, reserved only for my most fierce and loyal Shadowless. It takes you away from the battle on the solstice, however.'

'Sire,' Vultress began, interlocking her fingers and squeezing them so tightly they paled. Even from a distance, Ezra could see the hesitancy of her expression as she chose her next words. 'I am the strongest witch there is. You would rather take my imprinted cousin instead? Raeve is a traitorous wench. I don't mean to question you . . .'

'Then don't,' Mortem growled. 'I require the use of her just as I do the other Leaders, for a plan certain to capture my predictable brother. I wish to keep the imprinted by my side so they do not stray. But you are far more dangerous when unchained. Now, listen. There are some that may be able to resist my imprinting powers following the eclipse.'

'No such Elemental is powerful enough, Sire.'

'Shut up,' Mortem said with a bored shake of his head. His bluntness and Vultress's audible swallow in response forced Ezra to stifle a smile.

That was what it looked like to have power and authority. Ezra so deeply wished to command that too under Mortem's guidance, as he had been promised.

'As you know, I will spare my followers their autonomy. With the twins gone, I am granting you the position of my second-in-command. The Nekro and imprinted Shadowless will stay with me, but I want you to deploy groups of my faithful Shadowless to execute anyone who may try to oppose me. The Aevum's, Parashakti's, descendants of the Elemental Tribes . . . if they have the nerve, and few others.'

'It is a privilege, Sire. Of course. I will ready them immediately,' Vultress replied, her eyes gleaming with demented excitement, bowing once more.

'Good.' Mortem relaxed in his seat. 'Do not fail me, for your mission is essential if things do not go to plan during the solstice.' He jutted his chin in Ezra's direction. 'His powers aren't half as strong as the Lì girl's, but it'll have to do. Call him when you are ready.'

Mortem didn't even look at him. Ezra had been hoping that now was the time Mortem would recognise him as an asset. That he could treat him with respect or encouragement, just like he had when they first met outside of the Haven, when he told Ezra he was the key to their liberation and prosperity.

Now Ezra felt used. A fool. Regret bubbled inside of him. How could he have given it all up for this?

Mortem narrowed his eyes at Ezra.

'Yes,' said Ezra before hastily adding, 'Sire.'

With a single, short bark from Crescent, Mortem adjourned their meeting. As Ezra was leaving, he heard Mortem treat his new protégé to one final gift.

'Vultress. Should our plan, for any reason, fail – I should like you to visit one other family, but not until the time comes where the night is longer than the day. I have finally found *his* family. I think you know them. They were the ones who murdered your husband.'

Ezra couldn't see her face but he could tell that Vultress was smiling wickedly.

'Ezra.'

His heart leapt again. Mortem had remembered his name.

'See to our most important prisoner and get her powers under control,' he said, waving him away with a careless hand.

Ezra left without a word, a heavy weight dragging his feet as he made his way to the most secure part of the castle.

As he entered the prison cell, Ezra's eyes fell upon the

woman chained within. Shackles bound her wrists and ankles, fastening her to the bed. Needles and cannulae punctured the papery skin of her arms, the once healthy bronzed colour having diminished after years of captivity.

The woman did not move. She lay there, so still that she could be asleep, or even dead. Ezra could barely tell the difference sometimes. For him, that made her the perfect confidante.

'Something's happened upstairs,' he said, closing the chamber door behind him, sealing them both alone inside. He made his way over to the machine, his fingers resting over the button that would initiate the collection of her blood, her powers. Up close to the woman, he could see her eyes moving beneath the closed lids, the veins that bulged at her frail neck, even the individual strands of her shaved black hair.

'I never expected this.' He glanced around the vacant room before lowering his voice, fearful that Mortem or one of the Shadowless may hear him somehow. 'I've seen what Mortem has been preparing for the solstice. The Nekro, the Hybrids, the Shadowless army. The *Demons* . . . you should be grateful you can't see them.'

And still, the woman did not respond. She could not respond. She just lay there, silently awaiting the pain that always came. Ezra deliberated for a split second whether there was anything he could do to help her. He had voluntarily chosen to follow Mortem, so he still had access to his powers, unlike most prisoners.

Maybe he could teleport her somewhere within the fortress where Mortem couldn't find her. Maybe he could teleport her hundreds of metres up into the air and let her fall, giving her an end to it all. Did she have children or a family? Did they know what had happened to her? Would they want to know?

At the sound of a clang of metal in the far distance, ringing out along the dark, cold tunnels of the castle, the overwhelming sensation of terror flooded Ezra's body.

No. He had made his choice. Ezra reached out and pressed the button on the side of the machine. He stepped back as it hummed to life.

The woman on the bed seized up as she resisted the rough shackles that chained her. Rivulets of bright red blood slowly seeped through the clear tubes before entering the device. Ezra couldn't bear to stay any longer, the weight within his chest growing heavier ever still.

'I'm sorry,' he mumbled, watching as the black walls of the castle's chambers somehow darkened. Ezra didn't know if she could hear him, but he said one last thing before he left.

'Incantus and the Haven have no idea what is coming. Even with the Elemental Gems, the odds are against them. No one will come out of the battle or survive the Demons. Soon enough, they won't even have their shadow to keep them company.'

ACKNOWLEDGEMENTS

I want to start off by thanking you, the reader. Thank you for deciding to pick up my book. Some of you have been with me from the start of my online author journey, cheering me on and encouraging me to get the damn book out there. It's your undying support that has allowed me to flourish and take pride in being an author and a reader. I have so much love for you and I hope I wrote something you in turn love and cherish on your bookshelves.

Thank you to my family, my mum and dad, my two brothers, and our beloved dogs. You may not have always understood my story, but you always understood how much it meant to me and for that I am so grateful. I am privileged to know with utmost certainty what it feels like to be loved unconditionally. You have inspired me and my book directly and indirectly, and allowed me to write a story with a pen dipped in the ink of love and encouragement. I know I don't say it enough, but thank you for everything. Everything I am and all that I have to become is due to you.

To my love. Thank you for being my number-one supporter, my biggest advocate and loudest cheerleader. You may have joined my life long after the story of Alexis first came to me, but you have watched and been a part of its evolution. There is never a time where you don't hear out my rambling of potential plot ideas and character arcs and quotes. Loving you has made me a better man. Any success I have will be ours (yes, we can spend it on holidays).

To my friends. You know who you are. The ones who turn up and like and comment and share and support me. The ones who had tears in their eyes when I told them my book was finally getting published and who ran to pre-order it the moment I announced the news. Writing this found family couldn't have been easier, for the inspiration was all around me.

Thank you to my incredible editor, Yas Morrissey. Without you, this book wouldn't be getting published to be in bookstores all over the world. I will never forget the day we spoke and you said you saw a bright future for my book at Simon & Schuster. Your support and encouragement and expertise has transformed this from a Word document to a physical book in my hands! Thank you to the whole team at Simon & Schuster: the inspiring MD, Rachel Denwood; and powerhouse Publishing Director, Ali Dougal; to Laura Hough and Dani Wilson in Sales; Sean Williams in Design; Nicholas Haynes in Export Sales; Maud Sepult and Emma Martinez in Rights; the wonderful Jess Dean, Elizabeth Irwin and Ellen Abernethy in Publicity; the awesome Olivia Horrox and Miya Elkerton in Marketing; and Basia Ossowka in Production.

To my diligent copy-editor Genevieve Herr and proof-reader Lowri Ribbons, thank you for pulling out the best parts of my story. Thank you to Web HD for my beautiful website. A special thank-you to Katt Phatt for creating a stunning, eye-grabbing, magical cover for *The Light That Blinds Us*. Thank you to Alex Forrest for the breath-taking character art. Together, you have all made my dream a reality and it's everything I wished for and more.

Thank you to my beta-readers for your recommendations and honest truths and hype and advice. You made my book better and I am so grateful for you. Thank you to my author friends for welcoming me into the community, for supporting me in my debut journey and for advising me with your seasoned experience. You've made this overwhelming experience somewhat manageable!

Despite being a teacher, I am still always learning. Thank you to my Psychology PGCE mentor, Alison Wiggins, who taught me to shout even if my voice shakes. Thank you to my ex-patients and my students, past and present, who taught me the importance of patience, positivity, and never giving up. You made this impossible year worth it, and I see nothing but greatness in your futures.

Lastly, I want to thank the boy that made all of this possible. 13 year old Andrew who, back in 2013, spent too much time lost in other worlds, dreaming up his own. In every way, this book saved me. It dragged me out of my darkest times and guided me on to see the light in the world and the people around me. To see the light in myself. Thank you for giving me a purpose. Thank you for Alexis and his story, for putting the pen to paper (or fingers to keys), for sticking it through the plot holes and times of frustration and apathy and embarrassment and hopelessness. Thank you for every day that you worked to get this book written and published.

We did it. We finally did it. I hope I made you proud.

ABOUT THE AUTHOR

Andy Darcy Theo is a British-Greek Cypriot with an educational and occupational background in clinical psychology and teaching. Desperate to escape the Middle Child Syndrome and petrified of being forgotten, when he is not teaching, reading or talking about books, he is writing his YA fantasy series, Descent Into Darkness. He has been working on this complex psychological fantasy series for more than ten years, and after many changes in plot, characters and titles, he is ready to share it with you all.

Andy can be found on TikTok, Instagram and Twitter: @andydarcytheo and be contacted via his website andydarcytheo.com

The next book in
this epic series

COMING SOON